PRAISE FOR ELLE KENNEDY'S
KILLER INSTINCTS SERIES

"Heart-stopping, riveting suspense . . . for those who enjoy their romantic suspense on the dark and steamy side."
—*New York Times* bestselling author Christy Reece

"Dangerous suspense to quicken your pulse. Romance hot enough to make you sweat. Elle Kennedy puts them together and leaves you breathless."
—*New York Times* bestselling author Vivian Arend

"Hard-core romantic suspense loaded with sensuality."
—*USA Today*

"Relentless action, heated sexual tension, and nail-biting plot twists." —*Publishers Weekly* (starred review)

"An adrenaline-filled, exhilarating ride. The story is a thrilling, action-packed adventure as well as a tender story."
—Fresh Fiction

"As sexy as it is exciting . . . action aplenty . . . spellbinding romantic suspense." —Joyfully Reviewed

"Seduction, sex, and suspense—Elle Kennedy is a master at blending all three." —Romance Junkies

"Very good romantic suspense . . . all the right elements that I look for in a book like this." —Fiction Vixen

Also by Elle Kennedy

MIDNIGHT TARGET

A KILLER INSTINCTS NOVEL

ELLE KENNEDY

BERKLEY SENSATION
New York

BERKLEY SENSATION
Published by Berkley
An imprint of Penguin Random House LLC
375 Hudson Street, New York, New York 10014

Copyright © 2017 by Leeanne Kenedy
Penguin Random House supports copyright. Copyright fuels creativity, encourages
diverse voices, promotes free speech, and creates a vibrant culture. Thank you for buying
an authorized edition of this book and for complying with copyright laws by not
reproducing, scanning, or distributing any part of it in any form without permission.
You are supporting writers and allowing Penguin Random House to continue to
publish books for every reader.

BERKLEY and BERKLEY SENSATION are registered trademarks and the B colophon
is a trademark of Penguin Random House LLC.

ISBN: 9781101991312

First Edition: May 2017

Printed in the United States of America
1   3   5   7   9   10   8   6   4   2

Cover art by Kris Keller
Cover design by Katie Anderson

To all the fans of this series—
thank you for loving it as much as I do.

ACKNOWLEDGMENTS

I have been dying to write this book ever since I introduced Liam and Sully in *Midnight Alias*. And then, when I introduced Cate and Ash in *Midnight Action*, I was even more impatient to give these two couples their own stories. It took a couple of years to make it happen, but it finally did! *Midnight Target* was an absolute joy/emotional roller-coaster ride to write, and as always, I couldn't have survived this project without the help of some pretty awesome people:

Jen and Viv, for the feedback, encouragement, support, and, most important, their friendship.

Sharon, for her eagle eyes and always, *always* being there for me!

Tash and Nic, for everything!

Jess Brock, the biggest cheerleader for this series, as well as the funniest, sweetest, coolest publicist/friend/person I know.

Kerry Donovan, editor extraordinaire.

And finally, the readers and fans of this series. I write these books for *you*.

Chapter 1

Guatana City, Guatana

"How'd it go?"

Cate Morgan glanced over her shoulder to find a dusky-skinned beauty standing behind her chair. It always took her a second to remember that Riya Charan wasn't a movie star who'd wandered off the set, but an award-winning journalist with a scary number of battle scars from past high-risk assignments. After three weeks of being glued to Riya's side, Cate had developed a serious girl crush on the woman.

"Uneventful," Cate admitted as her colleague settled in the seat across from hers. "I'm loading the pictures now, but I don't think there's anything usable here." She gestured to her laptop, which she was using to import the photographs from her camera's memory card.

Unfortunately, her trip to the city center today had gleaned no results. She'd tailed the head of Guatana's naval defense ministry for hours, and the only shots she'd managed to snap were of the former general having lunch with his slime bag politician friends.

Riya frowned deeply. "Nothing? Really? Tomlin's intelligence is usually spot-on."

"I don't know what to tell you. Aguilar did go to the market like Tomlin said he would, but there was no hush-hush meeting. Here—look."

She spun the computer around and clicked on the photos that had already been uploaded. There was shot after shot of Felipe Aguilar in the nearly deserted promenade that made up Guatana City's sorry excuse for a market. A mere two years ago, the *Mercado Esmeralda* was a bustling tourist mecca crammed with booths and vendors, locally grown fruits and vegetables, and an array of merchandise at a low price. Now, with food and water shortages plaguing the small country, the market was a relic of a not-so-long-ago past.

The rapid decline of Guatana was the reason for Cate's extended visit. After she'd dropped out of college, it had taken a while for her freelance career to pick up, but this past year had been chock-full of opportunities. This latest gig was a major coup—providing the accompanying photographs for Riya's in-depth examination of the unsavory conditions in Guatana. The homicide rate was astronomical, as rival cartels jockeyed for power, all wanting to be the primary supplier of cocaine to the US. Politicians were either in the pocket of the cartels or backed by the military or both. Since freedom of the press was a joke in this country, the online articles painted a far rosier picture of the small South American nation, particularly concerning its rapidly collapsing economy.

If Cate's father knew what the conditions on the ground were like, he'd shit a kitten.

Yet, it was the most exciting assignment Cate had landed to date, and far more rewarding than she'd anticipated. Sure, the hotel was seedy. The streets were overrun with beggars. Locals were killed on a daily basis, usually caught in the cross fire of warring cartels. And yes, seeing all that turmoil broke her heart, but at the same time, someone needed to be here to capture this. To show the rest of the world what was going on right under their noses.

"Who do you think he's talking to?"

Riya's wary observation jerked Cate's attention back to the screen. The journalist tapped an unpolished fingernail on a picture that showed the general holding a cell phone to his ear. His brow held a deep furrow and there were unhappy lines around his mouth.

"No idea," Cate said, clicking through ten more shots of Aguilar on the phone. "But if Tomlin's right and Aguilar was supposed to meet someone, then maybe this is the other party. Calling to cancel the meeting, maybe?"

"Perhaps," Riya mused. Her dark eyes remained fixed on the screen. "Let's enlarge some of these and pay closer attention to the crowd. Maybe the mystery date is lurking in the background."

"I'm on it. I was planning on doing that after I finish uploading."

"Good."

When the other woman hesitated, Cate offered a frown of her own. "What's wrong?"

"Nothing. It's just . . ." Riya shrugged. "Still seems a bit silly to rely on my slightly above par sources when you've got a top-notch network to tap into."

Though it wasn't an accusation, it still raised Cate's hackles. Riya couldn't understand why Cate wasn't taking advantage of the resources at hand. Hell, Cate herself could see why that might confuse people. *Globe Magazine* was a powerful media outlet, but Riya's contacts weren't even remotely comparable to the ones at Cate's disposal.

No, at Jim Morgan's disposal.

And therein lay the problem, because Jim Morgan wasn't just a supersoldier—he also happened to be Cate's father.

Her father.

God, it still felt surreal at times, having a dad. Four

years ago, she was a seventeen-year-old girl living in France under her grandfather's thumb. Being forced to visit a mother who was brain-dead. Being told her father had abandoned her and eventually died.

But it had all been a lie, an elaborate story concocted by a man who'd turned out to be a criminal. The grandfather who'd raised her was an arms dealer who murdered anyone who looked at him wrong, and Cate never would've known the truth if Jim Morgan hadn't walked into her life and saved her from a prison of luxury and lies.

She had idolized Morgan on sight. Everything about him spoke to her: his commanding nature, his steely strength, his gruff tenderness. He was the kind of father she'd always dreamed of having, someone who loved her unconditionally, who protected her, who understood the strange itch she'd had all her life, that deep-seated need for action and adventure.

Or at least she *thought* he'd understood. These days, she wasn't so sure.

"I'm not involving my father," Cate said when she noticed Riya's expectant expression.

The other woman sighed. "Remind me again why?"

"Because he's a stubborn ass who refuses to treat me as an adult." She made an unflattering noise under her breath. "I told you—we're not speaking at the moment."

That got her a chuckle. "Seems like he's not the only stubborn one in this scenario." Riya's tone softened. "Look, hon, he's your father. Of course he's going to view you as a child. You *are* a child—*his* child."

"I'm twenty-one," Cate protested.

Riya laughed again. "Parents will always think of their kids as babies. Hell, I'm thirty-nine and when I go to Mumbai for a visit, my father still asks if I need help tying my shoes."

Cate laughed too. "So all dads are overprotective cavemen?"

"Pretty much."

Maybe there was truth to that, but Cate had a feeling Jim Morgan was a thousand times worse than Riya's father, who owned a cigar shop and was supposedly as gentle as a lamb. Morgan, on the other hand, was a black ops soldier–turned–mercenary. He could kill a man with his bare hands, and he was married to a woman who could do the same. Or maybe Noelle was worse, actually, because if Cate had to choose who was scarier—Jim or his wife—she'd pick Noelle in a heartbeat.

"All I'm saying is," Riya went on, "he's genetically programmed to want to protect you. But I'm certain that once this article is published, he'll get it. He'll understand that you belong out in the world and not in some lecture hall."

"I doubt it," she said glumly. "He acts like my photography is just an inconvenient hobby. And if he could get away with it, he totally *would* try to tie my shoes for me. He thinks I'm incompetent."

Riya snorted. "Incompetent? Hon, we never would've made it out of that village on the coast alive last week if you weren't so damn good at hot-wiring cars."

"Morgan taught me that," she admitted, albeit grudgingly.

"See? He wouldn't have armed you with all those crafty skills if he didn't believe you could handle yourself. And from what you've told me, he'd give his life for you and everyone else he cares about."

"Yes, but that has nothing to do with this assignment," Cate grumbled. "If I ask him for intel about Guatana and the cartels, he'll do the opposite of help—he'll fly out here on his jet and drag me kicking and screaming back to Costa Rica."

And she could *not* go back to Costa Rica. Morgan's compound, bordered by the jungle on one side and the mountains on the other, might be beautiful, but it was a damn fortress. Not to mention crowded. She couldn't walk out of her bedroom without bumping into someone. Her dad. Noelle. Abby and Kane, the married mercs on her dad's team. Ethan and Juliet, who'd also recently moved in. And, of course . . . Ash.

Goddamn Ash. She couldn't seem to go ten minutes without thinking about that jerk. And he *so* wasn't worthy of it. Nope, he didn't deserve even a nanosecond of her mental energy.

"We don't need Morgan's resources," she maintained in a firm voice. "We can do some more digging on our own. We know Aguilar is involved in shady deals with the cartels—it's only a matter of time before we find a concrete connection."

Riya looked unconvinced. "And if we don't?"

"Then . . ." Cate sighed. "Then I'll *think* about calling Noelle, my dad's wife. Or one of the twins—" At Riya's blank expression, Cate clarified, "Sean and Oliver Reilly. They're mercenaries now but they used to be information dealers. They have more contacts than the CIA."

"All right. Well, tomorrow we're driving up north, so hopefully we'll make some headway. Several of the northern villages are rumored to have ties with the Rivera cartel."

Cate nodded. "I'd like to get some photographs of Árbora," she said, referring to a small town that had been burned to the ground a month before.

According to Riya's contacts, Árbora had been swimming in riches thanks to a deal with the cartel. In exchange for cutting and packaging drugs, the villagers were provided with resources that citizens in the surrounding areas were being deprived of. Fresh fruit, plenty of grains, clean water. A rebel group in the area had caught wind of this and proceeded to torch the village, sending a clear message to the Rivera cartel and to anyone who chose to cooperate with them.

God, this entire country was in chaos. Civil strife, political bribery, citizens taking orders from drug cartels because officials were too weak or too corrupt to govern properly. Cate was both horrified and fascinated by it, and the latter only reaffirmed her decision to leave college. Why would she want to sit in a lecture hall and take notes about foreign conflicts when she could be experiencing those conflicts firsthand?

And why couldn't Jim Morgan, a man who lived and breathed action, who craved the adrenaline high and welcomed the danger . . . why couldn't he understand that she was cut from that very same cloth?

"Let's study the maps at dinner," Riya suggested. "We'll decide which areas are worth focusing on and plan our route."

"Sounds good."

Riya scraped back her chair. "I'll ring you in a couple of hours. Right now I'm in desperate need of a nap. I've been up since dawn."

"I'll see you later," Cate said, her gaze returning to the laptop as the older woman left the hotel bar.

It wasn't the most ideal place to work, but the hotel Wi-Fi was spotty everywhere but here. Upstairs, it was nonexistent, which was irritating as hell because Cate would've preferred the privacy.

She leaned forward in her chair and began sorting the day's pictures by time and location and transferring them to individual folders. When a waiter came by with another glass of water, Cate gratefully accepted it, then fought a rush of guilt after she'd drained half the glass.

It felt wrong chugging clean, ice-cold water when many of Guatana's citizens were dying of dehydration every single day.

But that's why she was here, right? To shed light on the injustice? People said a picture was worth a thousand words, and Cate always clung to that notion when she had her camera in hand. She'd captured brutal, heartbreaking images these past three weeks. Images of starving children and desperate parents. Of bread lines that evoked memories of Hungary and Great Depression America. Of heaps of garbage being used as housing.

Ironically, the photos she was currently studying were somehow the most gruesome of all. Felipe Aguilar, fat and tanned and clad in a thousand-dollar suit amid a crowd of disheveled, sickly locals. Aguilar handing over a crisp bill at a coffee stand, while ten feet away from him, three children scoured the dirty ground for loose change. Aguilar chatting on his cell phone, while—

Cate froze.

Was that . . . ?

Narrowing her eyes, she dragged two fingers across the trackpad to enlarge the photo on the screen. Then she studied it. Carefully. For what felt like hours. But no matter how many times she zoomed in and out, she still couldn't make sense of what she was seeing. As her heartbeat accelerated, she opened a Web browser and did a quick image search.

"Holy shit," she mumbled.

Instincts humming, she scrambled for her cell phone and pulled up Riya's name. She felt bad waking the woman, but if she was seeing what she thought she was, then Riya would want to be woken up.

"Hey," came Riya's response. Fortunately, she sounded alert.

"You need to get back down here. I have something to show you."

"Everything all right?"

"It's either more than all right—I'm talking scoop of the century all right—or I'm totally hallucinating."

There was a soft chuckle. "I'll be right down."

While she waited, Cate enlarged the photo and inspected it again. By the time Riya appeared in the bar, she was convinced this was no hallucination. And the wily journalist at her side instantly confirmed it.

"Oh my *fuck*," Riya breathed.

Cate sputtered out a laugh. "I know, right?"

The dark-haired woman bent over the screen, her eyes alight with excitement. "Jesus, Cate. It's really him. Or else it's someone who's fucking identical to him."

That gave Cate pause. "Ah, shit. Didn't he have a ringer during that raid last year? It was on the news, remember? The DEA ambushed some big powwow between the South American cartels and ended up killing a look-alike. What if this is one of his doubles?"

"Shit. Yeah, that's a likely possibility." Riya pursed her lips. "Let me call my guy at the Bureau. They might be able to run this through their facial recognition program. It'll take some time, though."

"How much time?"

"Days, most likely. They're not too quick about granting me favors."

Cate bit the inside of her cheek. Damn it. She knew someone with access to a program like that too. Someone who could offer results in a matter of minutes, not days.

"Fuck," she said with a sigh.

Riya's brow furrowed. "What's wrong?"

"This is a big deal, right?"

"Uh, this is huge, hon."

"Huge enough that we'd want confirmation as fast as we can get it?"

"Huge enough to win both of us a Pulitzer."

"Fuck," she said again.

"Cate—"

"Don't contact your FBI buddy," Cate interrupted. She released a resigned breath. "Morgan will have an answer for us before you even get off the phone with your guy."

Riya's lips twitched. "You sure about this?"

Cate was already opening her e-mail account. "You want fast results, this is how we get them."

She pulled up a new message, attached the photo, and quickly typed a few lines in the body. After she'd hit SEND, she reluctantly reached for her phone and shot off a short text as well.

E-mailing you a pic. Super important. Confirm that this is who I think it is?

She wasn't surprised when she received an instantaneous response.

Opening the e-mail. Stand by.

Cate rolled her eyes. For a man who spoke to her as if she were a military operative, he sure as hell didn't treat her like one.

Less than ten seconds later, a follow-up message popped up.

Jesus Christ, Cate. What the hell are you involved in??

She gritted her teeth and typed, Confirm or not?

After a long delay, Morgan texted back.

I'll get back to you soon. Sit tight.

Turtle Creek, Costa Rica

"Carbon Cola has announced it will cease production of its products, effective immediately, due to sugar shortages," announced a sober-voiced newscaster. "Meanwhile, inflation has increased by two hundred and thirty percent in the last month. Food bank lines grow longer on a daily basis, with all but a select few going home empty-handed." The screen split, and a pale-faced, suited man appeared on the right side. "Steven Cranston, you're an expert in Guatana foreign affairs—what do you make of this announcement?"

"Watching the news on a Friday night? I see that Jim needs to find something for you to do," a sultry voice drawled from the doorway.

David "Ash" Ashton looked up to find his boss's wife leaning against the doorframe. He muted the volume and flashed her his patented Southern smile full of wicked charm. "Does it involve you? Because if so, I'll be a happy man."

Noelle's blue eyes warmed from glacier cold to frosty. The only time those chilly eyes fully thawed was around Ash's boss, Jim Morgan. The Queen of Assassins took the King of Killers into her bed every night, and from the noises that came out of the bedroom, their lovemaking sounded more like a WWE wrestling match than a fuckfest. Ash always had an urge to cup himself protectively when she was around, but he refrained because he knew, as with any predator, that you couldn't let them know you feared them.

"You're a handful, Ash." She pushed away from the door and sauntered toward him.

Petite and curvy, with a face that belonged on magazine covers, more than one man had lost his head over her—literally. Noelle had put down more dangerous people than a platoon of Marines. She could get you off with one hand while tearing your heart out with the other. Ash surmised she'd done that to Morgan a few times before the two of them had called a truce.

"Feel free to fill your hand with me," he forced himself to say with a smile. He was a single Southern boy. Flirting was taught at the cradle. It used to come as naturally as breathing, but lately he'd found it hard to muster up any good humor. He'd become a moody shit. "I know Jim will kill me, but it'd be a worthwhile death."

Noelle stretched out an arm behind him and tangled her fingers in his hair. Most men would pop a boner the moment she sat down next to them on a sectional big enough to house half an army. His head acknowledged she was a beautiful and dangerous woman—the best kind for a mercenary—but his dick didn't get hard for anyone these days.

He had a feeling she didn't miss the fact that his downstairs was dead as a doornail as she ran her scarlet-coated fingertips through his hair.

"By all means, let's go upstairs and do the dirty right now." Her red lips curved into a smile.

Ash glanced down at his lap and prayed for something, anything to move, even though taking her up on her invitation would mean certain death. He wouldn't even get to lay a hand on her before Morgan would appear and rip him into pieces. Still, that would mean some kind of relief from the torment Ash had been suffering lately.

"Nah. I don't want the old man to look bad in comparison. If you had me, you wouldn't be able to go back. I like Jim too much to do that to him."

"Ah, I see. So, instead, you've blazed a path through all the local girls between the ages of eighteen and thirty-five. I've heard you've left quite a trail behind you."

Noelle's nails scraped along the back of his neck, a highly erogenous zone in the past. That and a light stroke behind his ears never failed to generate wood in his pants. Jesus. He was turning into a miserable human being. He couldn't even get hard when one of the most beautiful women on the planet was coming on to him. Yes, he knew it was fake. Noelle wouldn't actually fuck him. Not just because Morgan would kill them both, but because she had zero attraction toward him. And he wasn't interested in Noelle either.

But shouldn't he at least get hard? Shouldn't his cock stand up and acknowledge that a smoking hot chick was rubbing up against him?

"A gentleman doesn't brag about his luck with the ladies." Ash spread his legs so that his right thigh pressed against Noelle's knees. Surely that contact would rouse something in him.

"You've been staying home a lot lately."

She moved even closer. Close enough that he could feel her breath waft across the back of his neck. Still nothing.

"Didn't know you were keeping tabs on my love life," he said lightly.

"I keep tabs on everyone."

The way she said "everyone" made his short hairs prickle. "Everyone?" he echoed, trying to act nonchalant.

She smiled smugly. "Aw, honey, you want me to tell you all the dirty little secrets I know? Well . . ." She started ticking off her fingers, one by one. "Isabel and Trevor are trying for a baby—God knows why they'd want to bring a kid into this wretched world. Your boy scout Ethan likes to screw Juliet in the pool but thinks nobody knows what a naughty boy he is. Sofia's trying to convince Derek to give her a real wedding ceremony instead of the half-assed let's-go-to-the-courthouse-and-sign-some-papers shit he tried with her. Dubois knocked up his wife. Reilly's pulling a Sofia and harassing Bailey about marriage. Hmmm . . . who else . . . Kane and Abby kick the shit out of each other in the training room and then fuck like bunnies on the mats afterward."

"That doesn't seem like everyone," Ash noted. A bite of impatience he couldn't completely tamp down colored his words. Noelle was playing with him, but he wasn't sure why.

"Oh, who are we missing?" she drawled.

Fuck you, Noelle. She was going to make him say it, huh? And he didn't want to. For the past four years he'd tried to ignore his inappropriate lust for a girl he shouldn't be thinking about. He'd buried that lust deep down behind a dozen layers of self-control. He'd tried to fuck her out of his memory bank, burning through the local women, and then, when that failed, jacking off so many times that he swore he'd developed a callus on his right hand.

That only whetted his appetite instead of killing it off. Since then he'd tried to forget that she was alive. But it hadn't worked. Nothing had.

"No one, I guess. No one important," he muttered, drawing away from Noelle.

He was growing hard now, but it had nothing to do with Noelle and everything to do with the one person they weren't talking about. The one person significantly excluded from Noelle's exhaustive rundown of the entirety of her team of female assassins and Morgan's team of male mercenaries. The one person in the world who was off-limits to him.

Christ, if Ash thought Jim would castrate him for looking at Noelle funny, that punishment would be a birthday party compared to what Jim would do if he knew who starred in Ash's nightly—and daytime—fantasies.

And, as if thinking of *her* conjured up Morgan, the boss himself appeared suddenly in the doorway. "The two of you need to stop flirting and get your asses to the war room," he barked.

Ash jumped up as if the couch were on fire.

"Ash, honey, at some point, you need to decide that you want something more than Jim's approval," Noelle whispered as she slid off the sofa.

Ash followed behind with a bitter taste in his mouth. He knew that. The problem he'd always had was that he wanted both.

Jim's approval . . . and Jim's daughter.

Chapter 2

Three years ago

"They're back."

Ash watched as Ethan Hayes strolled up with a coil of rope over his shoulder. The two of them were headed for the training course to repair one of the rope climbs, but Ethan seemed more interested in the commotion beyond the front doors. His announcement was completely unnecessary, too. Jim Morgan and his daughter had been arguing loudly since they'd exited Morgan's Land Rover. From the sounds of it, they might have been arguing since Morgan picked Cate up from the airport.

Ash scratched his neck and pretended he didn't care that Cate was back, never mind that his dick started swelling at the first sound of her voice. "I'm guessing the college visits were a bust."

The two men shared a wince at the harsh slam of the door. That door was made of iron and wood. A man had to be really pissed off to hit the frame with that kind of impact.

"Would it fucking kill you to take this seriously?" Morgan thundered.

"I am taking it seriously," Cate yelled back. "If I take it any more seriously, I'll be getting my college degree on the fucking application process."

"Don't curse."

"Don't talk to me, then, you hypocrite!"

"Jesus Christ, Cate. I'm asking you to go out and experience a world that isn't full of guns and bad guys. Is that so wrong?"

"What's wrong with this life? Here with you and Noelle and our family?"

Ethan rolled his eyes and mouthed, *Family?* to Ash.

Yeah, they were a family. An unconventional one full of a bunch of head cases that wouldn't fit in any other life than this one.

But he didn't blame Morgan for urging Cate to seek a different path. Morgan's base of operations was a former drug lord's compound complete with booby traps, C-4, and three electric gates. Any loving father would want his daughter to live in a nice suburb where the biggest danger was someone's asshole dog pooping on your lawn instead of the threat of getting wiped out by a rival mercenary group.

"I want something better than that for you." Morgan's volume lowered a decibel and took on a weary note. "Anyone you're going to meet around here is a merc or a hired gun or an operative. You're better than that."

"Better than you?"

"Damn straight. The life span of a contract killer is short, Cate. So yeah, I want something better for you."

Ash's stomach dropped.

"Let's go, Rook," Ethan murmured.

Ignoring the twinge of shame in his gut, he followed the other man into the massive, modern kitchen and grabbed a pair of work gloves off the granite counter. "How long you going to call me that?"

"Until someone newer, younger, or rawer comes along," Ethan informed him.

"I'm recruiting tonight."

"Good. Fix now"—Ethan jiggled the rope—"recruit later."

"Okay, Ger."

"Ger?"

Both their heads shot up at Cate's question. They found her standing in the doorway, a wary smile on her lips.

"Short for geriatric." Ash winked at her while he quickly scanned her face. No signs of crying, thank fuck. Nothing was worse than seeing Cate cry, not even Morgan's implication that everyone in the household didn't deserve to breathe the same air as she did. "If I'm the rookie, then Ethan's a step away from the grave."

"Nah, that'd be Kane," Ethan joked as Kane Woodland, their second-in-command, stalked into the kitchen with Morgan dragging up the rear.

"What am I?" Kane grabbed an apple off the counter and bit into it.

"Old. Decrepit. Maybe senile," Cate volunteered with a pointed look toward her father.

Ash wondered if that would set off another round of fireworks, but Morgan merely snorted.

"What's so funny, old man?" Kane taunted. "We're nearly the same age."

"I'm not the one she's calling old."

"Oh you're old, Jim," Cate clarified helpfully.

"Not compared to Kane. I might be older than him in years, but I'm younger where it counts." Morgan smirked. "Ethan, what was Kane's time last run?"

"A little over nine minutes." Ethan was the keeper of all the team's times. The men could get a little competitive.

"Bullshit. I run that course in eight and under every

time." Kane turned to Ash. "Next time we race, I need you there to keep Ethan honest, rookie. I don't trust that kid."

Ethan just grinned.

"And you?" Kane said, turning to their boss. "You really think you can do better? You're slower than molasses."

Morgan raised a brow. "I could smoke your ass any day. Let's go. Right now."

"Bring it."

"I'm not kidding."

"Neither am I." Kane held out his arm. "After you, *sir*."

Morgan flipped him off before heading for the French doors that led to the huge stone terrace where the team liked to dine at night. The sun shone brightly above the lush green canopy of the jungle bordering the enormous property. As Ash watched in amusement, the two older men set off in a brisk march toward the tree line.

"Men," Cate grumbled from the counter.

Ethan snickered. "I can't believe they're actually going to race."

"You better get out there to time them," Ash told him.

"Hell no. Whichever one of them loses will kick me in the balls for being the time messenger. They can time themselves."

"Oooh, I'll do it," Cate said with sudden glee. "It'll be fun declaring Jim a big, fat loser."

Ash stifled a laugh as she practically pranced to the patio doors. "Oh, hey," she whispered as she passed by. "I need to talk to you later."

"About what?"

"College. Him." She jerked a thumb toward her dad's back as Morgan strode toward the jungle. "Please?"

It was the sad plea in her voice that did him in. "Course."

"Thank you." Cate squeezed his arm and then hurried down the terrace steps to catch up with the men.

Unwittingly, Ash's eyes drifted down to her ass, which was nicely encased in a pair of worn denim cutoffs. Christ. Her legs were criminally long. He stifled a groan.

"Better watch where your eye lands. People are noticing," Ethan murmured.

"Don't know what you're talking about."

"Seventeen's a little young, don't you think?"

"I repeat," Ash said stiffly, "I have no idea what you're talking about."

"Best keep it that way. Noelle's chameleons are adults and fair game. Jim's little girl? Completely off-limits, dude."

Ash didn't need Ethan to tell him. He already knew that. That's why he'd spent the past year keeping his thoughts to himself. All those dirty, inappropriate thoughts about how fucking pretty she was. How her lower lip was fuller than her upper one, how her hair was shinier than the one nice piece of furniture his granny diligently polished every Sunday. How her unbound breasts swayed under those infuriatingly thin tank tops she liked to wear.

He swallowed another groan. Fuck. What was wrong with him? He was eight years older than she was. He couldn't keep lusting after this girl, and not just because of her age.

He looked beyond Cate toward Morgan. The big man grinding his boot heels into the dirt had given Ash a new purpose in life after he'd left the corps. Morgan had taken him in. Mentored him, welcomed him into the fold. Morgan *trusted* him. But although Ash was good enough to watch Morgan's back, he'd never be good enough for Cate, at least not in her father's eyes.

He knew that. He respected that.

But that didn't mean he had to like it.

Chapter 3

Present day

Ash strode into the briefing room and closed the door behind him. He didn't miss the tension in Morgan's jaw or the way the man was glaring daggers at his wife.

"Did you know she was going to Guatana?" Morgan growled.

"No." Noelle rolled her eyes. "We were both at the same dinner, if you remember, when she told us that she was getting a travel assignment to Africa, and then the two of you argued about whether she'd be safe enough without a contingent of bodyguards. I distinctly remember some raised voices and a visit from the maître d', who told us that if we didn't use our inside voices, he was going to have to ask us to leave."

Morgan shoved a phone at his wife. "Then if she's supposed to be in Africa, why is she taking pictures of Mateo Rivera in Guatana?"

Ash nearly trampled his boss in an effort to see what was on the screen. When he did, his stomach plummeted to his feet. What the fuck? Mateo Rivera was dead. He'd been killed in a car bombing that was televised for three days on all the major news networks. The president of Guatana had stood in front of a pile of confiscated loot— cash, drugs, and guns weighing down a room full of tables. *Look here*, the headlines had screamed, *the war on drugs won*!

Yet the picture on Morgan's phone showed the round-faced, mustached South American looking fat and happy. Okay, maybe not happy, but sure as hell alive.

"Where'd she get that?" he demanded.

Noelle hid a smirk, but Morgan was too agitated to notice the panic in Ash's voice. "She said she took it yesterday in the city. Claims she was following up on rumors that a bottling plant was being shut down, but she's full of shit because this photo was clearly taken in the market."

"The plant thing isn't a rumor," Ash replied. His heart began to thud overtime. "It was just on CNN. Carbon Cola is ceasing production."

"Damn, conditions down there must be terrible."

Ash nodded grimly. Even in Iraq, in the middle of the war, soda trucks could be spotted everywhere. Bottling plants only shut down when a country was on the verge of collapse. When a water source was compromised, it was often better to drink the sugary, carbonated soda than anything running out of a tap.

"Is she on her way home?" Ash asked.

Morgan shot him a harried look. "She won't answer the damn phone."

Of course she wouldn't. Ever since Morgan had discovered and extricated Cate four years ago from a luxurious prison, he'd tried pushing her into a normal life—one filled with fraternity boys, college parties, and Starbucks. He'd even bought a house in Providence so Cate could have somewhere closer than Costa Rica to visit when she wasn't at Brown.

Cate, however, swore she hated coffee and college boys and dropped out of Brown to take photographs all over the world. Her initial assignments had been travel photography, and she'd taken spectacular, award-winning images of the cotton castles in Turkey, rice paddies in Yogyakarta, Indonesia, the wild animals in Chobe National Park, Botswana. With each award and each starkly beautiful image, Morgan's ability to dictate his daughter's future became less and less. And with the loss of control came increased agitation. The two of them fought more than they got along.

The mood around the Costa Rica compound was always dark after a Cate visit. The last one was four months ago. Ash had left the compound that night, got stupid drunk, and had his first—and only—episode of limp dick. He'd sworn off women since then.

"What's the last update we have on Rivera?" Morgan asked.

Noelle shrugged. "Other than he's supposed to have died in a car bombing? Not much. My people stopped tracking him. The power structure in Guatana splintered after his death, so I directed my resources to track the other cartels that are clawing for power."

"That was a mistake," Morgan snapped.

Noelle arched an eyebrow. "She's going to be fine."

Her husband's expression gleamed with accusation. "You always encouraged her to do this work."

"Because she's your daughter, Jim. She was never going to be happy sitting in your armed compound knitting scarves and taking pictures of the local flora and fauna." Unfazed by his icy glare, Noelle grabbed a burner phone and threw it on the table.

"Maybe if she'd spent less time around us, she'd have turned out different." Morgan ignored the phone and started pacing. "Instead, she spent day after day watching us practice hand-to-hand combat, shoot guns, and try to kill each other."

"And because of that, she can take care of herself," Noelle tried to soothe him.

Ash needed some soothing himself. His nuts were crawling inside his body with fear over Cate's safety. He wanted Jim to summon a chopper so that they could be in the air and in Guatana within two hours.

"She's a single girl. Alone." Morgan turned his angry eyes at Ash. "Did she tell you she was going to Guatana? I know she talks to you."

The boss definitely didn't know everything. Cate had stopped talking to Ash a long time ago. "She doesn't talk to me."

"Since when?"

Since you said you'd string any mercenary up by his gonads if he looked sideways at her.

Since I told her that I didn't want a little girl like her with her embarrassing inexperience.

Since I tore out her heart and trampled all over it.

It took effort, but he managed a careless shrug. "Sorry, boss, I don't know. We just grew apart."

"Shit." Morgan stopped pacing, a determined glint lighting his dark blue eyes. "Get your gear and let's be ready to go wheels up in thirty."

"On it. Who's coming with?"

"We'll take Kane, Ethan, and D."

Noelle made a disgusted sound in the back of her throat.

"What?" Morgan swung around. "You can come. I wasn't gonna leave you out."

"Cate's not going to be happy if you and your band of merry men go rushing in."

"So?" Ash said impatiently. "She'd be alive. That's what's important."

Noelle ignored him, directing her efforts on Morgan. "Your relationship with her is already touch and go.

Let's call your contact at the DEA and get some more information first."

Ash didn't like that at all. "That country is on the verge of an all-out revolution," he protested. "It's Poland in the eighties. Hungary after World War Two. Leaving her alone with a journalist is ridiculous."

Morgan's indecision was evident until Noelle placed a hand on his arm. "If you go in and pull her out—ruining whatever story she's working on—then it'll be a long, cold day in hell before she willingly comes back here to spend any off time with you."

The blunt words struck home, because Morgan nodded abruptly. "Let's get Greg Tripley on the line and find out what they know about Rivera. We can assess our risks then."

"Christ," Ash muttered. This was a mess. They should be on the first flight out of Costa Rica. Instead they were going to call some pencil pusher in DC?

Both Noelle and Jim ignored him. Noelle picked up the burner phone, typed something in, and then tossed the phone back on the table.

Ash crossed his arms and watched Morgan pace again as they all waited for this Tripley asshole to call them.

Five minutes later, after Ash's boss had nearly worn a channel into the tile floor, the phone finally rang. Morgan lunged forward and put the call on speaker.

"Morgan?" A nasal voice rang out in the room. "It's been a while."

As always, Morgan got right down to business. "Tripley," he barked, "I have a picture of Mateo Rivera looking like the picture of health, and if it wasn't for the fact that I know the photographer, I'd say this picture is bullshit. You gonna tell me that this is fake or Rivera's doppelganger?"

"The kids are great, Jim. Thanks for asking. Little Sara

is taking ballet now and Cameron is playing football with pads for the first year," Tripley said sarcastically.

"I don't give a damn if little Sara is in line to get the Nobel Peace Prize. We had solid intel that Rivera was dead and we pulled resources off him because of it. So is he dead or not?"

Tripley sighed. "Shit. We're not sure. At the time, the death info looked solid. The son—Adrián—is running the show now. But lately we've had reports of sightings of the old man. Initially we brushed them off as an Elvis phenomenon, but now we're thinking he might've faked his death."

"Why the fuck would he do that?"

"No idea. But in his absence, the drug trade in South America is now in upheaval. Maybe he's staging a dramatic reappearance."

"Is this dramatic reappearance going to coincide with a military coup and a lot of bloodshed?" Morgan asked grimly.

Ash's mouth turned dry as dust even before Tripley responded, because they all knew what the man was going to say.

"Yeah . . . if you have anyone you care about in Guatana, they should get out now."

It was nearing midnight. Despite the fact that she'd been up since dawn, Cate wasn't tired. Her brain was too busy replaying her last conversation with Morgan, in which he'd not so politely ordered her to come home.

"Get on the fucking plane, Catarina."

Ha. That's how he thought he'd win her over? By barking out commands and full-naming her? *No dice, Dad,* she thought as she angrily paced the hardwood floor of her hotel room. Technically, it was Riya's room, but the two women had switched because this one neighbored a suite whose occupants liked to get in screaming fights every night, which kept Riya up. Cate, on the other hand, could sleep through anything, so the switch hadn't been a hardship for her.

No, the only hardship at the moment was that her obstinate, sailor-mouthed father refused to respect her or her work.

She got it—he was protective of her. But that didn't give him the right to treat her like an idiot or undermine her abilities. Morgan had spent hours with her to ensure she could take care of herself. Target shooting, tracking, self-defense. Why had he bothered with all that if he was determined to lock her up in a cage like a helpless little bird?

On the small night table, her phone began to buzz.

Cate ignored it and kept pacing. She didn't need any more threatening texts from Morgan. She wasn't leaving Guatana no matter how many times he ordered her to "get on the fucking plane."

Mateo Rivera was alive, damn it. The facial recognition program Morgan's contact had run the photograph through had returned a perfect match. The most savage and feared drug lord on the globe hadn't died in a car bombing as the news had announced to the world. It didn't matter if his "death" had been staged or if the charred remains in that car had been misidentified. Either way, Cate and Riya's story was suddenly a million times larger in scope.

They were already reevaluating their plans for tomorrow. Rather than go up north, they'd discussed visiting Meldina instead, the village where Rivera's wife had grown up. There was a slim chance he was hiding out there while he . . . while he what? Ran his empire from the supposed grave?

Cate didn't know what the bastard was up to, but

whatever it was, it couldn't be good. Nothing in this country was good.

Sighing, she finally went to check her phone. Sure enough, a text from her father, demanding to know why she was ignoring his texts. She set the cell down and headed for the mini-fridge to grab a bottle of water.

She was just twisting off the cap when she heard the footsteps.

No, not footsteps. More like loud stomping. Even louder male voices were calling out to each other in Spanish, unconcerned that everyone on the floor was probably sound asleep.

With an annoyed curse, Cate stalked over to the door at the same time a horrified shriek pierced the air . . . followed by a gunshot that damn near vibrated in the walls.

She didn't have time to think. No time to panic. The adrenaline hit her hard, injecting into her bloodstream and surging through her veins, propelling her toward the dresser where she'd stashed her gun. She had the Glock in one hand and her phone in the other before the gunfire had even faded to silence.

But the silence didn't last long. It was rapidly replaced by more shouts, and though her Spanish wasn't as good as her French or German, she made out three unmistakable words.

"It's not her."

The voices were right next door. Oh fuck. Oh fucking *fuck*. They were coming from Riya's room.

A jolt of fear shot up Cate's spine. She flattened herself against the wall beside the door, her mind running a million miles a second. Those men were next door. They'd fired a gun at someone . . . that scream . . . Riya.

Had they shot Riya?

In the hall, a man continued to bark orders.

"She couldn't have gone far."

"Search every room on this floor."

"Don't let her get away."

"Kill anything that moves."

Cate's entire body grew icy with horror. Her. They were talking about *her*. She didn't know why she was so certain of it, but there was no doubt in her mind that the men out in the hall had come here for her.

Another scream echoed in the bowels of the hotel, along with another wave of gunfire. Muffled, but no less terrifying. Those bastards were shooting people. Killing people. Footsteps thumped up and down the hall, one set nearing her door. As her heart thudded wildly against her ribs, she dove across the room toward the other door—the one to Riya's adjoining suite.

They might still be in there! an internal voice warned.

Maybe, but any second they would be in *here*. Cate's gaze darted to the main door, her heart stopping when she saw a dark shadow fall over the light spilling in from the hall. Without a second's thought, she twisted the doorknob, raised her gun, and stepped into Riya's room.

The suite was empty.

No. No, it wasn't empty.

"*No*," Cate choked out.

Riya was half sitting, half lying on the king-size bed. The covers were gathered haphazardly around her waist, as if she'd been in the process of sitting abruptly before . . .

Before someone blew her head off.

Cate almost keeled over at the sight of her friend's brains painting the pillow crimson. Riya's dark hair was loose. Her eyes were wide open.

The top of her head was gone.

Bile coated Cate's throat, making it hard to breathe.

She stood frozen for a moment. She was going to be sick. She was going—

Later! a voice snapped. Morgan's voice, she realized. Her father was in her head, commanding her, spurring her to action.

She frantically looked at the half-open door. Dark-clad figures raced past it, a blur of motion that sent her pulse careening. The gunfire was still going strong, mingling with the frightened yelps, pleas, and screams reverberating through the hall like a gruesome symphony. People were dying. Those men out there weren't even stopping to check who they were shooting. They were armed with machine guns; she recognized the familiar *rat-tat-tat* of bullets being sprayed into the walls. Into flesh.

Move! her father's voice commanded.

Move. She needed to move. Run. But where? Her gaze landed on the door leading out to the small second-floor balcony. Half a second later, she was pushing it open and stepping into the humid night air. She studied the drop to the street below—eight feet, at least. No fire escape. No hand- or footholds. But . . . her heart jumped when she spotted the drainpipe running alongside the balcony all the way to the pavement.

There was a chance it wouldn't hold her weight.

There was an even bigger chance those killers back there would return to Riya's room and—

Cate cried out when something shattered behind her. The light fixture by the balcony door. Shit! Someone was in the room again and they were fucking *shooting* at her.

Without a single thought to what she was doing, she tucked her gun in her waistband, shoved her phone between her teeth, and heaved herself over the far edge of the balcony.

The pipe creaked in protest when her hands wrapped around it. She dug her bare feet into the rust-covered metal and slid down a few inches, then an entire foot. The slow and steady descent was cut short when she heard footsteps above her.

She didn't dare look up—she simply shimmied down as fast as she could. Her feet slapped the dirty pavement just as a bullet took out a piece of the wall right above her head. The bricks splintered, crumbled chunks raining down on her. A jagged shard scraped the side of her face but she ignored it. She was already running, zigzagging down the sidewalk the way her father had taught her.

Never give them a target, sweetheart. Keep moving. Make it hard for them to kill you.

A backward glance was all she allowed herself, but it was long enough to lock eyes with the man on the balcony. Tall and lanky, he had a head of thick black hair, eyes the color of charcoal. He looked . . . familiar.

Adrián Rivera.

Holy shit, it was Adrián fucking Rivera. Cate recognized him from the pictures in the newspapers. The young man had taken over leadership after his father's death.

Even from several yards away, she saw his frustration. The glint of anger and the feral set of his jaw. He raised an assault rifle and sprayed the cracked sidewalk with bullets, but Cate was out of his range and running again.

Her lungs burned with each desperate stride. This time she didn't look back. She didn't stop, didn't allow herself to think of Riya's dead body draped on that bed. She pushed forward, running until the soles of her feet were bloody and her body was reeling with exhaustion.

She wasn't sure how many miles she'd managed to place between her and the hotel. Between her and the men who'd come to murder her. It didn't matter—she'd never be able to run fast or far enough, not if those men were connected to the Rivera cartel. They would find her. They would find her and kill her and—

Stop it, Morgan's voice barked. *Panic gets you nowhere.*

Gasping for air, Cate ducked into a shadow-bathed alley and pressed her tired, aching body against the wall. Despite the late hour, cars continued to speed down the street. A honk broke the air. Voices drifted out of a nearby bar.

She drew a breath. Then another, and another, until the panicky fog cleared and she was able to think clearly again.

A safe house. She needed a safe house, somewhere to hide until she could find a way out of this mess.

She slowly uncurled her fingers, which were gripping her cell phone tight enough to leave an impression of the power button in her palm. It took several seconds for her hand to stop trembling but she still felt weaker than a kitten as she pulled up the familiar number. The phone seemed to weigh a hundred pounds as she raised it to her ear and waited.

"Dad," she whispered when his gruff voice slid over the line.

"Cate?" he said instantly, concern etched into his tone. "What's wrong, sweetheart?"

"I'm in trouble." She rested her head against the brick wall, the adrenaline in her blood dissolving into fatigue. "I . . . need you."

Chapter 4

Three years ago

"I need you. Stop laughing!" Cate yelled as she dangled over the side of the climbing wall.

"You're doing fine. Swing your leg up." Ash tapped his thigh. "You've got this."

"I hate you, David Ashton." But she swung her leg and caught the edge of the wall with her foot.

"Double-naming me. That hurts, sugar. Really hurts."

If Cate was confident enough to let go, she would've given him the finger, but she needed all five fingers clinging to the side of the twenty-foot-high wall so she didn't fall on her ass into the sand below.

After watching Kane and her dad race through this the other day, she'd woken up thinking that if she could beat Morgan's time, she'd somehow prove herself worthy of making her own decisions. Obviously that was the stupidest conclusion she'd ever come to, but she didn't realize the idiocy of it until now. After she'd army-crawled under what looked like a thousand spiderwebs, waded armpit high through swamp sludge, scaled a sixty-foot-high wall with a rope, and spun around tires with spikes in them, she'd been struggling with this wall for the last ten minutes.

Her arms felt like jelly. Her legs were scratched to shit. And Ash stood on the other side, hands on his hips, looking like he'd just taken a Sunday stroll in the park. She hated him. She hated his tall, built frame, his chiseled chest and those damn obliques that darn near begged for a girl to lick them from tip to tip. She hated his Southern drawl, which got thick when he was amused, as if his words were caked with syrup. She wondered how he sounded in bed, with a woman. When he said *sugar* to a girl he was touching, how smooth and slow were his words?

Most of all she hated that he seemed elusive.

There were plenty of boys around here that were hot to get into her panties, but not one of them affected her like Ash did. She'd let a few of those boys kiss her. A couple had even gotten to third base, but she was more turned on by just looking at Ash than by the fumbling advances of those guys.

Which was how she found the small scrap of energy to pull herself upright.

"Ha!" She raised her fists in the air and shook them. "I did it."

"You sure did." It sounded like *you shoore did*. He took a running jump and scaled the wall like he was a monkey.

She cast him a dark look as he settled in next to her. "Couldn't you have tripped at least once before pulling yourself up?"

"No, ma'am. Muscle memory." He tapped his biceps and Cate forced her eyes away so she didn't sigh like a teenage girl at a Bieber concert. "I've done this sort of thing too many times. If I screwed up, then I'd need to run this course a hundred more times. Because out there"—he gestured beyond them—"Ethan, Kane, your daddy, they rely on me to carry out my orders without hesitation or question."

Cate wrinkled her nose. "Is this your way of telling

me I need to suck it up and stop arguing with Jim about college?"

He shook his head. "I was explaining why I couldn't intentionally screw up climbing this wall, but since you brought it up . . . What's your problem with college?"

"I fell right into that trap, didn't I?" She twisted around and let herself fall into the sandpit.

Ash followed her down, his silence saying more than any words.

Cate sighed. "You know how the colleges are called the Ivy League?"

"Yeah. So what?"

"Well, they feel more like an Ivy tower. A place where Jim thinks he can lock me up inside and I'll never be hurt by the outside world. I think he forgets where I came from." She kicked her boot into the dirt. "There were kids protesting at one of the schools. I asked my guide what it was about and apparently they were upset that the cafeteria in one of the dorms was only offering one vegan choice instead of two."

"That sounds . . ." He was obviously struggling for something good to say and when he couldn't come up with anything, he threw up his hands and said, "Shit, sugar, there's got to be someplace you can go. If you don't go to college, what're you gonna do?"

"I don't know, but I want to do something with my life besides just sitting in a room listening to an old guy talk about how he thinks life should work in a perfect textbook world. You and I both know that nothing ever happens like you expect. What kind of muscle memory am I going to be building up? How to sit in a chair? How to pick up a pen?" She stopped ranting when they arrived at the cove.

"I kinda doubt that's the only learning you can do," Ash said, then frowned as he took in the grotto.

It was Cate's favorite place on the compound, where

a natural spring fed a small stone pool. Even better? The cameras that Jim had set up around the property had a blind spot.

She slid a mischievous smile toward Ash. She was tired of complaining. She'd argued with Jim for nearly the entire flight from Florida to Costa Rica and now she wanted to relax and enjoy herself with her favorite person. Her hands dropped to the hem of the long-sleeve shirt Ash had made her wear when she told him she wanted to run the course.

"Want to go for a swim?" she suggested.

He flicked his eyes toward a red dot high in a tree and then down to her frame. Oh gosh. Was that . . . *heat* she saw in them?

Only one way to find out.

"There's a blind spot here, you know," she whispered to him, even though there weren't any mics out here. The cameras were just visuals.

She watched as Ash took in the area and knew precisely the moment when he figured out where the blind spot was. His gaze fixed on a small depression in the back wall of the grotto. "You tell Morgan about this?" he said warily.

Cate beamed at him. "Now why would I do a silly thing like that?"

Of course she'd found a flaw in the system. That didn't surprise Ash in the slightest, though he did have to wonder if Morgan was truly aware of how shrewd and savvy Cate actually was. The boss had the tendency to underestimate his daughter.

"I hate all these cameras," Cate mumbled. The smile she'd been flashing faded as she slid through the water. "That's another reason I want to get away from here. I can't stand being watched all the time."

His gaze flicked up to the red dot again, then over to Cate, who was climbing the cliff wall like a mountain goat before settling into a niche right below the camera eye. The blind spot.

Well, Ash was going blind looking at the cotton of Cate's underwear plastered against her skin.

"Better safe than sorry." He toed off his boots but kept his clothes on, because his briefs wouldn't disguise his growing erection.

"Now you're just being a hypocrite. You've complained about the all-seeing eyes before," she reminded him.

"Yeah, but I also wasn't here when Morgan's previous base was torched, so I probably have a different perspective."

Before Ash's time, Morgan had lost a couple of people when his compound was attacked while he was chasing down a lead on Cate. Holden McCall, their tech guy, had lost his wife in the attack. Holden had gotten on a chopper and hadn't been seen since.

Morgan's new property housed not only his daughter but also his wife, and the man had no intention of losing either one of them. Thus the ten-foot-high walls, the intrusive cameras, and the sudden need to see Cate installed as a pretty coed in an American college. Ash totally got where his boss was coming from.

"Slowpoke," Cate called out to him, kicking out a stream of water with her foot.

Out of all the reckless, dangerous things Ash had done in his life, this had to rank up there at the very top. He spared one more look at the camera before tossing his phone beside Cate's abandoned clothes. Then he slid into the warm water and was at the rock formation with five broad strokes.

She scooted over to make room for him. "Not taking off your shorts?"

"I'm good." The heavy wet khakis felt uncomfortable enough to dampen his embarrassing response. Ash hoped it continued that way.

"Suit yourself."

He focused on clear green grotto water.

"I hate fighting with Jim," she admitted, pulling her knees up to her chest. "But all we seem to do lately is yell at each other. He probably wants me out of the house so there's finally some peace and quiet. I know everyone else is sick of it."

Ash tried hard not to notice that her smooth legs were rubbing lightly against his arm. Jesus. He was twenty-five, not fifteen. He did not get turned on by a little arm to leg contact.

"We've weathered worse," he told her.

Cate snorted. "Jim and I aren't even close to reaching our worst. By the middle of the rainy season, we'll make a tropical storm look like a walk in the park."

She tucked her head against his shoulder, filling his nose with the smell of vanilla and spice, and he had to fight to keep his arm from drawing her closer. He couldn't encourage her crush in any way. Morgan would fillet him from throat to dick if Ash so much as looked at her crossways.

"He loves you and you love him and that's why you guys argue. You only argue with the folks you love," Ash said gently.

"Is that right? Where'd you hear that?"

He shrugged. "If you didn't feel safe here, you wouldn't feel right about yelling at him. You'd do whatever he asked so he'd keep you close. That's how it works."

"I guess you're right." She paused. "You think I should go, don't you?"

"Yeah, I do." He started mentally running through the obstacle course they'd just left in order to maintain some control over his body. Cate's snuggling close did little to help with that effort. "Go a year and if you hate it, you can come back to Morgan with some real ammunition. Right now, all you've got is your opinion against his. Get some concrete facts to support why your plan is better than his."

"That seems like such a waste. Almost no one on Jim's team, or Noelle's, for that matter, has ever gone to college. Look at Bailey. She can run circles around anyone who has a computer degree."

"I don't know Bailey's story, start to finish, but I bet if she had the opportunity that Morgan's offering you, she'd have jumped at it. I know I would."

Cate jerked upright, nearly bashing the top of her head against Ash's face. "You want to go to college?" she asked in surprise.

"Well, not now. But back when I was in high school, my options were the military or working at the local copper plant. So yeah, if I'd had a free ride to college, I would've gone in a heartbeat."

She studied him, as if looking for signs of insincerity, but she wasn't going to find any. The military had been the only choice for Ash when he was eighteen, and he'd taken it. He didn't regret his decision or where it had led him in the years after he'd been discharged, but he completely understood Morgan's desire to see Cate have something more than racing around the world, rescuing dumb fucks or trying to prevent something tragic from happening—usually because of the actions of dumb fucks.

Beside him, Cate blew out a huge sigh. "Fine, but you have to visit me."

Something like regret pinched at his heart. Not seeing Cate every day when he was home would suck. He wanted to sigh, too, but figured he shouldn't show anything to her but approval.

"When I can."

"That's a terrible answer."

"No," he corrected. "A truthful one. If I'm working, I'm working. I'm still the youngest guy here. I have to keep earning my place."

"Jim's not getting rid of you. He likes you too much. So does Noelle." Cate leaned over and brushed her lips against his cheek. "Everyone likes you."

Ash gulped hard, fighting the urge to shift his head so that those soft, sweet lips would brush his lips rather than his cheek. He had to quit thinking like that, damn it. Morgan had saved his life by offering him a place on the team. No way would he repay Morgan by encouraging Cate, no matter how badly his body wanted her.

"Come on. We should go back," he said gruffly. "Your dad will be worrying about you."

Without waiting for her answer, Ash dove into the cool water and swam toward the bank, away from danger and temptation.

Chapter 5

It took Ash all of five minutes to get ready, and half of them were spent sprinting to his room. He grabbed the go bag that sat inside his closet and that he checked religiously every week, and then he was back in the war room ready for further instructions. Morgan was still on the phone, while Noelle was leaning over the shoulder of their security man, Bill, reading an e-mail on the screen.

"What's the holdup?" Ash wanted to be in the air—*now*. Cate's frantic phone call to Morgan had come in more than an hour ago. Why the hell were they still in Costa Rica and not on their way to Guatana?

At the interruption, Morgan frowned at him and turned away.

Noelle, however, glided over calmly as if they were planning a tea party. "We're gathering a team," she explained.

"For what? We go in, take her out, and we're done. You and I could do it." He jiggled his duffel impatiently.

"Jim wants to make sure that all the contingencies are covered. We don't have a secondary safe house there. He's been on the phone to see if any of our associates have locals on the ground so we can gather some intel and have a place to hide out if the first location is compromised."

Ash tightened his grip. "We don't need another safe house. Cate made it to the apartment you've got there, right?"

"Yes, but—"

"Then we fly the bird in, land it at the airport, take some kind of local transport to Cate's location, and then do it all in reverse. It's a cakewalk."

"You saw the news coverage. It's chaotic there." Noelle arched a perfectly shaped eyebrow. "A solid plan is the difference between success and failure. Dead and not dead."

"There are a dozen mercs living in this place. We could topple a government with them," Ash snapped.

Her mouth flattened. Clearly she didn't like Ash's testiness, but he didn't give a shit. "Not all of them are coming. Kane and Abby have a son. Someone will have to stay home and it'll take the two of them twenty minutes of arguing before they come to an agreement about who gets to fight the bad guys and who stays home with J.J."

Ash ground his teeth together. What would be the likelihood of him being shot down by Morgan's surface-to-air missile system if he commandeered the chopper and flew to Guatana by himself?

As if she could read his mind, Noelle shook her head in irritation. "Don't be stupid. Go and check on the med kit in the chopper. Make sure we have enough supplies."

Alarm spiked in his system. "Why? Is Cate injured?"

Fuck. What if she was? Morgan hadn't offered any details other than *Cate's in trouble. We need to get her.*

"No, but if you don't stop snapping at me, you will be. Now go."

Ash went, but only because he had no choice. The chopper's medical supplies were checked daily, but if that's what was going to get them off the ground faster, he'd inventory the hell out of the bandages, saline, and morphine syringes.

The task occupied twenty minutes of his time. They were short on syringes so Ash went to the supply room in the compound's basement and grabbed a new box. Then he had nothing to do but sit on the landing skids and wait for the rest of the team to show up.

Damn it, Cate, why couldn't you have stayed in college? Hooked up with a popped-collar-wearing frat boy and shot out the requisite two kids? Wielded a pen instead of a camera lens? Your dad would've bought you the house in the suburbs with the shiny pool in the back and you could be sipping mai tais on a playdate with the local moms.

He dragged a hand down his face, remembering how they'd swam together in that damn grotto in the back of the property. When she'd stripped down to nothing but her panties and bra and slid into the water to become all long legs, smooth skin, and bright, hungry eyes.

He'd wanted to take her up on the invitation she'd telegraphed every time she looked his way. Wanted to take her up on it so damn bad . . .

A buzz at his hip wrenched him out of the past. With a shaky hand, he pressed the TALK button. "Yeah?"

Noelle's voice was brisk on the other end of the line. "Ready? We're taking off in five."

"Just sitting here warming the chopper."

"We'll be out soon."

Twenty minutes later, the helicopter landed at the private airfield ten miles from the compound. Five minutes after that, Ash and the others boarded Morgan's jet, which would take them directly to Guatana. Yet even though they were finally doing something, Ash still couldn't relax.

Neither could his boss, who was a total wreck. Morgan couldn't seem to sit still for even a second. The moment the plane took off, he'd bolted from his seat to address the assembled team, which consisted of Noelle, Ethan, Kane, and Ash.

"You know I hate going in with guns blazing and no pre-ground prep, but according to our contact at the DEA, Guatana is going to hell in a handbasket. The cartels are in all-out war. Ballsy fuckers are killing people in the streets, and they don't give a shit if innocent civilians get caught in the cross fire. I spoke to my contact in the Guatanan military who said martial law will be imposed any day now."

In front of Ash, Kane and Ethan exchanged raised eyebrows. Martial law would make it harder to get in and out of the country undetected. Airspaces would become totally restricted as the military regime flexed its muscle and cowed all the people indoors.

"Do we have a staging area?" Kane asked.

Morgan shook his head. "No. A contractor is meeting us at the airport. He'll have two transport vehicles. Kane, you and Noelle will be in one. Ethan and Ash are with me. D's going to fly in and hold at the airport to make sure no one takes our plane."

Translation: if martial law got imposed, they'd take off regardless.

Morgan took a ragged breath and checked his watch, as if trying to will the plane to move faster. Ash had never seen the boss this tense before, which said a lot, because Ash had been present when Cate was discovered, and that entire op had been hella tense. He'd been the rookie then—still was, he supposed. At twenty-nine, he was the youngest man on the team. Jim hadn't expanded in recent years, even with the absence of Liam Macgregor and Sullivan Port.

"Any word from Boston these days?" Ethan suddenly asked, as if reading Ash's mind.

He wasn't surprised that Ethan was also thinking about their former teammates. On missions, the absences of their brothers were noticed most keenly. After Sully's capture two years ago, he'd disappeared on his boat and they hadn't heard from him since. Liam, or "Boston" as Sully had nicknamed him, had ghosted at the same time.

Sure, they still had the A-Team—Kane, Abby, Trevor, Luke. Derek Pratt, the scary asshole who'd somehow gotten a woman to fall in love with him and have his kid. Ethan, who'd been the rookie until Ash had come along. Basically your everyday assortment of former Rangers, SEALs, Marines, and Special Forces who lived off adrenaline and danger.

But they all would've felt better going in with Sully and Liam.

"Not holding my breath," Morgan replied before twisting his wrist to see the time again.

"If you look at your watch one more time, I'm ripping it off your wrist and throwing it out of the plane," Noelle announced, getting up to drag her husband back to his seat.

Winding a hand in his hair, she pulled his ear to her mouth and whispered until some of the tension left Morgan's shoulders. He gave her a quick, fierce kiss and then went to harass the pilots.

"Boss man is coming unhinged," Ash murmured under his breath.

"Not you, though." Ethan reached back and nudged Ash's knee. "Nerves of steel, right?"

"What's there to be nervous about?"

Ash was known for being calmest when the worst kind of shit went on. In his first tour of duty in the USMC, he'd cemented his reputation as the definition of calm, cool, and collected when he'd walked straight up to a suicide bomber strapped with enough C-4 to level a city block and took the detonator from the dude's hand. Ash had tried to explain to the guys in his unit afterward that if it was your time to go, it was your time to go. A guy with a bomb strapped to his belly wasn't going to make a difference.

Still, it helped to have the right training to guide fate along. When the bomber had hesitated in front of the café, where a mom and three young kids were enjoying an afternoon treat, Ash's antiterrorist training had kicked in. He'd known that the terrorist was weighing all that he'd been brainwashed about heaven and the instinctive human need to protect the young. Without the proper skill set, maybe Ash would've missed that window of opportunity.

He rose from his seat and went to crouch next to Noelle. "What's Cate armed with?"

Noelle batted her eyelashes coyly. "Why would she be armed? Cate's a photographer."

"I know you and your band of wicked women train with her all the time when Morgan's not looking."

Noelle was amused. "You think he doesn't know? He knows. He just likes to pretend it's not happening. She's got a Glock, a couple of tactical knives, and a few other tricks up her sleeve. She'll be fine."

"You think this is overkill, then?" He nodded to the two operatives behind him.

"No. This is Jim's daughter. He was without her for seventeen years. If he doesn't save her . . ." Noelle shook her head. "It would kill him. This would change him. So even if this is overkill, who the fuck cares."

Ash kept his smile of relief under wraps. No need to supply Noelle with more ammunition. "D's meeting us there?"

"Yeah, and everyone else is on standby. Callaghan,

Dubois, Castle and all the contractors on the B-Team. Nothing is too good for Jim's baby girl."

Ash's smile faded. "I know."

Which was why he'd stayed away. It wasn't just that Cate was jailbait when they'd first met, or the eight-year span between their ages. It was that he respected her dad too much. Ash knew the last person that Morgan wanted in Cate's bed was a merc.

"You have to prove that you're better than good."

He pasted on a cocky grin. "We all know I'm the best man here. Let's go on to the back and I'll give you enough material for a testimonial."

Her lips curved. "So you'll test the limits of Jim's patience with me but not with anyone else?"

"We both know you'd kill me in the sack before Jim even got his turn."

Noelle outright snickered before patting his arm. "You're my favorite little mercenary. Don't tell the others, though. They all have fragile egos."

"I'm fragile, too. Don't use the word *little* around me."

Noelle continued to laugh even as Ash returned to his seat.

Ethan cocked an eyebrow. "Gonna share with the rest of the class?"

"Nope." He settled into his seat and closed his eyes. The talk with Noelle did little to put his mind at ease. He wouldn't feel right until they were on the ground and en route to Cate's apartment.

No, strike that. He wouldn't feel right until he saw Cate with his own two eyes and made sure she was okay.

The airport was in chaos when they arrived. Air traffic control had no intention of allowing Morgan's private plane to land without prior governmental approval, so it took them an additional hour of circling before permission was granted. Ash didn't want to know how many favors Morgan had to call in for that.

"Hundred bucks says that the transport vehicles we were promised aren't at the terminal," Ash grumbled as they jumped down the jet stairs.

Ethan readjusted the shoulder strap of his bag. "Not taking that bet. How about we bet on how long it will take for the boss to lose his actual mind?"

"What's the over/under?" Ash grinned, although the effort to make it appear as if Cate's presence in this country didn't affect him the same as Morgan was getting more difficult by the second. The presence of heavily armed soldiers at the frickin' airport was doing nothing to alleviate his ball-shriveling anxiety.

"Say ten minutes?"

"I'll take the under." He surveyed the tarmac. The military was out in full force and tourists were casting longing looks at the planes that they'd just departed. *That's right, folks. You should climb back on your bird and fly away.*

"All these guns out here," Ethan observed. "Not a good sign."

"Understatement," Ash muttered. When you didn't bother to hide the danger of your country from tourists, shit was bad. His gut tightened and his pace quickened. The sooner they were out of here, the better.

The terminal was small, but the four mercenaries and one gorgeous assassin had gained a sizable audience. By the time the team passed through customs, there were five soldiers trailing them.

Kane whipped around. "Ash, you stay here and wait for D."

Not in this lifetime. "D's a grown-ass man. He doesn't need a babysitter." Ash walked right past him and out the doors. He wasn't sitting on his ass until D got to town.

"What the hell?" Kane began, but Ethan stepped in.

"I'll take airport duty," he volunteered.

Kane shook his head as he followed Ash outside. "There's something called chain of command, you know," he grumbled as they joined Morgan and Noelle on the sidewalk.

Ash shrugged. "I know. Are those our transport vehicles?"

A bearded man was leaning against the side of a black Land Rover with a matching one idling behind him.

"Looks like it. Let's go," Morgan snapped.

"Good thing Ethan isn't here or I would've owed him a hundred bucks."

Kane threw him an amused glance. "Didn't think—"

Whatever Kane was going to say was cut off by a bloom of blood appearing where the contractor's head was. The glass of the passenger window exploded. Swearing loudly, Ash drew his gun and charged forward, the other team members hot on his heels.

The second vehicle was already moving backward. Ash pointed the barrel at the driver, but the asshole kept moving away. Didn't matter. Another bullet struck the rear wheel tire and then another took the driver out.

"Sniper at three o'clock!" Kane yelled. "Top of the garage."

Ash dropped to one knee and swung around looking for a target. He caught a flash of movement at the ledge overhead, a blur of black and silver as the shooter darted back into the garage. He fired twice, then turned to see Morgan waving at him.

"Get in!" The boss threw open the back door of one of the Rovers.

Ash dove in, with Kane behind him. Noelle was already at the wheel. She slammed on the gas and whipped over the concrete median. Ash and Kane had their guns out, shooting at the remaining gunmen in the parking lot across the street.

"How many'd you get?" Noelle called back as she jumped a curb and entered the stream of traffic flowing away from the airport.

"Two. One wearing a suit and the other in a Windbreaker," Ash reported.

"I got the guy with the Windbreaker," Kane argued. "Right between the eyes."

Noelle shook her head.

"What was that all about?" Ash demanded, adrenaline still jolting through his system.

Morgan rubbed his chin. "Don't think it was about us. Must've been a preexisting dispute."

"Nice friends you have there, boss." He pulled out his magazine and started to reload. Beside him, Kane was doing the same.

"Like I said, this isn't how I'd ordinarily do things." Morgan might have said more, but his ringing phone interrupted him. "Cate?" he barked instantly. "We're on our way. We'll be there in—"

"Ten minutes," Noelle clipped out.

"Ten minutes." Morgan listened for a beat, then addressed the car. "She's still at the Bardera apartment. No suspicious activity on the street."

Ash's body sagged with relief. She was alive, then. Now it was just a matter of getting her safe and making sure she stayed that way.

Chapter 6

Cate kept the phone glued to her ear as she peeked out from behind the thin, musty-smelling drapes. She'd been holed up in Noelle's small city apartment for nearly five hours and the first light of dawn was beginning to wash over the derelict street four stories below.

Couldn't Noelle have picked a safe house in a nicer neighborhood? Bardera was a run-down, ugly part of the city, emanating an air of danger that was only made worse by the street youths loitering on the cracked sidewalks. From her upstairs sanctuary, Cate had already witnessed several drug deals go down. And either she had gunshots on the brain or that was actually muffled gunfire coming from a few blocks away.

Would her father hurry up and get here already?

"What's your ETA?" she hissed into the phone for the hundredth time.

"Less than five minutes," was Morgan's brisk response.

She swallowed her relief. "Are you going to tell me what happened at the airport?" She'd clearly heard Kane say something like "shit storm" and "airport" in the background.

"We ran into some trouble."

"What kind of trouble?"

"Nothing you need to worry about."

She gritted her teeth. She hated how he did that. He

always tried to shut her out, shield her from the perils of his job, even though she'd witnessed those perils firsthand when they'd met. Hell, within hours of leaving France, they'd had to jump out of a plane because some-one planted a *bomb* on it. An enemy had wanted to kill Morgan bad enough that they hadn't even cared how much collateral damage there'd be.

Cate fully understood that Morgan's life was dan-gerous. And she understood why he liked it—for it was the same reason she'd accepted all these assignments since she'd left school. The excitement, the adrenaline rush, the thrill of feeling *alive*. She was her father's daughter, all right.

She just wished he would recognize that.

"Just hold on," Morgan told her. "We'll be there soon."

"Who's we?"

"I've got Noelle, Kane, and Ash with me."

Damn it. She'd kind of hoped that he wouldn't bring Ash. But the guy lived on her father's compound, so she supposed it made sense, convenience wise, to bring him along.

Still, the thought of seeing Ash triggered some serious discomfort in her.

No, it triggered something else. It conjured up the mortification she'd felt the night she'd stripped naked and sprawled on Ash's bed like a pinup model, begging him to fuck her.

But he hadn't fucked her. Nope, he'd turned her down. He'd called her a kid, told her that he wasn't attracted to her. It still burned two years later when she thought of it, so she did what any sane person would do—she shoved those bad memories aside and focused on the present.

"Two minutes."

Morgan's voice penetrated the fog of humiliation caused by reliving Ash's rejection. "Any news about the hotel?" she asked, trying to distract herself.

But the question only made her heart clench, because she'd been trying so hard not to think about Riya's death. It must have hit the news by now. A well-renowned journalist brutally gunned down in Guatana? No way would that go unnoticed.

"Eleven dead," Morgan answered grimly. "All women."

Cate's stomach dropped. If she hadn't been convinced before that she was the target, she sure as shit was convinced now. Why else would they kill only women, and why had they gone to Riya's room first? Or rather, what was supposed to be Cate's room.

"No official confirmation yet that it was Rivera's hit squad," her father added. "But the Feds seem to think it was."

"Americans?" she said in surprise. "The police department involved foreigners?"

"The local police force is useless, you know that. Almost every officer is in the pocket of one cartel or another. So yeah, the officials called in outside investigators, and the preliminary reports are saying that the weapons used in the hotel shooting are consistent with what the Rivera cartel is currently armed with. A major arms deal went down a few months ago, a bunch of Russian AKs landing in the hands of Rivera's people. Casings and bullets they found at the hotel match those guns."

"I don't need a ballistics report to tell me it was Rivera," Cate said flatly. "I saw his son last night. He was shooting at me from the balcony when I escaped."

Morgan's tone sharpened. "You saw Adrián Rivera? Why the *fuck* didn't you mention that?"

"Because I had other things on my mind! Like the fact that I was getting shot at!" She exhaled a weak breath. "How did they know I was at that hotel, Jim? They knew my room number, which means they must know my name. Are they after me because I took that picture?"

"I think so."

Nausea coated her throat. "How did this happen? The only people I told about the picture were you and Noelle."

"The only person I told was my guy at the DEA . . ." Morgan let that statement hang.

Cate instantly knew what he was implying. There was a leak in the Drug Enforcement Agency. How else would her name have gotten back to the cartel?

"Are you tracking down the leak?" she asked in a tight voice.

"Already on it." He paused. "ETA—one minute."

She parted the curtains again and peeked out. Her heart stuttered when she made eye contact with a teenage thug sitting on the stoop of the building across the street. He leaned in to say something to one of his cohorts, and then both teens glanced up at her. She couldn't make out their expressions, but just the fact that they were so focused on her window made her uneasy.

"Start to head downstairs," Morgan ordered.

"There are some kids across the street," she whispered, then chastised herself for lowering her voice. It wasn't like those boys could hear her all the way up here. "They keep staring at this apartment."

"Did anybody see you enter the building when you got there? I told you to use the fire escape."

"I did," she assured him. Then she gulped. "There were a couple people in the alley, though. Looked like they were in the middle of a drug deal, but they were several yards away and I don't think they even glanced my way." But they were doing a hell of a lot more than *glancing* at her now. Their gazes were superglued to her window. "Does Rivera have people in this area?"

"Rivera has people everywhere," Morgan said grimly. "Come downstairs, sweetheart. We're almost here."

Releasing a shaky breath, Cate let go of the curtains and walked toward the back bedroom where the fire escape was located. She swung her legs over the narrow ledge, her bare feet protesting when they connected with the sun-warmed metal landing.

Fuck, her feet hurt. And her flannel pants and tank top were downright embarrassing. She didn't want her father to see her like this. Jim Morgan gave new meaning to the phrase *be prepared*. He would never have gotten blindsided the way she had back at the hotel, and he always, always had a jump bag with him. Hell, he probably slept with one on the bed between him and Noelle. The man could dress in seconds and be fully armed in even less time.

And here she was in her stupid pajamas, with all her identification and documents still in her hotel room. The only items she had on her were her phone and her gun, though Morgan might actually be proud of that. She'd managed to hang on to both as a means of protection and a means of communication. And, really, weren't those the only survival tools that counted?

She descended the ladder as fast as she could, breathing in relief when she didn't encounter anyone in the alley this time. The moment her feet met the pavement, she scurried along the side of the building just as a black SUV with heavily tinted windows pulled up to the curb.

The passenger door flew open.

When her father appeared in front of her, a gust of relief almost knocked her over. She soaked in the sight of his familiar blue eyes, dark cobalt just like her own.

His cropped hair, chiseled features, strong arms that drew her in for a quick hug.

"You okay?" he said gruffly, his breath fanning over her ear.

"I'm fine." She sagged wearily against him. "Let's just get out of—"

The squeal of tires cut her off.

Cate swung around in time to see two other vehicles skid in their direction. Another SUV, and a military Jeep holding four men, three of whom dove out before the vehicle had even come to a stop.

She didn't have time to blink or think or duck for cover. All she registered was the glint of metal shining in the early morning sunlight. All she heard was Morgan shouting at her to get down. From the corner of her eye, she saw the back door of Morgan's SUV burst open. Two men lunged out. Blond hair, dark hair. Kane and Ash.

Cate's heart flew into her throat as a tattoo-sleeved arm swung up to point an automatic weapon in her direction.

The next thing she knew, her ears were ringing like a carnival game and a heavy anvil was crushing her torso.

What the hell . . . ?

It wasn't until Morgan's hand clutched her shoulder and his entire body shuddered against her that she realized he'd thrown himself in front of her.

The man who'd been about to shoot her had hit Morgan instead.

"Dad!" Cate could barely hear her own shout over the deafening gunshots.

Morgan was like dead weight on top of her, but his eyes remained sharp and determined even as his hand trembled against the door handle.

"Get in," he croaked.

"You're hurt! Kane! Ash! He's hurt!"

But the men couldn't hear her. They were too busy diving out of sight while firing at the armed men who'd decided to conduct an all-out assault at six o'clock in the morning.

A bullet whizzed by Cate's head and shattered the back passenger window of the car, sending shards of glass into her hair and face. Ignoring the tiny nicks that scraped along her cheek, she snapped to action. It took all of her strength to push her father, all two hundred pounds of him, into the backseat of the SUV.

She probably shouldn't be moving him. That could make everything worse. But . . . but damn it, right now she was more worried that a bullet might find its way into his brain.

The car door suddenly slammed shut. A heavy thump shook the bare window frame and Cate caught a brief glimpse of Ash's face. His features were feral as he shouted at the driver.

"Go! Get him to a hospital! We'll take care of this."

They'd take care of it? Before Cate could ask how on *earth* they would take care of six men shooting at them, the car lurched forward. She saw a flash of blond hair from the driver's seat—Noelle, who didn't say a single word. The woman floored it and sped away just as the back windshield shattered, sending another shower of glass over Cate and her father.

Morgan was lying facedown, half-draped over Cate's lap, his big, muscular body barely fitting into the backseat. When she peered down, she was horrified to see that her hands were bright red. He was bleeding profusely.

"He's losing a lot of blood," she told her father's wife. "I don't even know how many times he was shot. How close is the hospital?"

"We can't risk going to a hospital," Noelle called

without turning around. Her laser eyes were focused on the road ahead, and Cate had no doubt she'd mow over any pedestrian that crossed her path if it meant getting Morgan to safety.

"Then where are we going?" Cate demanded, ignoring the frantic pounding of her heart. Jesus, she felt close to passing out.

"We have a contact. It's fine. He'll be fine. We'll get him to a doctor."

Cate pressed her palms on her father's left side, where he seemed to be bleeding the most. Almost immediately, her hands grew sticky, slippery with blood. She was about to remove her shirt, but then realized that her thin tank top would do nothing to staunch this kind of blood flow.

"Give me your shirt," she yelled to Noelle.

Even as she steered the SUV at a breakneck pace, the blonde quickly slipped out of her long-sleeve shirt, which left her in nothing but a bra. She tossed the shirt over, and Cate balled it up and held it to Morgan's wound. It wasn't long before the fabric was soaked through.

Oh God. What if he didn't make it? What if he—

No, he *would* make it. He was Jim Morgan, for fuck's sake.

Her breaths came out in ragged, fear-laced puffs. She applied as much pressure to Morgan's lower back as she could. She had no idea if he was even conscious. If he was even breathing. As the car bounced on the potholes of the unmaintained roads of this godforsaken country, Cate bent over and brought her lips to her father's ear.

"Stay with me," she begged. "You hear me, Dad? Don't you *dare* leave me."

*　　*　　*

Those fuckers had big guns and weren't afraid to use them.

Ash was mildly shocked that he wasn't riddled with bullet holes, though he probably would've been if Kane hadn't pushed him behind this concrete ledge at the side of the building's front entrance.

They were under siege. Bullets slammed into the low wall that Ash and his teammate were using as shelter. Cement splintered off the shoddily built barrier, jagged pieces of plaster snapping off it and onto the sidewalk.

As Kane provided cover fire, Ash bolted to his feet and fired his assault rifle in the direction of the men. One of the cars—the Jeep—was speeding away, and he caught a glimpse of one dark head behind the wheel. Didn't seem like the guy was going for help either. He was abandoning his comrades, the fucking pussy.

But Ash had bigger fish to fry than one coward who didn't have the balls to fight like a man. Another round of cover fire from Kane and he popped out again, this time managing to take out two of the men. That left three who were spraying the ledge with bullets. It wouldn't be long before it shattered completely and some of that lead found its way through the cracks and into Ash's body. He just prayed that Noelle and Cate had gotten Jim to safety.

It had all happened so fast, but Ash had been in combat before and he knew when another soldier was in trouble. By throwing himself in front of Cate, Morgan had provided a target for the shooters—his back. And that was a big fucking target.

Noelle will take care of him. You take care of these assholes.

He slid back down and flattened himself against the wall.

"Cover me," Kane barked. His face was streaked with dirt, his blond hair was mussed up, and there was a wild look in his eyes. It was hard to hear him over the unceasing racket of assault rifles. "Gonna make my way to the SUV, try to flank them."

Ash nodded grimly and reloaded his clip. Kane did the same. Pieces of rubble continued to splinter off the top of the ledge and fly past their faces. Those fuckers were just standing there and firing in a steady stream, as if hoping one of their bullets eventually found its mark.

These men weren't coordinated or precise. They were hired guns that had all the finesse of a herd of rampaging buffalo. Ash wasn't sure if they had more than a couple of functioning brain cells among the lot of them. Just fat trigger fingers, automatic weapons, and a shitload of ammo, which meant that because Ash and Kane were still breathing, it was going to be a cakewalk to take these assholes down.

Ready? Ash mouthed.

His teammate gave a brisk nod.

Ash slid toward the other side of the wall, while Kane belly-crawled toward the other. Their eyes met. On Kane's silent count, Ash flew up and fired at the three remaining gunmen.

He hit one in the arm. The guy's body twitched. Then he released an outraged roar and suddenly every gun was aimed in Ash's direction.

Adrenaline coursing through him, he dropped back down and fell onto his stomach like a snake while chunks of debris rained over him. The latest round of gunfire had taken out a piece of the building, but luckily none of the falling bricks landed on his head. When he dared to look up, Kane was gone.

A sense of sick satisfaction washed over him. Good. This would be over soon.

Very soon, in fact.

Less than five seconds later, Kane's booming voice echoed in the early morning air. "Drop it or he dies."

A bullet casing pinged off the pavement, and then silence fell over the sunshine-bathed street. Ash peeked out and grinned savagely when he saw Kane pressing the muzzle of a semiautomatic into the left temple of a tall, dark-haired man. He immediately understood why his teammate had targeted this particular man.

It was Adrián Rivera.

Fucking hell. The confirmation they'd yet to receive about the hotel massacre came loud and clear now: the Rivera cartel was after Cate. They'd sent another hit squad to terminate her—headed by none other than Mateo Rivera's eldest son.

"Shoot him!" Rivera growled to his men, but the two goons were flustered like a teenage boy on prom night.

"Drop your weapons," Kane snapped.

"Don't listen to him! He'll kill me regardless! *Shoot him*!"

They hesitated.

Ash didn't.

He flew up and popped each of them in the head, and before their bodies had even hit the ground, Kane had pulled the trigger on Adrián Rivera.

"Jesus," Ash murmured as he stared at the destruction they'd caused in such a short amount of time.

Dead bodies were strewn all around him. Blood pooled in the cracks and crevices of the pavement, shining deep red under the sun's rays. Bullet casings everywhere. Shards of cement, debris. It looked like a fucking war zone.

"You nuts?" he exclaimed when Kane threw open the driver's door of the cartel crew's SUV. "There's probably a tracker in that thing."

"Probably. But we'll ditch it in a few blocks. Right now we just need to get the hell out of here before the police show up. Get in, Rook."

Though reluctant, Ash climbed into the passenger side. A second later, Kane stepped on the gas and shot away, leaving the bloody scene in their rearview mirror.

Chapter 7

Two years ago

"You're leaving?"

Cate looked around Ash's bedroom in dismay. He had his pack by the door and all of his other gear laid out and ready to be stowed in another duffel.

"I didn't . . . Jim didn't . . ." She couldn't seem to form a complete sentence, thanks to the disappointment clogging her throat.

"It's a short trip. No more than a week or so." Ash threw the empty duffel onto the bed and started packing. "The actual rescue should only take a day, but we need to go in and gather intel first."

"I know that." Cate had been around Jim enough to know how these things went down. What she didn't understand was why Ash had been assigned to this mission. "But you just got back."

He shrugged, and Cate bit her lip as she watched the interplay of his muscles beneath his tight-fitting T-shirt. Back muscles like his were ridiculous. And don't get her started about the rest of his body. How could her father think she would ever be interested in those pasty-faced college boys when she was surrounded by men like Ash?

"Morgan asked me to."

It took her a moment to figure out what he was saying, because she'd been so caught up in lusting after his super ripped bod. "Why you, though?"

She perched herself on the bed next to his supplies. If she just sat on them, would he be forced to stay?

"Why not me?" He tugged a pair of cargo pants out from under her butt.

"Because you *just* got back. Because there are other people who can go." *Because I'm leaving for college in a week and I'm still a virgin.* Um, she should probably only offer the first part. "Because I'm leaving for college and wanted to see you before I left."

"Maybe we'll be back before you go."

Right. And pigs would fly.

Tamping down her rising anxiety, she watched as he packed away his stuff at an alarmingly fast rate. "Doubtful. But it's not just that you're going to be gone. It's that I'm always the one being left behind. Going to college is pushing me farther away." She swallowed. "This is my family. You're part of my family."

Ash zipped his pack closed and shoved it aside to sit next to her. "Why Brown, then? It's pretty far away. There are schools in Texas or Florida that are only a couple hours away."

She threw herself backward, letting the mattress catch her fall. "Do you know that you're the first person to ask me that?"

His face appeared above her. "Really?"

"Yup. I told Jim I was going to Brown and he said, where do I send the check."

"So you don't want to go to Brown?"

She closed her eyes. "I threw the applications on the floor and spun around until I fell on one."

"You're joking."

"Not even a little."

"Ah, sugar, why would you do that?" A light touch landed on her forehead.

Her eyelids flickered open to see Ash smoothing a wayward strand of hair away from her face, and her breath instantly lodged in her throat.

Last night, the men had been cleaning their guns on the terrace—Ash, Ethan, Kane, and Morgan. They were laughing about something. Cate had stood at the doorway, mesmerized by the way Ash had moved as he rubbed the oiled cloth over the gun barrel, over and over again. She'd watched his muscles bunch and release as he cleaned and gripped and pulled. She'd thought of all the ways he could do the same to her with his big, capable hands.

Her lips went dry at the memory. When her tongue darted out to wet them, she could swear she tasted him on the air.

Their eyes caught, and that connection she often wondered about, constantly fantasized about, took shape as the heat in Ash's gaze fired the need in her own. She became acutely aware that she was wearing nothing more than a thin, yellow cotton shift. It was hot and humid today, and she hadn't bothered with a bra. She never wore one if she didn't have to.

Cate reached up, a little surprised at her own brazenness, but . . . nothing ventured, nothing gained, right?

She was leaving.

He was leaving.

And she wanted him to have an idea of what he was going to be missing.

As her hand moved closer, Ash didn't duck away like he usually did. Cate's fingertips landed on the dark stubble of his cheek, the short hairs pricking her palm.

He stayed there, like she'd tamed him or captured

him, for one breath and then another, until Cate forgot she needed air.

"Ash." His name floated from her lips in one long exhale.

That sound was enough to break the spell. He didn't jerk away. No, he was too smooth for that. But his eyes shuttered as he took her palm, kissed it, and then, gently but firmly, laid it against her chest.

"I was in the Marines."

She blinked. "W-what? I . . . already knew that."

He repeated himself as if she hadn't spoken. "I was in the Marines, Cate, and I was discharged, other than honorably." With a stricken look, Ash got to his feet and slung the duffel over his shoulder. "Your father took a chance on me when no one else would. I owe him my life."

It was the answer to the question that she hadn't asked. Hadn't been brave enough to ask.

"Go to college, sweetheart. And when you do, trust me when I say that you're going to find something—or someone—that deserves you."

She lay there for a long time, listening to the echo of his boots as they walked away from her.

Those retreating footsteps rang louder in her ears than his words.

Chapter 8

Present day

The tiny hospital wing in Guatana's army base wasn't equipped for Jim Morgan's crew. The mercenaries filled up all the space, sucking the oxygen out of the rooms until Cate found it painful to draw a breath. She wondered if she was going to unravel, one atom at a time. And in front of Noelle, to boot, which would be the worst thing that could ever happen.

Over by the small window, Jim's wife stood with her arms crossed. Her beautiful face looked as if it were carved out of stone. Cate, on the other hand, felt like jelly—weak and soft and crushable. Essentially the opposite of everyone surrounding her.

She'd told Jim that she could handle herself in the field, but she was a hiccup away from breaking down. Riya was dead because of her. Morgan was injured because of her. All of this was because of *her*.

She hugged her arms tighter around herself and tried to concentrate on what Kane was saying to Derek Pratt, who'd shown up at some point during Jim's surgery.

"What's the ETA on the rest of the team?"

"Trevor and Isabel are already headed for the compound. Luke's still in Aspen but he's tracking down a charter. Bailey and the twins should be here in six hours. Juliet is landing shortly. I left word with Boston and Sully"—D shrugged, his broad shoulders shifting under a thin camp shirt—"but who knows? I'm going to check in with Castle and the contractors again, make sure they're still on standby."

"Supplies?" Kane asked.

"I'm on that duty," Ethan volunteered. "What do we want?"

"Everything. Ammo, electronics, vehicles. It's not hard to get our hands on anything we need. There's a black market here and starving people."

"I'll come with you," D grunted.

Ethan offered a quick nod and the two men took off, leaving Kane standing halfway between Noelle and Cate. It was obvious to Cate that he wanted to leave too, but she wasn't sure if it was because he was worried the women would get into a fight or if he hated hospitals as much as she did.

Kane dragged a hand through his hair. "Fuck, okay. We should—"

"Sorry to interrupt," a brusque male voice cut in.

Cate's gaze shot to the door as Timo Varela, the base commander, strode into the exam room they were using as a waiting area. Varela had been the one to greet her and Noelle after they'd driven past the heavily guarded gates onto the military base.

According to Noelle, he was a trusted contact of Jim's. Apparently the two men had known each other for years, and the stern-faced military leader had been aghast at the condition in which they'd brought Morgan to him. That had been four hours ago and there was still no word on Jim. The medical personnel had whisked him away on a gurney, leaving Cate staring after him with blood-stained clothes and tears in her eyes.

"I thought you'd like an update on Jim's condition," Varela said grimly. "I just spoke to the surgeon."

Noelle swung around, her ice-blue eyes finally revealing a hint of emotion: indignation. "Why the fuck can't we go in there and speak to the surgeon ourselves?"

Varela's tone was clipped. "As I've already told you, the operating wing is a restricted area. I'm sorry, but I can't bend the rules for you."

Her mouth flattened into a deadly line. "You've already bent the shit out of your rules by allowing us to use your base as our point of operation. Will it really make a difference if you let me see my goddamn husband? If you let his daughter see him?"

"It's a restricted area." His answering scowl was equally menacing. "And I'd like to remind you that I'm doing you a courtesy right now by allowing you to be here. One word from me and my men will kindly escort you out."

Noelle arched a brow. "You realize who you're talking to, right?"

The older man chuckled. "I'm well aware of it. But I'm confident that you won't harm a hair on my head—not as long as I'm of use to you."

"What's the update on my father?" Cate burst out, tired of their preamble. She appreciated Varela's assistance, but she wasn't in the mood to witness some bullshit power showdown between him and Noelle.

"Not good, I'm afraid." He softened his voice as he addressed Cate. "The surgeon removed two of the bullets. One narrowly missed his spine. Neither of them, fortunately, caused any internal damage. But the third bullet . . ." He paused.

Cate's heart jumped in fear.

"It left quite a lot of damage," Varela admitted. "The third bullet lodged between the C5 and C6 vertebrae, fracturing the left side of the bone. There's a lot of swelling and fluid buildup in the region, not to mention blood loss. He's struggling to breathe on his own so they've hooked him up to a ventilator. Because of the position of the bullet, the surgeon is leery of removing it at this point."

"What does that mean?" Kane snapped. "Because of the position of the bullet?"

"Because of the swelling and fractured bones, they're concerned about doing more damage and possibly causing paralysis. He's hoping that in a day or two, the swelling will go down enough to allow them to operate again. I'm afraid that's all I know. The surgeon said it'll be several more hours. We'll know more then."

Varela stepped forward and gave Cate's arm a gentle squeeze while casting a sympathetic glance in Noelle's direction. "I'm needed at a briefing soon, but I'll check in with you later. My men have been briefed about you and they'll give you wide berth."

"Thanks," Noelle bit out.

With a nod, Varela exited the room.

There was a split second of silence. Then, to Cate's disbelief, the others picked up their conversation right where they'd left it.

"We'll need to secure another safe house in case Varela decides to boot us," Kane said.

Noelle nodded. "Already on it."

"Seriously?" Cate blurted out, her accusatory gaze shifting between them. "Nobody's even going to address what the surgeon said?"

"The surgeon said shit," Noelle snapped. "All we know is that Jim's still being operated on."

"But paralysis—"

"He'll be fine."

"But—"

"He'll be fine," the woman growled.

But what if he isn't?

Her bleak thoughts were interrupted by the sound of footsteps. Cate knew whose feet were encased in those heavy black leather boots without looking up. She felt his intense green eyes fix on the top of her head and wished, with all of her might, that he would disappear. Or that she would. She'd take either option at this point.

But both were a coward's way out, and she wasn't a coward.

She forced her gaze to move from Ash's boots to his moss-green eyes. They were filled with sympathy and it made Cate want to fly over and slap him hard across the face.

Life was *such* a bitch. The first boy she'd ever had a crush on had been murdered by her grandfather for getting too close to Cate. Her second crush? Couldn't get away from her fast enough.

The last time she'd laid eyes on Ash, he'd taken the offer of her virginity and thrown it back in her face. It had been the single most humiliating event in her life, which said a lot, because she'd had several. Thanks to the bodyguards who followed her around most of her life, Cate had had a witness to all of her failures, from getting her first period in a public place—which required one of the guards to run to the pharmacy for sanitary pads—to the time she'd been caught gawking too long at a movie star in Monte Carlo and ended up falling face-first into a table of tourists.

Not one of her adolescent misadventures had left a mark like the one Ash's rejection had burned into her psyche.

Now, she stared at him coldly, wishing she could tell him to get the hell away from here, that he didn't belong. But Jim's men had more right to him than she did—they'd known him longer. Besides, she couldn't deny that things hadn't been good between her and Jim these last couple of years. He wanted to keep her locked up in a tower room. She wanted to live. Ergo, they fought—a lot—and because Cate hated fighting almost as much as she hated the man in front of her, she stayed away from the compound more than she visited.

Ash's gaze was wary as he took in the room. "How is he?"

"He's . . ." For a moment, Kane sounded lost. His longtime friend and leader was being cut open in some operating room right now, and even though Morgan's second-in-command knew what to do, he clearly didn't want to be in this position. Not under these circumstances anyway.

Cate didn't want him making decisions either. That was her dad's role.

"Kane?" Ash prompted.

"He's still in surgery."

"I left a message for Holden, like you asked. Is it that bad?"

Kane's eyes shot toward Cate. He lowered his voice but she could still hear him. "Yeah, it's bad."

"Of course it is," she snapped, tired of everyone pretending like she was too fragile to know the truth. "Kane wouldn't have called the entire squad and summoned them to this hellhole unless it was to say good-bye. That's what it is, right?" She jutted her chin out and dared Kane to contradict her.

He gave her a thin smile. "A few bullets aren't going to keep Jim down, but the boss would have my balls if I didn't launch a counterattack. No one touches you and lives to tell about it."

"Whatever, Kane. You can tell whatever lies you'd like, but I visited my dead mother for seventeen years. I know brain-dead when I see it."

Ash looked startled. "He's brain-dead?"

"No," she answered through gritted teeth. "But he's a lot more critical than everyone wants to admit." Her face hardened as she turned back to Kane. "Maybe you need to come to terms with it."

Kane flinched under her harsh words, but she wasn't at all remorseful.

"He's just thinking of all contingencies," Ash said tentatively.

Cate whipped around so she didn't have to face those eyes that seemed to see all the way inside of her. "Don't talk to me."

She shifted, putting her back to the two mercenaries, and stared at the empty hospital bed in the center of the room. They'd probably put Jim in here when he got out of surgery. God, she didn't even want to think about how he might look. She knew what death was. It looked like waxen skin, felt cold, and smelled of antiseptic. Her grandfather had kept her mom alive for seventeen years—but it wasn't alive. It was a form of grotesque necromancy. Cate had pulled the plug on her mother and she'd do it for her father if it came down to it.

Guilt and self-loathing swamped her. Yeah, she would make sure her dad didn't spend years on a ventilator, hooked up to bags of nutrition while a nurse changed his diapers every few hours or emptied out the cath bag. If Cate had to pull out every tube, IV, and wire to make him stop breathing, she'd do it. Then she'd be Cate Morgan, the girl who'd killed both her parents. Lizzie Borden had nothing on her.

The urge to fall apart was climbing up her throat again. Damn it, she would not cry. She would not break apart in front of these operatives. She would—

"You just had to come here, didn't you?" Noelle asked from the window.

Cate's jaw fell open. "Maybe you should've kept better track of your leaks. I was fine—Riya was *alive*—until I sent that picture to you."

"You came to us for information and we contacted our sources for you. It got out. All information does." Noelle tapped the end of her unlit cigarette against the windowsill. "Besides, what did you expect when you arrived? Guatana is a dangerous place. Bad things happen in dangerous places. Isn't that why you came here? Because it was oh so dangerous and you could show your father how *capable* you were."

Cate's cheeks burned with anger at the woman's mocking tone. "I came here because taking pictures is how I get paid. Because it's my job."

"If you say so, honey. But you never told Jim you were coming here because you knew what he'd do."

"Yeah, he'd be on the first plane to drag me back to Costa Rica where I would fossilize into old age in the jungle. If I wanted that life, I would've stayed with my grandfather."

Noelle opened her mouth to retort, but before she could unleash her cutting words, Kane stepped forward. "All right. Time out. You two go to your corners. Noelle—go outside and have a smoke before nicotine withdrawal makes you say things you regret. Attacking each other isn't going to make Jim come out of surgery any faster."

"We need to start making phone calls," Noelle muttered. "I'll contact Bailey again. Ash, call Luke and see if he's found a plane yet."

"I'll call Liam again," Kane said. "Maybe he'll pick up this time."

"I want in," Cate spoke up. "Jim's my dad. I have every right to be part of whatever action you take against Rivera."

She anticipated a fight. She got one.

"No way," Kane said immediately.

Ash wasn't far behind. "Agreed. Morgan would string us up by our nuts if you got hurt."

"Then I guess I'll just have to be careful, won't I?" Cate knew arguing with these men was futile. She needed to prove she wasn't going to be a liability. How she was going to do that, though, she wasn't sure. Her gaze flicked to Noelle, the only person in the room who hadn't issued a decree that Cate sit on her hands.

Noelle stared steadily back. "Go through every photograph and see if there's any additional information."

She nodded. She'd already done that once, before she'd sent the photo, but she'd go over them again. Maybe there would be a car or a license plate or someone else they could use. "On it."

"One more thing," Noelle called as Cate headed for the door.

She stopped in the doorway. "Yeah?"

"Take Ash with you."

Cate pressed her lips together to prevent a scream of frustration. This was a stupid, fucking test by Noelle. A test to see if Cate would follow orders. And if she didn't, then Noelle wouldn't allow her to set foot inside the briefing room again, because a soldier who didn't follow the chain of command endangered everyone on the mission. Jim had taught her that during one of the first nights they'd gone hunting together.

"Is that a problem?" Noelle arched an eyebrow.

"No. I've worked with worse assholes before." Cate left without looking to see if Ash followed.

He was, of course.

"So, that's how it's going to be," he said softly.

She didn't spare him a glance. "How else would it be?" she replied. Polite. Cool.

"I was hoping it would be . . . different." A note of resignation weighed on his tone. Then he cleared his throat. "I need to make those calls. I'll meet you in the war room."

Gee. She couldn't wait.

Chapter 9

"I can't believe I'm doing this."

The breathy voice vibrated in Liam Macgregor's body, because Penny's mouth was still on his dick as she whispered the excited words. He threaded a hand through her dark red hair and tipped her head back, peering down at her with a filthy grin.

"What? You've never given a blow job in a man's childhood bedroom before?"

Penny giggled. "No. And I also haven't done it when that man's entire family is one story below having Sunday brunch." She gave his shaft a slow tug, a worried look washing over her pretty face. "What if someone walks in on us?"

"They won't. I locked the door, remember?" He guided those pouty lips back to his groin, then moaned softly when her hot, wet mouth immediately enveloped him.

Fuck, he loved blow jobs. And it was almost fitting that his girlfriend was on her knees *here*, in his childhood room, because this was the one place where his dick had never seen any action. Growing up with strict Irish Catholic parents and seven siblings who were always underfoot made it impossible to have any privacy in this house. Sneaking girls in would've required

Houdini-level stealth, considering he'd shared this room with his two older brothers.

So yeah, he couldn't deny he was getting a sick sense of satisfaction right now, standing there with Penny working his cock like a pro—while on the wall across from him hung a huge oil painting of Jesus. Would it be sacrilegious to give the old guy a thumbs-up? Probably, but religion had never been Liam's thing.

His whole life, he'd played the part of the good Catholic boy, the altar boy, the mama's boy, but deep down, he'd always known he didn't fit in.

So why the hell are you back in Boston?

Shoving the question out of his mind, he focused on the tight suction on the tip of his cock, the delicate hand kneading his sac, and the sweet noises Penny was making as her head bobbed up and down.

He watched her—her swollen lips, flushed cheeks, copper hair streaming down her back. Each deep suck brought him closer to the edge and it wasn't long before his fingers tightened in her hair and he grunted out a quick, "Coming, baby."

He almost regretted offering the warning. He would've loved to find release in her warm, eager mouth, but Penny never stayed with him till the end. Her hand quickly replaced her mouth and he spilled into her palm on a choked groan, hips thrusting for several more seconds before his body grew still.

"Jesus," he mumbled as Penny got to her feet. "That was amazing."

At only five-one, she had to crane her neck to look up at him. Her brown eyes danced with mischief. "I aim to please."

Laughing, he wandered over to one of the night tables to grab some tissues. While he cleaned himself up, Penny dug around in her purse for her makeup bag, then examined her reflection in a small compact mirror.

"Ugh," she griped. "I definitely look like someone who just had sex."

Liam arched a brow. "You didn't have sex."

"Your dick was in my mouth—that's sex." She giggled. "And I told you we could find a way to make these Sunday brunches more fun."

He wanted to argue that the weekly Macgregor brunches *were* fun. Because they were.

But . . . they were also agonizing. Ironic that *fun* and *agonizing* could exist in the same realm, but it had always been that way with his family. He loved them deeply. His brothers, his sisters, his parents, the parade of nieces and nephews. He loved the laughter and the chaos and the good-natured ribbing. Yet, at the same time, it was all too . . . *normal* for him.

This two-story town house he'd grown up in had plenty of windows, plenty of doors. He wasn't, and had never been, a prisoner here. He could walk out at any time, and yet a part of him felt oddly trapped when he was home.

Before he'd joined the DEA all those years ago, he remembered sitting at that dining room table listening to his brothers talk about their day at the police station, celebrating his sister Rose getting her teaching degree, watching everyone fall in love, get married, have babies.

And it was all so unappealing to him. He'd dreamed of adventure. He'd wanted to shoot big guns and blow shit up. He'd wanted to feel that adrenaline high he got whenever he and Tommy G jumped off the Carson Beach pier into the South Boston harbor.

He hadn't felt alive, truly alive, until he'd left Southie and become a federal agent. And then, eight years after that, he'd resigned from the DEA and landed an even more exciting job—a soldier on Jim Morgan's mercenary team. He'd gotten to shoot guns and blow things up, all right. Being a merc had given him the biggest thrill he'd ever experienced and introduced him to some of the greatest people he'd ever met. Kane, Trevor, Luke, even that prickly bastard D. They'd become his brothers, but none more so than Sullivan Port.

Except Sullivan had been more than a brother by the end. He'd been . . .

Liam shut out the thought before it could take root.

"You ready to go downstairs?" Penny asked.

He mustered up a smile. See, *this* was the reason he couldn't think about Sully anymore. Penelope Doyle, the woman he'd been seeing for almost a year. When he'd returned to Boston two years ago, he hadn't intended on making it a permanent stay. He had every intention of going back to Morgan's compound in Costa Rica, where Liam had lived before that final mission in Mexico.

He'd come home to visit his family and recover from the memory of watching Sullivan get on that yacht, from the pain of knowing he wouldn't see his best friend for who knew how long, from the sorrow of realizing he couldn't be what Sullivan needed at that time. Liam would've done anything to help Sully kick the drugs he'd gotten hooked on during captivity, but his friend hadn't wanted his help. Sully had wanted to do it alone.

The thought of returning to Costa Rica without Sully had been too much to bear. So he'd stuck around in Boston. Eventually, a few weeks had turned into a few months, and suddenly it was a year and he was doing what he'd sworn he'd never do—working a nine-to-five job at the security firm his brother Kevin had opened after retiring from the force. It was pretty tame shit for the most part, though Liam always begged Kevin to give him the riskier assignments.

Yeah, so risky, bro. You're really straddling the danger line here.

Fine, so maybe the most exciting thing he'd done was accompany a CEO to Los Angeles for a three-day stretch of business negotiations. Terrifying shit, apparently, negotiations.

But he'd resigned himself to the fact that this was his life now. He wasn't a mercenary; he was a security consultant. And he was dating a lovely woman. Penny was smart, funny, and kinky enough to satisfy the wild sexual streak that ran through him. Plus his family adored her. She'd gone to college with his younger sister Becca, who was the one to introduce them.

"Liam?" Her voice jolted him out of his thoughts. "Are you coming?"

He nodded. The boisterous voices of his family wafted upstairs from the lower level, intermingling with the happy shrieks of his sister Monica's three daughters and his brother Denny's two sons. Only four of Liam's seven siblings were at brunch today, but each one traveled with an entourage of spouse and a minimum of two kids.

Liam's back pocket vibrated as he headed toward the door. "Hold that thought," he told Penny. "Let me check who this is."

He pulled out his phone and glanced at the screen. Kane.

Shit.

Kane was probably calling to beg him to come back again. A few months ago it was Trevor who'd made that call, a not so subtle attempt to bring Liam back into the fold. Trev had mentioned a tricky extraction in Colombia as an incentive, and Liam, who'd just come home after a boring day of providing bank security, had almost taken him up on the offer . . . until Trevor asked if he'd heard from Sullivan.

Just like that, the desire to reunite with his team had evaporated. How could he ever go back when the most important person in the world to him wouldn't be there?

"I need to take this," he said curtly.

Penny's forehead wrinkled. "Who is it?"

"Just an old friend. Give me a second?"

She hesitated, then stepped out the door.

Liam pressed TALK and brought the phone to his ear. "Hey," he greeted Kane.

"You still in Boston?" was the brusque response.

Liam frowned. Weird for Kane to forgo a hello like that. He wasn't Morgan, the tight-lipped bastard. Or D, who communicated through grunts.

"Yeah. Why? What's going on?"

"I take it you haven't listened to your messages."

"Nope, haven't had a chance. I'm at my folks' place."

"Gotcha. Well . . . if you can hop on a flight and get over here, it'd probably be a good idea."

Liam's stomach went rigid. Okay. That didn't sound good. "What's going on?" he repeated. "And where is *here*?"

"Guatana."

"The hell are you guys doing over there?"

"Cate ran into some trouble so we flew in to extract her. Shit went south."

His instincts began to hum óminously. "Who's hurt?"

There was a pause, long enough for Liam's palms to dampen. He expected Kane to say *Sullivan*. Expected to hear that Sully had rejoined the team and gotten hurt somehow. Or worse, that Sullivan was back on the drugs.

Those fears were put to rest and replaced with new ones when Kane said, "It's Jim. He got shot."

"How bad?" Liam demanded.

"Bad. Bullet lodged in his neck. Two others removed

from his back. He's still in surgery, but . . . ah, doctors don't know if he's going to make it."

His heart stopped. "Jesus Christ."

No way. This wasn't possible. Jim Morgan was frickin' invincible. He got shot, he got back up. Bullets didn't keep him down. Nothing did.

"So yeah . . . ," Kane said, his tone flat. "If you can afford to take the time off, I suggest you come here. Might be your only chance to"—a cough—"say good-bye."

Liam's heart started up in a fast gallop. Good-bye? Shit, this *was* serious.

"And if you have a way to get in touch with Sullivan," Kane went on, and that magic word—*Sullivan*—succeeded in making Liam tremble. "Do me a favor and call him for us. I can't get him on the radio."

"Will do. I'll be on the next flight out."

Still feeling shaky, he hung up the phone and collapsed on the edge of his bed. Well, technically it was his brother's bed. Denny had slept in the bottom bunk because Liam had claimed the top one—even back then he'd wanted to live on the edge. He remembered doing somersaults and flips off the top bunk while his brothers chastised him to stop. He hadn't stopped, though, and ended up cracking his forehead open one time and requiring twenty-two stitches.

He dragged one hand through his hair, unable to process what Kane had told him. But if it was true, then no way was he staying in Boston. He owed it to Morgan to go to Guatana.

Jim Morgan had given him the opportunity to live the kind of life he'd always craved. Because of Morgan, he'd made friends. He'd met Sully. He'd felt whole for the first time in his life. Not the way he felt here, like an empty shell that walked and talked and laughed and smiled on command, when a part of him knew he would never truly belong.

Morgan had done the same for Sullivan. Sullivan was an orphan and Jim had given him a family.

Fuck. Sully needed to know about this.

Liam's fingers shook as he pulled up his contact list. He had another way of reaching Sully that wasn't the radio. Before they'd parted ways, he'd given Sully a burner phone and promised his friend that he'd be the only one with the number. In that first year, they'd spoken several times, but they hadn't had any contact this second year. Hell, Sully might have tossed the phone overboard by now.

Praying that wasn't the case, Liam took a breath and made the call.

Chapter 10

San Nicolas, Aruba

Torture. The deep timbre of Liam's voice in Sullivan Port's ear was bloody torture.

And that was saying a lot, considering he'd literally been tortured not so long ago. For months on end, Sullivan had been trapped in a cell, pumped full of drugs, and raped by a woman he despised. He'd lived and breathed torture in Raoul Mendez's private island hellhole, and yet those gruesome memories didn't come close to evoking the unbearable pain he felt hearing the voice of the friend he hadn't spoken to in a year.

"Boston," he said, putting on a careless tone. Maybe if he pretended that no time had passed, then it wouldn't be awkward between them.

"Sully. Hey." It was impossible to miss the note of discomfort in *Liam's* tone.

Yeah, this was gonna be awkward, all right.

"Long time," he said lightly.

"Yeah." Liam sounded distracted now. "Look. I know we've got a lot of catching up to do, but that's not why I'm calling. You on the water or mainland?"

Frowning, he rose from his lounge chair and walked across *Evangeline's* upper deck. He stopped at the railing and stared out at the marina, at the gleaming hulls of the other boats bobbing in the calm water.

"Mainland," he answered. "I'm docked in a private cove off the coast of Aruba."

"Can you get a charter out of there?"

"Yeah," he said uneasily. "Why?"

"Kane just called. You weren't answering the radio."

"It's busted," he admitted. "It's one of the reasons I came to port. Need to get the bloody thing fixed. Why didn't he call this phone?"

"Because he doesn't know the number."

Sullivan blinked in surprise. "You didn't give it to him?"

"I promised you I wouldn't," was the gruff response. "You didn't want anyone to have it, remember?"

Yeah. Fuck, yeah, now he remembered. That was two years ago, when he'd still been a pathetic mess. Going through withdrawal, detoxing himself on the open water. It was a miracle he hadn't died, that some random fishing boat hadn't come across *Evangeline* drifting aimlessly in the ocean and found Sullivan's decomposing body below deck.

But he'd survived somehow, and he'd done it all by himself. He knew Liam would've come with him in a heartbeat, but it hadn't been his friend's responsibility to dry Sully out. And he hadn't wanted the rest of the team calling him every other minute asking if he was okay. He hadn't wanted to hear the pity in their voices. He fucking hated pity.

"What did Kane want?" he asked, pushing the bleak memories away.

"Morgan was shot in Guatana. Apparently it's bad. Critical condition. They don't know if he'll make it."

Sully sucked in a breath. "Bullshit."

"I know, right?"

"Jim Morgan doesn't go into critical condition. He's a bloody superhero."

A heavy sigh echoed in his ear. "No, he's a man. Mortal just like the rest of us."

He gulped. There was something so . . . sad in Liam's voice. Sully wanted to ask his buddy if he was okay, what he'd been up to since they'd lost touch, but it was too awkward, so he forced himself to swallow the urge. Ironic, because he was the one who usually spoke his mind without thinking. Liam was the calm, composed one. Liam assessed and analyzed, weighing every word before he said it, while Sully just blurted shit out, his words like gumballs popping out of a candy machine and flying haphazardly in all directions.

After several more seconds ticked by, Liam finally spoke again. "You stopped calling me."

Sullivan nodded, then realized his friend couldn't see him. He cleared his throat and said, "I know."

"Why?"

"I don't know." Fuck that. He did know. He knew exactly why he'd stopped calling his best mate.

Because Liam was bloody *in love* with him.

He'd wanted to give the guy time to get over it. He'd prayed that maybe with enough time, their friendship could go back to normal. Except he'd let the radio silence go on for too long. Weeks had turned into months and the next thing he knew, half a year had passed. By that point, Sully hadn't known what to say if he called. He'd hoped that Liam would be the one to reach out first, but that hadn't happened.

"Will you come to Guatana?"

The abrupt change of subject startled him. "Yeah. I'll find a pilot the moment we get off the phone. You?"

"Same." Liam paused. "He's gonna make it, bro. You know that."

"Yeah." Sully swallowed again. "Of course he will."

Another long pause.

He hated this. He really, really hated this. From the moment Liam had joined the team, the two men had been inseparable. They could talk about anything. Sullivan had told Liam about his past. He'd shared more details about himself than he'd ever done with anyone else, except maybe Evangeline. He'd never kept secrets from her.

Even thinking about Evangeline caused pain to ripple through his heart, so once again he pushed the memories aside. He was good at blocking out pain. Just ask Mendez. Ask Mendez's daughter, who'd taken great delight in sexually tormenting him.

Sully raked his free hand through his hair as the silence on the line dragged on. Lord, he'd thought he'd put all that bullshit on Mendez's island behind him, but evidently not. The memories were twisting his gut into knots.

He hated that he'd been that man—helpless, broken, trapped in a cell. And everything he'd done afterward still haunted him.

Killing Angelina Mendez with his bare hands . . .

Yelling at Liam . . .

Offering Liam sexual favors in exchange for heroin . . .

Jesus bloody Christ. He'd humiliated himself. Demeaned himself. How in the bloody fuck did a man ever come back from that?

Maybe he couldn't. Hell, maybe he shouldn't. His life had been a shit show since the moment his druggie mother abandoned him on the front steps of a church in Sydney. He'd been an orphan, a drug dealer, an addict, a total fucking mess. Nothing good ever lasted in his life. The one bright spot, the only happiness he'd been lucky enough to experience, had been stolen away from him.

And even after he'd cleaned up his act and joined the army, he'd still been a mess. Terrible at relationships, unable to sustain friendships. Except with Liam. That friendship had been different. Liam was different.

A tired sigh slipped out of his mouth, followed by three quiet words that Sully couldn't rein in. "I miss you."

There was a hitch of breath on the other end.

"Boston? You still there?"

After a painfully long pause, Liam murmured, "I miss you too."

The next round of silence stretched on even longer than the first, until Sullivan cleared his throat again. "Text me the team's location. I'll be there as soon as I can."

"Who was that?"

Liam's head jerked toward the door at the sound of Penny's shrill voice. For some reason, the suspicion flashing in her eyes irked him. His former boss was lying in a hospital bed fighting for his life and she was pissed because . . . what? She thought he was cheating on her? Over the phone?

"Just a friend." He stood and tucked his phone in the back pocket of his cargo pants. After a moment of hesitation, he said, "I have to go."

Her eyes narrowed further. "What do you mean, you have to go? Your mom's about to serve dessert."

"Well, I'm gonna have to miss dessert. There's somewhere I need to be."

Penny blocked his path before he could reach the doorway. She crossed her arms over her chest, luring his gaze to her ample cleavage. Christ, she had great tits. Big and bouncy. Add to that her tiny hips and firm ass and her body was a walking wet dream. The teenage boys at the Catholic high school where she taught probably jacked off to thoughts of her every night, confessed the sin every Sunday, and then repeated the cycle.

Not that he blamed them if they did—he enjoyed losing himself in Penny's body. But as much as he liked fucking her, and as much as he appreciated her company, there were definitely a few things he didn't like about her.

Like how she always demanded to know where he was and who he was with.

She got upset when he didn't text her back right away.

She'd told him she loved him after three months.

He'd overlooked all that, because, hell, were those really major red flags? He knew lots of women with clingy tendencies and they weren't all psychos. Besides, after lusting over someone who wanted nothing to do with him, it was a nice ego boost to be around someone who wanted to be with him all the time.

Right now, though? Not so nice.

"Where do you need to be?" she asked tightly.

He hesitated again. He didn't like discussing his former job with Penny or his family. They just didn't get it. When he'd joined the DEA, his father flat-out told him he was insane. *Why do you want to get shot up by drug dealers, you feckin' idiot?* The Irish brogue always came out when Callum Macgregor was angry or annoyed. Liam's mom, meanwhile, had clucked in worry, moaning about how she didn't want her baby boy to get hurt. His brothers, of course, called him stupid for not joining the police force like every other Macgregor male before him.

After he'd left the DEA and hooked up with Morgan's team, he'd kept the details about the new gig as vague as possible, telling his family he was doing contract work for the government. They would've flipped out if they found out what he was really up to. Jumping out of helicopters. Trekking through jungles and taking out rebel soldiers. Getting shot . . . though in his defense, that only happened once and that was because he'd been distracted by Sullivan's disappearance.

Either way, his family didn't need to know the specifics and neither did Penny.

"A friend of mine is in trouble," he finally answered. "He's hurt. I need to make sure he's okay."

"Oh, really? Do you tell all your friends you miss them?"

Liam froze. How long had she been standing outside the door?

"Yeah, I heard that." She crossed her arms even tighter, and her cleavage nearly spilled out of her thin V-neck sweater. "Who is she?"

Annoyance skated through him. "It wasn't a she. I told you, I was talking to an old friend."

"You're lying to me." Her expression clouded over. "You're keeping things from me, Liam, and you've been doing it since we started dating!"

"That's not true."

"Yes, it is! You hardly ever talk about yourself. I don't know anything about your past relationships or even the names of your ex-girlfriends." She huffed. "You know everything about *my* exes. I tell you everything."

"There's nothing to tell on my end." Frustration gathered in his stomach. Penny was still blocking the door, and he was tempted to plant both hands on her waist, lift her up, and forcibly move her out of his way.

That'd probably get him a slap to the face. Penny's family had Irish roots too, which meant she'd inherited the Irish temper. Not only that, but she was a redhead and that came with the redhead temper. Double whammy.

But Kane wouldn't have called if it weren't important, which meant Liam needed to go, ASAP. He had to track down a private charter. Commercial would take too long, and he had no idea if he could even find a place to land in Guatana. Last he'd heard, most of the private airfields in the region were either shut down or completely unreliable. The other month he'd had drinks with an old DEA buddy who'd admitted that the cartel situation in Guatana was getting unmanageable. A private airstrip had been blown up just a few months ago, the Rivera cartel's way of sending a message to a rival about who controlled the country's distribution channels.

"I heard your voice," Penny was saying, alerting him to the fact that she was still mid-lecture. "You weren't talking to 'just a friend.' It was someone you care about. And you told her you missed her!"

Liam clenched his teeth.

"And I heard the part before that too, when you wanted to know why she didn't call you anymore." Penny flattened her lips. "So who is she? Some girl you dated before me? Was it serious? Were you going to marry her? Just give me *something*, Liam! Who the hell is she?"

"*He!*" he burst out.

And regretted it instantly.

Penny's eyes widened. "What?"

He drew a ragged breath. "Nothing," he muttered. "Please"—he gently touched her arm—"I really need to go. A friend of mine is in trouble."

She ignored him. "What do you mean, *he*? He . . . as in . . . you were in a relationship with a *man*?"

Horror descended on her face, which only raised his hackles. "I wasn't in a relationship with him."

Her laser gaze pierced into him. He could see the wheels in her brain working overtime, her woman's intuition kicking into high gear.

"But . . . you had feelings for . . . him?" She shook her head in dismay. "For a man?"

He didn't answer.

"Are you gay?" The second she voiced the question, she glanced over her shoulder in panic, as if someone might be eavesdropping.

"No," Liam ground out. "I'm not gay."

Her breath came out in a hiss. "If you have feelings for a man, then that means you're gay, Liam!" Penny's jaw began to open and close in rapid succession, as if she couldn't quite form the right words. "Oh my God. Oh my God. This makes so much sense. This is why you've been holding back. This is why you haven't asked me to marry you—"

Marry her?

"Because you're *gay*."

He probably would've kept quiet if not for the disgust that flashed across her face. He'd known Penny was conservative—she went to church every Sunday like a good Catholic girl—but he hadn't taken her for homophobic.

"I'm not gay," he replied in a frigid voice. "But if I was? I sure as shit wouldn't appreciate the way you're speaking to me right now. There's nothing wrong with being gay."

Rather than acknowledge her insensitivity, Penny seemed to grasp only one thing he'd said. "You're not gay?"

His jaw tightened. "No. I'm attracted to women." He paused. "And men."

She gasped.

It took all his willpower not to snap at her again, because finding out someone was bisexual wasn't exactly gasp-worthy.

Though in her defense, it had come as a helluva shock to him too.

"And I haven't asked you to marry me," Liam continued, "because it hasn't even been a year yet. I'm an old-fashioned kind of guy."

"An old-fashioned kind of guy?" she echoed, her cheeks redder than the fire hydrant out front. "Old-fashioned guys—*Catholic* guys—don't go around screwing other men!"

"I don't go around screwing other men," he retorted through gritted teeth. "And if that's what you're worried about, that I've been cheating on you, well, I haven't. I haven't been with anyone since you and I got together."

"But before that?" she pushed. "Were you with a man?"

He hesitated.

"It's a yes or no question, Liam. Were you with a man?"

"Yes," he admitted.

"Oh my God." Tears glistened on her eyelashes as she weakly lowered herself onto the nearest bed. Her gaze turned pleading. "What am I supposed to do with this?"

A different man, or hell, maybe a better man, would have walked over, put his arm around her, and professed his undying love. But Liam stayed rooted in place. Great sex aside, his relationship with Penny had always felt like a way to . . . pass the time.

Shit. He was a grade-A jackass. That kind of attitude wasn't fuckin' fair to either one of them.

"Look at me," she wailed.

He briefly closed his eyes, then forced himself to meet her gaze.

And there it was again—the disgust. Seeing it evoked not only another spark of anger, but resignation too, because when he'd entertained those foolish ideas of him and Sullivan being together, he'd pretty much expected his family to react with the same revulsion Penny was broadcasting right now. Especially his father. Callum Macgregor was a good man. He was loyal and tough and he'd kill for his family, but he belonged to a different era. A generation that still threw around words that, nowadays, caused a national outcry if you so much as thought them.

"You really haven't been with anyone since we got together?"

He kept his eyes on hers. "It's only been you, Pen."

"Do you"—her voice cracked—"love me?"

His stomach twisted in discomfort. He'd never told anyone he'd loved them before. Not any of the women he'd dated. Well, if you could even call it dating. Most of his encounters hadn't lasted more than a few weeks. Ditto for friendships, at least not before he'd joined Morgan's team.

At the thought of Morgan, a sense of urgency overtook him. Fuck. He really needed to get out of here.

"Do you love me?" she repeated, leaning forward with her hands on her knees.

The new position caused her skirt to ride up, but not even the sight of her firm, creamy thighs could ease the tension hanging thick in the room.

"Because if you love, and if you tell me you see a future with me, then—" A shaky breath slid out. "Then maybe I'll be able to . . . overlook . . . this . . . this . . ."

She was stuttering now, as if it was impossible for her to fathom that the man in her life could be, God forbid, bisexual.

When he still didn't answer, her expression darkened. "That's all I need to know, Liam. Do you see a future for us?"

The back of his neck started to itch.

"Do you see us getting married? Having kids? Buying a house in Southie? Growing old together? Do you see that?"

Her voice rose at the end and he flinched at the screechy pitch. He was many things, including a liar when he needed to be, but he never lied to the people he cared about.

"No," he said hoarsely. "I don't."

Painful silence stretched between them. Ten minutes ago, Penny was on her knees with her lips around his dick, and now she was looking at him like he was a complete stranger.

"I can't believe this," she whispered.

Before he could blink, she shot to her feet, smoothed out the bottom of her skirt, and hurried to the door.

"Penny," he called after her.

"No," she snapped without turning around. "We're done here. You can go back to your boy toy or whoever the hell he is. Thanks for wasting a year of my life."

Panic hit him as she stomped out into the hallway. Yes, she had every right to be pissed. Sunday brunch was the worst time and place for her to have found out about his . . . history. But that didn't change the fact that his family was right downstairs. He didn't need Penny making a scene.

She was already halfway down the stairs when he caught up to her. "Penny," he said firmly.

She turned, visibly reluctant.

Liam nodded toward the lower landing. His father's booming laughter and the shrieks of his nieces and nephews pealed out of the living room. "My family . . . ," he started awkwardly.

Bitterness flashed in her expression. "What, they don't know you're a fag?"

A breath hissed out through his teeth. Christ. He hoped to hell it was the anger talking and that he hadn't spent the better part of a year with a woman who had that word in her vocabulary.

Penny's cheeks were flushed as she stumbled down to the landing. He took off after her again—only to freeze when he spotted his sister standing near the bottom of the staircase.

Becca was in her early thirties, a year younger than him, with the same blue eyes and jet-black hair that every Macgregor child had been born with. But at the moment, her usually rosy complexion was whiter than the wallpaper behind her head.

"Liam?" Becca said uneasily. "Pen?"

Penny marched past her friend without a word.

Liam helplessly stared over Becca's slender shoulders at the front door. All he saw was a whirl of red hair, and then the door slammed hard enough to rattle the frame.

"What did she mean by that?" Becca asked in a confused voice. "Why would she say that you . . . that you're a . . ." Her bottom lip quivered. "What did she mean, Liam?"

"Nothing. Just . . . nothing, okay?" He walked toward the front hall on unsteady legs.

"Where are you going?" his sister demanded.

"A friend of mine is in the hospital. I need to go check on him."

"Liam?"

Another voice stopped him before he could turn the doorknob. Jesus. Why couldn't he just leave this frickin' house in peace?

"What's wrong?" His mother had poked her head out of the kitchen and was eyeing him with deep concern. Her copper-colored hair was tied up in a messy bun atop her head and she had his sister Monica's one-year-old daughter on her hip.

Fuckin' hell. His mom and Becca and that damned baby were all fuckin' staring at him, and he'd never felt more suffocated in his life.

"I'm sorry, Ma," he mumbled. "Thank you for brunch, but there's been an emergency. I have to go."

"An emergency?" she trilled. "What kind of emer—"

He was out the door before she could finish, leaving their stunned faces in his wake.

Chapter 11

Two years ago

"Are you enjoying yourself?" Cate asked as she took a seat next to Ash on the stone steps.

The backyard of the Gateway Providence Country Club was lit up like an airport. Ash felt damn out of place here, but there'd been no changing Morgan's mind about this venue. The boss was still trying his damnedest to separate Cate from his life as a mercenary, which meant vacations were never spent at the compound in Costa Rica, but stateside. Ski resorts, beach getaways, country clubs. As if somehow, by stuffing Cate into these places, he could make her forget that the money that funded all of this came from guns and blood.

"Beer tastes as good here as anywhere," Ash said, carelessly raising his longneck bottle.

"My girlfriends are talking about you." She gestured toward a collective of pretty college freshmen all decked out in their nighttime best.

He followed her gaze and was instantly hit with a wave of undisguised female interest. The girls preened, flipping long swaths of hair over bare shoulders. Even in swanky resorts like these, Morgan's crew had no problem drawing attention. As the only single guy on the team, Ash knew he wouldn't have to spend the night alone unless he wanted to. It was crazy what these prim girls would do behind closed doors.

But he couldn't be less interested. These college chicks looked as bland as dry wheat toast. "Thought you had no friends," he reminded Cate. "Isn't that what you were saying in your last e-mail?"

She wrinkled her nose. "I said that I was tired of all the stupid, petty bullshit. Last week the girl in yellow—Emily—stopped talking to the girl in blue because the girl in blue—Natalie—sat next to Brock Gordon. Emily and Natalie have been friends since they were toddlers. I don't get it."

"I don't either. How could anyone name their kid Brock Gordon?"

"You know what I mean." She nudged him with her knee. "They think you're hot and dangerous."

Ash moved away slightly and stared out at the crowd to avoid the hurt expression on her face, but the last day he saw her at the compound was never far from his mind. He'd nearly made a mistake that day. One touch from this girl and all of his defenses crumbled.

He took a sip from the bottle of some designer beer that Ethan had foisted on him earlier, then said, "They're smarter than they look."

Cate rolled her eyes. "Those girls wouldn't know what to do with a man like you."

And you do? he wanted to ask. *You been with a man? You let one of these pansy-ass college boys touch you?* But he knew better than to go there. Plus, he had no right.

"Maybe it's the other way around," he suggested.

She didn't answer right away. Instead she reached forward to pluck a white blossom from a bush near the steps.

Ash tried to avoid looking directly at her tits, but it

was nearly unavoidable. The filmy printed crop top she was wearing pulled up, and he could see the lush under curve of her firm breast along with the shadow of her beaded nipple.

He hastily tipped the bottle back and drained it, but his mouth stayed dry, his tongue thick.

The image was branded in his mind. She was beyond beautiful. He wanted to slip his hand underneath her shirt and cup that perfect breast. The nipple already stood at attention. It wanted his hand, needed his mouth. His tongue tingled and swelled at the thought of drawing that nub between his lips.

He could imagine her straddling him in front of all these fine folks. Her lithe thighs would dangle on either side of his legs. She'd brace her hands behind her and curl her fingers around his knees. Her back would arch and her breasts would offer themselves to him like two ripe peaches aching to be plucked. Firm and juicy.

Christ almighty.

Ash dropped his hands casually between his legs, praying it hid his erection.

"I know more than you or Jim think I do," Cate finally said.

She leaned closer, sticking the flower into the button of his polo shirt. When her hands brushed against his pecs, he had to take a deep breath to remind himself that he could not throw this girl down on the steps of a country club and ravish her in front of her father and all her college friends.

"Just keep pretending for our sakes," he tried to joke. "It helps us sleep at night."

"When are you going to realize I'm all grown up?" This time the blossom she plucked off the bush ended up in tiny massacred pieces that she ripped apart in frustration.

"You're always going to be Jim Morgan's little girl, sweetheart. He looked for you for seventeen years. He wants to keep you safe. Making Noelle and you happy are the two things that motivate him."

"I know that. And I don't mean to be ungrateful, it's just . . ." She trailed off.

Ash knew she would've liked for him to jump in and ask exactly what she wanted, but he was afraid. He, a Marine who'd stared down armed insurgents, was more afraid of hearing exactly what Cate wanted than he was of any gun-toting maniac. Because he could fight the maniac. With this girl, he had almost zero defenses.

Lord, and if she said she wanted him? That she wanted him to take his callous hands and rub them all over her slender, golden body? He'd have a damn hard time saying no.

So he bit his tongue and swallowed down any and all encouragement.

Cate's frustration dissolved into a defeated-sounding sigh. "Thanks for the camera."

"It's just a point and shoot." He tried to downplay the significance of the gift.

Truthfully, it was the most expensive thing he'd ever bought, but the money seemed incidental when she'd opened the box. Her eyes had glowed like sapphires, sending a burst of unparalleled joy to Ash's chest.

"It's not just a point and shoot. It has a Leica lens and those are some of the best in the business. Plus it's small so I can take it anywhere." She rattled off a few more reasons, similar to the ones the guy at the camera shop had given when Ash went to find Cate's birthday present.

He was too fascinated by her mouth to pay attention to her words. Her pink lips moved, making circles and half-moons. They reminded him of cotton candy and his taste buds tingled at the idea of tasting them.

She smelled like the honeysuckle and roses that rimmed his grandmother's porch. Back in the day, he'd listen to his grandma chatter and drink whiskey-soaked sweet tea, getting mildly drunk one sugary sip at a time. That's what it was like with Cate. He was getting drunk on her voice, her company. While she spoke in glowing terms about lenses and apertures, he imagined that when she straddled him, she'd be soaked underneath that skirt of hers. Her arousal would drip out of her and coat her thighs. She'd be sticky and delicious, like a syrup made of the tree of life.

Maybe he'd make her stand up and he'd eat her out right there at the party. *Happy fucking birthday, baby girl. How's this for a present?*

God, he wanted to dirty her up. But if he did, if he gave in to his desire, Jim would kick him out on his ass. And Ash wouldn't blame him. Cate was one of those delicate, beautiful items that belonged on a shelf way up high so that everyone could admire it. If grubby hands like his got on her, they'd ruin her.

"I'm going to be a photographer."

Her abrupt announcement snapped him out of his booze-drenched fantasy. "What? I thought your major was English."

"I changed it."

"Does Jim know?"

She snorted. "What do you think has him in such a bad mood? I told him earlier today and he nearly had a coronary." She peeked at Ash under her long pale eyelashes. "What he doesn't know yet is . . . I'm quitting school."

Ash's eyebrows shot up. "What the fuck? Why?"

"Because it's a prison. And I already spent seventeen years in a cage, Ash. It was a beautiful cage, but it was still a prison. Jim—I mean, Dad—he's not much better." Her blue eyes gleamed with intensity. "I want to *live*. I want to go out and see the world. Experience it for myself instead of reading about it in books. You've all done that. You, Noelle, Dad, Abby, every one of you. You've been out there." She stroked a finger along the thin white scar that Ash had received in a knife fight when he was eighteen. "You've lived."

"Scars don't say you lived. They say you were stupid and allowed the other guy to get a drop on you." He pulled his hand away before he did something real dumb.

Over Cate's head, he saw a pair of blue eyes watching him. Shit. Could Morgan see the ache he felt for Cate? How he wanted to devour her? Carry her inside and take her violently? Lose himself in the hot sweetness of her innocence?

"Don't be an idiot, Cate. Get your degree and stop acting like a spoiled brat."

Her eyes widened, but Ash wasn't done.

"If you want to live, do it after you graduate. But don't ever take a free education for granted." He shuddered out a breath and got to his feet, painfully aware of Morgan's piercing gaze on him.

"Where are you going?" she demanded.

"To mingle," he said stiffly. "I suggest you do the same, sugar. And . . . yeah, we'll just pretend we never had this conversation. Because you're not dropping out of college."

He stalked forward, and now there were two gazes boring into him. A wary Morgan in front of him, an angry Cate behind him. The former made him edgy, but the latter . . . it scared him. Cate was unpredictable when she got mad, and he'd definitely made her mad right now.

He should've kept his mouth shut, damn it. Instead, he'd poked a tiger.

And God help them all when that tiger decided to poke back.

Chapter 12

Ash stared at the back of Cate's head as she flicked through photograph after photograph. Seeing her again after more than a year without contact was a punch in the gut. When he'd walked into that hospital room, he'd literally been without breath for a moment there.

"I'm not taking the blame for Jim's injuries," she muttered, almost to herself. "Rivera shouldn't have even known I had his picture. I called Jim because I thought it was safe."

Ash gripped the back of the chair so he wouldn't make a fool of himself by reaching out and trying to comfort her. That was an easy way to get a junk punch.

"We haven't done a lot of work for the DEA lately," he told her. "It's been mostly private corporations—tech firms and a couple of finance ones. DEA's been quiet."

"Maybe that should've been your first clue," she shot back.

"Maybe. But Tripley's been a good source for us. He seemed as surprised as anyone that Rivera was still breathing."

"Sounds like he's a good source for everyone," she answered sarcastically.

She advanced to the next picture, one that looked nearly identical to the last five she'd taken. As he recalled, Cate liked taking photos in burst mode, which allowed twenty or thirty frames to be taken of one image. She'd used that technique here but nothing in the photos was jumping out at either of them.

"What do you think the plan will be?" Her tone lost some of its hostility. "How we're going to attack Rivera, I mean."

He wasn't a fan of her use of *we*, but telling her to stay home would probably result in her sneaking off on her own, and they couldn't have that. "The goal is to stabilize Morgan and fly back to Costa Rica. D's going to arrange for Sofia to come and care for Jim—"

"Bullshit. Noelle just said that we're going after the cartel. She's not going to leave Guatana while Rivera's still breathing. So, I'm asking you again, how do you think it's going down?"

He shrugged. "We have to find him first," he reminded her.

Cate angrily clicked the mouse. "Yeah, well, I'm looking. I thought you were supposed to call Luke back—you said he didn't pick up, remember? And stop hovering like a bird. It's irritating."

"Right." Ash suspected everything he did irritated her these days.

Then again, did he really expect Cate to welcome him with a smile even under the best of circumstances? After their last encounter, he should be happy that she wasn't trying to cut his dick off. A guy didn't turn down a gift like the one Cate had presented and expect to be greeted with a banner and a brass band. Hell, even civility was a little too much to ask for. Intellectually, he knew he didn't deserve anything from her, but since he hadn't seen her in over a year, he'd take abuse over nothing.

Sighing, he moved toward the corner of the room to dial Luke Dubois, who answered on the second ring.

"Rook, what's the sitrep?"

"I'm calling for yours. Are you en route yet?"

"Yup. Managed to get a charter to the compound and now I'm sitting on another plane with Trev and Izzy. Our ETA is two hours."

"Try to land at a private airfield if possible. The situation at Guatana International is a clusterfuck," Ash warned.

"Copy." Luke paused. "How's the boss man?"

"Still in surgery."

"He's been in there for a helluva long time. What's taking so long?"

"He . . ." Ash paused when he noticed that Cate had abandoned her photos and was watching him closely.

He stared at her while he gave a brief description of Morgan's current status. Cate's mouth crumpled around the edges when Ash uttered the words "internal bleeding." He lowered his voice and finished with, "Prognosis is unclear."

"What's that fucking mean?" Luke demanded.

Cate's eyes were taking on a glossy sheen. "It's bad," Ash admitted. "Even if we didn't need you guys to go after Rivera, it's good you're coming down here."

"Damn." Luke exhaled slowly. "All right. We'll be there soon."

Ash hung up and tucked his phone away, then swept his gaze over the cramped office that they'd commandeered for their war zone. They'd carted out the desk that'd been in here and replaced it with two long metal tables and half a dozen chairs. Maps had been rolled out and Kane had already been coordinating with Noelle's tech girl, Paige, sticking red pins in the areas that housed all of Rivera's known properties and safe houses.

Ash was doing everything to avoid Cate's gaze,

afraid of the pain and worry he'd see in it, but to his surprise, she spoke up in a steel-edged voice.

"He's going to make it."

"Course he is," Ash agreed. He walked back to the table and planted a hand next to her laptop. "Morgan's too stubborn to die."

The *D* word set her off, causing her chin to drop to her chest. "Fuck," she whispered. "*Fuck*, Ash! He never wanted me to do this. He wanted me home and safe and if I'd listened to him—"

"If you'd listened to him, you would have gone crazy," he cut in. "You think Morgan would want you to beat yourself up over this?"

"If it meant I'd give up photojournalism, then yes, he would."

"No. That'd be Noelle's method. Jim's more straight-forward."

She gave a soft, watery snort. "True. Noelle's all about the head games."

"Speaking of head games, you know she doesn't really blame you for Morgan's situation either, right?"

"I know. She just wanted to make sure I didn't break down in front of you guys, so she made me angry." Cate smiled wryly. "Don't worry. I've had her number for a while."

He curled his fingers against the metal to keep from touching her. "He's going to be fine. You know Jim. He's not leaving you and Noelle by yourselves. He searched for you for seventeen years. A few bullets aren't going to keep him down."

She didn't move away. Her chest heaved, the side of her breast nearly brushing his arm as she exhaled heavily. "I hate that we're even talking about this. It's one thing to say you crave the danger, and another thing to come face-to-face with it. And it's not my life that worries me. It's other people around me getting hurt." She swallowed hard. "Dying."

Ash knew she was thinking of her journalist friend, and his heart ached for her loss. He hated the idea of Cate hurting in any way. From the moment he'd met her, he'd been overcome with a deep, relentless need to protect her.

"Riya . . ." She pressed her lips together. "Riya was a friend. She died because of me. Because of a stupid picture I took."

Ash shook his head. "She was a seasoned journalist, Cate. She knew the risks when she decided to come to Guatana. It's not a safe place."

"I know. But . . . I keep running through all these what-if scenarios. What if I hadn't taken that photo? What if I'd kept it to myself? What if I'd decided to go to Tunisia instead of here?"

"That kind of thinking is a one-way ticket to Crazytown."

"I know."

"How about what if Jim never found you? Wouldn't you rather have had these four years with him than nothing at all?"

When tears leaked from the corner of her eyes, Ash couldn't help himself. He slipped an arm around her and for one beautiful moment Cate forgot that she hated him and curled into him. Her hands clutched at his biceps and her face tucked into his neck. He could feel his collar getting wet as she cried silently in his arms.

He didn't tell her it was going to be all right. He wasn't that type of man. But he held her, soothed her in the only way he knew how.

"My dad died of a heart attack right after your nineteenth birthday," Ash confessed. "He was only forty-eight. I was in the middle of an extraction in North

Korea. A high-ranking business exec at some Silicon Valley tech firm wandered over the Chinese border and the North Koreans were holding him for ransom. Tech company didn't want to pay. I didn't hear about Dad until I got back. There were about a dozen messages on my phone."

"I'm so sorry." She peered up at him with sympathetic eyes, trying to pull away.

Ash's grip only tightened, pushing her head back into the crook of his neck where it belonged. He was going to pay for all this touching, but he'd worry about it later.

"He wasn't much of a dad. He spent most of his nights with his head in a bottle and most of his days sleeping off the booze, but I still felt guilty. Hard not to, so I get where you're coming from. But you can't let it control you. Can't let it make you do foolish shit."

He knew immediately he'd said the wrong thing, because Cate pushed away from him and glared with narrowed eyes.

"Just because I'm grieving doesn't mean I'm an idiot," she snapped. "I'm not foolish, but I'm also not going to sit on my ass while Jim's dying in there. I'm going to do something about it. So you can either help me or follow my trail."

She bolted off the chair and stomped out of the room, leaving Ash to stare after her in frustration. He always seemed to say the wrong thing with this girl.

Woman, an internal voice corrected.

Yeah. She wasn't a girl anymore, and it wasn't because she was twenty-one now, which officially made her legal. Cate had traveled the world since she'd left school. She'd gained experience. Confidence. That sweet innocence that had drawn him to her all those years ago was slowly fading with each assignment she accepted. She was still a fighter. Still had nerves of steel and fire to spare. But she was more hardened now, her hopes and dreams and emotions less accessible to him.

And knowing that she'd lost bits and pieces of her optimism in the time they'd spent apart only chipped away a huge piece of himself.

"I'm sorry, Father."

Mateo Rivera stared into his youngest son's unblinking eyes. He stared and stared and stared . . . until the flicker of emotion he was waiting to see slowly crept into Benicio's brown irises.

Guilt.

"Where were you?" Rivera finally asked.

He didn't raise his voice. He didn't sneer or spit or grab the pistol on the table and shoot every single man in the room, including his son. His wife teased him that he was scary when he yelled but downright terrifying when he remained calm. Camila knew him so well. So did Benicio, whose face paled as his father's quiet question hung in the air.

"I—I was across town speaking to the distributor in El Dalsa."

Rivera folded his hands in his lap. "Why?"

"W-why?"

"Yes, *why*. I could be wrong—I'm an old man, after all. My mind is starting to go—but I believe it's not your responsibility to speak to our distributors. That task falls to your brother." He ignored the twisting in his gut at the thought of his beloved son. "You, on the other hand, were asked to eliminate one nosy photographer, which you failed to do yesterday."

"Adrián wanted to handle it," Benicio mumbled, his gaze fixed firmly on his dusty boots. "You saw him last night, Father—he was so furious about the girl getting away. He ordered me to attend the meeting with Ortiz in his place so he could take care of the photographer himself."

"Look at me," Rivera commanded.

His son had been raised to be obedient and so his head flew up. Uneasy, shame-filled eyes locked with Rivera's.

"You're blaming your brother for this? You're blaming your brother for getting shot?"

"No," Benicio said quickly. "No, Father, I'm not. I'm just saying . . . he told me he could handle it. Like you said, it was one girl."

"But it wasn't one girl, was it?" He turned his attention to the lone man who'd managed to escape the scene of his son's murder. "How many?"

Pablo Perez shifted his feet under Rivera's unwavering scrutiny. He was one of the newer recruits to the organization. Adrián had taken Perez under his wing, insisting the young man would make a good lieutenant.

Rivera had yet to see Perez's potential.

"At least six of them," Perez stammered. "Four men, I think. Plus the photographer, and I think another woman."

When Rivera remained silent, Perez hurried on. "They were military, or maybe private contractors, but military at some point. The way they moved . . . They didn't expect the ambush but they reacted to it like soldiers would. I wasn't there when they"—his Adam's apple bobbed as he gulped deeply"—when they killed Adrián, but—"

"You weren't there?" Rivera cut in coldly.

The other man took a backward step even though Rivera hadn't so much as twitched in his chair. "There was a lot of shooting. I ran for cover in the Jeep and . . ." He glanced at his feet. "I was driving and I thought Adrián jumped in the back." Another gulp. "I didn't realize he wasn't with me until I was more than a mile away."

"So you left my son behind." Rage coated his throat. He slowly shifted his gaze to Benicio, who was even more ashen. "And you, you weren't there to begin with."

Silence hung over the large, musty-smelling room in which Rivera had been conducting his briefings since he'd gone underground. It wasn't the sprawling hacienda on the hill where he'd lived for the last three decades, where he'd married his wife and raised his sons. It wasn't the luxury he'd become accustomed to, the wealth and riches he'd clawed and bled and killed to accumulate.

But after three assassination attempts, and with Adrián so eager to prove himself, Rivera had decided it was time to retire. For years his wife had begged him to step down. She thought he was too old to run the business. As if one was ever too old to rule an empire! But, he supposed, what was the point in having an heir if not to leave him a legacy? And so, for the past two years, he'd been grooming his eldest, his pride and joy, to take over the family business.

And today, those sons of bitches had stolen Adrián from him.

A bolt of fury shot up his spine. Before anyone could blink, he grabbed the pistol, swung it up, and put two bullets in Perez's forehead.

The guards near the door didn't so much as flinch as Perez's body dropped like a sack of rotten potatoes. A puddle of blood pooled around the dead man's head onto the concrete floor. Rivera watched it briefly, satisfaction rising inside him, and then he shifted the gun barrel in Benicio's direction and watched his son's eyes fill with horror.

"Father," Benicio started.

He waited for the shock to turn into fear, but it didn't. He wasn't sure whether to be proud or more incensed. He'd raised his boys not to fear death. He'd raised them to be more than men—to be *gods*. To take what they wanted and never be afraid of the consequences. He supposed he shouldn't fault Benicio now for not cowering in the face of a gun barrel.

But boys, at the same time, were supposed to respect their fathers. Adrián would have had enough respect for the man who'd sired him to show some fear. His younger brother, however, proved to be as stupid as Rivera had always known him to be.

He lowered his weapon, chuckling when an audible sigh of relief slipped from Benicio's mouth. Ah. The eyes may not have conveyed the fear, but the body had felt it. Good.

"I want you to bring your brother's body to me."

Benicio's eyebrows shot up. "You want me to . . ."

"Are you deaf? I want you to go back to Bardera and collect your brother's body!" His lips tightened. "Unless you want to leave him there to rot like a dead whore in the street?"

Benicio gave a wild shake of his head. "N-no. I don't, Father. I'll get him right away." He took a hurried step to the door before halting abruptly. "What about the people who killed him?"

"I'll take care of that, don't you worry. Go. Bring your brother home."

The second Benicio was gone, Rivera signaled for his guards to leave him as well. Once the metal door clicked shut behind them, he reached for his bottle of bourbon and carefully poured himself a shot. He tipped his head back and drank, the burn of alcohol joining with the burn of rage in his gut.

He snatched one of the many disposable phones littering the table and dialed.

As he expected, the caller picked up right away.

"You gave me false intelligence," Rivera hissed in lieu of a greeting.

There was a sharp intake of breath. "I'm sorry? What are you . . . I . . . I don't know what you're talking about."

"You told me the photographer was a harmless girl. You said she was twenty-one, just starting out. You said she was estranged from her father."

"I said that because it's all true!" George Dale sounded flustered.

Good. He should be.

"I relayed everything that Agent Tripley told the team," Dale said desperately. "Cate Morgan was working on a story about corruption in Guatana. She's the one who took the picture."

"And her father?"

"I told you. James Morgan, a mercenary."

"Yes, and yet they are *not* estranged as you initially reported, because he flew all the way to Guatana to save the little bitch's ass. Not only that, but he brought a team of mercenaries with him."

"I'm sorry, I just . . . I don't understand why this is a big deal. She took a picture. It doesn't mean she knows anything. She doesn't. She's just a stupid girl."

"That stupid girl was resourceful enough to spot my face in a crowd of beggars. To connect me to Aguilar—"

"With all due respect, sir," Dale stammered, "you took a risk when you left your safe house. It's just bad luck that someone spotted you in the market."

Yes, bad luck, indeed. But the meeting with Aguilar had been unavoidable. For the past three months, the general had been dodging Adrián's attempts to meet, worried by the change of leadership in the Rivera power structure. As much as Rivera had resented Aguilar's reluctance to deal with Adrián, he'd also recognized that they needed the man.

For two decades the naval defense minister had provided the Riveras with unrestricted shipping routes, not to mention government protection. So, yes, they needed the sniveling fool. Coming out of hiding to facilitate a deal between Adrián and Aguilar, to offer reassurances to the general that their arrangement would continue in the smoothest of manners . . . it had been a risk, but also a necessity.

"We are not discussing me at the moment," he said coldly. "We're discussing *you* and your incompetence," he growled into the phone. "That little bitch sent my picture to your agency."

"The DEA already suspected you were alive," Dale protested.

"That's irrelevant!" he snapped. "It's the principle of the matter. It's the threat she poses. I don't need some nosy cunt in my business. It doesn't matter if she knows my location—what matters is that she exists." His fingers tightened around the phone. "What matters is that her people *killed my son*."

A shocked silence fell over the line. "Oh. I . . . I'm s-sorry. I d-didn't know . . . when did—"

"Stop stuttering like a fool!" Rivera drew a slow breath. "You screwed up once by not giving me the proper intelligence. This time you will not screw up."

"I don't understand what you're asking of me."

He gritted his teeth. "You're going to get me thorough intel on every single man and woman in that bastard Morgan's employment. I want their names, their histories. I want to know who their families are, who they're close to, who they're fucking. I want to know when they take a shit and when their families take a shit and when their motherfucking dogs take a shit.

And you're going to get me all this information by to-morrow morning."

Dale made a panicked noise. "Mr. Rivera, that's impossible. I don't have that kind of clearance! James Morgan used to be black ops. If there's a file on him, there's no way I'll ever be able to access it."

"Oh, I'm sure you'll find a way to be as resourceful as his bitch daughter. Do you want to know what will happen if you fail me again?"

Silence.

He could practically taste the other man's terror. The terror he'd wanted to see in Benicio's eyes and had been denied.

"Would you like me to tell you what I'm going to do if you don't get me what I need?" he asked pleasantly.

"No, sir—"

"Okay, I'll tell you." He smiled. "Unlike you, I'm quite skilled at gathering information, so I'm well aware that you have a lovely young wife. You only recently got married. Six months ago, I believe. The wedding was in Nantucket. Sounds like it was a nice ceremony."

"Please . . . ," Dale whimpered.

"What's your lovely wife's name again? Miranda? That's a beautiful name."

"Sir—"

"I'm very much looking forward to meeting your Miranda." His smile widened. "I don't know if she's going to enjoy meeting me—"

"P-please—"

"—but she's sure going to enjoy having my cock in her ass."

An agonized moan wailed over the line.

"Yes, I think I'll fuck her. I'll fuck her ass and I'll fuck her cunt and I'll fuck her mouth, and then I'll get my son to do it. And after he's filled her with his come,

I'm going to order every man who works for me to shove his big, dirty cock inside your wife's tight cunt. But it won't be tight when we're done with it, will it?"

"Please . . . no . . ."

Rivera grunted in disgust at Dale's choked sobs. Fucking weak bastard. Men didn't cry. And men certainly didn't cry over women. He loved his Camila more than he loved anyone. He would die for that woman, he would kill for her, but he would never cry over her.

"And once we finish fucking your sweet Miranda, I'll pull out my favorite knife and start cutting off pieces one by one. I think we'll start with her nipples. Pretty little pink nipples . . . They'll pop right off, I imagine. Then I'll drag my blade down to her loose, come-filled cunt—"

"Stop it!" Dale shouted, then immediately gasped as if realizing what he'd done. "I'll get you the information you need! I promise! But tomorrow morning might be hard. I'm begging you for a little more time."

"Tomorrow afternoon," Rivera relented.

"Thank you."

He hung up and reached for the bourbon. Men truly were puppets, so easy to maneuver if you knew the right strings to pull. And he'd pulled a lot of strings in his days. He was the most feared man on the globe for a reason.

But he was also a father.

So. Cockroaches had decided to take his son from him?

It was time to repay the favor.

Chapter 13

"Hey, Dad," Cate whispered to the unconscious man on the bed. "How're you doing?"

There was no response. No sound other than the hiss of the ventilator.

Swallowing a lump of heartache, she approached the hospital bed and dragged a metal chair closer to her father's side. She'd spent the morning in Guatana City with Bailey, so this was the first chance she'd had to check in on Jim. As she set the photographs she'd taken this morning on the bedside table, she found herself sheepishly checking for a reaction. Despite Jim's comatose state, he still was a commanding presence. Cate half expected him to rise up from the bed and glare at her for leaving the safety of the base today to take photographs of cartel spouses.

She released a rueful breath. "I guess the positive side of this is that you can't yell at me for taking pictures of Camila Rivera. Bailey and I saw her when we were getting coffee this morning."

Cate tapped the glossies they'd stopped to print out at the pharmacy, whose owner had been pathetically grateful for their money.

"Someone will be pissed, though. Ash, most likely. I blame all my problems with Ash on you, by the way." She was only half joking. "I mean, let's be realistic. He was the only guy around that was even close to my age.

Did you really think I'd be able to hang out with him all day long and not fall for him? Even Noelle likes him and she doesn't like anyone but you."

Her gaze drifted over Jim's prone form, hoping there'd be some kind of response, but there was nothing. There was no pleasure in trying to rile him up, no goading him out of the coma. She'd tried all those tactics with her mother for years—tears, both fake and real, screaming, begging, promises to be good, and vows to be terrible. All that had netted was pitying looks from the bodyguards assigned by her grandfather and disapproving stares from the nursing staff.

She sighed and rubbed a knot in her temple. "I know. If only I'd stayed in college and gotten my degree in . . . statistics or something boring and normal, you'd be fine, right? That's what you're saying in my head, but we both know you've lived every day on the edge. Who knew if you were going to come home in one piece?"

His disapproving silence hung between them at her not fully honest admission. She couldn't lie to Jim while he lay there and couldn't fire back at her.

"Okay, okay. I did worry, but that's not why I dropped out. I wanted something more than a college dorm room, but not this. I'm sorry. I never wanted to put anyone in danger."

Or get anyone killed.

The lump in her throat grew bigger. Riya had been shot to death because of her. Cate knew she'd have to live with that guilt for the rest of her life. But, God, she couldn't lose Jim too. One death on her conscience would break her. Two would crush her.

"Please," she whispered. "Just open your eyes, Dad."

There she was again—bargaining, pleading with someone who couldn't respond. She bit her lip. She couldn't make promises here, not when she knew she'd break them. She'd spent so many years sitting at her mom's bedside, listening to the hushed background voices accompanied by the drone of the machines that breathed for her mother, punctuated by occasional beeps and alarms. Was it any wonder that everything inside of her rebelled at sitting in lectures day in and day out? Doing was how she felt alive.

"The doctors are worried. They don't use those terms, though." She reached up to swipe some of the moisture out of her eyes. "They say things like your prognosis is uncertain and no definitive conclusions can be drawn at this stage. But we both know it's bullshit." She blinked through another rush of tears. "You'd hate this, but everyone has come to pay their last respects. If you were awake, you'd tell them to get the hell home—"

Her voice cracked and she couldn't go on. She bent her head low until her forehead was resting on the crisp hospital sheet. How many times had she talked herself hoarse in this very same scenario? It was too much. Just too much.

But maybe this was her cross to bear, and so she exhaled deeply and forced herself to keep talking. The nurses had always said she should talk to her mother, that coma patients could hear everything even if they didn't remember the conversations when they awoke.

"Do you know how many people you've touched? How many people love you so deeply? Even Holden is coming—he actually returned Kane's call after years of radio silence. Everyone's here for you, Dad. Everyone wants you to make it. Ash worships the ground you walk on. He won't take a breath without you giving him the okay. What's he going to do if you're gone?"

What am I going to do if you're gone?

God, this train of thought was getting her nowhere.

Cate took another deep breath and refocused back to the thing that would piss Jim off. If he were conscious.

"I was surprised to see Camila in the city today. She's very popular with the European tabloids. Her photographs are almost always somewhere glitzy and glamorous. Guatana is an economic wasteland—the only luxury goods here are clean water, meat, bread. So she's got to be here because her husband is here, right?"

She'd wanted to discuss this with Bailey earlier, but the woman had been uncharacteristically quiet, probably out of respect or concern. Cate wasn't sure.

A soft knock sounded at the door. "Am I interrupting?"

She looked over to find Liam Macgregor in the doorway, his gorgeous face creased with concern.

Cate shook her head, grateful for the company. "No, Jim is being maddeningly quiet. Did you just get in?"

He nodded. "Took a while. Total bitch to get here."

"I'm sorry."

"What for?"

"I don't know . . . inconveniencing you, I guess."

Liam gave her a gentle smile. "It's not an inconvenience. I need to be here." He moved silently across the tiled floor until he reached the bed. In a careful tone, he asked, "What's his condition?"

"A bullet in his neck. I think the swelling is causing his unconscious state. Reflexes all work, though." She tapped Jim's knee, and she and Liam watched as the leg moved involuntarily. "He's having problems breathing, which is why he's on the ventilator."

"Good news, bad news. It's a regular shit sandwich." Liam squeezed her shoulder in encouragement. "He'll wake up when he's ready, darling. In the meantime, we're going to salt the city with the ashes of the Rivera cartel."

Those words were more for Jim than Cate, judging by the look of steely promise he directed at the comatose man. Then he cleared his throat and turned back to her.

"Ran into D in the hallway. They're headed to the briefing room for a meeting." He cocked his head toward the pictures. "Are they going to need those? I can take them."

She bristled and swiped the pictures protectively to her. "No. I shot these and I'll show them to the team."

Liam raised his eyebrows at her sharp tone. "All right. Sounds like a plan."

"Sorry. It's been a rough few days." She dragged a hand down her face.

"I hear you, honey." He squeezed her shoulder again before gesturing for her to follow him.

Covertly, Cate studied Liam from under her lashes as they walked down the corridor. She'd always wondered how a man this gorgeous could have ever done undercover work. Well, unless it was on a movie set. He looked like an action hero—comic book Hollywood creation—but despite the fact that some women nearly fainted if Liam so much as cast an accidental glance in their direction, he'd never affected Cate in the slightest. He was just Liam, supersoldier, Boston native, with a sexy accent that came from a very sexy face.

Whereas with Ash, she only had to hear his name to get excited. The smell of his warm skin had her feeling too tight inside her own skin. If he'd happened to smile at her with a sort of fond affection like Liam had displayed in the hospital room, Cate would've been a puddle on the floor.

Hearts are stupid.

Liam's head jerked around.

She offered a sheepish look. "Did I say that out loud?"

He nodded.

She jutted her chin out defiantly. "Disagree with me?"

His lips curved upward in a sad smile. "Can't argue with you. I agree a hundred percent with that sentiment."

Then he ducked into the briefing room before Cate could ask him what he meant. She stared at his broad back, not quite sure how to take it. Hollywood had a love problem? That seemed impossible and probably spelled doom for the rest of the mere mortals.

"None of the leads are panning out. Everyone's mouth is clamped tight or they don't know shit," Ash was reporting when Cate and Liam entered the war room.

All the operatives minus Abby, who was home with her toddler, were present for the meeting, which meant that the tiny space was packed. It was standing room only, and Cate made sure to stand as far away from Ash as possible. She wouldn't be surprised if *he* was the one who'd decided to exclude her from this briefing.

"Macgregor." Noelle's blond head swiveled toward the newcomer. "Good. You're here. What's your DEA contact say?"

Liam didn't seem bothered that nobody took the time to say hello to him, but Cate noticed a few of the men tap his shoulder in greeting as he made his way to stand next to Kane. "Nothing," he reported with the grim shake of his head. "They're denying the leak came from them."

"That's a bunch of bullshit," Luke Dubois drawled. "No way that Rivera connects Cate with anything unless the photo is leaked."

"Never said it wasn't bullshit," Liam agreed. "But that doesn't change anything. I haven't gotten squat from the DEA."

"How about Aguilar?" Cate suggested. She stepped

forward and slapped down the stack of photos she'd printed out in Timo Varela's office before visiting her dad. The top one was a blown-up picture of Aguilar and another man.

"Where'd you get this?" Brow furrowed in suspicion, Ash looked at the table and then at her, clearly recognizing that this was a new photo and not one from the batch that had captured Rivera in the first place.

"Don't get your panties in a bunch," Cate answered, rolling her eyes. "Bailey was with me the entire time."

Sean Reilly, Bailey's husband, planted his hands on his hips. Accusation gleamed in his green eyes. "You said you were making a coffee run."

Bailey grinned. "We got coffee."

"What're we looking at?" Noelle pushed at Ash, who stood glaring at Cate. When he wouldn't budge, Noelle shoved him aside and examined the picture.

Cate flashed Ash a saccharine smile and got down to business. "The guy in the blue shirt is Aguilar. We saw him go into this cigar shop, which, according to the shopkeeper across the street, is owned by a known Rivera cartel sympathizer."

"Jesus Christ. Why not just offer yourself up to them?" Ash exploded, throwing his hands in the air.

"We took a few pictures and left, asshole," Cate spit back.

She was *so* tired of the team treating her like an imbecile. Every single one of them had gone target shooting with her. Jim had taken her into the jungle and trained her how to move soundlessly while tracking prey. Isabel had shown her the ins and outs of disguises—how it was more than just makeup and artfully used silicone implants, but the way you walked and talked and dressed. She wasn't a child anymore. Why wouldn't anyone see that?

She cast an angry glance at Ash. "We didn't go in."

"The coffee shop was across the street," Bailey offered helpfully.

Ash rubbed his forehead in frustration and backed away from the table. Cate wanted to yell at him, but knew that any outburst of emotion would be used against her. God, she was going to end up with zero molars after grinding them together so hard.

"Aguilar has always been our best bet," Noelle mused.

Kane gave her a rueful smile. "I hope you're not thinking of kidnapping the minister of naval defense in a foreign country and torturing the information out of him."

"We don't have any other options." Noelle pointed to the picture. "This guy isn't our best lead. He's our *only* lead."

D nodded. "She's right. We either pack up our toys and go home or we go after Aguilar."

"No one's packing up shit," Noelle growled. "Mateo Rivera sent a hit squad after Cate, and my husband was fucking shot. I want this motherfucker's *head*."

"Preaching to the choir," Luke murmured from his perch on the far table.

"We all want his head," Trevor said quietly.

She whirled toward him, blue eyes blazing. "Yeah? Then let's get off our asses and fucking do something about it!"

When Cate noticed several wary glances being exchanged, she bit her bottom lip in dismay. Noelle wasn't the type of woman to come undone, but right now the assassin's breathing was shallow and she was wringing her hands together. She was more worried about Jim than she was letting on, Cate realized, and that only made her own breaths go choppy.

What if Jim didn't make it?

Exhaling slowly, Noelle swept her gaze around the room. The color was returning to her face, and when she spoke again, it was in her trademark icy tone.

"We need to know everything there is to know about Aguilar. Snatching him will be easy—making him talk might not be. So we need leverage. We need to find out what he eats, where he shits, who he fucks. And we need all of that information now." She focused on the two gorgeous women near the door. "Bailey, Juliet, get some disguises. See if you can clean his house or office."

"I'm going to make contact with the Barrios cartel," Liam hedged in. "They might give me a meeting based on our history—I did business with them when I was deep cover. But I should probably have a product on hand, just in case. Do we have anything I can show them? Preferably an exotic?"

"I've got some African opium," Ash offered. When all eyes swiveled toward him, he shrugged. "What? It's good currency on the black market. I carry it in my go bag."

Liam's lips twitched. "I knew there was a reason I liked you."

Cate shoved down a kernel of reluctant admiration. Ash was always prepared, always thinking two steps into the future.

"There's no future between you and me."

Before she could stop them, the hurtful words he'd thrown at her the last time they were together flew to the forefront of her mind, turning her admiration to bitterness. God, what a dick. She *hated* him.

But what she hated even more was that she was still attracted to the asshole. That her body still wanted to surround itself in his strong embrace. Her stupid heart still thought he was the best thing she'd ever had the misfortune to lay eyes on.

Annoyed with herself, she forced her attention back to Noelle, who was directing the rest of the crew.

"D, Kane, figure out what kind of supplies we're going to need and how we're going to get them. Ethan, work the expat community. Find out who can be bribed and what their prices are. We'll need to get Jim out of the country without anyone knowing he's down. Ash—"

"I'm on watch," he interjected. "I'll stake out Aguilar's house tonight."

"Take someone with you." Noelle looked around the rapidly thinning room. People had taken their assignments and were leaving, the urgency of the situation not missed by anyone.

"I'll go," Cate volunteered.

"No way." Ash couldn't get his rejection out fast enough.

"Why?" She stuck her chin forward. "And don't say it's too dangerous, because all we're doing is watching. Unless you plan to kidnap a major military figure all by your lonesome?"

His expression darkened. "No, but this place is a hellhole and anything could happen. You shouldn't even be here, let alone running around taking pictures."

She met his angry gaze head-on. "Well, I'm here and I'm not leaving."

Ash turned to Noelle, who arched a brow and said, "Cate goes with you."

She didn't even bother hiding her pleasure. "I'll go get my camera," she chirped, then scampered out of the room before Ash could say no again.

To her irritation, he followed close behind, arguing the entire way to the room she was sharing with Noelle.

"Cate. Goddamn it, will you stop and listen to me? You're not coming with. It's too risky."

Risky, her ass. She was so tired of Ash telling her what she could and couldn't do.

"I was out there three hours ago with Bailey," she shot back. "And here I am, not a scratch on me. You can't hold me prisoner here. I have every right to—hey, stop that!"

She flew over and seized his arm before he could grab her bag from the bed. She'd had Kane pick it up for her from the hotel, and, luckily, all her documents were safe and sound. Apparently Rivera's goons couldn't be bothered to steal them.

Cate knew exactly what Ash was up to. He was going to try to take her passport, and that was *not* happening. But his arm was like steel beneath her fingers, and even when she dug her nails in his flesh, he didn't flinch or draw away.

Nope, he plucked her passport out of the canvas bag and stuck it in his pocket.

"You're staying here," he said firmly. "Your dad needs you."

"The hell he does. I've already watched most of my family die. Guess what? Not happening again. So either you take me with you or I go alone. You, of all people, should know that I make good on my threats."

"Then, I'll tell you now what I told you then: grow up. You're not an operative. You're a *photographer*."

Each harsh, judgmental word slapped at her. "And all we're doing is watching, unless you're planning to go rogue and take out the general yourself, which we both know you won't do because that would go against orders. And you never go against orders, do you, Ash?"

His jaw muscles ticked as he silently absorbed her insult. "You're not coming," he said finally.

"I'm still not hearing a good reason why not."

"Because I don't want you there," he growled.

Cate lifted a shaking hand to her mouth to cover a gasp. Had he really just said that? "What?"

"I don't want you there," Ash repeated.

Yes. He really *had* said it.

And those parting words were effective, because when he marched out of the room, she didn't argue or follow. Instead, she slumped onto the bed and dropped her head into her hands.

She should be used to his rejection by now. She really should be.

But she wasn't, damn it.

No, David Ashton still had the power to hurt her, more than anyone else she knew.

Chapter 14

After the briefing ended, Sullivan shouldered his duffel and trudged down the hallway of the dormitory-style barracks where Guatana's on-base soldiers resided.

Timo Varela was going above and beyond in proving his loyalty to Morgan. He'd offered up a block of rooms to Morgan's team, along with twenty-four-hour security in the infirmary where Morgan remained in critical condition. Sully had yet to meet Varela, but when he did, he planned on kissing the bastard's feet.

Without Varela's aid, Morgan wouldn't just be critical— he'd be fucking dead. And it was too risky for the team to stay anywhere else. In the current state that Guatana was in, the military bases were the most secure places in the country. Since those cartel bastards had already gone after Cate twice, the likelihood of them coming after her again was pretty bloody good, which meant that this base was the safest place for her, and for Morgan . . . if he made it through surgery.

Sully banished the unthinkable thought and approached the room he was going to be bunking in. His pulse sped up when he reached the open doorway.

Liam was sitting on one of the twin beds built into the wall. He was huddled over his phone, his dark eyebrows furrowed as he studied the screen.

Sully hesitated in the doorway, drawn to the deep crease in Liam's perfect forehead.

That word—*perfect*—pretty much applied to every inch of Liam Macgregor's movie star face. Chiseled features, piercing blue eyes, a tiny cleft in his strong chin. And his mouth . . . Sully had heard Trevor Callaghan's wife, Isabel, gush about Liam's lips more than once, how they had a perfect curve, just the right amount of fullness. He found himself staring at those lips now. They were pinched together, as if Liam wasn't happy with whatever he was seeing on his phone.

"You coming in or what?"

Liam voiced the question without lifting his gaze from the phone.

Sully wasn't surprised by that. His friend was former DEA—Liam always knew when he wasn't alone.

"Hey." He took an awkward step forward, shifting the strap of his duffel. "I'm gonna be crashing in here, if that's cool."

Liam nodded, then reached up and rubbed the back of his neck, drawing Sully's attention to his friend's sculpted biceps.

His gaze lowered to Liam's chest, which was hugged by a white T-shirt that stretched across the hard ridge of abs, and then to the pair of long legs encased in olive-green cargo pants. Fuck. The man had a great body. Sully had noticed it the moment they'd met, but back then he hadn't harbored any filthy thoughts about that body. Hadn't once thought about getting Liam's clothes off and running his hands over sinewy muscle and sleek skin.

Not until that gig in Paris, when tensions had run high and sexual awareness cropped up out of nowhere, leading to an impulsive kiss that Sullivan now regretted. That one stupid kiss had set off a sequence of events that had all but destroyed their friendship.

"How are you?" Liam asked quietly.

He offered a wry smile. "Why, does the answer to that question determine whether I can room with you?"

Liam cracked a smile in return. "We're still on that?" He gestured to the other bed. "Room away, dude. It's not like we're swimming in spare beds around here."

Sully's bag hit the floor with a plop. He sat on the opposite twin bed, forearms resting on his thighs as he leaned forward. Liam assumed the same position, and Sully would've smiled if it weren't for the grave look in his friend's eyes.

"I mean it, Sully. How are you?"

He sighed. "I'm not on smack, if that's what you're asking."

"Last time we spoke was a year ago. You can't blame me for wondering."

"Guess I can't. But don't worry, the drugs have been out of my system since I got on the boat in Portugal."

"And the cravings?"

He swallowed his discomfort. "They still come every now and then. Not often, though."

But when they did . . . Jesus. It usually happened in the middle of the night. He'd wake up from a dead sleep, sweating, shuddering, hands shaking as he remembered the euphoric thrill surging through his veins.

He wasn't sure if his addictive tendencies were hardwired into his genetic makeup or if he was just really fucking weak when it came to vices, but it'd always been that way for him. Alcohol, he could take or leave, but drugs, cigarettes, sex . . . he wasn't the kind of bloke who could have just one. One smoke? Nah, a whole pack. A joint? Sure, and maybe he'd snort some coke after. Blow job? Bring it, and then seven more rounds of sweaty, mind-draining animal sex.

He was addicted to pleasure. Or at least he had been

before he'd been locked up in Mendez's dungeon. Since then, he'd gotten a few BJs when he was on the mainland, but for the most part his libido had stayed dormant. Except for the nights when the cravings came. Those nights, he'd replaced the need for drugs with some serious jack-off sessions. Tried to distract himself by coming hard enough to make him forget about the high.

The only problem was, his fantasies were equally destructive, so eventually he'd stopped doing that too.

He couldn't remember the last time he'd gotten off. Six, seven months ago?

"Sully?"

Shit. He'd gotten lost in his fucked-up head again. "Sorry, what?"

His friend's expression was full of concern. "I didn't say anything. You just . . . look upset."

"I'm good," he said lightly. "I'm always good."

"Sure, man, if you say so."

"What's that supposed to mean?"

Liam shrugged.

"Tell me what you meant by that," he demanded.

"It means that you're full of shit," Liam retorted, a note of frustration in his voice. "It's not all good. Sometimes it is, but when it's not, you still say it is. You lie."

He arched an eyebrow. "You psychoanalyzing me now, mate?"

"No. Just stating a fact. I know you. You like to pretend that nothing bothers you, but we both know it does."

He didn't like where this conversation was heading, so he changed the subject. "How's Boston?"

Liam chuckled, seeing right through Sullivan's tactics. The man knew him too damn well. "Boston's great," he said vaguely.

Yeah, right. Sully knew Liam just as well, and he had no trouble reading between those lines. "You still working with your brother?"

"Yup."

"You . . . ah . . . seeing anyone?"

Liam's blue eyes went shuttered. "I was. Ended it before I came here."

"Why's that?" He kept his tone careless, but inside he was desperate for an answer.

Christ, he wanted to know if Liam was in the same depressing place as he was. If their friendship, that fucked-up attraction, had ruined him for everyone else too, or if it was just Sully who lay there at night, jerking off to the image of Liam's sexy mouth around his dick—

He quickly shoved the traitorous thought away before he sprung a boner. At one point, seeing Sully with an erection might've turned the other man on, but the indifference of his tone and the complete lack of desire in his eyes were a pretty big sign that Liam had gotten over him.

But hell, that was what he'd wanted, right?

Still, curiosity had him pushing, "Why did you end it?"

"It wasn't working."

"Why not?" Christ. Why was he badgering the guy? He didn't want to know this, damn it.

"Because it didn't." Liam paused. "She wanted me to propose."

She.

He fought a wry smile. Of course it was a she. Evidently Liam had reverted to the straight, Irish Catholic, pure hetero male that he was, which was exactly what Sully had known would happen. Liam Macgregor didn't screw men. Period.

Sullivan Port, on the other hand, had been attracted to both sexes as far back as he could remember. As a teenager he'd traded handjobs with a fellow drug dealer. They'd made out, fucked a few times. Brody was the first guy he'd ever screwed around with, but he sure as shit hadn't been the last. And the women . . . Lord, he'd had his fair share of those too.

But Liam, well, he hadn't even looked at another man until Sullivan had planted those ideas in his head, luring him into the world of threesomes and debauchery. But clearly the man had hopped back on the pussy train, just as he should. Liam wasn't cut out for Sully's lifestyle. That Irish guilt would crush him.

"Why haven't you? Proposed, I mean?"

"Not ready for that," Liam muttered.

"Uh-huh."

"What does that mean?"

"Means you're full of shit," Sully mimicked. "You haven't proposed because you don't want to get married. You've never wanted that."

That got him two raised eyebrows. "Since when are you an expert on what I want?"

A frustrated laugh flew out. "Are you kidding me? I know you better than I know myself, Boston. You don't want marriage and kids and some bullshit nine-to-five job. You're an adventure junkie. You want to travel the world and blow shit up." He offered a look of challenge. "Tell me I'm wrong."

Liam rubbed his hands over his knees and fixed his gaze on the floor.

"That's what I thought." Sully's chuckle died when the other man abruptly lifted his head.

"You know me, huh?" Those blue eyes shone with intensity. "All right. Then tell me, what else do I want?"

Sullivan gulped. Fuck. *Fuck*. Were they really going there? Right now?

His jaw felt like a rusty hinge as he opened his mouth, but he didn't get a chance to speak because footsteps sounded at the door. Thank Christ. Sully wasn't sure what he would've said, but he damn well hadn't been ready to have this talk.

"Jesus," he breathed when he spotted the figure in the doorway.

"Not quite," came the tired response. "Just little old me."

Holden McCall entered the room, causing both men to bolt to their feet.

Sully wasn't speechless often, but he had no idea what to say to the man standing in front of them. He hadn't seen his friend and teammate in four years. After Holden's wife was killed at Morgan's former compound, Holden had completely gone off the grid.

Liam was the first to say something. "Holden . . . ah, not sure if you remember me, but I'm Liam—"

"Macgregor," Holden finished. "The contractor."

It took Sully a moment to remember that Liam hadn't come on board full-time until after Holden was already gone. And now none of them were on the team. Life was a bitch sometimes.

"Hey, mate," Sully said to Holden. "It's been ages."

After an awkward beat, he pulled Holden in for an even more awkward side hug. Oh man, his old friend had lost a lot of weight. And there were dark shadows under his eyes. He looked like he hadn't slept in days. Or maybe years.

"When'd you get in?" Sully asked gruffly.

"About ten minutes ago. Decided to make the rounds before I went in to see Jim."

There was sadness in Holden's tone. Sully hated that it was Morgan's knocking on death's door that had drawn their former teammate back to the land of the living. "How've you been? Morgan said you moved back to Montana?"

A flash of pain crossed Holden's eyes as he shook his head. "No, I didn't. I've just been traveling around. Haven't stayed in one place for too long."

Another silence fell. Christ, this was bloody uncomfortable. What the hell were you supposed to say to a man whose wife had been gunned down in his arms?

"Have you met Cate yet?" Liam asked, trying to break the tension.

Holden finally cracked a smile. It was weak and frayed at the edges, but, hell, it was something. "You mean the furious blonde who just stormed past me while flipping the bird to some poor Southern boy? We weren't properly introduced, but I'd know her as Jim's kid from anywhere."

Sully chuckled. "Yeah, those two are scarily similar. And that poor Southern boy is Ash—he took Ethan's place as the rookie."

Ash's ears must have been ringing because he suddenly appeared at the door. His frazzled expression revealed that he hadn't left Cate's presence unscathed. "We're rolling out," he said stonily. "Get your shit together. Noelle's already in the chopper."

"Is Cate coming with?" Liam asked with a barely suppressed smile.

"No," the rookie snapped.

Sully fought his own grin. "You sure about that?"

"Don't care if I have to handcuff her to a pipe," Ash ground out. "She's not coming." Then he stalked off with a growl.

Holden watched the younger man go before turning to Sullivan. "Guess I have a lot of catching up to do," he remarked with a sigh.

He would always view her as a child.

It was a depressing thought, but Cate was no longer holding out hope that Ash would eventually see the error of his ways. Despite all the time and effort she'd spent trying to show him that she was all grown up, the stubborn jerk refused to let go of his first impression of her—that she was Morgan's teenage daughter, a helpless girl who needed to be saved and protected.

His staunch refusal to let her help with this Aguilar matter proved that.

The good thing was, Ash wasn't in charge. Noelle was, and she had no problem sending Cate into the field if necessary. Noelle had been recruited as a spy for the French government when she was only eighteen—she wouldn't let something as trivial as Cate's age stop them from finding Rivera.

Hell, the woman had already ordered Ash to take Cate with him on surveillance. Noelle was going to be pissed when she found out Ash had disregarded those orders, but the only reason Cate hadn't gone over his head again was because . . . well, because she didn't want to be anywhere near him right now, not after what he'd said to her.

I don't want you there.

Fine. Then she didn't want herself there either. Not if it meant taking Ash's abuse.

Still, she wasn't exactly thrilled as she paced the small room. She supposed she could take a quick nap, but she was too riled up to sleep. None of them had caught so much as a wink of sleep since they'd arrived at this base and probably wouldn't until they had some news about Morgan's condition.

I don't want you there.

She paced faster, all the while hating herself for letting Ash get to her like this. But that jerk had always had that effect on her.

When she'd first met Jim and moved to the compound, she'd viewed Ash as a friend, a big brother type. Once the shock of losing her old life had worn off and she'd adjusted to life on a mercenary compound, everything had changed. She'd gained confidence. She'd trained with Morgan and Noelle. And whenever she'd needed someone to talk to, she'd turned to Ash, who was always there to listen. They'd even had their own private spot in the jungle, for Pete's sake.

So yeah, it wasn't long before she'd stopped viewing him as a brother and started aching for him. Unfortunately, he hadn't ached for *her*. Because she'd been seventeen. And then eighteen. Nineteen. And Cate knew that until she was out of her teens, Ash would never give himself permission to touch her.

Except then she'd turned twenty, twenty-one . . . and it hadn't mattered either.

Bitterness clogged her throat. That man was a goddamn hypocrite. No matter how many times he reminded her how young she was, how he didn't want her, she knew he was lying. Over the past four years, she'd glimpsed heat in his eyes. She'd caught him staring at her when he thought she wasn't looking. She'd seen the desire he was trying to tamp down, and she'd hoped that one day he would give in to the attraction between them.

But he hadn't.

He wouldn't.

Her ringing phone snagged her attention, sending a wave of gratitude through her. Thank God. She didn't even care who was calling. Anyone would be a good distraction right about now. Ash didn't deserve the mental energy it cost her to obsess over him.

She snatched the phone from the desk under the small window. "Hello?" she said eagerly.

An unfamiliar male voice came over the line. "Hello, my dear. How's your father?"

"Who is this?"

"Do you really require a formal introduction? I assumed we were far past that by now."

A chill flew up her spine. "Rivera."

"Still so formal! Please, call me Mateo. And I'll call you Cate? I heard you prefer that to Catarina."

Despite the galloping of her pulse, Cate managed to keep her voice calm. "How did you get this number?"

"I have my ways." He chuckled. "And if you're thinking about tracking this call, don't bother. You won't be able to pinpoint my location, as I'm sure I won't be able to pinpoint yours."

He was right about that. Though she wasn't officially an operative, she still received the same perks as everyone else who worked for Morgan and Noelle, including an untraceable phone programmed with the techno voodoo of Paige, one of Noelle's assassins. Cate had no idea how it worked—something about dummy numbers and satellites and calls bouncing from tower to tower—but apparently Paige's tech skills were unbeatable. Even the CIA couldn't trace the team's phones, a fact that Bailey, a former agent, had cackled about to Cate once.

Although Rivera probably wasn't bluffing, Cate wasn't stupid enough to take him at face value. She grabbed a pen and notepad from the desk, already scribbling on the page as she marched to the door.

Making sure to keep her footsteps soundless, she

popped out into the hall in search of . . . shit, everyone was gone.

She forced herself to speak as she sprinted forward. She needed to keep the bastard talking. "Why are you calling?" she demanded.

"I thought I'd extend the courtesy of a proper introduction, seeing as we're going to be spending a lot of time together."

She ducked her head into the open doorways along the hall, one by one, but every room was empty. Damn it. "Yeah? What makes you think that?"

"Because I'm going to find you." Another low chuckle. "And when I do, it won't be quick and painless. I plan to drag out your punishment for days, hopefully weeks."

"Is that right?"

She reached the end of the corridor, which connected with the hall that led to the medical wing. When she turned the corner, she spotted a familiar face outside the door to Jim's room.

Holden McCall. They hadn't been introduced yet, but she'd heard the others talking about him before. Apparently he was the male equivalent of Paige, a whiz with computers.

Holden opened his mouth when he spotted her, but she held up her hand to silence him. She gestured to the phone, then shoved the notepad in his hand.

Frowning, Holden read the message she'd scribbled. Then he grabbed the pen from her hand and jotted down a note in return.

I need your phone number.

"You see," Rivera was saying, "usually I'm a reasonable man. I understand the concept of self-defense. I sent men to kill you, so of course you're going to try to protect yourself—I anticipated that, and I respect your sense of self-preservation. But no matter how admirable that is, there's one thing, to me anyway, that's far more important than self-preservation."

"And what's that?" she asked as she wrote down her cell number. She handed the notepad back to Holden, and he cocked his head, gesturing for her to follow him.

Silently, they moved in a brisk walk back toward the barracks.

"Family," Rivera answered. "Family is more important than anything else in this world."

"I agree," she admitted.

"Do you? Well, then you must understand why I'm so unhappy with you right now, my dear." He paused. "You killed my son."

Cate's breath caught. She'd been told that Ash and Kane had killed the cartel goons who'd ambushed them in Bardera, but nobody had mentioned that one of those men was Adrián Rivera. Had they been trying to shield her as always? Or had they just forgotten to tell her?

She was betting on the first one.

"Your son?" she echoed uneasily. "I don't know what you're talking about."

"You know exactly what I'm talking about. Your people gunned him down this morning." Rivera's tone remained deceptively pleasant. "He was my firstborn, you know." A pause. "He was a strong, intelligent boy. I was very proud of him."

"That's good to hear. A lot of parents feel nothing but disappointment for their children."

He laughed. "Are you speaking from experience?"

She followed Holden into a room near the end of the hall and watched as he removed not one but three laptops from a canvas bag on the floor. He placed them on the desk, his dark head bent and his features set in concentration as he began booting up each laptop.

"Is your father disappointed in you, little one?"

A lump rose in her throat. "No," she answered, although a part of her wasn't quite sure.

Morgan was certainly disappointed that she'd left school. That she'd chosen photography over her studies and was going on dangerous assignments. If it were up to him, she'd be photographing babies and awkward family portraits in a department store.

"No, I imagine your father is more open-minded than most parents," Rivera mused. "Killers usually are."

"My father isn't a killer," she said tightly.

"Oh, how naïve you are. Of course he's a killer. Your father, his wife, you . . ." There was a rustling of papers over the line. "Would you like me to list all the other killers in your father's employment? Kane Woodland, former SEAL, married to a woman who, on paper, has no identity, but I'm confident I'll uncover those details sooner or later. We've also got . . . Ethan Hayes, a Marine. Ooh Rah—that's what they say, right?"

Cate's blood ran cold. How the fuck did he know all their names?

"Shall I go on?"

She pressed her lips together.

Her silence only elicited another wave of laughter. "I see you've underestimated my resources, little one. Did you really think I wouldn't be able to find out who you people are?"

She adopted an indifferent tone. "We weren't trying to keep it a secret. My father runs a private military company. Most people who look into his background discover this right away."

"Perhaps. But I've only begun to scratch the surface of what I was able to learn."

At the desk, Holden was furiously typing something. One laptop screen showed a world map, while the other two displayed what looked like a satellite imaging system with flashing dots and lines that Cate couldn't understand. She knew every last component of her camera, could probably take the thing apart and put it back together like men did with their rifles, but other than a proficiency for graphic design programs, she knew shit-all about computers.

But Holden seemed to be making some sort of progress because he gestured to her in a *keep him talking* motion.

"What do you plan to do with all this information?" she asked politely.

"I plan to do plenty." Rivera sounded gleeful. Something creaked in the background, as if he was leaning back in a chair. "I'm very much looking forward to meeting you, my dear. There's no fear in your voice when you speak to me. I like that."

"Are most people afraid of you?"

"Of course they are. Do you think I got to where I am without being able to instill fear in people?"

"I guess instilling fear is an asset in building a criminal empire," she agreed.

"Indeed. But it gets boring, I'll admit. Standing in front of your enemy and seeing his pants dampen with piss as he stares down the barrel of your gun. Hearing him beg and cry for mercy before the blade of your machete slices his head clean off . . ."

She shivered.

"I prefer a challenge. You're going to be a challenge for me, aren't you, Cate?"

"You're never going to find that out." She laughed. "Because you're never going to find me."

He snorted. "Oh, the hubris of youth. I found you twice already. It won't be difficult to do it again." For the first time since this bizarre discussion began, his tone hardened to steel. "You're a meddlesome girl. Sticking your nose in places it doesn't belong. Taking pictures—"

"Is that really what this is about?" she interrupted with a harsh laugh. "One silly picture? What do you care, Rivera? Nobody knows where you are anyway."

"It might have started with a picture, but it ended with my son's blood on the street," he snapped. "Adrián would still be alive if it weren't for you. You *stole* him from me and you need to be punished for that, you stupid girl."

Fear skittered through her like a nervous animal. She'd seen pictures of what this man was capable of. The murders perpetrated by Rivera and his men were notoriously macabre. If he ever got his hands on her . . .

No. He never would. Morgan's people would find him long before that. If anyone was getting their head cut off, it was him.

"Anyway, as nice as it is to speak to you," Rivera said cheerfully, "I'm afraid I must go now. But don't worry. I'll see you soon, my dear."

The moment the line went dead, Holden let out an irritated curse.

"Did you get his location?" she demanded, ignoring the panic swirling in her belly.

He shook his head in frustration. "Yes and no."

"What the hell does that mean?"

"It means I narrowed it down to Guatana, which we already assumed is where he's holed up."

Cate slammed her phone down on the desk, angry at herself for not being able to keep Rivera talking for longer. But they'd had more than five minutes to work with, damn it. That should have been plenty of time.

"So what now?" she grumbled.

Holden offered a grim look. "We hope he decides to call you again."

Fuck. Yeah. She wasn't holding her breath.

Chapter 15

Two years ago

"Ash! What are you doing here?"

"I said I'd visit." The dark-haired, green-eyed devil dropped his hand from the door and sauntered inside. The small dorm room became positively tiny with his six-foot-four-inch frame filling up the space.

Cate drank in his appearance, hoping her giddiness didn't show on her face. She hadn't seen him in over three months and she'd really missed him. She'd hoped to spend some time with him when she'd gone home for Christmas, but to her dismay he'd been in Tennessee visiting his grandmother.

"Who's this?" her roommate asked in a tone that said she wanted the introduction made while she was on her back with her legs spread.

Cate didn't blame her. She wanted to throw herself into his arms, drag him down onto the bed, and rip his clothes off. Her first year of college had been one of celibacy, and it was time for her virginity to go.

She waved a hand in the general direction of her roommate. "Ash, this is Jessie. Jessie, Ash."

"Nice to meet you, ma'am." He gave Jessie a careless nod as he swung around, taking in the two twin beds and two desks that dominated the space. "This place isn't big enough to hold a cracker, let alone two girls. Morgan cheaping out on you?"

"It's what all freshmen get." Cate shrugged. It was a far cry from what she was used to but the lack of privacy was the least of her complaints. She reached over and grabbed a jacket. "Let's get out of here," she suggested. She always felt like she was suffocating in this room and it wasn't merely because of the lack of space.

"Don't leave on my account," Jessie called.

"Not a fan of your roommate?" Ash asked as they stepped out into the afternoon sunshine. Despite the clear skies, it was cold.

"She's all right." Cate shivered. She'd spent two years in the tropics and only a few months in Northeast winters. She wasn't acclimated yet.

"I think that's what my gran would say is damning with faint praise." Ash reached over to pull up the collar of her down coat.

When his knuckles brushed against her neck, she shivered again, and this time it had nothing to do with the chilly temperature.

"Let's get you out of the cold." He took her elbow and led her toward the coffeehouse that sat opposite her dormitory.

"How's your grandma?" Cate forced herself to tread lightly. She didn't know what Ash was thinking and was a tad afraid to throw herself at him. Again.

"She's good. I keep waiting for age to set in and slow her down but she's too strong for that." He chuckled to himself. "I'm probably responsible for that. We fought a lot when I was growing up. She wanted me to do certain things and I wasn't interested in her way. I was a little punk, always thinking I knew best."

Cate glanced over at him, wondering if he was directing a message toward her, but he was busy opening the door. She slid under his outstretched arm and into the coffee shop. A bell jingled merrily as Ash closed the door behind them.

On their way to the counter, Cate could feel the eyes of all the girls in the room swing toward Ash. They wanted to know who he was and how they could get his clothes off, and Cate wanted to throw a sign over his head that declared him off-limits. Except he wasn't. She knew that he slept with local girls down around the compound. There'd been times when he'd leave to hit a club and wouldn't return until the next morning, wearing the same clothes he'd left in and a satisfied look on his face.

Cate tried not to let it bother her too much. If she wanted Ash to see her as a woman, she couldn't be whining about the fact that he had sex. She simply needed to make herself be seen as the best option in his book. She'd hoped to do that at Christmas, but he'd been gone.

"What do you want to drink?" she asked.

"Coffee. Black."

She ordered for the both of them and shoved his money aside when he tried to pay. "It's four dollars. I think I can manage that."

He hesitated. "My gran wouldn't like it."

"And if you pay then *I* won't like it, and I'm the one standing in front of you."

"When you put it that way . . ." He grinned and stuck his money back into his wallet.

"You don't like making anyone mad, do you?" Cate teased as they waited for their drinks.

"I think it's more like I don't want to disappoint people. I don't mind pissing some folks off. That's actually fun, depending on who they are. But people I care about? I'd prefer it if they were happy."

"And me? Where do I fall?" Cate blurted out before she could stop herself.

"You're on the top of the list of people I want to see happy." He paused and Cate swore he was about to say something else when their names were called. Ash abruptly turned from her and grabbed the foam cups. "Let's find a place to sit."

"Did you come from a job?" she asked as he wrangled two chairs together. There weren't any empty tables, so he created a makeshift seating area in the corner near the window.

"Yeah, had one over in Hong Kong."

"An exfil?" she said hopefully before taking a sip of her hot chocolate.

She hated it when Ash went undercover, because, well, she knew what happened during those undercover missions. Sometimes operatives had to sleep with marks. Hell, Cate herself was the product of one of those honey traps. Her dad had slept with her mom in order to infiltrate an arms dealer's organization. As a result, Cate's mother had gotten pregnant, and then, in a shoot-out between Cate's criminal grandfather and American military operatives, her mom had suffered the head wound that had left her brain-dead.

The rest of that story wasn't at all pretty. Nope, because her sick grandfather had decided to keep her mom hooked up to machines for seventeen years—until Cate had finally had enough and pulled the plug.

She wondered if anyone else at Brown had a backstory as *interesting* as hers.

Cate almost laughed at the thought. Yeah, right.

"You're thinking about something bad. Your mom?" Ash guessed quietly.

She sighed. "How'd you know?"

"You always get that look on your face. And no, it

wasn't an exfil. More of an information-gathering trip. Counterfeiting is a big-time operation in China, you know?"

Cate nodded. "Yeah. So?"

"So a US tech firm asked us to go in, find out which groups are running these counterfeiting ops, and leave a couple well-placed messages. I didn't spend much time doing anything other than follow a bunch of businessmen around."

Meaning, he'd kept his jewels tucked away. At least, that's what Cate hoped it meant.

"How about you? How're you enjoying college?"

"It's not as great as you promised me it would be. I don't relate to any of these people. And classes are . . . they're classes, you know? Old profs standing up and talking for hours about the dullest subjects. I didn't know people could talk that much about one thing."

"I always wanted to go to college," Ash admitted. He kicked out his long legs and draped an arm around the back of her chair.

"You did?"

"Yeah. But I was dirt poor and had crappy grades. It was either the military or working a bunch of shit jobs. Factory work down where I come from was about the highest a kid could strive for, but getting one of those jobs required knowing folks, and Gran and I didn't know a soul. Not in the way you needed to."

Cate hung on his every word. "This is the most you've ever shared about yourself," she informed him.

"Really?" He cocked his head, but he didn't deny it.

"Really. You and I have talked a lot, but it's mostly about me. You know everything there is to know about me. All of my ugly past."

"Your past wasn't ugly," he said softly.

"Are you kidding me? Of course it was. That's why

I can't be here. I don't belong with the rest of these kids. I'm not cut out for sitting in classrooms and working a desk job." She bit her lip. "I can't believe Jim even wants that for me."

A burst of laughter sounded from the neighboring table, only highlighting how out of place Cate felt at this college. She wasn't a laughing, bubbly girl, and never had been.

Ash sighed and set down his untouched coffee cup. "Come on. Let's find a quiet place."

"My roommate is still in the room."

"I've got a rental."

Damn. For a second there, she'd thought that by "rental" Ash had meant a room. But as he led her to a visitors' parking lot, she realized with disappointment that he'd meant a rental car.

"Climb in." He held the passenger door open while she settled into the seat, but he didn't start the car after he got in.

"Do you have a hotel room?" she asked, almost timidly.

"No. This is just a stopover."

Her disappointment grew. "Oh. I thought you might stay for a while."

He shook his head. "I gotta get back. Morgan will be wondering where I am. Mission ended two days ago."

Cate looked down at her lap to hide her unhappiness. Then she snapped out of it, injecting herself with some much-needed confidence. So what if he'd only planned for a stopover? She could *convince* him to stay.

It would require a level of sophistication she wasn't sure she had, but she'd just have to brazen through it. According to Noelle and her troupe of female assassins, guys were largely controlled by their dicks. Which was what made Noelle's team so successful. Men regularly underestimated women and were easily susceptible to a suggestive come-on.

Then again, Juliet and Isabel and Noelle dressed like they were models out of Femme-Fatales-R-Us, while Cate—she ruefully glanced down at herself—was bundled up in a coat that made her look like she was hiding a herd of penguins next to her chest.

When Ash reached into the backseat, she covertly unzipped her jacket, hoping to make herself look a little more . . . doable.

"Here," he said awkwardly. "I picked something up for you. Sorry I missed the holidays."

Her expression brightened as she accepted the small package and shook it lightly. It made a satisfying thud inside the box. "Oh, thank you! You didn't have to get me anything." She paused. "I left your present at home."

"Uh, yeah . . ." A pale pink tinge appeared on his cheeks. "Morgan gave it to me."

Cate groaned. "Oh my God! Did you open it in front of him?"

"Sure did. And let's just say he . . . had some questions." Ash shrugged, as if receiving a fire-engine red Speedo was completely normal. "I told him it was a joke."

"It was no joke, buddy. I'm tired of you keeping your pants on every time we swim out to the grotto. Figured with the proper attire, you might change your ways." She grinned at him. "What'd Jim say?"

"That we needed to work on our senses of humor."

"You're still alive, so that must mean good things," Cate said lightly, but inwardly she cringed. No wonder Ash was a little stiff—he was embarrassed over the gift and the fact that his boss obviously knew about Cate's feelings for him.

But, she took heart that he was here and had a gift for her in return, which meant she'd been on his mind while he was on a mission. And then he'd stopped to see her before he went back home. *That's* what she should be focusing on.

"He sent me on a two-month job on the other side of the world, so yeah, it's all good."

Cate couldn't tell if Ash was being sarcastic but she was encouraged that she hadn't received a ranting phone call from Jim ordering her to stay the hell away from his men.

"Yeah." She swallowed, then slid as close as the bucket seats of the cheap rental allowed and laid a hand on his arm. "It's all very good, Ash."

He froze and then moved his arm away. "Open the present," he said gruffly.

Ignoring the pang of hurt evoked by her touch being dismissed, Cate tore into the wrapping, lifted the lid on the small box, and then frowned. "What is this?"

"It's a pen."

"A . . . pen?"

What in the hell was she going to do with a pen?

"It's a fountain pen," he explained. "For you to, ah, do your homework with."

"Oh. It's really nice," she said faintly, too surprised to hide her confusion.

She wasn't a writer. She didn't keep a journal. She'd complained to Ash regularly about homework and college and he bought her a *pen*? It was thoughtful, sure, but she wasn't ever going to use something like this.

Didn't he know her at all?

She closed the box and leaned over the console. "Thank you. I'll treasure it." And she would, because Ash had given it to her. Swallowing again, she leaned in to embrace him, but he drew away.

And then, instead of accepting even a hug from her,

he started the car. "I need to get to the airport. You okay walking back to the dorm alone?"

It took some effort to keep her jaw closed. Seriously? This whole trip was bizarre. Him showing up out of nowhere, spending less than an hour in her company, and then giving her a pen?

"What's going on, Ash?"

That pink flush still rode on the tops of his cheekbones. "Nothing's going on. If you don't like the pen, I'll return it."

"Return it? I thought you bought it in Hong Kong?"

"At the airport, actually."

Cate slumped back against her seat. Oh God. He'd bought the pen at an airport gift shop. He hadn't been thinking of her on the op. He'd just stopped in Rhode Island, bought the gift in some duty-free shop, and then popped over to Brown.

Something else suddenly dawned on her. He'd stopped because Jim had told him to.

Embarrassment heated her cheeks. Yep, that was exactly what this impromptu visit was about. Because Ash would do anything and everything that Jim Morgan asked of him, even dropping by on a layover after a long mission to check up on Jim's little girl.

"Got it," Cate mumbled, averting her gaze. "Feel free to report to Jim that I'm alive and well."

"I'm not here because Morgan told me to," Ash said through visibly clenched teeth. "I'm here to visit a girl I care about."

"I'm not a girl," she snapped. She was so damn tired of hearing that word come out of Ash's mouth. "I'm a woman. I'm nineteen, and I know what I want."

He released a ragged breath. "I should go."

Her lips tightened. "Why? Because this conversation

is getting a little too uncomfortable for you? Fine, cover your ears if you want, but I'm still going to say this—I want *you*, Ash. That's all I've ever wanted."

She could swear she saw a glint of heat in his eyes, a flicker of longing, but it faded before she could be sure.

When he didn't utter a word, Cate repeated herself. "I know what I want." She flashed him a look of challenge. "Do you?"

She knew those were the wrong words to say even before they left her mouth, but she couldn't stop them.

His eyes darkened and his chin hardened. "Yeah. I do. And I'm sorry, Cate, but you're always going to be a girl to me. Nothing is going to change that you're nearly nine years younger than me. Even if you weren't Jim Morgan's daughter, I'd still walk away." He took a deep breath and then gave a smile that made Cate sick to her stomach. He reached across the console, and instead of touching her, he opened the car door. "Go to your dorm room. Forget about me. Fall in love with one of these college boys. Trust me, sweetheart, you'll be a lot happier."

"I never took you for a coward," she said stiffly, climbing out of the car. "But obviously you are."

Ash frowned but didn't say a word.

"And I don't want to be with a coward, so I guess we're even."

She slammed the door and stomped off, the tears in her eyes making it hard to see. But she heard the engine roar as Ash sped out of the parking lot. And she thought she heard a shout of frustration too, but . . . that was probably the one in her own head.

Chapter 16

Present day

"You'll be happy to know that your daughter is pissed off at me." Ash yanked the chair away from Morgan's bed before dropping his large frame onto its rickety base. "Then again—what else is new?"

He rubbed his tired eyes, wondering what the heck he was doing in here instead of catching a few hours of much-needed sleep in his bunk. It was five a.m. and he'd been watching Aguilar's house all night. The general and his wife had woken up at three o'clock for a late-night quickie, but aside from that, there'd been no activity from the Aguilars. Which only brought a pang of guilt to Ash's stomach, because, in light of tonight's uneventful stakeout, there was really no reason why Cate couldn't have come along.

Well, other than that he didn't want her anywhere near this Rivera mess.

"She was running around chasing after Aguilar and Rivera's wife with her camera this morning."

His jaw ached from holding in the world-class ass-chewing he wanted to deliver to Cate. Why did she always have to run *toward* danger, damn it?

"Maybe you were too strict with her," he muttered to Jim. "If you'd loosened the reins a bit, taken her around the world to see things, maybe she wouldn't be so determined to—ah, hell, what am I talking about? Girl had more stamps on her passport at the age of seventeen than most seventy-year-olds."

Which was one of the many reasons he needed to stay away. It wasn't just for shits and giggles that Morgan wanted Cate to have a normal life. Cate had grown up the pretty, pampered princess of a sick man who forced his granddaughter to pretend her dead mother was alive. And then she'd watched that man die in a gun battle between her real father, Noelle, and a bunch of hired thugs.

So yeah, Cate definitely deserved a dose of normal. And Ash knew the value of that because it was something he'd never had. His life had consisted of drunken shouts from his dad, insults from his peers about how every man in his dead-end town had dipped their wicks between his mom's legs, and a grandmother who'd struggled to make ends meet to support them. Normal sounded pretty damn perfect to Ash.

What *wasn't* normal was a twenty-five-year-old panting to get into a girl's panties when she was only seventeen. What wasn't normal was fucking some of the most beautiful, willing, flexible women on the planet and thinking about that jailbait teen back home. What wasn't normal was having a hard-on from just looking at her.

Yet at the same time, he didn't regret a single second he'd ever spent with Cate. They'd become close fast, and even knowing it was wrong, Ash hadn't done anything to stop it. He hadn't wanted to stop it. Their friendship had become one of the most important things in his life. *She* had become one of the most important things in his life.

But his need for her had always been superseded by one thing—his loyalty to the man lying in front of him.

He wanted Morgan to wake the hell up so that they could talk, so he could finally tell the man that Cate was all grown up and she should be allowed to choose who she wanted to be with. Of course, that would be met with Morgan's boot in his ass. And Cate would probably slap him silly. She might've wanted Ash at one time but he'd ground that affection beneath his boot heel. At best, Cate might want a revenge fuck where she'd rock his entire world and then leave him begging for more.

Sad truth was, he'd take it. He'd snap that chance up in a heartbeat if he knew it wouldn't result in everyone hating him. He wasn't sorry about much about his past, but he sure as hell regretted not taking Cate up on her offer. He'd dreamed too many times about having her to turn her down once again.

"Your doc said we should talk to you. Apparently you can hear things and if you hear things it'll make you wake up faster. So you're faking it? You're lying there, enjoying a good ol' rest? How about I tell you that I'm gonna go down the hall, strip your daughter bare, and give her what she begged me for years ago?" Ash taunted.

Morgan didn't move.

"Fuck me." A hollow laugh escaped. "We both know that threat won't fly, because I'm not going to do shit. Jesus. I feel like a fool." He scrubbed his face with both hands.

It wasn't the loss of his home that Ash feared—it was the loss of Morgan's trust. Jim had given Ash a chance when the rest of the world had turned its back on him, and he refused to repay Morgan by taking his only child. Morgan didn't deserve that. Cate sure as hell didn't either. She deserved someone good and decent. Someone like Ethan or Kane. Ash was . . . well, he wasn't any of them.

He was good at following orders, most of the time. He was good with a gun. He didn't mind getting shot at because he figured every day he was alive was some sort of gift.

He knew he wasn't good enough for Cate. Morgan had seen it immediately and all his warnings that he didn't want Cate to end up with a merc had been meant for Ash.

He knew that, but he didn't take offense. Morgan loved his daughter and wanted the best for her—like any good father would. It was just another reason why Ash admired him so damn much.

"You're a good man, Jim," he said hoarsely. "Decent. Real decent. When I was discharged and I went home, there was no hero's welcome. You once asked me if I was tired of people thanking me for my service. No one thanked me there. The news of my discharge beat me home."

Ash propped his elbows on his knees and stared at his hands. The ones that killed people. The ones that engaged in casual, meaningless sexual encounters. He wanted to mold his hands against Cate's curves until he could map them in his sleep. He wanted to dirty that girl up until all she saw when she closed her eyes was his face, his body—*him*.

He wanted her to look at him with that undisguised desire and worship because he had the same feelings churning him up inside.

"You'd kill me right now if you knew what was going on in my head," he whispered. "I stayed my hand so many times because I respected you. Still do. I kinda want you to rise from the bed and smite me."

He'd never had a lot of affection in his life. There were girls. Always girls, but that wasn't affection. That was . . . a back scratch. A temporary relief for an ongoing, dull ache. His gran hadn't been very warm. His mom wasn't around. His dad's idea of affection was not beating on Ash.

"I had a crap dad, you know," he informed the unconscious man. "I'm not going to be him—drinking, slapping people around, shitting on the people he's supposed to love." A lump formed in his throat. "You did good with Cate. I know you've been fighting, but forcing her to go to college was the right thing to do. She had these ideas in her head about what the world was like—all fucking adventure and fun times. But you and I know that it's full of garbage and Cate's the opposite of that. She's *life*, Jim. And this world is only worth breathing in if she's alive." He swallowed hard. "So while you're taking your nap, I'm going to protect her, even if it means she hates my guts. I can live with that. What I can't live with is her dying. I think that's how you've always felt too."

Ash pushed to his feet, feeling unsettled. He wasn't much for talking about his feelings. The only person he'd ever really shared with was Cate.

He placed a palm on Morgan's arm. "You're a good man," he repeated. "The best I've ever known and you're the only real father I've had. I—"

A shuffling sound at the door had his head shooting up. He found Sully standing there, a frown on his face.

"Here to confess your sins?" he asked his old friend, forcing out a small laugh.

The Aussie cleared his throat. "Actually, you're the guy I wanted to see."

Ash raised an eyebrow. He wasn't sure what Sully needed from him. They hadn't seen or spoken to each other in two years. "Sure. What's on your mind?"

Sully's gray eyes flicked toward the bed, down to the floor, and then back up at Ash. "I just wanted to talk to you about, ah, what you heard me say a couple years back."

"About what?" Ash experienced a beat of confusion before understanding hit him.

Two years ago, Sully had been captured, raped, and pumped full of heroin. Luckily, the man was a modern-day superhero, managing to escape by himself and kill his rapist. And then, after the mission wrapped up, he'd taken off on his boat to parts unknown. Before he'd left, though . . . Ash had overheard Sullivan desperately offering his best friend a blow job in exchange for smack.

"Oh," Ash murmured. "Gotcha."

"Yeah, about that." Sully's voice was full of self-directed disgust.

"Nah, man, you don't need to say anything about that. That wasn't you."

Sully shoved his hands in his pockets and blew out a stream of frustrated air. "No, it *was* me, and it's bloody humiliating when I think about it."

"Then don't," Ash advised. "I don't think about it. And I don't see that person when I look at you."

Their gazes locked awkwardly before hastily shifting around their surroundings. Damn. If Ash thought talking about his feelings to an unconscious man was uncomfortable, then this scene was exponentially worse.

He struggled to find the right words to reassure Sully. "What happened back then is your past. You look behind you a lot when you're sailing?"

Sully tilted his head. "Don't we all?"

He was talking about more than sailing, obviously. "I suppose we do, but we probably shouldn't."

"Easy to say, but it's a lot harder to live by, isn't it?" Sully's perceptive eyes signaled he'd heard some of what Ash had been telling Morgan.

It was Ash's turn to stare at the ground. "The past has a loud fucking voice," he finally said.

Sully barked out a sharp laugh. "Fucking truer words were never spoken, Rook."

He snorted. "How about we both try moving forward? Starting with you calling me Ash, you old fuck."

"I can try. Not making any promises, though."

Ash headed for the door. "I should probably get some sleep. It's been a long day and even longer night."

"Good luck with that. I'm pretty sure Noelle and Cate are keeping everyone in the barracks awake with their bickering."

His shoulders went rigid. "Why are they bickering?"

"You didn't hear? Cate got a call from Rivera tonight and decided to wait to tell Noelle about it. Said she didn't want to interrupt the lady killer's recon."

"Are you fucking kidding me?" Ash shouted, then instantly lowered his voice when he remembered where they were. "She spoke to Rivera?"

"Apparently so. Holden tried to trace the call but he wasn't able to pinpoint the loca—"

Ash was out the door before Sullivan could finish the sentence. His boots pounded the floor as he tore down the maze of corridors, pushing through doors until he was in the barracks wing of the building. Anger pulsed in his blood the closer he got to Cate's door. Mateo Rivera had phoned Cate and she'd decided to sit on the news until the team returned to base? She couldn't have phoned in the fucking update?

Ash flew into the room without knocking, catching the tail end of Noelle's sharp request. "—to repeat the conversation for me."

His gaze traveled from Noelle's irritated expression to Cate's resigned one. "Rivera made contact?" he snapped, directing his accusatory gaze to Cate.

"Yes. He did." She crossed her arms tightly over her chest. "And I'd appreciate it if you kept your lectures to yourself. I've already heard them from Noelle."

The blond assassin flattened her mouth. "You should've called."

"Why? It wasn't urgent, and I didn't want to distract you guys when you were on surveillance. Holden traced the call as best he could but Rivera didn't stay on the line long enough for us to get anything other than that he's in Guatana. We couldn't even narrow it down to a neighborhood."

"Tell me what he said," Ash commanded.

Cate looked like she was gritting her teeth, but rather than argue, she dutifully recited everything she and Rivera had spoken about. As Ash listened to her relay the man's taunts and promises of finding her and torturing, his pulse raced faster and faster. And the vow he'd just made to Morgan about keeping Cate safe suddenly became a whole lot more crucial.

"Any background noise that you can remember?" Noelle asked. "Sounds of traffic? The market? An echo?"

Cate paused in thought. "No, just his voice. He was somewhere quiet, either alone or else everyone in the room had their mouths zipped shut. The only thing that stuck out to me was that he was somewhat breathless, like he'd been laughing or running. It wasn't obvious, but . . . it was there."

Ash frowned. "Laughing?"

"He just sounded more excited than I thought a mastermind criminal would sound. You and Jim are always so cool," she told Noelle. "The only time you get riled up is with each other."

Noelle nodded slowly. "He's emotionally invested in us. Our emotions only go haywire when it involves someone we care about. Obviously he loved his son. And . . ." She pursed her lips. "He's got the other kid, right? Benicio. Stands to reason Rivera worships that one too. He'd take extra care in making sure his remaining son is protected. I think we need a tail on him."

Ash nodded in agreement. The problem was that even with the entire team in Guatana, they still didn't have enough manpower to cover a wide stretch of area without any fore planning. They were running blind and undermanned.

"I'll talk to Kane," he said. "Maybe we can put Castle and some of the other contractors on Benicio Rivera." His fists clenched as he glanced over at Cate. "And if he calls you again, you're not the one who gets to decide whether or not it's *urgent*."

Her blue eyes flashed.

"I fucking mean it, Cate. Anything related to this op comes up, and you get on the goddamn phone and report it in. End of fucking story."

He spun on his heels before she could answer, Noelle's soft chuckle tickling his rigid back on his way out the door.

"It was a lovely service." Camila slid into the bedroom and gently closed the door behind her. She wore a simple black dress and not a trace of makeup, with her hair arranged in an elegant bun at the nape of her slender neck.

As Rivera watched, she began removing the pins from her hair. She laid each silver needle on the night table, then fluffed her hair with both hands until it flowed past her shoulders. There were no streaks of gray in those long tresses. At forty-four, she was still a beautiful woman, with pristine posture and a youthful air to her.

The nearly twenty-year age difference between them had never bothered him before, but nowadays, with his sixty-year-old bones aching from arthritis and his hair almost completely silver, being around Camila made him feel like an old man.

"Any unwanted guests?" Rivera asked his wife.

"There were some suits there," she admitted.

His gaze sharpened. "Government?"

"I think so. Some military too. But they kept their distance."

That didn't appease him. Those sons of bitches had no right showing up at his son's funeral, especially when Adrián's own father wasn't able to attend. Now that every government agency out there knew he was alive, Rivera couldn't risk leaving this safe house again.

The cocksuckers would be actively pursuing him; President Flores would demand it. That idiot had made too big a production after the car bombing that "killed" the infamous Mateo Rivera. Press conferences, photo ops, sound bites touting his victory against the cartels. Flores was a peacock puffing out his feathers and pontificating about change, when the only thing he truly cared about was his image. If the world discovered that Rivera had not perished in those flames, the good president would look very, very bad.

"We expected intruders," Camila reminded him when she glimpsed his irate expression. "Don't let them tarnish our boy's memory, *querido*. Today is a day to remember Adrián, not to bother ourselves with government rats."

A lump of pain rose in his throat. "You dressed him in the gray wool suit? The one that belonged to my father?"

She nodded, her elegant features equally pained. "He looked strong. Proud." She smoothed out the front of her dress. "Father Ruiz delivered a beautiful eulogy."

"Good. I'm glad."

"It was a lovely service," she repeated.

Rivera heard more than what her words conveyed. "But?" he prompted.

His wife's dark eyes slitted dangerously. "But it lacked one thing."

He waited.

"Blood."

An unwitting smile sprang to his lips.

"I want their blood, Mateo." Her voice was calm, as was her stride as she walked over to the bed. "I want the people who killed our son."

He patted the mattress and she lowered herself beside him. "You'll have it, *mi amor*," he promised.

They both fell silent for a moment, sitting side by side on the edge of the thin mattress. Rivera didn't miss the way his wife's nose turned up slightly as she swept her gaze over his living quarters. He understood her disdain. This dark, musty basement was starting to close in on him, making him long for their sprawling hacienda with its dozens of rooms.

Here, he had only this bedroom, a sitting room where he did his reading, and the meeting room where he conducted his business. In the three months since he'd staged his death, he'd been moving money to various offshore accounts while grooming his son to take over the business. Everything had been on schedule. The money, the transportation, the private island where he and Camila would live out their retirement.

But that nosy little photographer had changed all that. Now, he would not leave Guatana until he exacted his revenge. Until he'd run his blade over every inch of Cate Morgan's lily-white skin. Until he'd ripped her hair out by the roots, one strand at a time. Tore off her fingernails. Cut off her nipples, her arms, her legs. Maybe he'd take her head to the island with him and display it in the great room of his villa.

He couldn't deny that he'd enjoyed speaking to the girl, but he hadn't appreciated her insolence. She could afford to learn some manners. Perhaps he'd teach her some before he cut off her head.

"I didn't see Benicio upstairs," Camila remarked. "And he left the church before me. He should be back by now."

"He was already here. I sent him to take care of a dispute at the shipyard."

She raised a brow, but Rivera didn't elaborate.

"Perhaps he'll actually get the job done this time," he mumbled under his breath.

But Camila didn't miss that. "You need to have more faith in him," she said firmly.

"He has yet to show himself worthy."

She made a tsking sound with her tongue. "He's your son. That makes him worthy." Sighing, she leaned closer and rested her head on his shoulder. "Adrián was my firstborn, and I loved him. I'll always love him, *querido*. But Benicio has spent his whole life trying to prove himself to you, to show you that he can be as strong and as capable as his brother. He has potential, Mateo. I don't know why you refuse to see it."

"All I've seen," he said stiffly, "is a spoiled, entitled boy who thought I would give him an empire simply because we have the same blood running through our veins. He's yet to show me that he has what it takes to lead." He grasped her chin and tipped her head up. "Do you remember the dog?"

An exasperated look crossed her face. "He was just a boy," she protested. "You asked too much of him."

"No. I didn't." He released his wife and stared up at

the ceiling. "He doesn't have it, Camila. He doesn't have what we have."

She took his hand, brought it up to her lips, and kissed it softly. "Perhaps not, but maybe his way is just as good as ours. Maybe you don't need to spill blood to rule the world."

He gave her an indulgent smile. "We both know better than that, *mi amor*."

Benicio might be his son, but the boy lacked the thirst for bloodshed that was required of all leaders. Rivera had killed his first man when he was only ten years old. His father was the one who'd handed him the knife, encouraged him to spill the blood of their enemy. Feeling that blade slice into that vermin's abdomen had given Rivera a thrill he'd never experienced before.

Adrián had known that same thrill. Camila, too, knew the unparalleled satisfaction that came from taking a human life. But not Benicio.

Benicio was weak.

Rivera stood up and walked over to the side table. A stack of files sat on the weathered wood, and he picked it up and returned to sit by his wife.

Camila's manicured hand slid over the front of the top folder before slowly opening it. The first page was a photograph of Cate Morgan.

"This is her?" Camila asked.

"Yes."

One fingernail traced the girl's heart-shaped face. "She's beautiful."

"Yes."

She shut the folder and opened the next one. And then the next one, and the one after that. She did the same thing with each one, tracing the faces with her fingers, and when she'd gone through the whole stack, she placed the files beside her and turned to meet his eyes.

"These are the people who killed our boy?"

"Yes."

"I want all of their heads."

Rivera smiled and lifted his arm, and his wife slid closer and tucked her head in the crook of his neck. His grip tightened around her. This woman . . . She was magnificent.

From the moment he'd laid his eyes on her, he'd known that he was going to make her his wife. She'd been gripping a knife in her hand, pushing the blade deep in the gut of the local punk who'd tried to rape her. She'd twisted that blade and left it in his flabby flesh, then wiped her bloody hand on the front of her paisley dress, leaving a streak of crimson on the fabric. When she'd turned to find him standing in the mouth of the alley, she'd jumped in surprise.

And then she'd smiled at him.

He was thirty-three. She was seventeen. Their ages hadn't mattered. Nothing had mattered except that Mateo Rivera knew, with bone-deep certainty, that he was staring at his soul mate.

"Mateo," she said, drawing him out of his memories.

"Yes, *mi amor*?"

"Give Benicio one of these folders."

He hesitated.

"Please." Her tone softened, her warm breath fluttering over his shoulder. "He's not like us, but he's still our son, and he's the only son we've got left." She paused. "Give him the opportunity to show us what he's capable of. For me, *querido*. Do this for me."

Chapter 17

After two days of round-the-clock surveillance on Felipe Aguilar, Ash was dying for some action. But for a woman who'd demanded they bring her Mateo Rivera's head on a spike, Noelle had taken her sweet-ass time giving the order for them to grab the naval defense minister.

Which meant forty-eight straight hours of recon on a dude who spent most of his days going from the ministry offices to his palatial home, where he ate dinner, had two bottles of wine post-dinner to wind down, and was then entertained by his young wife well into the wee hours of the morning. For a sixty-year-old, Aguilar had a lot of energy.

As excruciatingly boring as it was, the surveillance had led Ash and the others to the conclusion that Aguilar—shockingly enough—might actually love his wife. He'd had a couple of mistresses on the side before he'd married Renata, but he seemed to have set them aside. Granted, twenty-six-year-old Renata was Aguilar's third wife, but Bailey, Isabel, and Juliet had utilized various covers to gain access to the man's house and office and had found no evidence that he was fucking around on the girl.

His wife appeared to be their best leverage, which was why she was currently gagged and bound in the trunk of Ash and D's car.

"This snatch-and-grab is taking too long," D muttered

from the passenger seat. "They should've checked in by now."

Ash kept his gaze on the windshield, monitoring the deserted street for any suspicious activity. "Hey, it's not easy to take out a convoy," he said in the rest of the team's defense.

If everything was going according to plan, then the others were currently in the process of staging a car accident in order to ambush the general on his way from his home to his office. The twenty-five-minute drive never varied, which would make it easy to catch Aguilar five miles from his estate in the hills and right outside of town.

D snorted. "I could do it in my sleep."

"I have no doubt," Ash said, rolling his eyes. "All you'd have to do is stand in front of the guy's car and glare at the driver and they'd piss their pants in surrender."

He was only half joking. With his coal-black eyes, big frame, and multitude of tattoos, Derek Pratt was a scary motherfucker. Most men cowered at the mere sight of him.

D tapped his fingers impatiently on the dashboard. "They're taking too long," he repeated.

"Would you just chill?" Ash grumbled. Then he laughed, because asking a man like D to "chill" was fucking absurd. D had probably never known a moment of relaxation in his life. "How about we pass the time with some conversation?"

The other man looked bewildered. "Why would we do that?"

"Because that's what people do," Ash answered in exasperation. "They *talk* to each other. How's Sofia doing? And the kidlet?"

"Sofia's good. Kid's good."

A conversational genius, this one. "Glad to hear it. Gabby walking yet?"

At his daughter's name, D's harsh features softened. Just slightly. "Yeah. And she's fucking *fast*, bro. One second she's there, the next she's running off to cause trouble. Drives me batshit crazy."

Ash laughed. "Wait until she's old enough to date. Then you'll really go nuts."

D smirked. "She'll be a virgin 'til the day she dies. Guarantee it."

"Aw man. You're gonna be one of *those* dads?" He paused. "Wait—what am I even saying? Of course you will. I already feel bad for poor Gabriela. She's gonna hate you, dude. Straight-up hate you—"

"We're on our way," a sharp voice interrupted.

Both men snapped to attention at Noelle's report.

"See?" Ash said. "Told you they'd get it done."

D harrumphed, then touched his earpiece. "Any hiccups?"

"Negative," Kane replied. "Went off without a hitch."

"Didn't even have to kill any of his guards," Noelle muttered, and Ash grinned at the disappointment he heard in her voice.

"Be there in ten," Kane said before the feed went quiet.

D reverted to his silent self as they waited for the others to arrive, leaving Ash to sit there in tense anticipation. Ten minutes could feel like a lifetime when you were on waiting duty, and it wasn't long before Ash's mind wandered toward subjects he'd been trying hard not to think about.

Like Morgan, who was still unconscious even after two days out of surgery and whose doctors couldn't explain why that was or whether it would change.

And Cate, who'd barely said a word to him since he'd refused to let her accompany him on surveillance and then chewed her out for delaying reporting Rivera's phone call to the team.

But what the hell else was he supposed to do? Let her come along? Take the risk that she might get caught in the cross fire of this war they'd started? If a bunch of cartel scumbags were capable of taking Jim Morgan down, then how the fuck did Cate think *she'd* fare?

With Morgan fighting for his life at the moment, someone needed to watch out for his daughter. And Ash had dubbed himself that someone, whether Cate liked it or not.

He just wished she'd stop freezing him out. He wished Morgan would open his damn eyes. He wished . . .

Wishes don't always come true, Davey.

Ash gulped as his grandmother's blunt voice filled his mind. Yeah, Gran had never pulled any punches with him. Brutal honesty was that woman's forte, and she'd given him many doses of it over the years.

Your dad's a drunk, Davey. The booze will always be more important to him than you.

Your mama's not coming back, kiddo. She done and left ya.

You're a good kid, Ash, but those daddy issues—hoo-boy, they're gonna screw you up big-time if you don't deal with 'em.

A smile sprang to his lips. Edie Ashton was one tough broad, but Lord, he loved that woman to death. He wouldn't be half the man he was today if it weren't for her.

"Go time," D rasped.

Ash straightened his shoulders when he spotted the approaching vehicle. The headlights were off, but he glimpsed a blond head at the wheel—Kane. The SUV stopped at the curb and Ash saw several shadows get out. The busted streetlights made it easy for Ash's teammates to haul Aguilar from the car to the dingy shack they'd secured for this op. But even if the sidewalks were lit up like Times Square, Ash doubted the residents of this slum were going to pay any attention to what their neighbors were doing. These were folks who were too busy worrying about buying bread at the grocery store.

Noelle's voice drawled in his ear. "Bring her in."

He and D wasted no time. They jumped out, popped the trunk, and were greeted with the muffled yelps of their captive.

Ash reached in for the bleached blonde, who was trussed up with zip ties around her ankles and wrists. Her mouth had been covered with tape and he lifted a finger to his lips when their eyes locked.

"Don't make a sound," he warned.

She thrashed around and yelled a few curses against the duct tape.

He sighed. Captives never did what you asked them to. He grabbed her ankles and threw her over his shoulder, clamping one arm around her legs. D slammed the trunk closed, and then the two of them headed for the shack, Ash effortlessly carrying Renata's thin, squirming body.

Inside, they discovered that Noelle, Kane, and Trevor had been busy. Felipe Aguilar's hands and feet were duct-taped to a metal chair, and there was a bandana tied around his mouth in a gag. A square table had been dragged near his chair and someone had already laid out their supplies on it. They were going low tech with this interrogation—piano wire, a car battery from the general's own Mercedes, and a set of electrical leads.

D walked over to the table and picked up a length of wire. "Do we want to save her or start with her?" he said brusquely.

Noelle gestured for Ash to bring Renata to the second chair. "Start with her. We don't have time to dick around."

With a shrug, D squatted down in front of Aguilar and ripped the gag off.

Immediately, Aguilar started to shout, "Don't hurt her! She has nothing to do with anything! She knows nothing!"

Ignoring him, Ash dragged the sobbing woman over to the chair and dropped her into it. Kane silently joined him, his features hard as stone as he attached one of the leads to the battery and then threw the ends to Ash.

"We don't want to play games," Noelle told the stricken-faced couple as she watched Ash attach one lead to the pulse point of the neck and another to the woman's wrist. "Mateo Rivera is still alive. He sent out a hit against an American photographer." She smiled humorlessly. "We aren't fans of that. So tell us where Rivera is and you and the missus get to walk out of here alive, with all of your body parts intact. If you don't, we're hooking your wife up to a few thousand volts of electricity."

Renata moaned, and while part of Ash felt sorry for her, the rest of him was mostly contemptuous. This woman sat in her air-conditioned palace eating imported berries and wine while her country fell to pieces. Renata Aguilar belonged to a corrupt rich upper class that skimmed all the wealth. Meanwhile, the rest of Guatana lived in squalor with hardly enough food and clean water to keep one person alive, let alone the large families that were housed together.

So yeah, did he feel bad that they were threatening

to hurt this woman? A little. But if it meant officially putting Mateo Rivera out of commission, he'd do whatever needed to be done.

D shifted on the balls of his feet. "Can you shut her up? She's annoying me."

"She's got tape on her mouth already," Ash pointed out. "I think it's your guy's sniveling that's making all the noise."

"He's right," Noelle snapped. "Let's make the asshole talk."

Without delay, she tapped the wire to the battery and the girl nearly flew out of her chair. Tears streamed down Renata's face, matching the ones rolling down Aguilar's cheeks.

Ash exchanged an incredulous look with D. He had a feeling this was going to be the easiest interrogation they'd ever conducted.

Kneeling down, he peeled the tape off the woman's mouth and said, "Tell your man to help us out and you can both go."

"Please, please, Fefe, tell them! Please!" she begged.

Aguilar gritted his teeth. "She is young. Let her go. She knows nothing."

Noelle sent another bolt of electricity through the woman's body.

When Renata screamed high and long, Ash raised his eyes to the ceiling. They were using a twelve-volt battery, hardly enough to make a person flinch, let alone wail like a tormented banshee.

"Don't waste my fucking time," Noelle barked.

"Please, please," Renata cried.

Aguilar shut his eyes and turned his face away. That earned him a scream from his wife, but this time it was out of outrage.

"New plan," Kane suggested. "Let's hook this bad

boy up to Aguilar's nuts and shock him until either his dick falls off or he starts talking."

D gave a savage grin. "I like that. Get it over here."

As Ash stripped off the leads, Renata disparaged Aguilar's parents, grandparents, his prowess in bed, and most of all, his weak-ass cowardly self. Aguilar, however, was too busy watching Ash, his expression growing increasingly uneasy.

"I predict this marriage isn't going to last long after tonight," Ash remarked as he kicked the battery over to Aguilar's chair.

Behind him, Noelle was retaping the wife's mouth.

"You might need counseling," Trevor said conversationally.

Chuckling, Ash kneeled down and stuck a lead onto Aguilar's shaking knee. "I've heard it's helpful. Hey, D—you and Sofia ever go to counseling?"

"No. We fuck."

Kane snickered. "That's what keeps a marriage alive, right?"

Trevor threw in his two cents. "That, and not wanting her to suffer any pain."

"That's a given." D took out his knife and flicked it at Aguilar's crotch. When the man jerked backward, almost tipping his chair over, D smirked at the general. "Just cutting your pants off, bro. No need to lose it."

"I don't know where he is!" Aguilar blurted out. "A street boy brings me a message to meet him!"

Ash and the others nodded in satisfaction. "Good start," Trevor said. "What does Rivera want from you?"

Aguilar looked down at the knife against his groin and then at the wires that Ash was holding. A second later, he reluctantly started talking again. "Sometimes it's protection. Sometimes it's information."

"What kind of information?" Noelle asked.

"What other countries are requesting. What rivals are doing. That sort of thing."

"Why'd he fake his death?" That probably wasn't important but Ash was curious.

"I don't know. I guess he wanted to retire." Aguilar hesitated. "His son is in charge now—Adrián." He made an embittered noise. "Mateo wanted me to co-operate with the boy. I was reticent. We arranged to meet to discuss it further."

Ash shook his head. "Sorry to be the bearer of bad news, but Adrián Rivera is dead."

Aguilar looked startled. "W-what?"

"Dead as a doornail," Kane confirmed. "I took him out myself."

Noelle stepped forward impatiently. "None of this matters. Tell us where he is."

"I don't know," Aguilar sputtered. "I swear, I don't know."

"D," she prompted.

Quick as lightning, the tattooed mercenary pulled the M45 from his waistband and swung it across Aguilar's jaw. Blood, spit, and maybe a tooth flew across the room.

"We're done playing around," Noelle growled. "Where do we find Rivera? I know you would've sent one of your goons to follow those messenger boys."

"He'll kill me," Aguilar sobbed. "He'll kill me."

Noelle smiled. "And I'm going to order these nice boys to peel the skin off your cock and make you eat it if you don't tell us what you know. Ash . . ."

He held his open palm toward D, who slapped a KA-BAR into his hand. Before their captive could even blink, Ash shoved the blade into Aguilar's shoulder.

The man let out a high-pitched shriek. "A ware-house!" he cried out. "I know of a warehouse on the west end—Santino Road. I think they do deals there. Maybe it's where they bring the product. But someone there would know where Rivera is. They must!"

Noelle's smile widened. "Now, was that so hard?"

Ash pulled the knife out, wiped it on his pants, and tossed it back to D. "Sit tight," he told Aguilar. "We'll be back if the information you gave us isn't accurate."

"It is. I swear it!" Aguilar yelled, but he was talking to their backs.

Ash and the others were already walking away.

"Should we kill him?" Ash murmured on their way out the door.

"Why?" Noelle shrugged and kept walking. "The cartel will do it for us."

Ash returned with blood on his hands. Most of it had been wiped off but there were smears around his knuckles, and Cate's heart seized up as she inspected him covertly.

The team had gone out without her—again. Noelle, Ash, and the others had moved against Aguilar tonight, while Cate was once again relegated to the base to watch Jim lie like the dead in his hospital bed. Not one of these operatives would want to be in her shoes. It sucked to wait and wonder and worry. Couldn't any of them see past their own noses to recognize that?

"Do I want to know?" she asked Ash as everyone congregated in the war room for a briefing. She strove for a casual tone, even though she felt like punching him and everyone else in the face.

He flashed her a grin. "Not my blood."

Cate hid her relief. She wasn't supposed to feel anything toward Ash—not relief, not fear, not love, not hate. "Did you get any information from the Aguilars?"

"Maybe." Noelle tossed her handgun and a couple

of knives onto the table. "He gave us the location to a warehouse that Rivera may or may not be using as his hideout. How's Jim?"

"He's still out. Doc Palmer says we need to wait it out. They've given him something to keep him unconscious until the swelling goes down."

Cate bit the inside of her cheek until she tasted blood. Seeing her dad lie there so still and motionless, so much like her dead mother, pushed her emotions right up to the edge, but the entire group already thought she was a weak link. She wasn't going to enforce that notion by breaking down in front of everyone.

"You okay?" Ash asked softly.

Damn this man. He always saw too much. "I'm fine."

Noelle caught Cate's eyes and jerked her head to the door. "I need to wash up. Come join me." She glanced at the others. "We'll do the briefing in five. Go take a potty break or something."

D snickered as the two women slid out the door. Cate bristled at first, because she thought Noelle had postponed the meeting for Cate's sake. But when she looked over at the older women, she noticed that Noelle's face was haggard and drawn, grief making her beautiful features look sharp and hard.

"He'll wake up soon," Cate murmured, but they both heard the lack of conviction in her voice.

"He'd fucking better." Noelle sounded tired.

They entered the small bathroom at the end of the hall. Cate watched as Noelle pulled off her black tank top and started splashing water over her face and neck.

"You and Ash still fighting?"

Cate met the woman's eyes in the tiny mirror over the sink. "When do we ever *not* fight?"

"Didn't always used to be that way," Noelle reminded her.

"Yeah, well, things change."

The blonde grabbed a towel and patted herself dry. "High-pressure situations can bring out a lot of emotions in people. Both good and bad. And sometimes those feelings aren't real. It's just adrenaline masking itself as something different and intense."

Her mouth twisted in a scowl. "Yeah? So you're saying Ash doesn't actually think I'm a weak little girl who can't take care of herself?"

Noelle rolled her eyes. "Of course he doesn't think that."

"He's got a funny way of showing it."

"Because he's a man. Men are stupid, honey."

Cate hesitated. "You don't think I'm weak, do you?"

"Oh, please." Noelle tossed the towel back on the hook and then leaned against the wall. "Unlike your father, I don't believe that we should continue protecting you. People can't learn how to protect themselves unless they've experienced some pain."

"Pain," she echoed warily.

"Yes. We need the pain. It's the negative response that kids get when they stick their finger in a light socket or over a hot surface. The brain tells the little shits not to do it again."

"I have no idea what you're telling me," Cate admitted. "But if you're warning me against involving myself in this mission, it's too late. I'm already part of it. Rivera knows my name. He's coming after me—he said so himself."

"You've always had a good head on your shoulders." Noelle gave her a rare smile, one that actually reached her eyes. "I'm not going to exclude you from anything because, yeah, you're already involved, and I know how fucking stubborn you can be. But you do need to listen and follow orders. A couple of years out in the field with a camera isn't on the same level as years of training."

"I know that."

Noelle sighed. "Jim doesn't want you to get hurt, physically or emotionally. He's been trying to shield you ever since he met you. But pain is what defines us. Too much of it and your barriers become too hard. I've been there. Jim's been there. Almost all his men have been there." She offered a pointed look. "You have to decide whether what you want is important enough to fight through those walls. But that's your call."

Cate frowned, not at the advice itself but because of who was dispensing it. She reached for Noelle's arm before the woman could walk out the door. "Why are you being so nice to me?" she asked suspiciously.

Noelle frowned back. "What, I can't be nice to my own kid?"

She inhaled, sharp and fast. This was the first time Noelle had ever implied—no, flat out stated—that she viewed Cate as her daughter. Yes, the woman was technically Cate's stepmother, but their relationship had always been more of a friendship than anything.

"I'm your kid, huh?" She couldn't fight a smile.

"Oh, wipe that smug look off your face," Noelle grumbled. Then she let out a breath, and her voice grew surprisingly gentle. "Of course you're my kid, asshole. You think I'd invest all my time and wisdom on just anybody?"

Cate snorted.

"Even if Jim doesn't make it—which he *will*—I'm still going to be here for you. So if you had any ideas about ever getting rid of me, you can forget about those, fuck you very much."

A rush of emotion warmed Cate's heart. "I love you too," she said quietly.

"I know."

Cate's eyes felt hot as they left the bathroom. They

stepped into the hall and nearly ran into Ash, who'd taken the time to clean up. A fresh T-shirt clung to his defined chest. His face looked slightly damp, as if he'd washed up in a hurry.

Cate drew in a deep breath, searching for the anger that she'd nursed for years. It was her best protection against this man, and at times like these, when she was at her lowest, it was her *only* protection.

There'd been nights when she was on assignment in foreign locations that the loneliness would eat away at her until she closed her eyes and saw Ash smiling at her, heard his Southern drawl telling her that she should slow down, that life was still going to be there tomorrow. In those low moments, she'd longed for him.

And now, while her superhuman father lay unconscious for the third straight day, a part of her wanted to throw herself into Ash's arms and scale those barriers that Noelle talked about.

But he wasn't worth the effort. She'd already offered him everything she had and he'd refused it. No, he'd spit on it, turned his back, and then refused it.

Cate wasn't going to ever put herself in that position again.

"Can we talk?" he asked, his green eyes fixing on Cate.

"The briefing—"

"Hasn't started yet," he finished.

Cate looked to Noelle for assistance, but the woman just shrugged and said, "Take your time. We'll see you in there."

A jolt of desperation shot up Cate's spine as she watched Noelle walk away. Reluctantly, she turned back to Ash. "What do you want?"

"Is it so wrong for me to care about what happens to you?"

She forced herself not to be affected by the thick emotion in his voice. "It is when you're trying to shut me out of this mission." She stuck her chin out. "I'm a part of this, Ash. Noelle has already agreed to that."

His jaw hardened. "Not with me you're not."

"Then I'll be with someone else. Bailey—"

"Goddamn it, why won't you just let the professionals do their jobs?"

"Because that's my dad in there." She jabbed a finger down the hall toward the medical wing. "And he's all I have left in this world."

Her voice quavered, which she hated, particularly in front of Ash. She couldn't look weak in front of him. He'd leap on that excuse, go running to Noelle, and have Cate kicked off the team before she'd even strapped on a gun.

"Cate—," he started.

"You want me to be safe?" she cut in. "Then you have to include me. You *have* to. Because if I'm forced to sit here and watch another parent die, I guarantee you I'll go insane."

"And what if something happens to you?" He glared down at her. "What then?"

God, she could get lost in his eyes. Had gotten lost in them. Those green, green eyes that reminded her of the lush plants in the jungle held a banked heat that she'd never seen before.

"I'll be careful," she found herself whispering. Her hands reached up to press against his chest—to calm, to caress, she wasn't sure. He felt warm and alive and she had to fight hard not to throw her arms around him and hold him tight.

"There's no such thing." His voice was as low as hers, the tone as raw as she'd ever heard from his lips.

She opened her mouth. "Ash, I—"

"You guys coming?" a deep voice said from behind them.

Cate closed her eyes in relief at Kane's appearance. She'd been so close to making a mistake, saying things she shouldn't, and she'd never been more grateful for the interruption.

"Yep," she said lightly. "Heading to the war room now."

"In a minute," Ash corrected. "We'll be right there."

Kane arched a questioning eyebrow at the two of them before giving a nod. "See you in there."

Cate tried to follow him but Ash tugged her back. "Wait," he said. "What were you going to say?"

Somehow, she found a reserve of steel and straightened her spine. She hadn't avoided her only home for two years to lose all of her self-control—and self-esteem—in one awful moment. "That you're not in charge of this mission," she lied. "Noelle is, and she's agreed that I can be a part of it."

She didn't wait for his response. Nope. Instead she scampered after Kane into the war room, where the team was once again assembled.

"There's increased cyber chatter between tangos," Holden was saying. "Comm channels indicate that the Barrios cartel is taking credit for the attack at the hotel, which is bound to piss off Rivera. There's probably going to be a retaliation strike."

"Yeah, Isaac Barrios has a habit of riding in on someone else's coattails," Liam said with a nod. "He's a lazy son of a bitch."

"Have you made contact with him yet?" Noelle asked.

"In the process of it," Liam answered. "I never dealt with Barrios directly when I was undercover—I mostly did business with Niko Vega, one of his lieutenants. I've already left Vega a message, so we'll see what he comes back with. Shouldn't be an issue to set up a meeting, though."

"About that . . ." Kane exchanged a look with Noelle and then squared up to face Liam. "We got a call from the DEA. They heard you were going back in and want you to stand down."

Liam glowered. "How'd they hear about that?"

"Must be a mole inside the cartel," Kane replied with a shrug.

Liam clearly didn't like this one bit. "What do they want us to do? Hold our dicks while they leak more information than an oil tanker in the Gulf?"

"No. Fuck them," Noelle retorted. "We're going in regardless. Set up the meeting, Macgregor. But for now, we need to plan an attack on the address Aguilar gave us. As of right now, you're all on recon." Her deadly gaze swept around the room, making Cate shiver. "We strike tomorrow night."

Chapter 18

"You don't call me anymore." In the passenger seat, Bailey sounded more upset than angry as she twisted her body to look at Liam. "And you haven't answered my last few texts."

"I know," he said ruefully.

She crossed her arms over her chest. "Care to explain why?"

With a sigh, Liam turned away from her concerned gray eyes and focused on the windshield, under the guise that he was surveying the area.

But the street was quiet and deserted, and had been for hours. It was also pitch-black, courtesy of the broken lampposts lining the cracked sidewalk. The lights weren't out due to power outages—the bulbs had been smashed, shattered glass strewn all over the pavement. Liam wasn't sure if that was a result of neighborhood kids throwing rocks at the lights, or something more sinister, like cartel scumbags requiring the shroud of darkness for their illicit activities.

Either way it made their job easier. He and Bailey were in the front seat of a beat-up Volkswagen, a vehicle chosen specifically to fit in with the other shitbox cars in the area. They'd been assigned street surveillance, while the rest of the team was posted on the perimeter they'd set up around the address that Aguilar had given them, a two-story building with a sagging tin roof and very few windows.

So far, they were simply watching. The problem was, the building's handful of windows were boarded shut, so they had no line of sight to the interior. Abby had called in a request from a CIA contact for satellite images, but no one had gotten back to them yet. For now, all they could do was wait until they received more intel.

Normally, Liam would be thrilled to work alongside Bailey. The two of them had become close during the Paris job four years ago and had kept in touch ever since. Regular phone calls, long e-mails, funny texts. He adored the woman, and he'd been the first person to fly to Ireland when Bailey had needed help getting Sean Reilly out of a jam.

She was right, though. He *had* been ghosting for the last while. But he supposed it was too much to hope that Bailey wouldn't question him about it.

"What? Have you unfriended me?" she demanded. "Am I not cool enough for your Boston lifestyle?"

He chuckled wryly. "Nah. If anything, you're too cool for it."

Which was the absolute truth. His life in Boston didn't include gorgeous female assassins. Hell, he could just imagine what his parents would say if Bailey dropped in for a visit. If she showed them how good she was at transforming into other people. If she revealed all the men she'd killed with her bare hands. Paula and Callum Macgregor would have simultaneous coronaries.

"I've kind of lost touch with everyone," he confessed. "My life is boring now."

"Well, that's no fun." She grinned. "You don't do boring, L. You're built for action."

He shrugged. "Maybe I had too much action before.

I'm getting old, B. Maybe this nice stable security gig is just what I need."

"And the nice steady girlfriend? She still in the picture?"

He shifted uneasily.

"What's her name again?" Bailey pressed. "Penelope?"

"Yeah. Penny." He glanced over. "She dumped me."

Bailey's jaw fell open. "Are you fucking kidding me? *She* dumped *you*? Has she *seen* you?"

He couldn't help a laugh. But his voice lacked humor as he said, "Oh, she saw me, all right. She saw too much, apparently."

Bailey leaned over and placed her hand on his knee, stroking it gently. "What happened?"

Before he could answer, an Irish brogue filled his ear. "The fuck are you doing, luv? Giving him a handie?"

Liam snorted, while Bailey narrowed her eyes at the sound of her husband's irritated voice. Sean Reilly was positioned on the roof across the street. He'd be providing cover for them if they were compromised and needed to make an escape. But it looked like he was monitoring his wife as well as their car.

"I'm just comforting my friend," she retorted. "If that makes you mad, then too fucking bad."

"That rhymed," another voice piped up. Luke's Cajun drawl. "And why do you need comforting, Boston? You been off the grid so long you've forgotten how to conduct simple recon? Are you crying right now? Bailey, darling, give the man a tissue."

Liam touched his ear to activate his mic. "Hey Reilly, tell Dubois what I'm doing with my hand right now."

Reilly snickered. "He's flipping you the bird, mate."

Luke made a sound of mock pain. "Fuck, that hurts.

Reilly, send your wife my way. I'm the one who needs comforting now."

"Fuck the lot of you," Sean replied pleasantly.

"Boys," Isabel said. "Let's play nice."

"Let's not play at all," Trevor spoke up, sounding annoyed. "How about we all remember what's at stake here?"

Liam instantly sobered and the feed fell silent. No one ragged Trevor for being a buzz kill because the reminder was just what they needed. Rivera had sent armed thugs after Cate. Those thugs had put three bullets in Morgan's back. Noelle might have been the one to declare war, but every man and woman who cared about Jim Morgan wouldn't rest until Rivera was dead as a fuckin' doornail.

Liam once again assessed his surroundings. The pale glow of lights in the windows of nearby buildings, the muffled sound of music pouring out of an open window. At the building next to their target, an older man stood on a balcony, puffing on a cigar while he murmured into a cell phone. Lucky bastard. Most of the people in this country didn't have food or water and this fucker could afford a cell provider.

"Seriously, though," Bailey murmured from the passenger side. "I miss you, Liam."

His throat tightened. "I miss you too."

More than she would ever know. And he didn't just miss her—he missed *this*. Despite the circumstances that had brought them to Guatana, he loved being with his team again. Loved knowing that Luke and Isabel and Sean were lying on nearby roofs with sniper rifles. Loved knowing that the rest of his teammates . . . D, Trev, Kane, Ethan, Ash, Sullivan . . . that they were all on the ground, armed to the teeth, and waiting for the order to strike.

He'd missed the camaraderie. The chatter over the comm. The way they moved together like a well-oiled machine.

"You're worrying me."

He looked over again. "Why? Because I'm not feeling chatty?"

"You're never feeling chatty, honey. That's Sully's job—he's the one who can never shut up." She pursed her lips. "But you've both been worryingly quiet since you got here." Her gray eyes probed his face. "The relationship ended because of him, didn't it?"

His jaw twitched. Goddamn this woman. She was too fuckin' perceptive. "I told you. Penny dumped me."

Bailey rolled her eyes. "Yes. I got that. But she dumped you because of him, didn't she?"

"Not exactly."

"That means I'm right."

Christ. He wanted to drag both hands through his hair in frustration, but if his hand got too close to his ear he would activate his mic and then the whole team would hear this awkward conversation, so he curled his fingers over the steering wheel instead.

"She found out I was bisexual," he muttered. "She didn't like it."

"So she ended it?" Bailey shook her head in disgust. "That's it. I hate her."

He had to smile. "You don't even know her."

"Doesn't matter. I hate her. Anyone who hurts one of my best friends deserves to get punched." She paused. "What about the guy?"

Oh, for fuck's sake. Discomfort twisted Liam's stomach. Couldn't he have been paired up with anyone else? Just his luck that Kane had teamed him with Bailey, a woman who was way too skilled at prying.

"What guy?" he said lightly.

She gave him a pointed look. "The *guy*, Liam. You know who I'm talking about."

He swallowed a sigh. "What about him?"

"Who ended that? You or him?"

"Me."

"Why?"

"Because it didn't feel right."

"Because it didn't feel right, or because *he* didn't feel right?"

"Does it matter?"

"I guess not." Even as her watchful gaze continued to scan the street, she reached over again and touched his cheek.

A growl sounded in both their ears, but they ignored it. Fortunately, Sean didn't pipe up again.

"I hate seeing you unhappy," she said quietly.

"I'm not unhappy."

Liar.

Fine. He was fucking miserable. And seeing Sully again wasn't exactly helping matters. He wasn't sure how he'd expected their reunion to go down, but it hadn't been this awkward sort of indifference. It was as if they were operating in a weird state of denial. Other than that one charged moment in the barracks when they'd almost ventured into territory that scared the shit out of him, they hadn't had a single meaningful conversation.

But maybe that was for the best. Maybe they didn't need to talk about any of that shit. Sullivan hadn't wanted to start something up in the first place, and it had taken Liam two years to reach the point where he didn't lie awake at night fantasizing about his friend.

Except . . . two days back in Sully's presence, and Liam had reverted to the pathetic, confused mess he'd been before they said good-bye two years ago.

What made it worse was that Sully didn't look like the man Liam had left in Portugal—he looked like the man Liam had lusted over before Sully's abduction. He'd cropped his blond hair, shaved the beard, bulked up. And unlike the last time they'd seen each other, his silvery eyes were sharp and alert again. He really was sober these days, and although that made Liam eternally grateful, being around the pre-captivity Sully— that vibrant, gorgeous man who oozed sexuality—just reignited the attraction Liam had fought so hard.

He didn't need to feel that lust again. He didn't need to remember that night in Dublin, after Sully had been injured in a car bombing. Liam had slid into bed with him that night, wrapped his hand around his friend's cock, and—

Fuck. No. He couldn't let his mind go there. It had been a onetime thing. A random sexual encounter designed to make Sullivan forget about the pain he'd been feeling.

"CIA just got back to us." Kane's voice cut over the feed.

Both Liam and Bailey snapped to attention.

"What are we looking at?" Ash asked.

"We've got two floors—"

"No shit," D grunted. "We've been staring at those two floors for six hours."

"You gonna let me finish?" Kane asked in amusement.

"Sorry," D muttered. "Proceed."

"Bottom floor is showing nine distinct heat signatures. All in motion—I'm thinking it's a crew packaging up the coke."

"Top floor?" Oliver Reilly, Sean's twin, asked.

"Only two heat signatures. One prone, northeast corner. Another standing near the west wall."

"Think it's Rivera?" Luke piped up.

"Could be," Kane answered. "Obviously he's been lying low since he faked his death. Stands to reason he'd be holed up in some safe house."

Ethan's skeptical voice joined in. "One as lightly guarded as this one?"

"Lightly?" Ash echoed. "Try not at all. We've got no exterior guards, for fuck's sake."

"Could be a trap," Sean said flatly.

"Or a strategic move on his part," Trevor countered. "Posting an army out here would be like a neon sign that there's something—or someone—important inside. Rivera might not want to draw that kind of attention to himself."

"Either way," Kane spoke up, "there's no way to verify the identities of the second-floor tangos unless we go in."

"Then we go in," D said with impatience.

The team leader paused, then barked out a series of commands. "Everyone get in position. D, set the charges. You, Sully, and Ash penetrate from the front. Door in the back looks like reinforced steel—we'll need to blow that too. Ethan, Reilly Two, I want you posted out there in case anyone makes a run for it. Bailey, Boston, cover the front. Luke, Izzy, Reilly One, take the bird's eye. Me and Trev will drop in from above. Skylight looks flimsy—we can blow that with one charge."

"Just the two of you?" Oliver asked warily.

"We're only dealing with two tangos. We need the rest of you downstairs to handle the bulk on the first floor. Trev, make your way up to me."

"Copy."

"Everyone ready?" Kane said grimly.

A chorus of *yessir*s rang over the line.

"Good. Wait for my word."

There was nothing worse than being assigned to provide cover fire but Liam didn't object to Kane's orders. A former SEAL, Morgan's second-in-command had planned and executed hairier ops than this one—Kane knew what he was doing.

Still, Liam wasn't thrilled as he slid out of the car and got in position. As he checked the magazine of his assault rifle, he heard an answering click and saw Bailey doing the same. She was crouched behind the rear door near the trunk, while he was hunched behind the side of the hood.

"D," Kane barked. "Charges set?"

"Affirmative."

"Ethan?"

"Ready when you are."

Liam tensed at the brief silence that followed. He raised his rifle and aimed at the front door, catching sight of D's shadowy figure slithering away from it. Red lights blinked from the detonators D had stuck over the knob and on each corner of the door. And although Sully and Ash were too good to be spotted, Liam knew they were nearby, hiding in the shadows.

"On my count," Kane finally said. "One."

Liam adjusted his grip.

"Two."

His trigger finger itched.

On Kane's *three*, a burst of blinding light illuminated the street like a bolt of lightning in a black sky. The front door was blown off its hinges, releasing a wave of shrapnel that flew in all directions. It didn't come close to hitting Liam and Bailey, but he felt the heavy thud made by the door as it crashed onto the pavement a few feet from them.

Almost immediately, three black-clad figures advanced on the hole that the explosion had left behind. Ash or Sully must have thrown a smoke bomb because suddenly Liam couldn't see anything but a white-gray cloud that swallowed up his teammates as they moved inside.

Up above, a plume of smoke floated through the air; Kane and Trevor had blown the skylight. And from Ethan's brisk report, the back door had been taken out too.

"Going in," Ash reported.

"We need them alive," was Kane's brusque reply. "Incapacitate, don't kill."

"Roger that."

Liam had never felt more ineffective in his life as he stared at the smoke pouring out of what used to be the front door. Sully, D, and Ash weren't activating their mics, so he had no idea what they'd encountered inside. His spine stiffened when he heard shots, but the gunfire didn't last long. As it died off, it was replaced by muffled shrieks from the building's interior. Shrieks that were too high in pitch to have come from men.

He and Bailey exchanged a puzzled look, but neither of them so much as moved. They had their orders, and their weapons remained trained on the door.

Another wave of gunfire filled the night. It sounded like it was coming from above, which meant Trevor and Kane had breached the second floor.

Sure enough, Kane reported in a second later, and he didn't sound pleased. "It's not him," he growled. "Just some punk-ass kid jerking off."

"Literally," came Trevor's dry voice. "Walked in on him with his hand around his dick."

Liam didn't know whether to laugh or curse. *Fuck.* The cursing won out. Because if Rivera wasn't one of the two tangos upstairs, chances were he wasn't downstairs either.

"Ash," Kane prompted. "Report in."

After a short pause, Ash's Southern drawl filled Liam's ear. "No one of value down here. Our contact at the CIA was right—this is a packaging facility. We're looking at a bunch of low-level grunts. And they didn't even put up a fight. Surrendered the second we came in."

Sean chuckled. "You mean D didn't get to shoot anyone?"

"Shoot them?" D echoed. "You know I prefer a knife."

"Right. Forgot what a sick motherfucker you are, mate."

"On our way down," the team leader spoke up.

Liam frowned at Kane's report. "What about Mr. Dick-in-his-hand?" he demanded.

"He doesn't know shit. Said that Rivera's other son is calling the shots now and that Mr. Dick was assigned to head security for this warehouse. Apparently Rivera Junior holds all his meetings in one of the warehouses by the docks."

"We gathered intel on all those facilities," Trevor added. "They all deal in cargo. Rivera wouldn't be hiding out at any of them."

"Do we believe the jerk-off boy?" Ash asked.

"Yeah, I think we do, Rook." Kane made a disgusted noise. "He pissed all over himself when we came in through the roof. Started talking immediately, and he didn't set off my bullshit meter. Kid didn't know anything."

"And the guard?"

"KIA. He fired at us."

"Jesus," D growled, his impatience unmistakable. "Let's stop wasting time with this chatter and torture these fuckers. One of them has to know something."

Liam touched his ear. "You guys need me in there?"

"Negative," Kane replied. "We've got it covered. Maintain your position."

He swallowed a rush of disappointment. He'd come to Guatana for Jim, to potentially say good-bye to a man he loved and respected, but now that they were on a mission, he craved the action. He hated being banished outside like a guard dog.

Bailey caught his eye knowingly. "Stop pouting, sweetie."

"I'm not pouting," he grumbled.

But yeah, he kind of was. This fuckin' sucked.

And who knew what was going on inside, because the comm had gone quiet again. It seemed like he'd been waiting an eternity, but a glance at his tactical watch showed that only five minutes had passed.

"Kane," he said when a report still hadn't surfaced. "Anyone squeal yet?"

"No, and they're not going to either. These are just minions. They know shit all." Kane sounded annoyed. "We're sending a few of them out. Hold your fire."

Liam and Bailey exchanged another look. They were sending out hostages? What the fuck was that about?

Half a minute later, several shadows darkened the cloud of smoke that was beginning to thin out, and then three women came tearing through the doorway like bats out of hell. Wearing nothing but bras and panties, with their hair tied back in bandanas, the trio of females stumbled onto the sidewalk.

Liam raised his rifle, only for Bailey to hiss at him. "He said hold your fire."

"I'm not firing. Just preparing."

"They're not armed."

"They're still part of the crew." They had to be, judging by their state of undress. There'd been too many instances in the past of cartel employees trying to steal the drugs they were cutting and packaging, and sneaking the product out in their clothing. Nowadays, it was protocol to force the crews to work in their underwear. The Barrios cartel had done the same thing when Liam was undercover with them.

Across the street, the three women were no longer dazed and unsure. They sprinted down the sidewalk, their sandals slapping the pavement with each frantic step they took to put distance between themselves and the warehouse.

"We're coming out," Kane said a moment later.

Liam watched as several of his teammates stalked out of the gaping doorway. They dispersed quickly, heading for the various vehicles on the street or ducking into nearby alleys. As Ethan reported that he and Oliver were still watching the rear, Sullivan and D darted across the empty road and joined Bailey and Liam behind the car.

Liam didn't miss the streak of soot on Sully's chiseled face, which probably got there during the initial explosion. And though now was probably not the time to notice how hot Sully looked, it was impossible not to.

D, meanwhile, wore a satisfied, savage expression, which made Liam wonder if he'd gotten to use his knife in there after all.

"Luke," Kane said over the feed. "Release the Kraken."

Liam barely had time to smother a laugh before a puff of blue whizzed past his peripheral vision.

Luke, who was on the roof of the building behind them, was armed with a rocket launcher and he obviously got off on using it because a loud whoop echoed in Liam's ear seconds before the warehouse went *boom*.

"What about the men inside?" Bailey shouted over the loud explosion that rocked the building.

"They work for Rivera," was D's implacable response. "They kill for Rivera."

Liam saw Bailey bite her lip in dismay as she gazed at the wall of orange flames across the street. He knew she didn't condone killing unless it was absolutely necessary, and, truth was, killing a bunch of cartel minions *wasn't* a necessity.

But he also knew that they were all feeling a little bloodthirsty tonight. And if they couldn't get their hands on Mateo Rivera, then they might as well send him a message that he'd never be able to misinterpret.

James Morgan's people were not to be fucked with.

Chapter 19

"How did you let this happen?" It was difficult for Rivera to hold his son's gaze when the entirety of his vision was a red haze.

"I . . . don't know," Benicio whispered.

He didn't *know*? The incompetence of this boy, his goddamn *seed*, was so incredible it had Rivera biting back hysterical laughter.

But the acidic rage burning his intestines took precedence to any humor he might find in Benicio's absurd explanation. The report he'd just received was eerily similar to the violent events he'd faced during the early days of his reign. After Rivera's father had stepped down, their rivals crept out of the woodwork, eager to wrest power from the Riveras. They hadn't believed little Mateo could fill his father's big shoes. They hadn't viewed him as a viable threat. But little Mateo had proved them wrong and taken extreme pleasure in doing so.

After his own retirement, he'd watched Adrián face the same obstacles. Enemies who didn't think he was smart enough, deadly enough. Adrián, however, had wasted no time squashing the minor skirmishes before they could escalate.

Now, less than a week at the helm and Benicio had lost one of their most profitable packaging facilities. And not even to another cartel!

"They ambushed us," Benicio began. His voice trembled on the last word, and that was the word that got Rivera's attention.

"Us?" he echoed. "Your use of that word, son, implies that you were present for this ambush, which you were not."

"I was at the docks inspecting the new shipment, just like you requested," his son protested.

"And you didn't think to assign security to the packaging facility?"

"Augustin was there," Benicio said weakly.

Rivera slowly rose to his feet. "Let me ask you a question. When your brother was in charge, did he ever place useless twats in charge of warehouse security? Or did he, perhaps, select capable lieutenants, like Hernandez or Kafari or Ortiz, men he knew could execute proper evacuation protocols and preventative security?" The rage bubbled up to his throat, hissing through every word. "Men who *wouldn't let our facility get blown up*!"

"Augustin wanted the responsibility, Father. He wanted to prove that he could take on a greater role in the organization."

"So you put him in charge of security?" Rivera roared. He took a breath, struggling for calm. "Tell me, did Augustin assign any guards to the perimeter?"

"No, but—"

"How many guards did he post on the main floor?"

"One, but—"

"One!"

Benicio flinched. "He checked in with hourly reports, Father. He assured me that the area was secure. I didn't realize until later that he'd reassigned the facility guards to the warehouse in Toro."

"You didn't realize . . ." His breathing thinned. "He was nineteen years old! A child! *That's* who you chose?"

Rivera slammed both hands on his thighs. "He *deserved* to burn to a crisp in that warehouse! That's what happens to incompetent children!"

Benicio visibly gulped. "I'm sorry."

"What does your apology really do for me, boy? Will it bring back the hundreds of thousands of dollars that were reduced to ashes? Will it bring back the burnt corpses of the men and women who have loyally served us for years? Will it bring back our product?"

Benicio cringed at each angry word that was hurled at him. "No, Father, it won't."

Useless! This boy in front of him—no, he was twenty-four years old. That made him a *man*, not a boy. But he might as well have been a toddler in diapers walking around with shit stuck to his ass, too useless and stupid to wipe it himself. Benicio had allowed James Morgan's people to waltz into a facility that should have been heavily guarded. He'd placed a bungling teenager in charge of security.

Camila was wrong.

There was nothing worth redeeming about this pathetic child.

Rivera turned away. He was done with this. Clearly Benicio was—and would always be—a failure.

"Your brother would have never let this happen." Clenching his jaw, he stalked out of the bedroom.

In the briefing room, the enforcers he'd dispatched were waiting for him. These were his most trusted men, having proven their loyalty and proficiency with their blood and sweat. They shifted uneasily when he stalked out. A few gazes flickered toward Benicio before returning to Rivera.

"I'm relieving my son of his duties," he announced to the crew.

Not a single man registered so much as a trace of surprise. Rivera curled his fists to his sides. Yes. They were smart men. They all recognized that Benicio wasn't worth a second's thought.

"James Morgan's people blew up my warehouse. I will not stand for that." He marched over to the table and picked up the files he and Camila had pored over the other night, then walked back to his men and began slapping folders in each of their hands.

"There's only one objective," he said coldly. "Destroy these people. Are we clear?"

"Yes, sir," they said in unison.

He turned to the stocky, mustached man at the end of the line. "Hernandez, you're in charge of security of all our current facilities. Dispatch the appropriate men. I assume you won't let what happened tonight occur again?"

"No, sir." Confidence rang in Hernandez's tone. His expression held a trace of disgust as he glanced over Rivera's shoulder at Benicio.

"Kafari, I want you to speak to the head of my wife's security team. If Morgan's people are coming after us, I want her safe. She needs extra guards." He smiled. "You can take them off Benicio's security detail if needed."

A strangled noise came from behind him.

He didn't turn around. There was no point in protecting his son any longer or wasting further manpower on him. And while he would protect his investments for the time being, the moment he eliminated James Morgan and his people, Rivera would take his money and his wife and retire to his island. The other cartels could fight over the remains of his empire like the scavengers they were.

Without a true heir to leave it to, the empire meant nothing now.

Rivera looked at the other men. "These people, their families . . . send them a message that the Riveras do not forgive nor forget. Show them the meaning of suffering."

He clapped his hands and the crowd dispersed, the room emptying until only Rivera and his son remained.

He walked to the bar on the other side of the room and poured himself a glass of bourbon. Benicio stood frozen near the bedroom door, his dark eyes warily tracking his father's movements, his face paler than snow.

"Father," he began, "what should I do?"

A harsh laugh escaped his lips, poisoning the air in the room. "What should you do? You can stay in this safe house, keep your mouth shut, and do absolutely nothing." Sarcasm dripped from his tone. "I'd like to believe you couldn't screw *that* up, but you're quite skilled at proving me wrong."

Shame flickered in his son's eyes.

"Now get out of my sight," he snapped, baring his teeth. "It's time to let the grown-ups work."

Cate pushed open the door to Morgan's room and peeked in. When she saw the chair next to the bed was empty, she made her way inside. Noelle usually was in here between recon shifts, so if she wasn't with Morgan at the moment, that meant she'd probably snuck out to take a smoke break.

"Noelle's smoking again," Cate informed her dad. "This is your fault. If you were up and about, you'd be riding her ass hard." She paused and grimaced. "Probably literally. Ugh, I can't believe I just had that thought about you and Noelle. Unfortunately for you, I have sex on the brain." She tapped his knee, just to watch it jerk.

She knew from experience with her mother that it didn't mean anything. Sensory reflexes happened even with patients who were brain-dead, but Cate took her encouragement where she could find it these days, and the small movements of Jim's leg or arm or fingers gave her solace.

"Ash is here and I can't stop looking at him or watching him. Even when he's cruel to me, I still want to be near him." She laughed ruefully. "It's sick. I know that. He was so awful to me the last time we saw each other. I should hate him for that, but I know why he did it. I know he did it for you."

She took a shaky breath. "I guess no matter how far away I run from him or how many guys I let into my life, I can't wipe those feelings away." And she wasn't sure if she wanted to. Being in such close proximity to Ash and seeing his torment and worry about her well-being was driving her nuts, tearing down all those barriers she thought she'd built against him.

Jim didn't respond.

With another sigh, she rose and kissed him on his forehead. "I love you, Dad. Get better."

In the hallway outside his room, she rested her forehead against the wall and tried to find some composure. The stress and guilt were eating away at her. Her eyes felt scratchy from all the tears she'd been keeping at bay and her throat was sore from all the words she wanted to say but couldn't.

She didn't know how long she'd stood there before a soft male voice called her name.

"Come on, Cate, you need a drink."

She wheeled around to see Holden watching her in sympathy. She almost wished he had a scowl on his face. It'd be easier to take. "Hey. Can't sleep?"

A faint smile ghosted across his face. "I haven't been able to sleep for some time. I'm going to the mess hall to get a drink."

"If you promise that it's not milk, tea, or juice, then yes, I'm game."

"I was thinking scotch. You like scotch?"

"No. I hate it. Pour me a double."

He snickered, and they headed out of the main building to the small one beside it, which housed the base's dining hall. The place was empty when they walked in, so they had free range of the large, slightly dated kitchen.

In the end, there was only enough scotch to fill two glasses to the halfway point.

"We're not getting drunk tonight," Cate observed as she swirled the amber liquid around in her glass.

"I can tell you from experience that drinking only temporarily dulls the ache." Holden shrugged. "But sometimes the temporary fix gets you to the next day." Then he tossed back the entire glass in one gulp.

If there was anyone who knew what it took to survive, it was Holden, so Cate followed his lead by taking a big gulp and breathed through the burn.

"Your dad still sends me checks every month, did you know that?"

She shook her head, but she wasn't surprised to hear it. Jim was loyal to his core. He was probably treating Holden's absence from the team as an extended sabbatical.

"He does," Holden confirmed. "With a message that the door is always open. I cash the checks because not cashing them will earn me a visit that I don't want or need, but I haven't spent a dime. I'm probably going to give the money to some charity. Beth loved animals, so I'm thinking the Humane Society or something like that."

Cate marveled that Holden could say his dead wife's name without breaking down. "I bet she'd like that."

"I suspect she would." He nodded toward the glass

in her hand. "You drinking that or painting the sides of the glass with it?"

"You want?" She pushed the glass toward him. "I wasn't lying about hating scotch."

"It's an acquired taste. Beth didn't like it either. She was a red wine lover, the drier the better. She hated any kind of aftertaste. Me? It's the heat at the end that I like."

"I wish I'd met her."

"She would've mothered you to death. Sometimes you need that." His dark gray eyes were piercing, as if his loss gave him a special insight into Cate's wounded soul. "You've suffered a lot in your life. Another girl wouldn't be so strong."

"I'm not a girl." The protest was automatic by now. "I haven't felt like a girl for a really long time."

He picked up her glass and took a contemplative sip before saying, "Yeah, I suppose you're right." With his elbows on the table, he leaned toward her. "Jim and his crew think that Beth dying in my arms was the worst thing that could've ever happened, but when I look back, I feel like that was the only way to go. I mean, I loved her hard that night, and the minutes leading up to her death were ones I don't regret at all. It's the other times—where we spent stupid hours arguing about jackshit. Or when I was gone on missions and she was back home alone. It's the time apart that I regret. Not the time that we were together."

The air was so thick with emotion, so full of Holden's memories and his wise words that Cate could only stare back at the man. There was a message there between the words, and it wasn't simply to live life to the fullest. It was something more, but she couldn't seem to decipher it.

Holden held her stare for a long moment before rising to his feet. "This is South America. They've got to have some wine in this joint somewhere."

While he was rummaging through the cupboards, Liam wandered into the kitchen, exhaustion creasing his gorgeous face. "Is this the meeting of the pre-insomniacs?" he asked, ruffling Cate's hair as he walked past her chair.

"Or the pre-alcoholics anonymous," Cate joked.

"If you find something, pour me a double." Liam dropped into an empty seat. "Any news on anything?"

"No. Jim's the same. I think Noelle is smoking on the patio, plotting Rivera's castration."

Holden joined them at the table, bringing a jug of something that smelled like sour grapes. He poured three full glasses, but Cate made no move to touch hers. Liam didn't either.

"There's so much illegal activity going down, I can't make out what's related to Rivera and what's just general unrest in the city," Holden admitted. "People are making deals just to get food, so anything that Rivera is doing easily passes under the radar."

"Damn," Liam said. "Well, I've got a meeting with the Barrios cartel tomorrow night, so hopefully that gives us some kind of lead. I don't like being here. I've got an itchy feeling about this shit."

The other man nodded. "Yeah, it's not a good place."

Cate could hardly believe it. Two of Morgan's men were actually talking operational shit right in front of her. Maybe they *did* believe she'd grown up.

She was on the verge of doing something stupid, like thanking them, when her phone rang. And the moment she saw *unknown caller* flashing on the screen, she knew exactly who it was.

Rivera.

"I think it's him," she hissed to Holden, who instantly hustled to his feet.

The three of them pushed their chairs back and damn near sprinted to the war room where Holden had his equipment set up. When Holden gave her the signal, Cate quickly jammed her finger on the TALK button.

"Hello?" she answered coolly.

"Cate!" a voice boomed jovially. "It's your friend Mateo. I hope I didn't wake you."

"I don't see how you're my friend," she drawled. "A friend would meet me in person."

Rivera let out a laugh so loud Cate had to pull the phone from her ear. Beside her, Holden typed furiously into his computer.

"You're trying to lure me out. I like it. You're a precious, delightful girl."

She bristled. "I'm a woman, thank you very much, so if you like girls, you're barking up the wrong tree, you twisted pedophile."

Her insult only made him laugh harder. "I think if I had a child like you, I would not be so worried about the future of my business."

"Oh dear. Your son isn't living up to your expectations?"

It was Rivera's turn to reply with frost in his voice. "Have you lived up to your parents'?"

So, his sons were a sore point. She tucked that bit of information away. "My mother is dead, which you probably know, and Jim doesn't care what I do," she lied.

"All good parents care about their children's future. Perhaps your father doesn't express any interest in you because he doesn't love you."

"God, Rivera, that's weak. Suggesting I have daddy problems? Be more original and pay attention. Obviously he does or he wouldn't have come to Guatana to save my butt."

"You're not a parent, so you cannot know whether obligation or love drives him. When you have a child, your whole perspective on life changes. Your children become an extension of yourself, a reflection."

"Ah, I see. And you don't like what your mirror is showing you? Is that the problem? Your kids aren't big and strong like you?"

Liam shook his head at Cate's combative tone but she knew instinctively that this was what Rivera wanted from her. A sniveling woman wouldn't get the same reaction from this cruel, sick man.

He gusted out a sigh. "Do you believe in nature or nurture?"

"Both," she answered immediately. "I think they're inseparable."

"This is a sign of your immaturity. You see, it's nature. I have two children and one is not like the other. If it was nurture, they would be the same, but they are not."

She found herself oddly curious to know more. "What makes them different?"

Rivera paused for a moment. "When Benicio was nine, a rabid dog found its way onto our property. It was sick and needed to be put down, otherwise it could have infected the other dogs and pets around our home. I gave Benicio a gun and told him to save the other animals. But Benicio refused. He thought he could aid the dog, perhaps save him. He went to the dog to try to feed it. What do you think happened?"

"The dog bit him," Cate said with absolute surety.

He made an approving sound at the back of his throat. "The dog was ill. It saw Benicio as a threat and reacted. He bit off a chunk of the boy's forearm—Benicio still wears the scar of that encounter. My son

Adrián walked over his brother's screaming body, picked up the gun, and shot the dog's head off. That, my dear, is nature over nurture."

Cate disagreed. She thought the story showed that Benicio had a compassionate heart while Adrián was as sick as the dog, but she knew that theory wouldn't fly with Rivera. To him, Benicio's kindness was a flaw.

She sought a different reason, one that would fit better with the man's worldview. "Maybe it shows that Benicio likes to find a way where everyone wins."

"That itself is a fallacy. There is only one winner. The rest are losers and cowards, and those people should be put down. Which one are you, Cate?"

"I'm a winner," she spat out. "And you, Rivera, will be the loser."

"We shall see." He chuckled, then murmured, "Good night, little one. I'll see you soon."

As the call disconnected, Cate anxiously turned to Holden, who was bent over his laptop. "Anything?" she demanded.

He lifted his head and cursed. "Nothing. Didn't have enough time."

From his perch near the door, Liam didn't look at all surprised by the report. "Rivera's too smart to allow his calls to be traced. If we're going to find him, it'll be through intel on the ground, not cell towers."

"Then get us some intel," Cate said in a firm voice, locking her gaze with Liam's. "Squeeze the Barrios people tomorrow until they give you something—" She halted, blushing self-consciously when she realized she'd just barked orders at him like she was the one in charge.

But Liam simply flashed her a grin and raised his hand to his forehead in a salute. "Yes, ma'am."

Chapter 20

The pulsing bass line pounding from inside the nightclub was so loud that Sullivan could feel it vibrating in the cracked sidewalk beneath his wing tips. He could swear the walls of the building were shaking. It was a bloody awful song too, some Spanish pop bullshit. He was a classic rock guy. Dance music just gave him a headache.

Or maybe the throbbing in his temples right now had nothing to do with the shitty music and more to do with the insanity they were about to walk into. He hated going into an op blind. Fucking hated it.

"There has to be another way," he told Liam. Then he made the mistake of glancing over, and, just like every other time he'd glanced at Liam in the past hour, his body tightened in a very unwelcome way.

Liam Macgregor was attractive on a good day, but when he was decked out in a suit? When his hair was slicked away from his face, emphasizing his strong forehead? Jesus. Talk about sex personified.

Sullivan, on the other hand, hated wearing suits. His shoulders were too broad, his chest too muscular. Every time he had to wear one of these bloody things he felt like an overstuffed sausage.

"It'll be fine," Liam assured him. "I practically lived here when I was undercover."

"I didn't realize you were assigned to Guatana."

"Not exclusively. South America was my territory,

but I spent most of my time in the north. Venezuela, Colombia, Ecuador. I always hated this country the most. It was a shithole back then and it's a shithole now."

"You sure the Barrios people will deal with you?"

"I don't see why not. I made them a lot of money when I was undercover." He offered a wry grin. "I also cost them a lot of money, but they don't know that."

Despite the spark of curiosity that Liam's remark triggered, Sullivan didn't press for details. He'd never asked questions about the man's work with the DEA, but he was aware that Liam had left the agency because he'd felt like he was losing himself, getting too deep with the criminals he was supposed to be friends with.

That was all sorts of messed up, because Liam Macgregor had *good guy* written all over him. Sully couldn't imagine his buddy ever consorting with scumbags, and so convincingly that they'd considered him one of them. But he supposed they all had their secret talents. God knew he'd been pretty bloody good at dealing drugs.

"What exactly was your cover?" he asked, giving in to the curiosity.

"I dabbled in sex."

Sully's eyebrows flew up. "You whored yourself out?"

"No." Liam sighed. "I had girls who did that for me."

"Jesus. You were a bloody pimp?"

"Yep."

His jaw fell open. He couldn't fucking believe what he was hearing.

There was an awkward silence before his friend finally spoke again.

"I didn't mistreat the girls who worked for me. They were all over eighteen. They were all clean and sober—I made sure of that." Liam's voice softened. "I helped a lot of them off the streets, actually. That wasn't part of the job, but I couldn't just let them go out there and do what they were doing . . ." He trailed off. "I mean . . . fuck. On one hand, I believe it's a woman's right to choose what to do with her body. If prostitution is what she wants, then fine. But a lot of these girls, they sold their bodies because they didn't think they had any other options. So, if I could, I'd give them another option."

"How?" Sully's voice sounded hoarse to his own ears.

Liam shrugged. "Helped them continue their education. Found them other jobs whenever I could. And the ones that worked for me, I made sure nobody hurt them. I gave them protection, a place to stay if they needed it." He sounded sad. "I guess I was a very good pimp."

The shame in his friend's blue eyes tugged at Sullivan's heart. "Hey. We've all had to do things we're not proud of. I told you about my time on the streets."

"Yeah, but that was different. You were an addict. You didn't choose to be an addict."

"No, but I chose to deal drugs. I chose to feed other people's addictions. And I chose to sample my own merchandise. I made those decisions, mate. At least with you, you were following orders."

"Like that matters," Liam scoffed.

"It does in a way. A government agency was telling you it was okay. And you said so yourself—you helped a lot of the girls. Plus, you took out a lot of scumbags in the process. You did good, Boston."

"Not good enough."

Before he could stop himself, Sully reached out and touched Liam's arm. It was meant to be a soothing gesture, but the moment his palm made contact, curling over that band of muscle, his pulse sped up and his mouth ran dry. He couldn't remember the last time he'd touched his friend. They hadn't even shaken hands earlier this week when they'd seen each other for the first time in two years.

Time seemed to freeze as Liam's gaze slowly lowered to Sully's hand. He stared at it for a long, silent beat. Then he cleared his throat and eased away from Sully's touch.

"Anyway, I hooked up with the Barrios cartel under the guise that I wanted to get into the drug game. Offered up my girls as drug mules, and we came up with an arrangement that suited both of us—"

They were interrupted by D's voice on the comm line. "We doing this shit or what?"

Sully's brain quickly snapped back to business mode. Their teammates were stationed on the perimeter, waiting for them to make contact with their target. Luke, Ethan, and Juliet were already inside, keeping an eye on the crowd. Only thing left to do was go in and take this meeting.

"You ready?" Sully asked.

Liam nodded in resignation. They'd only taken one step when he halted. "Sully," he started.

"Yeah?"

"Anything I say in there . . . or do in there . . . it's part of the cover, okay? It's just . . . I need you to know it's not me."

Ignoring the jolt of alarm that shot through him, Sully nodded in return and followed his friend to the entrance. He would be playing the part of Liam's new associate, which he knew his teammate wasn't thrilled about. Liam had wanted to do this alone but Sully had put his foot down and Kane and Noelle had agreed.

Liam had been out of the game for years—who knew how these fuckers would react to seeing "Mac Mulligan" again. He needed backup, whether he wanted it or not.

There was no line out front. After they'd paid the cover charge, the bouncer waved them through without a second's glance. The moment they stepped into the club, they were greeted by a blast of music that nearly shattered Sully's eardrums. Jeez. The tunes were even worse in here. Another pop song, this one featuring a female vocalist who was way too shrill for his liking.

The crowd seemed to love it, though. The dance floor was jam-packed with an array of couples grinding up against each other. The women wore skimpy clothing, many of the men didn't have their shirts on, and everyone was so caught up in their vertical fuckfests that it made it easy for Sully and Liam to move unnoticed through the throng of dancers.

Sully gave the room a quick once-over. At the bar in the far corner, a stunning brunette, tall and statuesque, was surrounded by a mob of salivating men. He hid a smile. Juliet Mason-Hayes couldn't go anywhere without making dudes drool. He wondered if Ethan was lurking in the shadows, fuming at all the attention his smoking-hot wife was getting.

He didn't see Ethan, but he did spot Luke leaning against the wall. The man's dark eyes were ostensibly undressing the group of scantily clad women to his left, but Sully didn't miss the shrewd glint in that sensual gaze. Luke was aware of everything and everyone in the room. A few sexy broads weren't about to distract the former SEAL.

"Where to?" The music was too loud, so Sully was forced to bring his mouth close to Liam's ear. He could swear the other man flinched.

"Follow me." As Liam tilted his head to whisper back, his clean-shaven cheek brushed Sully's chin.

A shiver ran up his spine. Fuck. This was so not the time.

They threaded their way through the crowd, moving across the stuffy club that reeked of sweat, perfume, and stale beer. The main room branched off into a secondary bar area, where the music was just as deafening. No dancing, though, just tall tables scattered throughout the room.

As they walked past the bar, a familiar face caught Sullivan's eye. Ah, so this was Ethan's post. Neither he nor Liam so much as glanced at their colleague as they marched past him toward the saloon-style doors at the opposite end of the room.

With utter nonchalance, Ethan pushed away from the counter and shifted to the end of it, providing himself with a better vantage point of his teammates.

Sully raked a hand through his hair and tapped his ear to activate his mic. "About to make contact," he murmured without moving his lips.

"Copy," came Kane's voice. "Snipers are in position outside. Rookie, Trev, and I are on the street if you need backup."

He let his fingers drop and shoved both hands in his pockets, the epitome of casual as he and Liam approached the black-clad man barring the doors.

Liam raised his voice over the music. "I'm here to see Niko."

The guard's menacing expression didn't waver. "Name," he barked.

"Mac Mulligan." Liam's Boston accent became more pronounced as he spoke. "He's expecting me."

The guard clicked his black earpiece and relayed Liam's name. A second later, he moved to the side and gestured to the doors.

Liam took the lead and neither of them said a word as they marched down a corridor with fluorescent lighting. The bulbs flickered in and out, casting ghostly shadows on the shoddily painted walls. Man, this place was a shithole. Sully couldn't believe the Barrios cartel conducted most of its business in nightclubs like this one, but he supposed it made sense. Illegal operations required a front, and the club served as a legitimate business to conceal the not so legitimate activities of the scumbags who ran it.

At the end of the hall, another armed thug appeared. "Weapons," he said in a monotone.

Liam made an annoyed noise but didn't object. He simply reached inside his black suit jacket and slid his Beretta out of its holster. He handed it to the guard, then glanced at Sullivan, who pretended to balk. He'd known this was coming but he still had a part to play.

"I'm not giving up my gun," he protested.

Liam cast him an impatient look that bordered on disgust and was just caustic enough to startle Sullivan. He'd been warned that his friend would become a different person, but he'd never seen this kind of contempt in Liam's gaze, especially not directed at *him*.

"It's routine," Liam growled. "Give him your weapon. Now."

With feigned bluster, Sully disarmed and handed his gun over. Then, with a sullen look, he stood there like an obedient toddler while the guard patted him and Liam down. After the thug was satisfied that they weren't carrying any other weapons, he gestured for them to follow him.

"Niko will see you now."

Thirty seconds later, they were entering a dingy room that stank of sweat and urine. Three men sat at a round table in the center of the room, a deck of cards and a pile of poker chips littering the tabletop. Against the far wall, a half-naked woman was sprawled on a ratty couch. From the hazy look in her eyes it was obvious she was high on something.

And as fucked up as it was, Sully experienced a pang of . . . Jesus, envy. He hated himself for it, but that blissed-out look in the young woman's eyes called out to him like a siren's song.

He tore his gaze away from her and studied the rest of the room. There was one door, which led out to the alley behind the club. Liam had done business here before and knew the layout, so they'd come prepared—D was already out there, monitoring the alley. Two guards manned that door; two more were posted at the one they'd just entered from.

At their appearance, one of the men at the table rose to his feet. He had golden brown skin marred with pockmarks, a fat cigar sticking out the corner of his mouth, a gun in his hand, and a knife at his belt.

"Mac Mulligan," he drawled in accented English. "Welcome back."

"Niko Vega," Liam drawled back. "Long time."

As Liam held out his hand, a knot of tension formed between Sully's shoulder blades. He carefully watched Vega's expression, waiting to see what kind of welcome mat he'd be rolling out. According to the dossier Noelle's sources had compiled, Vega wasn't the head honcho of the Barrios cartel, but damn close to it. He was Isaac Barrios's second-in-command, running drugs through this club and the various whorehouses and bars the cartel owned throughout Guatana.

Noelle had also warned them that Vega had a sadistic streak, particularly when it came to women. Apparently he liked a little knife play with his sex, and rumor had it he'd accidentally killed several hookers during his violent fucking sessions because he hadn't realized how much blood they'd lost. Liam hadn't even blinked when Noelle had revealed that grisly tidbit, which told Sully that his friend had already known all about Vega's extracurricular activities.

After an interminable delay, Vega finally stepped forward and gave Liam's hand a hearty shake.

"Motherfucker!" he crowed. "You went and retired on me! Broke my heart." He paused, raising one bushy eyebrow. "And now you've come crawling back because . . . what is it you need, Mac? What brought you out of retirement?"

Liam grinned. "Retirement brought me out of retirement."

Again, that Boston inflection seemed thicker than usual. Sully suspected Liam was putting it on, that it was part of his role as Mac Mulligan, the American pimp who'd dreamed of dabbling in the drug world.

"Wicked boring," Liam went on. "I went back to the States, lived like a king for a few years, even got married."

Vega gave a robust laugh. "You? Married?"

"Divorced now. I was fuckin' bored, Niko. You know me—I'm not cut out for a life of leisure."

"Is that why you're here? You want back in the game?"

"Among other things."

"I'm intrigued." Vega narrowed his dark eyes at Sullivan. "Who's this?"

"I told Bobby all about him over the phone." Liam nodded at a silent man at the table. From the dossier, Sully recognized him as Roberto Silva, a Barrios enforcer. "This is Jake Sullivan, my new partner."

"Partner, huh? And what sort of business are you two boys running?"

Liam smirked. "What else? Sex." He gestured to one of the empty chairs. "May I sit?"

"By all means. Sit. Take a load off."

As Liam pulled out a chair, his gaze raked over the dark-haired girl on the couch. "Who's the bitch?"

"Pia." Vega's lips curved in a filthy smile. "Hot little thing, isn't she?"

"Very. Is she business or pleasure?"

"Both. She's Carlos Mendoza's little sister."

Sully had no idea who they were talking about, but Liam seemed to know. "No shit," he said in surprise. "Guess I've missed a lot since I've been gone. You're chummy with the Mendozas now?"

Vega threw his head back and released a roar of laughter. "Hardly. That motherfucker broke the rules and tried to steal a chunk of my territory. So I stole his sister." His expression was downright gleeful. "I fuck her every night and get Bobby here to film it. I send the tapes to Carlos and he can't do shit about it. *Dios*, Mulligan, she's got the tightest pussy I've ever fucked."

"Yeah?" Liam got a lewd look on his face.

Sullivan pretended to be unfazed, but inside he was more than a little ruffled. Liam was acting like a slime bag and he didn't fucking like it.

Vega laughed again. "I knew you'd like that. You always liked sticking your dick in a tight hole."

What? Jesus. What the hell had Boston done when he was undercover?

Vega snapped his fingers. "Pia, come here and give our guest a kiss hello."

Despite her cloudy expression, the girl on the couch still had enough of her mental faculties to heed Vega's orders, but her limbs lacked coordination as she stumbled off the cushions and made her way toward Liam. Once she reached him, she stood frozen in place, uncertainty on her face.

Sully's chest tightened. She was a pretty girl, not older than eighteen or nineteen. Her thin arms and legs were marred with bluish bruises, and she looked so unbelievably fragile standing there in nothing but her flimsy bra and panties. He wanted to rip off his jacket and wrap her up in it, shield her from the crude smiles of these men.

And Liam was one of those crude men. Spreading his legs, he patted one knee and said, "Come here, darling."

She hesitated.

"Go on," Vega urged.

Nobody in the room missed the steel in his tone.

Visibly swallowing, Pia awkwardly settled on Liam's knee. When he shifted slightly, she almost fell off, and her slender arms instantly wrapped around his neck for balance. Sully suspected Liam had done it on purpose.

"Well, aren't you a pretty little bitch," Liam murmured, tracing her delicate jaw with his thumb.

She shivered, and Sully knew damn well it wasn't out of desire. When his friend curled a hand over her jaw and drew her face closer, her trembling intensified.

It required serious effort to contain his repulsion as he watched Liam's lips close over Pia's rosebud mouth. The flash of tongue he glimpsed had him clenching both hands on his thighs. He breathed deeply in an attempt to calm himself, but it didn't work, because Liam's other hand was suddenly cupping one small tit. Then that brazen hand tugged the girl's bra down, and when her breast popped free, Liam pinched her nipple between his fingers.

Pia made a strangled sound of dismay, which summoned a chuckle from Liam and more raucous laughter from Vega.

"Told you—hot little thing," Vega teased.

"Oh yeah." Liam gave her breast one last squeeze, then smacked her hip as if she were an animal and ordered her off him.

Pia shuddered with unmistakable relief as she darted back to the couch.

"Shall we get back to business?" Vega said, his lips twitching.

"I suppose." Liam was grinning again. "Though I appreciate the distraction."

Vega clasped his hands on the table. His handgun lay inches from his right hand. Beside him, Bobby the enforcer was palming a silver Glock.

Sullivan felt naked without his own weapon, but he wasn't concerned about all the firepower he saw in the room. Along with Vega and Bobby's pistols, he and Liam were dealing with assault rifles from the door guards and a deadly-looking hunting knife in the hand of the third man at the table. Another enforcer, Sully suspected.

Didn't matter, though. If it came down to it, he could disarm one of those fuckers in a heartbeat.

"So what can the Barrios cartel do for you, Mac?" Liam reclined in his chair, the picture of relaxation. "Protection."

Vega chuckled. "You can buy rubbers at any bodega in the city. You don't need us for that."

One of the guards snorted.

"Not that kind of protection. As I mentioned, I have a new business venture. Jake and I are running a whorehouse in Toro."

Vega raised a brow. "Rivera's territory? Are you fucked in the head?"

"I didn't realize Rivera had laid claim to Toro until the transaction had already been brokered. Needless to say, this is a clusterfuck," Liam admitted. "The fuckers are playing power games with us, jacking up the price of protection and operating licenses."

Operating licenses? Sully swallowed a laugh. Well, fuck. Who woulda thought the cartels were so business savvy?

"It's fuckin' extortion. Highway robbery," Liam grumbled. "And I'm not putting up with that shit."

"I see. And what do you think I can do about it? Like I said, it's Rivera's territory."

"Then let's make it Barrios territory," Liam said carelessly.

Vega looked startled. "Meaning?"

"Meaning I'm here to propose we eliminate a mutual threat." Liam leaned forward, a feral glint in his eyes. "I want you to help me take out the Riveras."

A shocked silence fell over the room. Even the guards looked bewildered.

Finally Vega answered, his voice slow and laced with interest, "And how would we do that?"

"The Rivera Empire is already on shaky ground. Rivera Senior is dead. Word is his oldest son just got iced too. That means the younger son is in charge now— Benicio, who I'm told is a moron. How hard would it really be to eliminate him? And you know what happens when you cut off the snake's head. The rest of Rivera's people will either scatter or fight each other for power. The cartel will be in shambles."

Vega rubbed the stubble on his chin and repeated his earlier sentiment. "I'm intrigued."

"Good. I want you to be. So what do you say, Niko? You know I've got cash to spare. I'd be willing to part with some of it to hire a private military company if needed, trained mercs that could lay siege on those motherfuckers. Once Benicio and his lieutenants are eliminated, the Barrios cartel steps in and collects its spoils. You absorb what's left of the Riveras, and your territory is doubled, if not tripled."

"What do you get out of it?" Vega asked coolly.

"Sex."

"I'm flattered, but . . ."

Liam rolled his eyes. "Fuck off. You know what I mean. I want exclusive rights to the sex trade in your territory and whatever territory you get from the Riveras. Whorehouses, brothels, gentlemen's clubs—I want to be the only game in the market."

"I see," Vega said again.

"So? What do you think?"

"What do I think . . ."

As Vega trailed off thoughtfully, the tension returned to Sully's body. It stretched his back, pinched the nape of his neck. Shit, that wasn't good. As a soldier, he'd been trained never to ignore his instincts, and right now they were humming like a cheap air-conditioning unit.

"I think that sounds like a very good plan," Vega finished, smiling slightly. "And it's a plan I would be happy to take to Isaac . . . if I trusted the man who was proposing it."

Liam's features tightened. "What the fuck does that mean? You don't trust me? Since when?"

Vega's smile widened.

"You fuckin' know me, Niko." Liam's tone grew increasingly incensed. "Have I ever screwed you over?"

"No . . . Mac Mulligan has never screwed me over," Vega relented. He paused, cocking one brow as he fixed Liam with a toxic look. "But I'm not so certain about Liam Macgregor."

Sully froze.

Fuck.

Fuck, fuck, *fuck*.

They'd been made.

Chapter 21

Liam could have faked astonishment. Maybe voiced a denial. But he knew when an op had been compromised, and he wasn't one to waste time that could be used saving his own skin. Besides, men like Niko Vega weren't the type to *talk* through their issues. No, Vega's gun was already swinging upward, leaving Liam with very little time to react.

Fortunately, he and Sully didn't require more than a split second. One moment they were seated, the next they were diving in opposite directions, removing themselves as targets. As Liam slid onto the floor, he brought the third enforcer down with him, relieving the man of his knife.

Then, with perfect accuracy, he hurled the blade and sent it flying into the center of Vega's throat.

A gruesome gagging noise echoed in the room. Liam vaguely registered a red arc spurting from Vega's throat, but he was too busy taking cover to pay it much attention.

Almost instantly, bullets started flying. Sharp rifle blasts cracked in the air. Casings pinged off the floor. Chunks of plaster broke off the walls, raining down on Liam's head. He rolled over so that the enforcer's back was pressed to his chest, providing himself with a human shield when Bobby Silva fired at him. Silva ended up putting two bullets in his colleague's gut, and the muscular man jerked on top of Liam like a fish out of water, crushing him to the floor.

Breathing hard, he adjusted their angle so he could slip the man's gun from his holster. As Silva fired another round, Liam pushed the enforcer off him, rolled again, and shot at Bobby's kneecap.

The big man staggered, his groan of pain slicing through the gunfire. From the corner of his eye, Liam saw a blur of motion. Gray wool and a flash of blond. Sullivan had disarmed the guard at the door, taken out the other one, and was now opening fire on the ones at the exit.

The entire shoot-out lasted all of three seconds—the two guards dropped to the floor in a pool of blood at the same time that Liam blew Bobby's head off.

But the man whose knife and gun Liam had stolen wasn't dead yet, and the motherfucker suddenly possessed superhuman strength even while bleeding out. Before Liam could blink, the enforcer flew forward on his knees and head-butted Liam's forehead with enough force to make him see stars.

Something wet dripped down his face, sliding over his cheek. He tasted copper in his mouth and realized he was bleeding. The asshole had split his eyebrow. Awesome.

Fortunately, it didn't matter how much rage-induced strength the bastard had. What he *didn't* have was a weapon. Liam did. Two shots to the chest and one to the head, and the remaining Barrios thug crumpled to the dirty linoleum floor in a bloody heap.

The only sounds remaining in the room were Liam's steady breaths. Sullivan's soft footsteps as he walked to the back door. And something else. Something that made Liam's shoulders go rigid. Soft wheezing. Throaty gurgling. Terrified gasps.

He glanced over and spotted Pia curled up in a ball

on the couch. She was cradling her left arm, her bare skin soaked with blood.

Liam shot to his feet and ran over to her, but his heart sank the moment he reached her. Those gurgling noises could only mean one thing—she'd been shot in the lung, probably from an errant bullet.

"Boston," came Sully's sharp voice. "We gotta go."

"She's hurt," he called back. He dropped to his knees and gently moved her arm, cursing when he glimpsed the round bullet hole above her right breast.

"Easy, darling," he murmured in Spanish when she began to thrash and protest under his touch. "You'll make it worse."

As she went still, he tipped her body forward and searched her shoulders and back for an exit wound, but there was none. The bullet was still inside her, most likely lodged in her lung.

Fuck.

"Boston," Sully commanded.

His helpless gaze traveled from his friend to the bleeding woman on the couch. She would die any second . . . or she would spend several more agonizing minutes drowning in her own blood, choking on it. Either way, she wasn't going to make it.

With regret that sliced right down to his bones, he slowly brought the Glock to her left temple. He stroked her cheek with his free hand, rubbed her bottom lip, smoothed her damp hair back. Then he peered into her brown eyes, which were growing unfocused by the second.

"Close your eyes, darling," he whispered.

The words penetrated the state of agony she was in, because those delicate lids fluttered shut. After a beat, Liam closed his own eyes and pulled the trigger.

He flinched at the gunshot, then froze for several seconds, inwardly condemning himself despite knowing that he'd done the right thing. He took a breath, reminding himself that the girl would've died regardless. At least he'd given her a painless death.

Exhaling slowly, he got to his feet and hurried toward the door that Sullivan was holding open. When the two of them burst out into the dark alley, they were instantly joined by D and Ash.

"You okay?" the rookie asked, focusing his concerned gaze on Liam's face.

He swiped at the blood again. "Fine. Got head-butted by an asshole."

"What happened in there?" D barked.

"My cover was blown," he ground out. "Someone must have tipped them off."

"DEA?"

"No fuckin' idea. Maybe DEA, maybe Rivera. Either way, Vega knew who I was. He knew we were playing him."

"Any loose ends?" D cocked his head at the door.

"Nah, we took care of it," Sully answered.

D nodded, then swung around and took off walking. Without a word, they followed him to the edge of the alley, where two black Ducatis were waiting.

"The others are already on their way back to the base," Ash reported.

Since Liam and Sully's car was stashed two blocks away, Liam tapped D on the arm and said, "We'll meet you at the rendezvous. Thanks for the assist."

"Not that we needed it," Sully piped up. "Boston and I are superheroes, didn't you know?"

"Sure, Aussie, whatever you say." Rolling his eyes, D swung a leg over one of the bikes, revved the engine, and then he was gone.

Ash followed suit a moment later, chuckling as he sped off.

Liam glanced at Sully and then they were on the move again. Not quite at a run, but a brisk pace, because who the fuck knew what was happening back at the nightclub. He doubted anyone had heard the shots over the music, but one of the guards on the main floor could be scheduled to check in with Vega at any second. Someone could be walking into that room right now, discovering the gory scene, and calling for the cavalry.

They needed to be long gone before that.

With Sully in the lead, they raced down another alley, hopped a chain-link fence, and made a loop around the area to where they'd stashed their vehicle.

Drops of blood continued to trickle down Liam's face, soaking his lips, and maybe it made him a twisted motherfucker, but he welcomed the metallic flavor that coated his tongue. He welcomed the pain in his eyebrow. The stickiness of his palm when he wiped at the blood. The adrenaline still coursing in his veins. The way his heart was pounding, not from fear but a sick sense of excitement that someone might be chasing them.

It was such a stupid thought that he stumbled to a stop a few feet from the car, clutching his side as a wave of laughter overtook him.

"Boston?" Sully sounded both puzzled and amused as he stared at Liam doubled over. "You lose your bloody mind?"

"No," he choked out between laughs. "I'm pretty sure I found it."

"What the hell does that mean?"

"It means . . ." More laughter tickled his throat, making him gasp for air.

Jesus. This felt so good. So liberating.

He dragged his tongue over his bottom lip, licking away at the blood as he straightened up and met his friend's eyes. "I missed this."

Sully's mouth twitched. "Missed what? Getting shot at?"

"Yeah. I did. It's fucked up, I know, but security sucks balls, Sully. I hate it. I hate my job. I . . ." He began to laugh again, rubbing his fists over both eyes. They were starting to water. "I miss the action. I miss the guns. I miss the blood. I miss the—"

He stopped, his breath hitching as he realized Sully's face was only inches away from him. His hands dropped to his sides. His heart began pounding for a whole new reason. The look in Sullivan's eyes was . . . familiar. It was how he'd looked in Paris after he'd guessed that Liam was attracted to him. And rather than recoil in horror, Sully's eyes had taken on this exact gleam. Seductive. Hot. Lusty.

Liam's vocal cords seized. He didn't know what was happening right now. Couldn't make sense of it. All he knew was that Sully's large hand was moving toward his face . . .

His whole body swayed when Sully ran his index finger over the blood staining Liam's lips. When he drew back, the pad of that finger was stained red.

The air seemed to . . . change. It thickened. Liam didn't move. Couldn't move. But Sully *was* moving. Not his hand this time, but his mouth, traveling closer and closer, until, finally, warm lips collided with Liam's.

Jesus Christ.

What the fuck was happening right now? What the—

A strangled sound slipped out when he felt his friend's tongue prod the seam of his lips. The surprised noise caused his mouth to open, allowing that wet tongue to enter with a greedy, savage thrust that sent a shock wave of lust to Liam's cock.

Despite his thickening erection, he didn't return the kiss. He didn't swirl his tongue over Sully's. Didn't grip the man's shoulders or breathe in that familiar spicy scent. His mind was racing as fast as his heartbeat. Why the fuck was Sullivan kissing him? After all the protests Sully had put up, all his efforts to push Liam away, all the times he'd insisted that giving in to the attraction would destroy their friendship . . . after all that, he suddenly had his tongue in Liam's mouth?

As a dose of anger injected into his bloodstream, he growled against Sully's hot mouth, then planted both hands on his friend's chest and gave a hard shove.

"Don't fucking do that," he snapped.

Gray eyes widening, Sully staggered backward, looking as stunned as Liam felt. "Shit," he whispered. "Fuck. I'm . . . sorry."

"Yeah." Liam couldn't taste the blood anymore. It'd been replaced with the sour taste of bitterness clinging to his throat. "Yeah, you should be."

Then he pushed past Sullivan, threw open the driver's door, and got into the car.

Even though he was in desperate need of sleep, Sullivan was doing his bloody damnedest to avoid his and Liam's room. Since they'd returned to the bunker, he'd spent thirty minutes shamelessly flirting with Juliet, another forty-five playing dice with some of the Guatanan soldiers, and now he was walking into Morgan's hospital room despite the fact that it was past one a.m.

He'd been checking in on the boss several times a day since he'd arrived in Guatana. Not to say good-bye, because fuck that. James Morgan wasn't going to die. The visits were usually quick—he just poked his head in and ordered Jim to wake the fuck up. But tonight Sully approached the bed and sank down in the chair beside it.

Morgan's face was pale, his broad body motionless.

The doctors had taken him off the drug that had been keeping him in his comatose state and they had no clue why he hadn't regained consciousness yet, chalking it up to one of those unexplained medical mysteries. Still, the longer Morgan remained out of it, the harder it was for Sully to control his worry.

He didn't reach for Morgan's hand. Nope. The boss would kick the shit out of him if he woke up and found his operative clutching at his fingers in some wimpy nursemaid act. But Sully did lean closer to rest his forearms on the edge of the thin mattress, giving Morgan a pleading look that the man couldn't see.

"You need to wake up. Seriously, mate, you're starting to freak everyone out."

No response. Not even a twitch.

Something akin to desperation bubbled in his throat. "You can't keep doing this, lying here like a sack of potatoes. I don't know what's happening in your stubborn brain right now, but just open your eyes, man. Your daughter needs you. Your scary-as-fuck wife needs you. And I need . . ." The helplessness spilled over. "I need to get the fuck out of here," he choked out. "I need you to wake up so I can get out of this goddamn country. So I can get away from . . ."

Liam.

It always came back to Liam.

Sullivan couldn't be around his old friend anymore. The temptation was too strong. The longer they were around each other, the greater the danger that he would do something stupid.

Like kiss the guy again.

He swallowed a silent groan. He still didn't know what had come over him earlier. It was like the devil on his shoulder had reared its horny head, taken possession of Sully's tongue, and shoved it inside Liam's mouth. There was no good reason for why he'd done it. Liam had just looked so bloody sexy. Literally bloody— his face streaked crimson, blood dripping from his bottom lip. And Sully had wanted to *taste* him. To be part of whatever feral experience Liam had been going through in that moment.

Two years ago, it had been Sullivan who'd pushed Liam away. Sullivan who'd insisted how stupid it'd be to let lust ruin a friendship that mattered so much to both of them.

Tonight, it had been Liam's turn to put a stop to it. Only, Sully knew his friend hadn't done it for the sake of their friendship.

Liam hadn't wanted that kiss. The bloke had spent the past two years in Boston. He was straight as an arrow again, sticking his cock in a woman, not a man. And that was how it was supposed to be.

"I can't be around him," he confessed to Morgan. "I can't be here anymore."

Jim didn't answer. The only sound in the small room was the steady hiss of the man's breathing tube as it moved air in and out of his lungs.

Sully curled his fingers, bunching the starched sheet tight between them. "I *kissed* him," he bit out. "I kissed Liam tonight."

A squeak came from the doorway.

His head swiveled toward the sound.

Bloody hell.

Cate was standing there. Her eyes, the same dark shade of blue as her father's, were wide with shock.

Sully rose from his chair with uncharacteristic embarrassment. After one last glance at Jim, he slowly walked over to Cate.

"You didn't hear that," he murmured wryly.

"Not a thing," she murmured back.

He nodded in gratitude and stepped toward the threshold, but Cate stopped him before he could leave. She latched a small, warm hand onto his forearm. "Sully," she said softly. "Are you all right?"

"Of course, love." He kept his tone light. "I'm always all right."

Before she could call bullshit, he ducked out of the room and made his escape.

Except now he was right back to where he'd been two hours ago—trying to find reasons to avoid Liam, who would definitely want to talk about what happened earlier.

Or hell, maybe he wouldn't. Sully was having trouble reading the guy. They used to be able to tell each other anything, but these days they were acting as if they were total strangers.

Not tonight, though. Tonight, Liam hadn't felt like a stranger. When their mouths had collided in that mind-melting kiss, the only thought running through Sullivan's mind had been *home*.

He'd felt like he'd come home.

His legs were unusually wobbly as he trudged toward the barracks. The door to their room was closed and no light spilled from underneath it. Maybe he'd gotten lucky and Liam was asleep. God knew he ought to catch some shut-eye himself. They'd just executed three back-to-back missions in the span of three days. Eventually even the best soldiers needed to rest and Sully's aching body and grainy eyes warned him that he was pushing himself too hard.

Gulping, he turned the knob and entered the dark room.

Shit.

He didn't need to see the shadowy figure sitting up in bed to know that Liam was awake. He'd always been able to sense Liam's energy. Crazy, but true. Every part of him was highly attuned to Liam Macgregor, which was probably why they worked so well together. Why Kane and Trevor and Morgan always paired them up in the field.

As his vision adjusted to the darkness, he made out the accusatory gaze being aimed at him.

"You done avoiding me?" Liam asked politely.

He went over to his bed and sat down. "I wasn't avoiding you."

"Bullshit."

Sully stifled a curse. "Okay, fine. I was avoiding you. Is that what you want to hear?"

"No. I want to hear what the fuck you were thinking earlier."

He dragged one hand through his hair. It was shorter these days, so he couldn't get a good grip. Which sucked, because right now he felt like tearing it out by the roots.

"I wasn't thinking," he mumbled.

"Really? That's your answer?" A mocking note colored Liam's voice.

"What other fucking answer do you want, Boston?" The powerless sensation he'd been fighting all day returned in full force. "That's my MO, right? I don't think before I act. Never have, probably never will."

"So there's no explanation for why you decided to stick your tongue down my throat other than you weren't thinking?"

Sully's jaw stiffened. He didn't like Liam's tone or the hostility poisoning the air. He and Liam never fought, or at least they hadn't in the past.

"I felt like it, all right? I don't know what else to say. I felt like it and I acted on it and I'm sorry for that." As exhaustion washed over him, Sullivan bent over to unlace his boots. He kicked the first one off, speaking without looking at Liam. "I get it. You didn't want it. My bad. I won't do it again." He shucked the other shoe. "So go to bed and close your eyes and if you're still feeling freaked out, go ahead and jerk off. Think about pussy or whatever it is that gets you off. I need to sleep."

He whipped off his shirt. When his head popped free, he was startled to find Liam looming over him. He hadn't even heard the other man move, which was a testament to Liam's training.

"Are you fuckin' kidding me? You think I pushed you away because I was freaked out? We're long past that, Aussie. Kissing a man doesn't scare me."

Shock filtered through him. He didn't know what to say to that, but fortunately Liam didn't give him a chance.

"I wasn't freaked out. I was pissed."

"Pissed?" Sully echoed hoarsely.

"Yeah, pissed."

"At what?"

"At *you*, you goddamn asshole! The last time we were in this position, you all but threw me to the curb. You told me you didn't want to get involved. You told me if we fucked it would be like lighting a match to our friendship and setting it on fire. Remember that, Sully?"

He could see his friend's broad frame shaking with anger. Feel the heat of those blue eyes as they blazed at him.

"So what the fuck changed?" Liam snapped. "Suddenly it's okay for us to go there? Suddenly it won't ruin our friendship?"

"What friendship?" he roared back.

Liam jerked as if he'd been struck, but Sully didn't give a shit, because he was angry now too. He rapidly shot to his feet, advancing on Liam until their faces were inches apart.

He didn't miss the way the man's gaze darted down to his bare chest, resting briefly on the horseshoe-shaped scar on Sully's biceps. Liam had sewn those stitches himself. In Dublin, after shrapnel from a car bomb had torn off a chunk of Sully's flesh. The scar was just a reminder of what happened later that night—Liam sliding into bed with him . . . his big hand circling Sully's cock . . . jerking him off to one of the most intense orgasms of his life.

He knew Liam was thinking about it too, because a spark of heat lit his eyes.

It triggered an answering spark in Sully's groin, which he forced himself to ignore. "We don't have a friendship," he said flatly. "We haven't spoken in a year, haven't seen each other in two. So I repeat—what friendship, Boston?"

They were both breathing heavily. Liam cleared his throat, but his voice was still hoarse when he said, "You're right."

Sully blinked.

"We have no friendship. We have nothing." Liam shook his head. "So I guess that means there's nothing stopping us from doing *this*."

Liam erased the rest of the distance between them and slammed their mouths together.

The kiss was hot, primal. No tenderness or finesse. Just the hungry joining of their mouths, the reckless battle of their tongues. Sully shuddered when Liam palmed his chest—not to shove, but to caress. Long fingers glided over hard ridges of muscle, calloused fingertips skimming Sully's nipples before sliding down to his waist. Strong hands dug into his flesh hard enough to bring a sting of pain.

Jesus. Sully had never been manhandled like this

before and he couldn't deny that he enjoyed it. *Craved* it, especially from Liam.

This man was a bloody force to be reckoned with when he allowed himself to let go. Liam's Catholic upbringing had required him to tamp down his base urges for most of his life. Sully had helped him unleash them when he'd invited Liam to spend the summer on his yacht. He'd lured the man into raunchy sexual experiences, and he couldn't deny that witnessing Liam give in to the wild streak he'd always kept tightly reined had turned Sully on something fierce.

And tonight . . . he'd loved the sight of Liam's face covered in blood, loved seeing the man surrender to the joy that violence brought him.

But *this*? His friend's greedy mouth pressed against his . . . the way Liam sucked on his tongue and then bit it . . . It was almost too much.

When Liam's hand shifted and his fingers grazed the waistband of Sully's cargo pants, it triggered a bout of panic. "What the hell are you doing?" Sully ground out.

"What does it look like I'm doing?"

He swallowed rapidly, but it didn't help to erase the flood of moisture that pooled in his mouth, making it impossible to speak.

"We're both gonna go our separate ways the moment we take out Rivera and make sure Morgan is safe. Chances are, we're never gonna lay eyes on each other again. So all those fears you had about ruining our friendship? Forget them, Sully. There's nothing to fuckin' ruin."

Pain arrowed into his heart. No, that couldn't be true. That couldn't—he sucked in a breath when Liam undid the button of his pants.

"Boston . . ." Those two syllables came out on a wheeze.

"Shut up."

Sully's brain damn near imploded when he felt a strong grip around his cock. Liam gave him a slow, measured stroke, twisting the head before gliding back down to the base. There was no tentativeness in the touch. It was confident, deliberate.

Suspicion pricked Sullivan's chest, but he didn't get a chance to dwell on the odd sensation because Liam was pushing him backward, tugging him down until Sully's ass hit the mattress. A hot, eager mouth descended on him, sucking him so deep that he fell back on his elbows, weak with shock and desire.

Jesus motherfucking Christ. So good. So bloody good.

Liam sucked him down to the base with skill that astonished him. Sully knew he was well endowed. Most women—and men—couldn't handle all of him, but Liam seemed to have no trouble. Which only triggered another jolt of wariness.

"You've done this before," Sully choked out.

The other man lifted his head and arched one dark eyebrow. "So what if I have?" Then he licked a hot circle around the head of Sully's dick and drew him deep again.

As jealousy speared into him, a million questions burned at Sullivan's tongue. When? Who? How many times? But he wasn't able to voice any of them because Liam was doing the most incredible things to his body.

His eyes rolled to the top of his head as his friend fisted his shaft and gave it a slow pump. Heat tingled in the base of his spine. It had been so bloody long since he'd had someone's mouth on him. Someone's tongue tracing the underside of his shaft, licking its way down to his balls. And it was made all the hotter because it was Liam's mouth. Liam's tongue.

It broke his fucking heart to think that the only reason Liam was doing this was because he thought there was nothing left between them. That their bond had been severed. But that didn't stop Sully from cupping the back of Liam's head and urging the man to take him deeper.

The unspoken command didn't get him the desired result. Liam simply released him, letting his lips hover over the tip. "You want me to suck this?" he taunted. "You want me to suck it hard and fast until you're coming down my throat?"

Lust arrowed a path straight to Sully's balls. Who the fuck was this man? Where was Liam Macgregor?

"Yes," he said weakly. "Yes, that's what I want."

"Beg for it." Liam's voice was silky, low.

He didn't know whether to laugh or cry. This was his doing. The Liam he'd met in New York all those years ago wouldn't have dreamed of saying shit like this. Sully was the one who'd unleashed the man's filthy side, and now he was paying the price for it, gasping and trembling as Liam jacked him in a fast stroke punctuated by a tight squeeze, hard enough to bring black dots to his vision.

"Beg," Liam growled.

He was helpless. Mindless. "Suck me." His voice rang with anguish, his throat tight with desire. "Please, Boston, suck me off."

With a dark chuckle, Liam lowered his head again. One hand maintained its grip around the shaft, while the other slid lower, wicked fingers brushing over a sensitive spot that had Sully's hips arching upward. Then Liam swallowed him up again and his entire world was reduced to *more* and *oh fuck* and *don't stop*.

He couldn't breathe. Couldn't think. Couldn't do anything but pump his hips and thrust into Liam's hungry mouth. The impossibly tight suction was almost too much to bear. And that finger, Jesus Christ, that finger . . .

The orgasm sizzled up Sully's spine, pulsing through his body in powerful waves that had him groaning with abandon. He didn't give a fuck if the entire base heard him. It felt too damn good.

Too. Damn. Good.

Liam stayed with him until the end, eventually slowing his strokes and easing the pressure of his tongue. Teasing, lazy licks guided Sullivan back to earth, and when Liam raised his head and swiped his tongue over his wet lips, another shudder overtook Sully's body. Holy fuck. That was the hottest thing he'd ever seen in his life.

Neither of them spoke for a second.

"That was . . ." He trailed off. There were no words to describe how amazing he felt right now.

The other man looked smug. Hell, he had every right to look like that. He'd just sucked Sullivan's brains right out of his cock, so deftly and assertively that he deserved a bloody medal.

Sully's shoulders tightened abruptly. Thinking about Liam's skilled blow-job technique sent another hot streak of jealousy through him. "You said you've done this before," he muttered. "With who?"

Liam's expression grew veiled. "No one you know."

The answer didn't appease him. The jealousy was in his throat now, scorching his esophagus. "Who?" he pressed.

"Doesn't matter." Liam made a disparaging noise under his breath. "What? You're pissed? Jealous? You're the one who told me you didn't want to be my sexual guinea pig, remember? You said if I wanted to experiment with dudes, I should find someone else to do it with. So I did."

With a harsh laugh, the dark-haired man got to his feet and headed for the door.

As it clicked shut behind him, Sully lay there on his back, his cock still out and semi-hard, his heart ravaged by the thought of Liam with anyone else.

Chapter 22

"I can feel you judging me," Cate said without turning to look at Ash. She kept her eye glued to the viewfinder of her camera, as she'd been doing for the last hour.

Against Ash's numerous protests, Noelle had assigned him and Cate to city surveillance this morning. He clearly wasn't happy about it but Cate didn't give a shit. She was finally being given the opportunity to go out in the field and she wasn't about to let Ash's sulking spoil that for her.

"I haven't said a word," he grumbled.

"You don't have to. The air is full of your disapproval."

Rather than deny it, he fell silent.

Good. She hoped he continued to keep his mouth shut because in such close quarters it would be kind of hard to pull her arm back far enough to land a good punch.

For the past hour, the two of them had been kneeling in a tiny roof alcove of a three-story building overlooking the city center, searching for signs of Rivera from the rooftop. Ironically, the unrest in Guatana was making it easier to do their jobs because most of the streets were empty. The once bustling capital showed little signs of commerce. Most of the businesses were closed, except for government and military offices, and since few people had money, there was no foot traffic in the market.

So far, the only people Cate and Ash had seen were employed by the state. Felipe Aguilar was not one of those people. The day after his interrogation, D had been dispatched to take inventory of what was left inside the shack where they'd left Aguilar. He'd reported back that word on the street was that a high-ranking official had been garroted in a slum along with his wife and another woman. The other woman was likely a plant by either Rivera's cartel or another cartel.

Cate was surprised nobody had claimed responsibility for Aguilar's death yet, but Noelle had sagely told her that no matter how much power you had, it was never a good idea to piss off the military. And at the moment, the Guatanan military was the only source of authority left in the country.

Beside her, Ash shifted his sniper rifle and Cate tried to focus on anything other than the sexy flex of his biceps. Damn him. He was making it impossible to concentrate. Plus, he smelled amazing—soap, lemon, and a hint of spice. She wanted to lean over and lick his arm.

Get a grip, an internal voice warned.

Right. She couldn't be thinking these kinds of thoughts. If anything, she ought to be fantasizing about taking her camera and smashing it across the top of his head.

"You enjoying this?" he mocked. "Sitting up here and having the sun bake you into the tar?"

"Better than sitting at home," she answered coolly, as if they were inside a fancy hotel having afternoon tea instead of sweating like two pigs in August.

"This is boring as shit. I'd rather be in air-conditioning, drinking beer."

"Then go do that," she snapped. "Is this what stake-outs with you are like? No wonder Noelle put me with you. No one else probably wants to work with you."

"I'm awesome to work with. *Everyone* wants to work with me."

"I can't see why. You're crabbier than an old lady. And when you're not complaining, you're brooding so hard I'm getting a headache from it."

"Then leave," he muttered.

Argh. All this arguing and sniping and waiting was turning her inside out. Maybe she shouldn't have fought so hard to come on this stakeout. Being around Ash was torture. He looked too good and smelled too good and the simmering anger and violence he was radiating only whetted her appetite and made her want him more.

She wished she could shut off her hormones, make her body see that Ash wasn't worth its time, but her desire stubbornly refused to subside. And whenever his green eyes so much as flicked in her general direction, her heart did an infuriating flip.

What was it she'd told Liam the other day? Oh right. That hearts sucked.

At the thought of Liam, Cate suddenly remembered what she'd overheard in her father's room late last night, and decided that yes, hearts certainly did suck. The anguish on Sullivan's face when he'd confessed to kissing Liam, to needing to get far away from the man, had been almost unbearable to see. Ash had admitted to her once that he suspected there was something going on between those two, but she hadn't really believed it until now.

"What's the matter? Can't think of a bitchy enough comeback?"

The taunt made her stomach clench. She truly did hate fighting with him. "I'm all out of comebacks," she said with a sigh.

"Yeah? Then why do you still look mad?"

"I'm not mad." She paused. "I'm sad."

Her quiet admission caused his features to soften. "What's wrong?"

"Nothing. I was just thinking about . . ." She shook her head. "Forget it."

"Tell me what you were thinking about," he pressed, a note of intensity in his voice.

"If you must know, I was thinking about Sullivan and Liam and how bad I feel for them."

A furrow creased his strong brow. "Why's that?"

"Because . . ." She let out a tired breath. "Because I think they're in love and it makes me sad that they can't tell each other that, okay?"

Ash looked startled. "Oh. Ah, okay."

"You disagree?"

"No. I don't. I think your assessment is spot on. Those two have been dancing around each other since the day I joined the team."

"Four years," she murmured. "That means they've been fighting this . . . whatever it is . . . for four years. And my dad and Noelle fought each other for *twenty* years. Can you imagine? Not allowing yourself to be with the person you love for that long? Noelle was—" She stopped, her breath hitching as something occurred to her.

"What is it?" Ash's voice was low, gentle.

"I just realized . . ." Cate swallowed to moisten her suddenly dry throat. "Noelle was seventeen when she first met Jim. He was twenty-five."

Ash's eyes went shuttered but not before Cate glimpsed a flicker of emotion in them. She knew he was reading between the lines, seeing the parallels she hadn't intended to draw. But she couldn't deny how spot-on the comparison was. She'd met Ash when she was seventeen. He'd been twenty-five.

Were they destined to follow in Jim and Noelle's

footsteps? Allow the hatred between them to stew and fester until they spent their days fantasizing about ways to kill each other? And then, twenty years later, finally drop their guards and fall in love again, both of them regretting all the time they'd wasted?

Granted, to fall in love *again* meant that they were in love *now*. Which they weren't. Or at least, Ash wasn't. Cate wasn't sure how she felt about him anymore, but yes, she had loved him at one point.

He'd never loved her, though. To him, she'd been nothing but a little girl with no experience—wasn't that what he'd told her the night she'd thrown herself at him?

"Cate," he started, his voice hoarse.

Her pulse sped up. "What is it?"

"I—" He stopped, his eyes narrowing. "Hey, isn't that Camila Rivera?"

His words were like a cold shower. "Where?"

"Five o'clock, near the bank building."

She swung her head toward the bank, clicking her camera to take multiple shots of the slender brunette in high heels and a form-fitting dress. "Might be, but it's hard to tell when all we can see is her profile."

The woman turned just then, and Cate snapped several more pictures, excitement thrumming in her blood.

"It's her," she confirmed.

Ash lowered his gun. "You sure?"

She nodded emphatically. "Ninety-nine percent sure. It'll be a hundred once I blow up the pictures for a better look."

Without another word, Ash sat up and started dismantling his gun.

"What are you doing?" she demanded, her annoyance rising. "You don't believe me?"

"What? No, I'm packing up because we're going to follow her."

"We are?"

A burst of happiness replaced the knot in her chest. She couldn't believe he wasn't going to force her to go back to the base while he finished the recon on his own. He was actually trusting her to be a part of this.

"Yep," he said. "Get your gear and let's go."

She fought a teeny jolt of suspicion. "Just like that?"

"You second-guessing yourself?" he asked as he snapped his rifle case shut.

Cate shook her head slowly. "No. I'm right. It's definitely her."

He shrugged. "Then let's roll."

Liam dunked his head under the shower of the barracks' communal locker room, but the hot water sliding down his naked body didn't do a damn thing in easing the tension he'd been riddled with since returning from surveillance duty with Ethan.

With every lead relating to Rivera's whereabouts leading to a dead end, the team was now running reconnaissance throughout the city in the hopes that Rivera might surface somewhere. But although Liam and Ethan had watched the market for hours today, there'd been no sign of the cartel leader.

Still, Liam would've been happy to sit on that rooftop all morning, day and night if it meant avoiding this base. He'd had to choke down his disappointment when Cate and Ash arrived to relieve him and Ethan, leaving them no choice but to come back to base and report to Noelle.

The queen of assassins was getting increasingly frustrated with the lack of progress they were making. She wanted Rivera dead for what he'd done to Jim and Cate, and the longer he stayed out of her reach, the more unpredictable she became. Liam wasn't sure he wanted to be around when she finally lost her trademark cool.

He reached for the bar of soap in the built-in tray on the tiled wall and started lathering up. He was just rinsing himself clean when footsteps sounded from the door.

Anyone but Sullivan. For fuck's sake, let it be anyone but—

It was Sullivan.

Yeah. Somehow that didn't surprise him. After what went down between them last night, he'd known that Sully would eventually track him down.

Their eyes met across the steam-filled room. Liam's throat ran dry as Sullivan flicked the lock on the door.

"Really, mate? You seriously think you can suck my cock and then walk away like that?"

Sully took a step. He wore camo pants and a white T-shirt, but the clothes didn't stay on for long. As Liam watched in dry-mouthed dismay, the man peeled off his shirt, exposing his heavy, muscular chest. Then he kicked off his boots and removed his pants.

Liam's heart stuttered. Sully wasn't wearing any boxers. He was buck-naked, all golden skin and rippled muscles and an impressive erection that stirred Liam's groin.

Ignoring the pile of clothes at his feet, Sully stalked forward in predatory strides.

By the time Sully reached him, Liam's erection was at full mast. Neither man addressed their state of arousal. Their gazes remained locked.

"Where'd you sleep last night?" Sully's voice was smooth as cream and laced with accusation.

"I crashed in the comm room. Left at dawn for the city with Ethan."

The big blond man nodded.

Liam didn't know what that meant. And he was valiantly forcing himself not to look at his friend's crotch.

No, his *former* friend's crotch. The days of their tight-knit friendship were long gone—that was the only reason Liam had allowed himself to succumb to temptation last night.

He wouldn't have touched Sully if the man hadn't made it abundantly clear that there would be no consequences. No friendship to ruin, no awkwardness to deal with. Liam had no doubt Sully would disappear right after this job, the way he always disappeared. He'd run off and hide on his boat, where he'd pretend he didn't give a shit about the world.

"What do you care where I went?" Liam asked quietly. "You looked more than satisfied before I left last night."

"Satisfied?" Sully made a disgruntled sound. "Why? Because I came in your mouth?"

His cock twitched at the dirty memory.

"You think I just rolled over and fell asleep?"

"Didn't you?"

"No, mate, I didn't."

With feigned nonchalance, Liam turned to face the shower, letting the water soak his face. He rubbed his palms over his cheeks and then slicked his wet hair back. "Why's that?" he asked without looking over.

"Because we weren't done last night." There was a pause. "We're not done now."

He jumped when he felt a warm, male hand on the small of his back. Then, before he could blink, Sullivan twisted him around and pressed him up against the tiled wall, his mouth landing on Liam's in a harsh kiss.

The greedy stroke of Sully's tongue sent lust surging through his blood, and he was gasping for air by the time the man released him. Gray eyes, burning with desire, pierced Liam's face, speeding up his pulse. This was such a stupid idea. It would lead nowhere. It always led nowhere. But he still wanted it. He wanted it more than he wanted his next breath.

From the hot look in Sully's eyes, he wanted the same damn thing.

Without a word, he slowly brought his mouth back to Liam's, but instead of another tongue-tangling kiss, he dragged his tongue over Liam's top lip and lapped at the droplets of water clinging to it.

Liam shivered.

Sully chuckled.

"You made me beg last night," the blond man murmured, bringing his lips close to Liam's ear. "I don't like to beg. But I did. For you. And now you're going to do it for me."

He shuddered when sharp teeth nipped at his earlobe. Oh sweet Jesus.

The temperature in the shower spiked about a hundred degrees and it had nothing to do with the hot water pouring from the spray or the steam hanging in the air. Breathing hard, Liam tracked the lazy motion of Sullivan's hand as it glided down his body and wrapped around his cock.

The strong grip made him moan. "Sully," he started.

"Shut up." Sullivan gave a firm stroke that indeed shut Liam up.

He stared into the other man's eyes as that hand began to move in a slow, torturous rhythm. Base to tip, squeezing, caressing, fondling. Sully dragged his thumb over the little slit on the sensitive head and toyed with the moisture pooled there, teasing and rubbing until Liam's knees grew weak.

A hot mouth latched onto his neck, a soft hiss of breath that brought goose bumps to his flesh.

"We're not friends," Sully rasped. "Not anymore."

"I know." It pained him to say it, but it was true. Or at least it felt true.

"You want to know what we are?" Sully's breath tickled his throat.

He gave a helpless groan when Sully bit down on the hypersensitive tendons there. Oh fuck. His cock swelled in Sully's hand. He was actually close to coming.

The other man seemed to sense that because he slowed the pace of his strokes. "Want to know what we are?" he repeated.

"What are we?" Liam managed to ask through the gravel in his throat.

"We're just two blokes who want to fuck each other's brains out."

He sucked in a breath. His hips shot out involuntarily, thrusting his dick hard into Sully's fist. With a filthy smile, Sully released him.

And then he sank to his knees.

Liam glanced down and immediately went lightheaded. His gaze soaked in every detail: the gray eyes peering up at him, the moisture clinging to Sully's chiseled features, the dark-blond stubble shadowing that strong jaw.

Sullivan Port personified sex. He oozed it. And he was really fuckin' good at it. Liam had seen this man make dozens of women scream in ecstasy.

His mind suddenly flashed back to the last threesome they'd indulged in, conjuring up the memory of Sully's face buried between a redhead's legs. She'd been gobbling up Liam's cock at the time, her moans vibrating through his shaft. He remembered the way she'd writhed in mindless pleasure as Sully's tongue flicked her clit. The way she'd thrashed and squirmed and begged Sully to make her come.

Now that tongue was on *him*, circling the head of his cock, bringing him pleasure he'd never imagined. He was aching. He wanted to thrust deep, wanted to fuck Sully's mouth and shoot down his throat. But Sully had other ideas. He tortured the tip with featherlight licks, while his big fist squeezed the shaft, preventing Liam from pushing into his mouth.

Low, tormented noises rang in the steamy air. It took Liam a second to realize they were coming from him. He was shaking with need, so consumed by it he could barely stay upright.

"Sully," he said in agony.

The man didn't reply. He couldn't—his lips were wrapped tightly around the head of Liam's cock.

"You're driving me crazy," Liam groaned.

Now those lips curved in a smile, and then, with his gaze fixed on Liam's, Sully took him in one inch at a time.

"Oh fuck," he croaked.

The suction. The heat. He was buried so far down Sully's throat that every time the man swallowed it sent shock waves up Liam's dick. But just as he began to move his hips, Sully retreated.

"Don't stop, damn it."

Husky laughter rippled in the shower as Sully tilted his head. "Beg."

Oh Christ.

"Please," Liam said weakly.

He shuddered when Sully cupped his balls and began fondling them, languidly, as if he had all the time in the world.

"Please. Make me come."

Sully laughed again.

Liam's cock bobbed impatiently, seeking the man's mouth, but when he tried to guide it back to where he wanted it most, Sullivan turned his cheek. He pressed his lips to Liam's thigh and bit him again.

Liam let out a strangled groan. *"Please."*

"Sure, baby, whatever you want."

The careless response startled him but he didn't have time to gripe about the mind games Sully was playing because that wicked mouth was taking him deep again.

And that tongue . . . it was scraping along his shaft, licking and torturing.

And that hand . . .

And that finger . . .

He froze when the tip of Sully's finger breached the one place he'd yet to grant anyone access to. Not even Joe, the man he'd hooked up with in Boston, had touched him this way.

"Relax," Sully whispered.

Even over the water running, every sound in the room seemed to be magnified. Liam's shallow breaths. His pounding heart. The wet suction of Sully's mouth.

And all the while, that finger kept prodding. Maybe if he weren't so distracted by the fact that his cock was stuffed down Sully's throat, he would have protested, but right now he couldn't muster up a single objection. This was too . . . fuckin' . . . good. Liam didn't expect to like it, but when that finger slipped inside him and rubbed a particular spot, the pleasure was so intense he lost his footing.

Sullivan abruptly pulled his mouth away. "Easy," he warned, reaching up to grasp Liam's waist to steady him before resuming the task of sucking Liam dry.

There were no strokes of the hand this time, just a hot mouth sliding over him and a talented finger teasing that spot deep inside, over and over, until Liam gasped in pleasure.

"I'm coming," he ground out.

Sully responded with a hum of approval as he drank up Liam's release.

Holy mother of God. It was the most powerful climax of his life. The best blow job of his life. Nobody had ever come close to making him feel this way. To leaving him so limp and sated he wanted to slide down to the floor and collapse in a happy heap.

Wiping his mouth with the back of his hand, Sully got to his feet and flashed a cocky smile. He was still harder than steel, his cock jutting proudly, and although Liam's mouth watered at the sight, he didn't reach out to touch that massive erection.

Instead, he searched the other man's face and whispered, "What the fuck are we doing, Sully?"

"I don't know," his friend admitted.

"You know it's not going to go anywhere."

"I know."

Neither of them sounded convinced. Liam wasn't sure why that was. Of course this wouldn't go anywhere. They'd part ways as usual and pretend it never happened.

His heart ached at the thought.

"I don't do relationships, Boston."

The hoarse confession triggered a jolt of shock.

"I hurt people," Sully went on. "I get bored and my eye wanders and . . . and then I hurt people. It's easier to walk away before it gets to that point."

Liam adopted a careless tone. "You can't hurt me, Aussie. Because we're nothing to each other, remember?"

"Right."

Tension gathered in the air, thicker than a radiation cloud. Liam didn't know what to say. Didn't know if there was anything *to* say. But even if he'd managed to come up with something, he didn't get the chance to voice it because of the sudden commotion in the hallway.

"You can't stop me. Damn it, Trev, I need to go!"

"You're not going anywhere. That's what they fucking want—to draw us out!"

Just like that, any traces of lust or regret or discomfort were extinguished. Liam charged out of the shower area with Sullivan hot on his heels. It sounded like Trevor and Isabel arguing out there, and those two never raised their voices at each other.

Liam grabbed the towel he'd left on the bench and dried off as fast as he could, but his body was still damp as he shrugged into his shirt and shoved his pants up to his hips. Sully dressed in a hurry beside him. Neither man bothered with boots or socks. They just ran barefoot to the door.

They flew out to see Trevor and Isabel facing off in the middle of the hall. Trevor looked upset, but not half as upset as his wife, whose face was ashen and whose body was visibly trembling.

"I have to go," she insisted.

"What's going on?" Liam called out.

The couple spun around, startled to find them there. Trevor glanced briefly from one man to the other. Liam knew Trev didn't miss their damp hair, their bare feet, but there was no question or judgment in the man's eyes. His gaze held nothing but deep concern, directed at his wife.

"What's wrong?" Sully asked when neither of them answered.

Isabel's blue eyes glistened with unshed tears. Her lower lip shook for a moment, and then she let out a shuddery breath and said, "Rivera killed my father."

Chapter 23

One year ago

The pitter-patter of tiny toddler feet greeted the team as they piled out of the two Land Rovers onto the compound's paved driveway.

"Daddy!" J.J. squealed as he barreled out of the house and threw himself into his father's arms.

Kane caught the small boy and laid a big smacking kiss against his cheek as Abby floated down the front steps to join her men. Soon, the courtyard was filled with happy couples. Ethan had his arms full with Juliet, and even Morgan had his face tucked into Noelle's neck for a moment.

A pang of envy struck Ash. Although he'd called this place home for the last four years, no one was waiting with their nose pressed against the window for his arrival. Hell, even that scary bastard D had been wearing a sick-ass smile from some text he'd gotten from his wife. He'd barely said good-bye to the team in his haste to hop on another plane to get home to Mexico.

Ash rubbed the back of his neck in discomfort. Ethan and Kane had talked about grabbing dinner and a beer in town tonight, but he didn't think that was happening now. He wondered if he should wait around or head to the barracks. At one point he'd had a room in the big house, in one of the posh suites on the third floor, but the lack of privacy up there had eventually gotten to him and he'd moved into one of the outbuildings.

Back when the compound was owned by a drug lord, the barracks had housed his private army. These days, it was just Ash, and the loneliness was starting to get to him. It was why he'd stopped in Rhode Island last month. After the gig in Hong Kong had wrapped up, he hadn't been in a hurry to get home. But that visit turned out to be a fuckup.

He reached inside the Rover and grabbed his pack. The prospect of eating by himself wasn't thrilling, but he was definitely feeling like a third wheel.

Before he could separate himself from the crowd, Morgan hailed him. "Ash, good work on the op."

He gave him a half-smile in return and mentally shook off his melancholy. He had a good life here in Costa Rica. He didn't need a woman—there were several in the city that had no problem taking him into their beds. And he had a family. When Morgan had hired him, it wasn't just to do a job, but it was an invitation to be part of a band of brothers. So yeah, his cup was full, he had to remind himself. He didn't need anything more than this.

"Thanks. It ended up being a lot less dangerous than I thought."

The job in Trinidad to help suppress a coup had been successful with almost no casualties on either side. They'd diffused a bomb, captured two of the rebel leaders, and left with a fat paycheck and a happy client.

The older man nodded, looking a tad pensive. "Good planning and good intel helped." He cast an uncharacteristically tense glance toward his wife, and Ash wondered what that was all about.

"You should stick around, honey," Noelle cooed. A small smile played around her lips. "We're having pejibaye soup."

Ash felt a jolt down his spine as the mystery of Morgan's strained expression was solved. The creamy soup made with the locally grown pejibaye palm fruit was a favorite of one particular person—Cate Morgan.

"Pejibaye?" he echoed, and tried, nonchalantly, to scan the grounds for signs of her. When he came up empty, the itch of discontent roared to life again. He returned his gaze to Noelle, who was now grinning outright.

"Yes. Inna made it special for Cate. She's home for the long weekend. It's Martin Luther King Jr. weekend in the States. Brown doesn't have classes on Monday." Noelle turned to Morgan and placed a scarlet-tipped hand on his chest. Her expression remained casual, as if she were pretending not to notice that her husband was turning as stiff as a board.

Images of the red Speedo flashed in front of Ash's eyes. He suspected Morgan was thinking about the same thing.

"Dinner will be ready in about two hours," Noelle told him. "Gives you time to clean up."

"Noelle," Jim said in sharp warning.

"What? You just got back from a successful mission. It'll be nice to have a family dinner, won't it?" The mocking note in her voice couldn't be missed.

Morgan made a growling noise, which Ash decided to ignore.

"I'm going to unpack my gear. I'll let you know about the chow later." He had a couple of hours to decide whether he'd be eating a sandwich in the barracks or dining with the rest of the crew.

He knew what he *wanted* to do. It was more of a matter of what he *should* do.

"You do that," she murmured, then allowed herself to be drawn away by a question from Abby, leaving Morgan glaring at Ash.

"I'll walk with you," Morgan said. It wasn't a request.

Ash tightened his grip on his pack before giving his boss a nod and making his way toward his quarters. Morgan followed him, not speaking until they were well clear of the house and out of Noelle's earshot.

"You did good work back there in Trinidad," Morgan said, breaking the silence. "You're a valuable asset to the team."

"You fixin' to fire me?" Ash drawled.

"Not yet," Morgan grunted. "Don't give me a reason to either. I like you, but . . ."

"But what? Don't come to dinner or I'll be looking for a new job?" He sounded testy, but hell, he *was* testy. He'd kept his hands off Cate all these years and it had been damn hard. He couldn't be held responsible for the girl's feelings or her inappropriate gifts.

Morgan sighed. "Cate grew up with a shitty grand-father. Now she's here, and let's face it—I'm not much of a dad. She has no shot at a normal life. She says she wants to run around the world and do crazy stuff, but that's because she hasn't experienced anything different." His voice went gruff. "She's a beautiful girl, but she's still only a girl."

"I know that," Ash ground out.

He'd always restrained himself. Always. And Morgan getting up in his face, suggesting that Ash was in-fluencing Cate in the wrong direction, was not fucking appreciated. For the last year he'd been intentionally hurting Cate in an effort to maintain some kind of distance. Like the pen fiasco? He'd stood in that airport shop for an hour, obsessing over the exact right gift. The one that said, *I think of you and you should think of me, but in the most casual and least meaningful way.*

Morgan's features hardened. "All I'm saying is, I want the best for Cate."

Which meant while Jim trusted Ash to have his back, he didn't want Ash's dirty hands anywhere near his daughter.

"Don't worry," he muttered. "I'm keeping my pants zipped if that's what you're worried about. I do my fishing in the city, not here."

He turned on his heel and marched toward the squat concrete building that served as his home. Thankfully, Morgan didn't follow. He didn't need to. Ash had gotten the message, loud and clear.

But fuck, he was tired of disappointing Cate, of being forced to say things that hurt her feelings. After he'd left Brown, the look of disappointment on her face when she'd opened his gift had eaten away at him. He'd passed up an expensive camera he'd wanted to buy because he knew that would've been encouraging her in the wrong way. So he was doing everything Morgan had asked of him and more.

As he pulled open the barracks door, he sighed with frustration. Hell, maybe Morgan was right to be suspicious. Ash shouldn't have gone to Brown in the first place. What was he trying to do? Compete with all the preppy assholes that strutted the sidewalks at that fancy college? He had no rights to Cate and he wasn't in any position to claim her either.

Screw dinner. He'd stay away from the main house tonight. He'd go into the city, find some willing woman, and try to forget the one he really wanted. He owed that to Morgan.

All his good intentions drained away the minute he opened his bedroom door.

In the middle of his bed, lying on the forest green comforter, was an angel—a naked one. She was a tumble of long blond hair and acres of golden skin. Behind those closed lids, her eyes were deep blue. She looked like a girl from the tropics rather than one who'd spent the winter bundled up in wool sweaters and mittens.

He should look away. That would be the right thing to do, but he couldn't move. Lust anchored him to the floor as his eyes devoured Cate's perfect body. Her round, perky breasts sat high on her chest. Her long legs were muscled and smooth. One arm lay across her stomach while the other was flung over her head as she slept quietly on his bed.

He could go to her, part her legs, and dive between them. His tongue darted out and licked along his lower lip as if he could taste her from here. Christ, he wanted to consume her. Fall on her, cup her tits, feast on her nipples, drown himself in her honey until he was drunk.

As need throbbed in his groin, he closed his eyes and slumped against the doorframe. Even if he didn't owe Morgan everything, he couldn't touch Cate. Because her father was right—she deserved the chance to experience a life different than the one she'd grown up with. A normal, regular life away from violence and seclusion.

If he took her up on her offer, he might bind her to him permanently, and as much as his body and his heart rejoiced at that thought, he needed to reject his selfish impulses. If he cared about her at all, he needed to push her away.

His gran once told him you had to be cruel to be kind. She'd caught him feeding some ducks in a nearby pond when he was about five or so. She'd slapped him silly and said he was going to kill those birds if he kept sneaking them food; that they needed to learn to hunt for grub on their own because he wasn't always going to be around.

With that hard lesson in the forefront of his brain, Ash threw his bag on the ground forcefully. It landed with a loud clink against the terra-cotta tile, generating the intended result. Cate jerked upright in surprise, her hair falling down her breasts.

He pushed himself away from the door, forcing a nonchalant look on his face as if he didn't have a raging hard-on. He couldn't prevent that, but he could pretend like it didn't matter.

"What are you doing here?" he asked with feigned indifference.

"I—I . . . ," she stuttered, not fully awake.

Her hand went to brush the hair out of her face, but froze mid-air when she realized she was nude. She began to cover herself up, then halted, as if remembering that her intention was to drive him out of his ever-loving mind.

"Noelle told me you were coming home today. I'm here on break."

"That's nice, but it doesn't answer the question of what you're doing here without your clothes on." He stopped by a chair and took in the pile of clothing before shifting his cool gaze to her.

Cate's eyes widened at his unwelcoming tone but then a smile curved her lips when she noticed the unmistakable bulge in his pants.

"I think it's obvious why I'm here." She rose to her knees, putting her mouthwatering body on display for him.

Ash locked his legs as they threatened to give out. She looked like a goddess, and he was only a man.

Cruel to be kind, asshole . . .

Right. He had to be strong. He couldn't surrender.

"You need to leave." He leaned down, swiped a pair of dark blue jeans from the chair, and tossed them to her. "We're having dinner in an hour. I need to shower and shave." And jack off.

Cate moved toward him. "I'll shower with you."

"No, you won't."

"Why not?" she challenged.

"We're having dinner," he repeated.

Her hand dropped to her thighs, mere inches from her smooth, bare sex, and Ash's brain short-circuited. His heart beat frantically with worry and want. If she touched herself? He wasn't going to be able to do what he needed to.

"I don't want dinner. I want you." Her tone was so matter-of-fact that Ash wanted to give her some acknowledgement of the courage it took for her to do this.

Instead, he remained silent.

She powered on. "I was at a frat party a week ago and there were these guys there. This one guy, Eric—he's a Sigma Chi. He liked me. We did stuff."

He struggled to maintain his indifferent expression. But inside, he was seething. Stuff? He wanted to bash Eric's head in.

Sounding less confident than before, Cate went on. "But I ended it. I didn't want Eric. I want *you*." Her voice wobbled. "You should be my first. My only."

Ash stalked over to his dresser and pulled out a clean set of clothes.

"I know you want me too," she blurted out. "Damn it, I can *see* how much you want me."

He channeled all his self-loathing, all the anger he felt toward Morgan, and injected it into his voice. "Don't flatter yourself, sugar. My dick gets hard when I see a naked woman. It's a physical reaction. I'd get hard for Noelle and Juliet and Abby too if they were flashing their tits at me."

"Bullshit."

"Truth," he shot back. "Look. Cate." He drew a breath. "You're beautiful, okay? Not gonna deny that. But here's the problem—I have no desire to sleep with a virgin. Little girls with no experience don't interest me. So if you came all the way from Brown for sex, you're shit out of luck. Go back to Eric. That's where you belong."

Her gasp of pain hung in the air between them.

Ash stared past her because he couldn't bring himself to look her in the eye. Not after the hurtful lies he'd just spewed.

"Ash," she whispered, and he heard the sob that caught in her voice. "I—"

"Get out, Cate. Go back to the house. I don't want you in here."

Before she could object, he stalked across the hall to the bathroom, where he turned the shower on full blast and proceeded to bend over the toilet and vomit until all that was left in his system was acid-coated bile.

Yeah. If she didn't hate him before, she sure as shit hated him now.

Chapter 24

Present day

"We found something!" Cate announced when they returned to the base three hours later. "Camila Rivera is here and she's staying at the Westin."

Not a single person in the briefing room spoke in response. It took her a second to realize that she and Ash had walked into something . . . and it wasn't good.

Trevor had his arm around Isabel, whose face was drawn. Noelle stood near the desk, arms crossed, features hard. D was stone-faced as usual, while Sullivan, Liam, and Kane just looked concerned.

Ash placed a warning hand on Cate's arm before addressing Noelle. "What is it?"

The blonde let her arms drop to her sides. "Isabel's father was killed this morning."

Cate rocked back on her heels. She didn't know much about Isabel's dad other than that he'd held a position of power in the East Coast mob and was now incarcerated in Sing Sing. As the number three man in the DeLuca crime family, he'd been untouchable on the inside, or at least that was what Isabel had always maintained.

"Rivera?" Ash said grimly.

"Looks like it." As Noelle gestured to the collection of photographs splayed on one of the tables, Cate noticed that the woman seemed to be making a conscious effort to avoid Ash's eyes.

What the hell was going on? What did Isabel's father's death have to do with Ash?

Warily, Cate walked over to look at the photos, then regretted it instantly.

Holy *hell*. Killed? *That* was the word Noelle had chosen to use? The pictures didn't show a killing—it was a bloodbath. Messy. Gruesome. A total hatchet job.

Cate's stomach churned as she and Ash examined the photos. Bernie Roma's entire body was covered in stab wounds and there was blood everywhere. The attacker must have hit a main artery.

But it wasn't the blood that disturbed her—it was the missing fingers. On Bernie's right hand, all five fingers had been chopped off at the second knuckle. Judging by the ragged ends, the blade that was used hadn't been very sharp.

Cate studied another picture and nearly threw up when she realized that the dismembered digits had been shoved inside Mr. Roma's mouth. The thumb was sticking out grotesquely from the corner of his lips.

Behind her, Ash cursed softly. "Looks like Rivera's work, all right. When did this happen?"

"Late last night," Kane told them. "It was an inside job. Rivera must've paid off one of the other prisoners to do the deed."

Isabel's head jerked up. "I'm going back to New York," she declared.

Her husband shook his head. "Absolutely not. That'll play right into their hands. They want to split us up, make us weaker."

"I need to make funeral arrangements." Her voice was strong and steady. "I'm the only family he had left, Trev."

"He doesn't need a funeral," Trevor snapped. "Especially not one planned by you. And that bastard doesn't deserve your tears, Izzy. Not by a long shot."

Although she flinched at his bluntness, Cate understood where Trevor was coming from. From what Jim had told her, Isabel's father had basically disowned her when she'd joined the FBI. They'd been estranged ever since, and, according to Jim, Bernie Roma hadn't been a very nice man.

"He might've been a bastard, but he was still my father," Isabel shot back. "I owe him a proper burial."

Trevor threw a helpless look at Noelle, whose expression grew pained. "Do what you have to do," she told Isabel, albeit reluctantly.

D shifted restlessly behind them. "I gotta get back to Sofia."

"I need you here," Noelle argued, the tiniest hint of panic in her voice.

The two locked eyes until D finally gave her an abrupt, unhappy nod.

"Fine. I'll send her and Gabby to the compound for now. Until I feel she's unsafe, I'm with you."

Cate could tell Noelle didn't like that answer much, but she didn't complain. Her gaze flickered toward Ash before she hastily pulled it away again.

Something else was going on. Cate felt it in her bones but was hesitant to question Noelle in front of everyone. And Ash didn't seem to be picking up on the nervous energy Noelle was throwing out.

Trying to ignore the strange tension, she asked, "Why would Rivera target Isabel's father?" Before anyone could speak, a gasp of anguish stalled Cate's breath and then she answered her own question. "Oh God. Rivera told me he was coming after all of us—I didn't realize what that meant."

Ash reached for her arm. "Cate—"

"This is my fault."

"It's not your fault," he said firmly. "It's the DEA's fault. And Rivera's. Not yours."

Isabel quietly spoke up. "He's right. It's not your fault, sweetie."

"Bullshit." She blinked rapidly through a rush of tears. "None of you would be here in the first place if it weren't for me. Riya died because of the picture I took. Rivera knows who you guys are because of *me*." She swiped at her wet eyes. "I never thought he'd go after your families."

"That's what men like him do." Ash dragged one hand through his dark hair. "That's how he controls people. He doesn't kill you, he kills everyone you love."

"Ash," Kane started, taking a step forward. "There's something—"

"No," Noelle interrupted. "I'll do it."

Cate's alarmed gaze flew to Noelle. Oh shit. She hadn't been imagining the tension. Something *was* up.

"What's going on?" Ash glanced from Kane to Noelle.

The woman grabbed a cigarette pack from the table and tapped out a smoke without meeting Ash's gaze. "Bernie Roma wasn't the only casualty."

He stiffened. "What does that mean?"

Noelle lit up and took a long drag, reluctance etched into every inch of her beautiful face.

Ash raised his voice in anger. "Somebody tell me what the *fuck* is going on."

On a long exhale, Noelle said, "Your grandmother was killed last night."

Silence crashed over the small room. Ash stood frozen in place. Cate, meanwhile, grabbed the nearest chair and sank onto it in horror. Maybe Ash didn't feel like the world had kicked his legs out from under him, but Cate sure as hell did.

Kane took over for Noelle, his sympathy unmistakable. "Three men were seen entering your grandmother's house last night while she was attending a book club at the library. An emergency call was placed around ten o'clock. Came from a concerned neighbor. The cops found your grandmother in the kitchen. Beaten, throat slashed, and, uh, there were signs of sexual assault. The sheriff is willing to send us copies of the crime scene photos, if we want."

Ash didn't say a word.

Noelle ashed her cigarette in a nearby coffee cup and finished for Kane. "Someone used a permanent marker to write the words *payment in kind* on her refrigerator."

Cate's stomach turned over.

The man beside her finally made a sound—a long, heavy breath that echoed in the room. "She goes to bed at eight thirty every night. Has for as long as I can remember."

Cate marveled at the evenness of his tone, the way his hands didn't even clench at his side. Didn't he feel *anything* right now? She knew he was close with his grandmother. He didn't speak of her much, but when he did, it was with grudging respect. Once he'd described himself as a "little shit" who hadn't known the meaning of authority and command until his gran had whipped it into him.

"Yeah," Kane said with visible discomfort. "Apparently that was still the case. The neighbor called the sheriff's dispatcher because she was suspicious that all the lights were still on that late."

"Small towns," Ash replied, utterly expressionless. "That's how it is. If it hadn't been for the refrigerator note, I might've said it was meth heads."

The room went silent again.

"Ash," Isabel finally said, grief in her eyes. "I'm sorry for your loss."

He shrugged. "Sorry for yours." And then he was back to business, turning toward Noelle. "I assume we're moving Jim?"

She nodded. "Jet's being gassed up right now. Doc says Jim shouldn't be moved but I think he's a sitting duck here. I'm not sure how much longer we'll be able to stay at this base without word leaking to Rivera. If he can get to Isabel's dad in a maximum-security prison, then . . ." She trailed off.

"He's got a lot of resources," Ash finished for her.

"Exactly. So I say we move him. It's only a few hours from here to Costa Rica. Kane will be on the flight." Noelle's gaze was fixed on Cate as she spoke.

Cate moistened her lips. "Are you asking me for permission?"

"He's your father."

"He's your husband."

Noelle ground out her smoke. "We make this decision together or we don't make it at all."

She gulped as all the petty arguments she'd had with Jim came rushing over her. Her demands for freedom. Her rejection of every one of his suggestions after her disastrous first year at college. He'd only ever wanted her to be happy but it was always on his terms. Now, she was in the terrible position of making decisions for him, and she didn't want that.

"We should take him home." She bit her lip. "I'll go with him."

To her bewilderment, Noelle shook her head. "We can't risk it."

"Risk what?"

"We're sending most of the team back to the com-

pound. They've got families to think of. Sofia and
Gabby. Luke's flying Olivia and his mother-in-law in
from Colorado. Kane's parents are coming in from
Michigan. J.J. will be there." Noelle sighed. "If it wasn't
for the kids, I'd be fine with you heading home, but . . ."

But your presence would endanger the children, was
the unspoken rest of that sentence.

Ash let out a low angry sound. "Cate's a kid."

"The hell I am." She rose from her chair to face him.
"I'm the one Rivera really wants. And I don't know
about you, but I wouldn't be able to live with myself if
I led that psycho and his death squad home to where
J.J. and Gabby are staying."

"Then I'll take you somewhere else," he shot back.
"I can hide Cate for as long as we need to." The last bit
he directed at Noelle, who looked back with regret.

"No, I need you here. With Kane and Luke leaving,
we're going to be stretched too thin. And if Isabel is set
on going to New York—"

"I am," Isabel cut in.

"Then that means Trevor is leaving too—"

"Damn straight," Trevor said, protectively squeezing
his wife's hand.

"Which means that they'll need backup," Noelle finished, sounding tired. "Callaghan, take Bailey and the
twins to Manhattan with you. And for the love of God,
don't leave the safe house unless it's absolutely necessary. Rivera's hit squad is probably still in the city."

"Fine," Ash snapped, "but that still leaves you with
D and Holden. Ethan. Jules. And"—he gestured to
Liam and Sullivan, who'd remained silent for most of
the briefing—"Boston and Sully. It's a small crew, but
it's not unmanageable."

"It's not enough," Noelle snapped back. "I need you
and Cate here."

A muscle in his cheek ticked a few times as he stared at Noelle. Then he did a very un-Ash-like thing—he picked up the coffee cup that Noelle had been using as an ashtray and hurled it against the wall.

Cate flinched as pieces of ceramic exploded into the room. "Ash . . ."

"God fucking dammit!" he yelled, and then he threw open the door and disappeared, his heavy boots echoing in the tiled hallway.

"I always wondered what would make him lose his cool," Kane murmured. "Guess now I know."

"I'll go talk to him," Cate said quietly.

Noelle offered a nod. "I'll talk to the doc about transporting Jim and let you know what he says."

Cate ducked out of the room and hurried down the corridor in the direction of the barracks. At the last second, she made a detour to the kitchen. Holden had caught her the other morning and informed her that he'd found a bottle of whiskey and if she had trouble sleeping, it was in the cabinet by the fridge.

If anyone needed a shot of liquor right now, it was Ash.

Five minutes later, she tracked him down in his room. He was sitting on the bed, long legs stretched out in front of him, a rifle resting against one knee. Cate didn't say a word as she carefully moved the rifle to the side and offered him the whiskey.

Jerking his head in gratitude, he took the glass and downed the entire contents in two seconds flat. "Sorry about the mess downstairs," he mumbled. "I'll clean it up later."

"Liam is doing it." After a moment of hesitation, she settled in beside him on the bed.

His mouth turned down at the corners. "You shouldn't be here with me. I'm not in a good mood."

"I know." She took the empty glass from him and set it on the floor. "But Noelle is saying good-bye to Jim and I think she deserves some privacy."

He exhaled heavily and shifted his legs around. His big boots came to a rest close to her small sneakers and he studied the contrasts for a moment before raising his gaze to hers. "I'm sorry for calling you a kid. It was a knee-jerk thing. I just want you to be safe."

"I know that." The ache in his eyes prompted her to slide off the bed until she was kneeling between his legs. She placed both hands on his knees as if to steady him, even though he was already sitting down. "But we live in a really unsafe world. You can't protect everyone you care about all of the time."

His hands fisted on the tops of his thighs. Cate hesitated, then let her fingers creep over his, slowly, waiting for him to draw back. To her surprise, he didn't. He relaxed, flattening his fingers under hers and tipping his head back against the wall, as if her simple touch soothed him.

She took that as a sign of encouragement and cleared her throat. "I wish I'd met your grandma."

"She would've liked you." He smiled sadly. "It was men she wasn't fond of. She once told me that if God had intended for my old man to screw all those women, he'd have given him more than one penis."

Cate choked back a laugh.

"No, go ahead and laugh. That shit's funny." Ash peered down at her, a half-smile playing around his lips. "She had choice things to say about her own daughter too. 'Your mom don't have the sense of a tick when it comes to men.'"

"But you . . . she was proud of you," Cate hedged. "For going into the military. You told me that once."

"I remember. I think that was the time I asked you for a good memory of your grandfather and you said that you didn't have any."

"That's because he was a maniac who kept a dead woman alive and made his granddaughter visit the corpse every week. Oh, and he had his granddaughter's best friend killed. It's hard to remember a good time with him," Cate said flatly.

She didn't like thinking about her grandfather. He'd kept her from Jim for too long. Seventeen years too long, and now she was on the verge of losing her father just when she'd found him.

Forcing those awful fears away, she turned her attention back to Ash. "When's the last time you saw her?"

"Over Christmas. I went home for a visit because she hadn't seen me in a while and kept leaving me messages asking if I was still breathing. But you're right. She *was* proud that I enlisted. I never told her what I did after I got out and she never asked. Probably because she didn't want to know the answer."

"You've always done good things, Ash."

"Have I? I don't think I have. Like right now? There's not a good thought in my head."

His voice had taken on a dark note, one full of hunger. And beneath his absurdly long lashes, there was unchecked heat. It stole the air from her lungs.

"You shouldn't be here," he said roughly.

She bristled. Was he seriously going to kick her out again? After she'd come in here to comfort him?

"In Guatana," he clarified when he caught her expression. "You've got a huge target on your back, sweetheart. I don't want . . ." He took a breath. "Fuck, do you realize what Rivera wants to do to you?"

"Yes. Kill me."

"Kill you," Ash echoed. His face went bleak. "Except before he kills you, he's going to rape you a few hundred times and then cut off your fingers and shove them in your mouth."

A cold shiver ran up her spine. "I won't let him."

"You shouldn't be here," he said again.

"And where exactly should I go? You heard Noelle— if I go home, I risk leading Rivera to everyone we care about. I'd never be able to live with myself if something happened to any of them."

In the blink of an eye, Ash yanked her up into his lap and cupped her chin with both hands. "And you think *I'd* ever be able to live with myself if I lost you?"

Her jaw fell open, shock slamming into her chest at the same time Ash's mouth slammed against hers. She could feel the rapid beat of his heart, the unsteady breath in his lungs, as he kissed her hard and deep.

Her moan filled his mouth and he answered with a guttural noise of his own. After all this time, after all these years of restraint, Ash was finally letting go, and his kiss was as addictive as she'd always known it would be.

He spread her lips with his tongue and drove it inside, kissing her with a passion that sucked the breath out of her lungs. And as she gasped for air, his hands delved under her shirt and cupped her breasts, thumbing her nipples over her bra.

"Fuck," he choked out. "I have to taste you." He pushed her shirt up high enough to release her breasts from her bra, then dipped his head and sucked one nipple hard into his mouth.

Lost in exquisite sensation, Cate ground her lower body against the prominent bulge beneath his zipper. God, now wasn't the time for this. Not after he'd just received news that his grandmother had been murdered. Not when more than half of the team was taking off to secure the safety of their loved ones. Not while Jim lay unconscious a few corridors away from them.

But the feel of Ash between her legs, the touch of his lips against her own, his hot mouth around her nipple . . . she'd dreamed about this for years.

She cried out when he captured her other nipple between his teeth, nipping gently. Her fingers scraped against his scalp to keep his head against her breasts, and the urge to rip off his clothes, to remove any barrier between them, was burning all her rational thought to dust.

"Not enough," he muttered. "Need more."

He fell backward and pulled her on top of him, his hands clawing at her waistband. Just before he could undo the button, Noelle's voice sounded from behind the door.

"Cate," the woman called. "We're loading Jim up in five minutes."

A curse got lodged in her throat. Every inch of her was throbbing, aching for Ash, but it was difficult to hold on to that arousal at the mention of her father.

Obviously Ash felt the same way because he swiftly pushed to his feet and held out his hand to hoist Cate off the bed.

Neither of them spoke as they smoothed out their rumpled clothing on their way to the door. But their attempts to de-sex themselves failed miserably because Noelle wore a slight smirk when they joined her in the hall.

"Sorry to interrupt," she said mockingly.

"It's fine," Cate answered, averting her gaze in embarrassment. "We were just . . . talking." She moistened her lips, which felt swollen from Ash's greedy kisses. "So the doctor said it was safe to move Jim?"

"He wasn't thrilled, but he signed off on it. Our bigger concern right now is smuggling Jim off this base without alerting Rivera. That bastard has eyes all over this city."

Noelle walked off without delay, leaving Cate and Ash to hurry after her. When they reached the medical wing, the blonde was already in Jim's room, standing at the end of the bed glaring down at him.

"If he wasn't already out of it, I'd smack him upside the head for making this more difficult than it has to be," she growled without turning around.

"That's Jim for you. Always trying to get you to do things his way," Cate said lightly.

"Right. Asshole." Noelle knocked her fist against the metal frame at the foot of the bed. "Say your good-byes and be quick about it. We're on a tight schedule."

With her heart in her throat, Cate nodded and stepped toward the bed. She picked up Jim's large hand with its many scars and calluses and hugged it to her chest. This man had been such a powerful presence in her life—both before and after she'd met him. It was too soon for him to go, though. She'd only just begun to know him.

"Jim . . . Dad. This is no time to be sleeping on the job. Noelle's going to leave you. And me?" She pulled the limp fingers to her lips. "Get better soon or I'll marry the worst, baddest mercenary alive and we'll send our operatives out to crash all your missions and steal all your clients."

"D's already taken," Ash remarked dryly.

Cate glanced over and grinned at him but the humor faded as she gently laid Jim's hand back on the bed. "Do you want a moment?" she asked, gesturing toward Jim.

"Nah. I'll say something to him when he wakes up. I can be the one person to tell him that I never once thought he was going to kick the bucket. Maybe he'll give me a raise." Ash thumped his fist against the bed frame. "You hear that, old man? Stop being a dick and wake up. No prince is going to come along and save your ugly mug."

Cate snorted.

"We're ready to roll," a voice said from the doorway. Holden appeared, wearing a blue jumpsuit. When he strode past Cate, she saw that the words "CableVision" were stitched along the back.

Kane and D walked in a moment later, wearing similar jumpsuits and holding a backboard that they lined up next to the bed.

"On my count," Holden said. "One. Two. Three." On *three*, he and Ash lifted Jim's body and shifted him from the bed to the waiting backboard.

Holden unhooked the IV and laid the bag at Jim's side. At his sharp nod, Kane and D carefully maneuvered Jim out of the small room and down the hallway. Cate followed silently, her heart aching at the sight of her big, strong father in such a vulnerable position.

Out in the main courtyard, two satellite trucks idled on the dusty ground. Timo Varela was already out there, clad in military fatigues and sporting a regretful expression.

"I really am sorry I can't let you use one of our choppers," he was telling Noelle, "but it would raise too many red flags, especially since you want to leave the country unnoticed."

"It's fine," she answered briskly. "We're more comfortable taking our own jet anyway."

Varela glanced at Jim's unconscious body in dismay as the men carted the stretcher toward one of the waiting trucks.

Cate noticed that Noelle looked equally distressed, which told her the woman must really be worried, because she never revealed a sliver of emotion if she could help it.

Swallowing, Cate walked over and touched Noelle's arm. "You should go with him."

Noelle bit her lip.

"Go," Cate urged. "I know you trust Kane—I do too, of course—but you'll feel a lot better if you're with him. And it's only a few hours there and back. You'll be back in Guatana before midnight."

After another long beat, Noelle gave a decisive nod. "You're right. Fuck it. I'm going."

She hid a smile. "Good. Now get in the truck and make sure nothing happens to my dad—"

Noelle was marching off before Cate had finished her sentence.

A soft chuckle had her turning her head. She found Ash standing beside her, looking amused. "I swear, you're one of the few people who can get away with giving that woman orders. Anyone else, she'd pull a gun on."

"I'm very skilled at dealing with alphas," Cate said with a sigh.

She started to shift her gaze back to the trucks but Ash lightly grasped her arm to stop her. "Cate. About what happened before Noelle interrupted . . ."

Her shoulders tensed. Of course. He was about to tell her what a big, fat mistake it had been. That he'd kissed her, touched her, because of some bout of temporary insanity. That she was an inexperienced little girl and the mighty David Ashton didn't fuck girls—he fucked *women*.

"What about it?" she said tersely.

"I don't—"

"Ash," Kane called from across the courtyard. "Need to talk to you before we go."

Resignation flashed in his eyes. "We'll talk later," he murmured before darting off in Kane's direction.

Cate stared after him in frustration. *I don't* . . . He didn't *what*, damn it? Didn't regret kissing her? Didn't want to do it again? He couldn't have finished that one measly sentence instead of leaving her here to wonder?

She was so tired of Ash walking away from her. One of these days she was going to tie him down, though what she was going to do with him once she had him secured, she wasn't sure. Either fuck him or kill him.

Maybe both.

Chapter 25

It was just past nine o'clock when a soft knock sounded on Cate's door. She barely heard it over the loud thumping of her heart, the hum of anticipation in her blood. She'd been riddled with anxiety all day and evening, wondering when Ash would come to see her. *If* he'd come to see her.

Despite his assurance that they would "talk later," he'd kept his distance ever since the others had departed. Cate had spent the day studying the pictures she'd taken of Camila Rivera, searching for any clue that might lead them to the location of the woman's husband.

Another rap on the door alerted Cate to the fact that she hadn't responded. "Yeah?" she called.

"It's Ash," he said unnecessarily.

"Come in."

Nervously, she smoothed her hands down the front of her shirt. With Ethan, Juliet, and D handling surveillance tonight, Cate had no reason to leave the base, so she'd already changed into pajamas, which consisted of a tank top and teeny cotton boxers, both thin enough to make her feel like she wasn't wearing anything at all.

Ash opened the door and shut it quietly behind him. He was still dressed in pants, boots, and a tight T-shirt, but his hair was wet. Had he showered? On closer inspection, she realized his chin was clean-shaven too. The perpetual scruff he sported was gone.

Cate rose and walked over to him. In an almost involuntary reflex, she reached up to touch his face. The skin felt soft beneath her fingers. "You shaved," she said dumbly.

He rubbed a hand over his jaw. "Yeah."

Her core began to throb. A man didn't shower and shave for the fun of it. This could only mean one thing.

Heart thudding a million miles a minute, Cate searched his eyes and found what she was looking for. Heat. Desire. "What were you going to say earlier? Before Kane called you over."

Ash didn't shy away from her imploring gaze. "Twenty years."

She blinked. "What?"

"I was going to tell you that I don't want to be like Noelle and your dad." His throat bobbed as he swallowed. "I don't want you and I to dance around each other for another twenty years."

Warmth flooded her heart. "Neither do I." She started to reach for him but he took a maddening step back.

"No." When her mouth opened in outrage, he corrected himself. "Not yet. I mean it, Cate. If we're really going to do this, we need to talk about a few things first."

"Seriously? I might not be a man whisperer like Noelle's chameleons but since when do men want to *talk* when they can be *naked*?"

Ash snickered before going serious again. "Humor me, okay? Because this needs to be said."

"Fine." She waved a hand. "Talk away."

He drew a deep breath, then exhaled in an unsteady puff of air. "Last year . . ." He inhaled again. "The night I found you naked in my room . . ."

Her stomach twisted at the memory. "What about it?"

"I lied to you that night. Every single word I said was a goddamn lie, sugar." Remorse floated across his handsome face. "I was trying to push you away. I knew Morgan didn't want the two of us hooking up, and I said all that shit because I wanted you to hate me. I wanted you to get over me."

"I suspected as much." Another knot formed inside her. "But . . . it hurt, Ash. It really fucking hurt."

"I know." He moved closer as if he was going to touch her, changed his mind, and took a step back. "You have no idea how sorry I am. That look on your face when I . . ." He swallowed. "It haunts me."

She fisted her hands on her hips. "So you pushed me away back then. Why aren't you pushing me away now? It's not like Jim is suddenly waving around a flag of approval. What's changed?"

"Twenty years," Ash repeated through clenched teeth. "I just told you—I'm not willing to torture the both of us for twenty fucking years. I want you. I wanted you from the moment I met you, and I don't give a shit if it's wrong."

A smile curved her lips. "Then why are you still not touching me?"

His low growl heated the air. "Because I'm not done talking."

"Do that again."

"Do what?" he said warily.

"That growling thing. It's hot."

Now he grumbled in frustration. "Would you just let me finish?"

"Sorry. Go on." Her hand made a zipping motion across her mouth.

"So yeah . . . I told you how I feel," he said awkwardly. "Now I need to tell you how I am."

She eyed him in confusion. "What does that mean?"

"It means I'm not like those young college guys you're used to." His cheeks hollowed as if he was grinding his molars together. "I'm not gentle or sweet when it comes to sex. I have a filthy mouth. I can be rough. I—"

"Why are you telling me all this?" she interjected, sputtering with laughter.

"Because I want you to know what you're getting into. What I'm like in bed." He shifted his feet. "I want to make sure you can handle it, that it won't scare you away."

Grinning, she gripped the hem of her tank top and slowly dragged the thin material upward. "Tell me—do I look scared?"

The shirt hadn't even cleared her head before Ash was on her. His hands fondled her bare breasts roughly, summoning a gasp from her lips.

"This what you want, Cate?" he demanded. "What you really want?"

"Yes," she answered breathlessly.

"Yeah? You want my cock inside your pussy? You want me to suck on your tits until you squirm and then fuck you with my tongue? Because once I start, I'm not gonna fucking stop."

She curled her fingers around his biceps, her body clenching in desire at every lust-drenched word. But she couldn't be passive here. Ash already thought that she was too young for him, too inexperienced. She had to meet him word for word, thrust for thrust.

"What about you, Ash?" she challenged. "You want my mouth on your cock? You want my fingers in your ass?"

His expression lit up. "So it's going to be that way, is it?" he said with a chuckle.

"Yeah. It's going to be that way."

Still laughing, he pulled his T-shirt off with one hand while the other dropped to his pants. Somehow he was able to toe off his boots, ditch the pants, and back her toward the small twin bed in one fluid motion. Then he reached down and gripped his impressive erection.

"You sure about this?" he muttered, his eyes blazing with unadulterated lust. "Because I haven't had a woman in a long time and I need this so fucking bad. Three days from now you'll still be aching from the pounding I'm about to give you. This isn't going to be sweet or pretty. Last chance, sugar."

His Southern accent crept in, slurring his words together like melted syrup. Cate wanted to lie back on the bed and bathe in them. And his intentionally coarse words did nothing to scare her off. They only wound her up tighter.

She smiled at him. "I don't care." Then she threw herself on the bed and spread her legs. "Do your worst, baby."

He growled again, and damned if that didn't make her hotter.

She'd never felt so ready in her life, and yet when Ash climbed onto the bed, kneeling above her like some conquering lord, a frisson of apprehension spiked into her. She'd never seen him like this. Features stretched harshly across his skin, dark red color riding high on his cheekbones, pupils black with arousal. And his cock hung heavy and hard, sending a rush of moisture to her core.

Cate's inner muscles clenched in anticipation. She'd wanted this for as long as she could remember. She'd spent four years fantasizing about this moment, and she was reveling in the fact that he hadn't been with anyone for a long time, that he was going to take her rough and hard.

"Fuck me," she begged when he still hadn't moved.

The words acted like a switch. One moment he was still and the next he was curling his lean, muscular body over her. He palmed one breast as he took the other

one in his mouth, the deep suction sizzling right down
to her pussy. Her knees came up to trap him between
her legs. The throb in her core needed his thigh, his
hand, his tongue. Shit, anything.

She writhed in agitation as he bit and sucked and
kissed every inch of her breasts. He tongued her nipples
until they were so hard it was almost painful. They were
aching. Everything was aching.

"Ash, please."

"You hungry, sugar? You need something?" His
words were mocking but his face belied the light tone.
Every taut plane of his body screamed of a man in need.

"You," she whispered. "I need you. Inside of me. Now."

Her hands fumbled with her boxers, but he brushed
her fingers away and wrenched the shorts down. He left
her lacy panties on.

"Jesus. You wear these skimpy things all the time
under your clothes?"

A strong hand cupped her and Cate squirmed
against the grip. She wanted him to remove that last
layer between them and shove something, *anything* inside her. "Y-yes. Why?"

"Those college boys see this, Cate? You show these
fuck-me panties to those punk-ass, pink-shirt-wearing
boys?"

"What?" She couldn't understand what he was talking
about. Her mind was foggy from arousal, spurring her
to desperately reach between them for his cock.

He shifted out of reach. "Answer me," he ordered.
"How many of those assholes have seen you like this?"

"None," Cate hissed. "None of them. I didn't let even
one of them touch me."

No, it wasn't until she'd been in the field that she'd
finally accepted that Ash wouldn't be her first. She'd

given her V-card to a reporter, more out of loneliness than desire, and it had never, *ever* felt like this. She'd never felt this alive. Every nerve ending tingled. Every cell crackled with awareness. Every part of her was desperate for release.

"Right answer," Ash drawled, and then he shoved her panties aside and thrust two fingers inside her.

The orgasm came without warning. Cate couldn't help it, couldn't stop it. Ash had detonated the fuse that had been burning for four years, and her back arched off the bed as a wave of pleasure rocked through her.

"Fuck. You are so fucking tight."

Her eyes flicked open to see him staring at his fingers tunneling in and out of her. His teeth were clenched and sweat beaded on his forehead. The muscles in his chest and arm rippled as he pumped her with his hand.

"Give me more. Don't hold out on me," she pleaded. The man had her pinned to the bed with two fingers, but she still wanted more. She needed, lusted after his cock. And she wasn't leaving this bed until she got it.

Chuckling, he withdrew his fingers. "Just making sure you're ready."

Was he kidding? She'd never felt more primed in her life. But when he nudged the broad head of his cock against her opening, she felt a twinge of panic. He was a lot bigger than she'd realized.

"Take it slow," she whispered.

He gritted his teeth but nodded, and they both began to sweat as he started the slow, torturous process of sliding inside of her.

"Relax, sugar. This is going to feel good." Ash braced an elbow next to her cheek and slipped his hand under her head, enough to raise it so he could plunder her mouth. His kiss was urgent, but somehow tender. A marked difference from the rough but thrilling way he'd handled her before. It was as if now that she was under him, he was allowing himself to slow down.

Had he worried she'd turn him away? After all those times she'd offered herself up to him and he'd rejected her? She was the one who should be worried. She was the one—

"Hey there, where'd you go?" He stroked her cheek. "You still with me?"

Her eyes flipped open to find a sea of dark green filling her vision. Even if she'd wanted to wrap a cloak of indifference around herself, she wouldn't have been able to.

"I'm with you," she assured him.

His eyes grew heavy-lidded. "Remember that," he said fiercely, and in one powerful movement he closed the distance, driving his hips forward until he was seated all the way to the hilt. "You're with me now."

She gasped and arched into him as he palmed her ass and held her in place while he hammered into her, making good on his promise to leave a mark. There wasn't a cell in her body that wasn't affected by him. The hand under her head had moved to her neck, one thumb pressing heavily against her pulse point. Each deep thrust brought her closer and closer to the brink, need coiling tighter and tighter inside her until she was shaking wildly beneath him.

"You need to come, don't you?" he rasped against her ear.

Yes. Right now would be nice. Right now would be glorious. But she wasn't able to voice the words. All she could manage was a helpless moan.

He responded by slipping his hand between them and pinching her clit, and the bright burst of pain against the drenched backdrop of pleasure brought her off the bed with a wild cry.

She climaxed in waves, the orgasm rolling through her body, over and over and over until she sagged, limp and wrung out, to the mattress.

Ash rose on his knees, lifting her bottom up without losing their connection, without halting his relentless assault. He draped her legs over his shoulders and took her in punishing strokes until the hunger rose in her again. She met him thrust for thrust, clutching every hard, furious inch of him until she was lost again. And this time she took him with her. He groaned his release and a flood of heat filled her core as he spilled himself inside of her.

With shaky arms, he set her legs back on the mattress and withdrew, and they both moaned at the loss. Cate registered the wetness on her thighs. There was something vaguely wrong with that but she didn't want to focus on it. She wanted to hold this moment of bliss tight against her heart.

Still breathing hard, Ash settled on his side next to her. The bed was barely big enough for her, let alone the both of them, but they made it work. Their bodies were pressed together as he stroked a palm over her sweaty forehead.

"I didn't use a condom."

Oh crap. That explained that sense of wrong she'd felt. "I'm on birth control," she replied. "And I had a physical before I came to Guatana. I, ah, had all the regular STD tests done."

"Me too." His tone was slightly awkward. "I can show you my results. They're on my phone."

Cate nodded, although she trusted him when he said he was clean.

"I'll use one next time," he promised.

"Next time? I don't think I can handle a next time," Cate murmured. She was so worn out she could hardly move.

"Next time," he reiterated, nudging her earlobe with his lips. "I'll give you a thirty-minute nap and then we're going again."

She was laughing even as her eyelids fluttered shut. Drowsiness crept over her and she fell asleep with the imprint of a hardening erection at her side.

Next time.

That sounded way too good to be true.

After grabbing a late-night bite at the mess hall, Sullivan returned to the barracks and entered his room to find Liam pacing the floor like a madman. The man had a cell phone pressed to his ear, his handsome face creased in frustration.

"This isn't a fuckin' joke, Kev," Liam was snapping. "I need you to get everyone out of town. Ma, Dad, Denny, the girls, the kids. Fuckin' everyone."

Sully eased inside and closed the door. Kevin was one of Liam's brothers, and the fact that Liam was pacing even faster now suggested that he didn't like what the guy was saying.

"Jesus!" Liam burst out. "I'm not telling you to leave the country, just to get out of town for a few days, a week tops. Move the family to a safe house while I take care of this cartel mess. I have two locations you guys can use—one in Connecticut and one in upstate New York. You just can't stay in Southie."

There was another long pause. Liam's fingers tightened over the phone.

"You of all people should appreciate the importance of security! I'm not messing around here . . . no, I'm not

back with the agency . . . this is a private matter . . . no . . .
my former company. The mission went south and now
we've got a fuckin' cartel after us." Liam listened, then
cursed angrily. "People are dying, Kev. You need to
leave the state. You can't—damn it!"

Sully flinched when Liam whipped the phone on the
bed. "Did he hang up on you?" he asked.

"No, he's going to talk it over with Denny and call
me back." Liam shook his head. "But I know my brothers. They're not going to skip town."

"Did you tell them about the rookie's grandmother?
Izzy's dad? About the bullets they put in Morgan's back?"

"Yeah. I told them everything."

Liam collapsed on the edge of the bed. Sully joined
him, but kept a foot of distance between them.

"You don't know the Macgregors, man. The whole
family is a bunch of stubborn Irish fucks. They don't
run. I called my dad first and that's what he said—
Macgregors don't run. They fight."

"You gotta admire that," Sully said carefully.

That earned him a scathing look. "Admire it? People
are getting killed. My brothers and sisters have *kids*.
Little kids. And they're willing to risk all their lives just
to abide by some family motto? That's fuckin' bullshit."

Liam looked so frazzled that Sully couldn't help
himself—he reached for the guy's hand. Then he took
a breath and squeezed Liam's knuckles, half expecting
his teammate to recoil in horror. But Liam surprised
him by lacing their fingers together.

Discomfort soared up his throat. Were they seriously
sitting here holding hands?

Bloody hell. Sucking each other off was one thing,
but this was a level of intimacy that made the back of
his neck itch.

And yet he didn't pull his hand away.

"My family is a goddamn pain in the ass."

Sully swallowed. "I hate to play the orphan card here, mate, but at least you have a family."

Liam's expression instantly sobered. "I know. And I love them, I really do. I just wish they had more sense. I wish they took this warning seriously." He sighed. "I wish they took *me* seriously."

"They do."

"No, they don't. I'm the family fuckup, the one who didn't follow in Dad's footsteps and join the force. The one who didn't get married and knock up his wife. The one who took off and left them all behind." Bitterness colored his voice. "The one who likes to fuck men."

Sully froze. "Do they . . . know about that? You told them that you were . . . ?"

"Bisexual?" Liam supplied. "Nah, they have no clue. Well, my sister Becca suspects. She's been texting me for days demanding answers."

"Answers about what?"

"Before I left . . ." Those long fingers tightened in Sully's. "I told you about the chick I was dating?"

He nodded.

"She ended it after she found out I was bi," Liam mumbled. "It disgusted her. And, ah, she called me a fag in front of my sister."

"You shitting me?"

"Nope. I guess it was too much to hope for tolerance and understanding from the woman I was with for a year."

"Guess so," Sullivan said wryly.

"But yeah, Becca keeps asking what Penny meant by that."

"What have you told her?"

"Nothing. Said it was just a misunderstanding."

Of course Liam would say that to his sister. As much

as the man griped about his family, Sully knew that their opinion meant the world to him. Liam hated the thought of them finding him lacking or being disappointed in his life choices. They wanted him to wind up with a nice Catholic girl and pop out the requisite number of rugrats. Anything less than that was unacceptable to the Macgregor clan.

So yeah, no surprise that Liam was still keeping his family in the dark. But what did amaze Sully was that his friend no longer seemed conflicted. Liam had referred to himself as bisexual. He'd insinuated that he'd experimented with men. And fine, as jealous as that made him, Sully also felt deep pride.

Liam had faced his confusion head-on. He'd worked through it and reached acceptance about who he was and what he wanted. So it didn't matter if the Macgregors disapproved. Sully was simply glad that Liam was no longer fighting himself.

"I'm going to tell her, though. Probably when I get back to Boston."

"You are?" Sully said in surprise.

Liam nodded. "Of all my siblings, I'm closest with Becca. She's the only one who's not married—yet, anyway. She's got a serious boyfriend and I'm sure he's going to pop the question any day now. But she's thirty-three. The rest of them all got married in their early twenties, so she and I were kind of the rebels for a while there."

Liam began rubbing the pad of his thumb on the center of Sully's palm. Sully didn't think the other man was even aware of it, but the featherlight caresses sent a wave of sensation through him. Heat, and the strangest rush of tranquility. He didn't look down at their hands because he was afraid it would alert Liam to what that thumb was doing.

"I've always been able to tell Becca everything. She's

the kind of person who doesn't know the meaning of judgment, you know? Like, I could tell her I want to take up figure skating and she wouldn't even blink. She'd just ask me when we're going shopping for skates and glitter."

Sullivan chuckled. "So why didn't you tell her the truth when she asked?"

"Because I was on my way here. It's not the kind of bomb you can just drop and then waltz off to board a plane. I'd rather do it in person, have time to talk it through."

"Would she tell the rest of your family?"

"Not if I ask her not to. But I figure if there's anyone in the family to confide in, it's her. And then, based on her reaction . . . I don't know." Liam let out a heavy breath. "Then maybe I'll have the balls to tell the rest of them. They'll . . . be okay with it." He went quiet for a beat, as if he was inwardly trying to convince himself of that. "Or at least Becca will be. She's always accepted me for exactly who I am."

Sully was startled when his teammate suddenly pinned him down with serious blue eyes.

"You ever had that before?" Liam asked.

His brow creased. "Had what?"

"Someone who accepted you unconditionally, completely. Someone you could talk to about anything and know that you were, I don't know, safe, I guess? Have you ever had that?"

A lump rose in his throat. "Yeah . . . With you."

Liam's lips parted slightly. "Just me? Nobody else?"

His throat was almost completely clogged now. No air seemed to be getting in. "There was someone else," he admitted.

"Who?"

"Evangeline."

"Your boat?" Liam said with a snort. "I know you've got her name tattooed on two different parts of your body, but that doesn't count, bro."

"No, not the boat." Sully slowly disentangled their fingers and reached around to pat between his shoulder blades. "The tat back here? That one's for the boat. This one . . ." He turned his forearm and traced his fingers over the black script inked on the inside of his wrist to his elbow. "This Evangeline was real. A living, breathing woman. Well, a girl."

"Who was she?"

"Someone I loved."

"Someone you . . . loved."

Sully smiled at the confusion he saw on his friend's face. He'd expected it. Every time they'd spoken about love in the past, he'd always maintained that it was over-rated, that he had no interest in it. So he knew his words were coming as a complete one-eighty.

"I just turned seventeen when I met her. I was living on the streets, dealing drugs, taking drugs. And this one night, I snorted some bad coke and wound up in the hospital because of some fucked-up reaction." He breathed deeply as memories he normally kept locked up spiraled to the surface. "Evie was a nursing student, two years older than me. Her class was at the hospital that night doing rounds with the other nurses. She was in my room when I woke up."

His chest ached as he pictured Evangeline's big green eyes sparkling with life. The light brown hair that she'd worn long, with messy bangs that constantly fell into her eyes. He'd loved sweeping that soft hair off her forehead. Stroking her impossibly smooth cheek as he leaned in to kiss her.

Fuck, he hadn't deserved her.

"We started talking. She made me laugh. And the

next day she helped me get into rehab. When I got out two months later, she was waiting for me." A self-deprecating smile touched his lips. "I have no idea what the hell she was doing with me. I was a street thug. No place to live, no money, no prospects. She could've had anybody she wanted, but she chose my punk ass." He shrugged. "Maybe she just wanted my dick."

Liam laughed. "I doubt that. You need to give yourself more credit, man."

"Hey, I'm awesome, no doubt. But . . . you didn't know this girl, Boston. She was kind. Drop-dead gorgeous. And smart, so fucking smart. She had her entire life in front of her. I truly don't know why she was wasting her time on me."

"What happened to her?"

"She got sick. At first, it was complaining she was tired or that she couldn't breathe. She'd bump into a chair and get a nasty bruise. It worried me, but I didn't push her to see a doctor until she collapsed one night."

His windpipe tightened to the point of suffocation, the mental picture of Evangeline's rosy cheeks and sparkling eyes slowly dissolving into images of a gray complexion, deadened eyes.

"She was diagnosed with acute myeloid leukemia. There were too many white blood cells in her bones and it spread so bloody fast." He shook his head in dismay. "The doctors couldn't keep up with it. It's not one of those cancers you can cut out. It was everywhere, in every bone marrow sample they took, in every test they ran."

"Shit." This time it was Liam who reached for Sully's hand. He cupped it between both of his, infusing his warmth into Sully's cold flesh.

"The chemo did shit. So did the radiation. They gave her three months to live. There was this other treatment they could've tried, but she was so weak by then and she refused to try it. And, I don't know, she wasn't herself anymore. She shut down, not just physically but emotionally. Mentally. She moved back in with her mother and wouldn't leave her room. Wouldn't get out of bed, refused to eat. I could feel her slipping away and there was nothing I could do about it."

"I'm sorry," Liam said quietly.

"But yeah . . ." He cleared his throat. "She was one of those people you mentioned. Someone who would never judge you. She knew I dealt drugs and didn't condemn me for it. She tried to help me instead. Helped me get my GED. She was the most beautiful person in this whole world. Inside and out."

"They gave her three months . . ." Liam hesitated. "Did she last that long?"

Agony rushed up his throat. "No. She . . ."

"It's fine, you don't have to tell me."

He jerked when his friend leaned over and cupped his chin. A callous thumb swept over the line of Sully's jaw.

"No, it's okay. Might as well finish this sob story, huh?" He choked down the pain and released a short breath. "After she got sick, I moved into their place to help take care of her. Her mom didn't like me at first, but she warmed up after she realized how much I loved Evie. She said we were soul mates, and yeah, I know we were young, but I think she was right. Evie was my entire world." His chin sagged into Liam's hand. "So I was staying there and, well, those treatments were expensive, so I started dealing in scrips. Bigger amounts, harder shit. Every cent I made, I handed over to Evie's mom to use to pay for her medical bills."

"She must have appreciated that."

"She did. And I think that's why she didn't object to me living there. But the thing is, I couldn't exactly stash huge amounts of product like that on the street. So all the pills I was dealing, the oxy, painkillers, all that shit . . . I kept it in the house, in Evie's room."

A warning note entered Liam's voice. "Sully, you don't have to tell me the rest."

"She was in so much pain and she'd given up. She didn't want to lie in bed for another two months and just wait to die, so she took matters into her own hands. She got into my stash, took whatever she could swallow, and OD'd. I got home from my deliveries that night and she was already gone."

"Fuck. I'm sorry."

Sullivan bit the inside of his cheek. "After she died, I fell off the wagon. Started popping pills again, getting high so I wouldn't have to feel anything. Kept dealing, too, and then I got busted for possession. That's when I met Tom—I told you about him, remember? The cop who took me in? He gave me a place to stay, helped me get clean again, and encouraged me to enlist in the army. And . . . yeah, you know the rest."

Liam's blue eyes flickered with sorrow. "You named your boat after her."

He nodded. "Before she got sick, we used to talk about what our life together would be like. She wanted to live on the water—that was her dream, to eventually buy a place on the beach in a small town. She'd work as a nurse at some clinic, and I . . . well, who the fuck knew what I'd do. But that was our dream. She wanted a boat, and on weekends we'd take it out on the water. So . . ."

"So you gave her the dream," Liam finished hoarsely.

"Yeah, I guess I did." A humorless laugh slipped out. "Maybe it's a good thing we never got to live that dream together. Sooner or later I would've broken her heart."

"What makes you say that?"

"You know me, mate. Have I ever been able to keep

my pants zipped? I would've gotten bored with her eventually, stepped out on her. I would've hurt her." He bristled when he noticed Liam studying him intently. "What?" he said defensively.

Liam didn't answer. He just kept staring, as if he was trying to figure something out.

For the life of him, Sully didn't want to know what it was, so he stood up and ran a hand over his cropped hair. "Call your family back. Keep working on them until they agree to leave Boston."

"Sullivan—"

"Rivera's targeting families," he muttered, avoiding Liam's eyes. "The only thing you need to be worrying about right now is keeping yours safe."

Chapter 26

Cate woke up to the sound of Ash's soft, steady breathing. He was lying beside her, one arm thrown over the top of his face, the other loosely embracing her. The darkened window indicated it was still nighttime, but she wasn't sure how late.

She thought she'd feel euphoric after sex with Ash, but the multiple rounds of it had only exhausted her body. After the last orgasm had washed over her, she'd felt hollowed out emotionally. Throughout all the sex, he'd said a lot of things. Filthy, erotic, exciting things, but none of them had indicated that what they were doing was anything more than a physical release.

She supposed that was exactly how she needed to treat it—as a purely physical experience that had everything to do with their bodies and nothing to do with their hearts. He wasn't suddenly in love with her. That kind of thinking was precisely what had led to her seventeen-year-old heart getting crushed.

But she wasn't a child anymore. She wouldn't let Ash crush her again. Even if he walked out the door right now, she was *not* going to let him take her heart with him.

As a flicker of panic ran through her, she sat up in bed and rubbed her face, wishing that Ash didn't have this power over her. The power to turn her into an emotional mess.

"What's wrong?" His eyes snapped open, his hand already moving to grip the weapon that wasn't at his side.

Cate wasn't sure if he'd been awake or if his military training had kicked in by her movement.

"Nothing's wrong," she assured him. Then she drew the sheet up to her breasts, feeling awkward with her state of undress now that the passion had cooled like the sweat on her body. "Noelle should be back soon, right?"

Ash cast her an unreadable glance from under hooded eyes before swinging his legs out of bed. Unlike her, he had no problem waltzing around nude. He casually and slowly picked up his pants and shirt, tossing both on the bed.

Cate silently chastised herself for the way her heart sped up and her core throbbed in anticipation. One would think that after the third . . . or was it four times? Whatever the number, her body should be revolting against another bout with Ash. Instead, it wanted to stand up and declare its availability.

Ash flipped his phone over and checked the screen. "Noelle's on her way," he reported.

Cate watched as he picked up his pants and pulled them on. Then he plucked the shirt off the sheet and tossed it over his shoulder, not bothering to fasten his pants.

"I'll see you in the morning, sugar."

Grabbing his boots, he made his way around the side of the bed, planted a breath-stealing kiss on her mouth, and then sauntered out of her room.

I'll see you in the morning, sugar?

What kind of half-assed statement was that?

Cate threw herself down on the mattress with a huff. The sheets smelled like him. *She* smelled like him. But instead of getting up and washing herself off, she rolled over, buried her face in the pillow, and breathed him in. God, he was so sexy. And so damn good in bed. But she'd known it would be like that with him. She'd known it when she was seventeen—that he was the right guy to take her virginity.

Ash might be an asshole, but tonight he'd proven that he was utterly unselfish in bed, and . . . Cate suddenly felt cheated. Instead of an experienced, patient lover for her first time, she'd gotten inept fumbling in some dirty hotel room in Jakarta with a drunk journalist who'd bragged about how he was a stud in bed but in actuality turned out to be a total letdown.

The guy's technique had consisted of three steps: wham, bam, and thank you. As in, he literally thanked her as he rolled his body off hers. She should've known better, though. Another journalist there, a woman, had warned Cate about the guy, but in her own drunken state, she'd viewed the yellow flag the fellow female had thrown up as a sign of jealousy.

The second time she'd had sex, she'd been sober. It hadn't hurt, and the guy had lasted longer than the first, but it hadn't felt like she thought it should. She hadn't burned for him. There'd been no energy between them. It was dinner, a little fondling, some kissing followed by penetration, and then it was over.

Was she wrong to want more than that? To want passion? She wanted someone who stormed the castle, who was so overcome with need that he'd tear down the walls to get to her. Maybe it was archaic to crave that, but she did.

Of course, she also wanted her freedom and independence. Was that even possible? To have it all?

Noelle's dry voice sounded from the door that Ash had apparently left ajar. "From the looks of your bed, I'd say you and Ash worked through your issues."

Cate allowed herself one silent moan of embarrassment before flipping over on her back. She was a grown woman, damn it. She had nothing to be ashamed of.

"We had a lovely chat," Cate replied, grateful that the darkness hid the flush on her cheeks. "So Jim made the trip okay?"

"Yeah. He looked peachy when I left. Sofia had him all hooked up to his needles and IVs and that fucking ventilator." Noelle dropped her gun on the other bed and sat down, looking rattled. "You got my text, right?"

Cate nodded. The text had come through in between rounds two and three of her and Ash's sexcapades. Her thighs squeezed at the memory because she was pretty sure that was the round when Ash shoved her up against the wall and pounded her from behind. There might still be plaster stuck to her breasts from that particular session.

"Well, like I texted you, Sofia said the swelling is going down. Good thing we bought that MRI equipment last year or I might've been tempted to haul him to a hospital." Noelle clenched her fists on her knees. "When we find Rivera, I'm going to gut him from his neck to his dick. No, to his groin," she corrected. "Because I'm chopping off his dick and feeding it to him before I fillet him like a fish."

Cate was fully on board with the bloodthirsty tactics. She wanted Rivera to pay too. "What's the plan?"

"Same as it's always been—find the asshole. We need to follow the son and the wife, but we don't have the resources for both." Noelle sounded exhausted, not just from the trip she'd just taken, but all of it. "Rivera has eyes everywhere, it seems."

"How'd he get to Ash's grandmother?" Cate wondered out loud.

"Best guess is that he's pulling favors from gangs in

the States. There's a motorcycle club that runs drugs and guns from Mexico across the border into Texas. They serve as a pipeline for gangs in the central US. I spoke to an FBI source earlier and he said that the prisoner who iced Bernie Roma is connected to a rival family on the East Coast—New Jersey, maybe Boston."

"Boston . . . Doesn't Liam have like a thousand family members in Boston?"

Noelle nodded.

"You think he'll go home?"

"He has to be thinking about it."

Cate pursed her lips in thought, her mind running over the options—the very few options—available to them. "The wife," she finally said, surprising herself with the confidence in her voice. "We should focus our resources on Camila Rivera."

"Why do you say that?"

"A couple reasons. Family is obviously important to Rivera, because he's targeting *our* families—"

"The son is family too," Noelle pointed out. "And this whole clusterfuck is retaliation for the other son's death."

"Yes, but I don't think Benicio means as much to him as Adrián did," Cate countered. "You didn't hear him on the phone—he sounded so disgusted when he spoke about Benicio. He basically called him a coward."

"Did he mention the wife?"

"No, but I find it super fishy that she's resurfaced in Guatana out of the blue like this. I did some research, and she spends most of her time in Monte Carlo and the Caribbean. Suddenly she's back in Guatana? At the same time her supposedly dead husband is photographed in the market?"

"You're saying she's here to see him," Noelle mused.

"My gut says yes."

The other woman nodded. "All right. We go with your gut, then. You and Ash can tail her while Macgregor and Port toss wherever it is that she's staying."

Her and Ash on another mission? Oh boy. Cate didn't know if she could handle it, but if she wanted to convince everyone that she was a capable adult, complaining about being paired with someone she'd slept with would not be the right way to go.

"Sounds good," she said, and her voice was a bit hoarse because her heart was in her throat.

When she'd arrived at the compound four years ago, Jim's people had gone out of their way to welcome her. Abby showed her how to throw knives. Isabel taught her how to apply makeup and use clothes as a weapon. Jim took her on tracking lessons. And Ash, before he'd driven her away, had been her constant friend.

But she'd never felt like she was one of them . . . until tonight. Noelle had not only listened to her, she'd actually acknowledged Cate's instincts and was using them to formulate a plan.

For the first time in her life, Cate felt like she truly belonged.

The next morning, Noelle outlined the plan and gave credit to Cate, who basked in the glow of approval. She knew it was silly but she loved knowing that today's mission to tail Camila Rivera was her doing.

"Holden, what do we have in terms of eyes on the ground?" Noelle turned to the tech man. "Can we tap into the local surveillance?"

He shook his head. "At least eighty percent of the city's surveillance cameras have been busted, disconnected, or just aren't working because of a tech failure.

I'm thinking we use a drone. The model I brought has a two-mile radius and can fly up to an hour at a time. I've got two of them, so we can have one in the air while the other is charging up."

In the seat next to Holden's, Liam frowned. "How noticeable is it?"

"And aren't those fuckers noisy?" Sullivan asked from the doorway. He appeared to be trying to position himself as far away from Liam as possible, which brought a pang of sadness to Cate's belly.

Every time she saw them, the tension between them seemed a thousand times greater. She wished they'd just talk through their issues, whatever those issues even were. Why did men have to be so damn complicated?

Case in point—Ash. He was leaning impassively against the wall, making a studious effort to avoid her gaze. He'd stopped by her room in the morning but Cate had been busy getting ready and so he'd given her an indecipherable look and left. She had no clue what was going on in his mind, and unfortunately, now wasn't the time to try to figure it out.

"Got these from an Army contact." Holden reached into his bag and pulled out a small bird-shaped object with a propeller attached to the top. The thing was no longer than Cate's hand. "It'll look like a bird unless you're on top of it. And it's got regular and thermal cameras, so if she goes into a building, I can track her general movements."

"Two miles is a good distance," Liam remarked.

"Ain't technology grand?" Ash drawled. It was the first thing he'd said all morning.

Cate's eyes flew to him and he gave her a cool look in return. Damn it, how did he feel about last night? Was he regretting it?

"Not grand enough," Noelle replied briskly. "Drones aren't going to flip the hotel room where Camila is staying." She addressed Liam. "How are you getting in?"

"We've got it covered. Paige is helping us out."

Sullivan spoke up in a light tone. "You sure you don't need me on the ground?"

Noelle shook her head. "No, the others have got it covered. You're with Macgregor."

Cate didn't miss the unhappiness on his handsome face. Liam wore a similar look, though she suspected his displeasure came from the fact that Sullivan clearly didn't want to be paired up with him.

And as messed up as it was, the fact that these two easygoing guys and best friends were having problems suddenly made her feel a little better. Maybe her insecurity as it related to Ash had more to do with general relationship bullshit than any immaturity on her part. Or maybe it was her own feelings of inadequacy that were causing her to feel uncomfortable after last night.

The buzzing in her pocket interrupted her unhelpful thought process. She pulled out her phone and then swore under her breath.

Unknown caller.

"Rivera," she told the group.

Holden immediately darted over to his laptops. Ash, meanwhile, pushed away from the wall and stomped to Cate's side, as if Rivera was going to reach through the phone and grab her.

Although, hadn't he done that already? By killing Ash's grandmother and Isabel's father, that psycho had touched them all. Yesterday, there had been palpable fear in the air. Kane and Luke couldn't get home fast enough. Isabel had taken an entourage to New York to plan a funeral. Even D had ultimately bailed on the op, insisting he needed to be with Sofia even after telling Noelle he would stick around.

Cate couldn't let herself underestimate Rivera, and as much as she might be loath to admit it, having Ash's big frame by her side brought her a sense of comfort.

No one spoke as she answered the call. "Hello, Mateo."

"Hello, little one. How are you this morning?"

"Feeling pretty good," she lied.

"How do you like my welcoming committee?"

"Are you talking about when we shot up your airport or when we killed your son?"

There was a short silence before Rivera spoke again. This time his voice was tight and a lot less jovial. "I was referring to the deaths of your loved ones."

"I think it goes to show how weak you are, coming after old people like that."

Ash stiffened.

She could tell by the way he was glaring at her that he didn't like her aggressive stance, but playing the weak victim wouldn't result in mercy from Rivera. They'd killed his son. In retaliation, he was threatening to destroy each and every one of their families. He wanted them to be emotionally destroyed because it would feed his giant ego. The better tactic was to get him to overplay his hand or at least send him into a rage.

Jim always said that staying calm was the one way to gain an advantage over an opponent. Or maybe he'd said the key was *appearing* calm? Cate hoped the latter was accurate, because under her serene exterior, her heart was galloping like a racehorse.

"You'd prefer I struck closer to home?" he countered with a laugh. "I thought I was being kind. I was told that Bernie Roma despised his daughter—I did her a favor, no? And Mr. Ashton's grandmother was feeble and ill. That was a mercy killing."

Lord, she was glad Ash wasn't able to hear that. He'd have ripped the phone out of her hands and gone tearing into the street after Rivera.

"I was telling someone the other day," Rivera continued, "that young people today lack gratitude. I'm teaching you an important lesson, *querida*. I find that women respond to sexual violence the easiest. They don't mind getting their fingers broken, but rape them and they break like fragile china."

Holden gestured for her to keep Rivera on the phone longer.

Her palms were sweating over the obvious delight in Rivera's voice at the prospect of raping her. Somehow, she forced out a natural tone. "And how did Camila respond? Does she approve of you sticking your dick in someone else to punish them? Is that how you justify your infidelity? Because that's a new excuse. 'Oh, no, dear, it wasn't an emotional thing at all. I don't love her like I love you,'" Cate said in a mocking tone. "But you do love it, don't you? You get off on having that kind of power over people. Though is it really power when you prey on people weaker than you? That's what you do, right? You hide and attack the weak and old?"

"You shut your vile mouth, little girl," Rivera growled into the phone.

"Or what? You'll shut it for me? Teach me a lesson? I already have a dad, so I don't need your input, thank you very much."

"You're testing my patience."

"My deepest apologies for that."

"When I find you—"

As Holden snapped his fingers, Cate interrupted Rivera with a cheerful laugh. "Oh darn, I'm afraid I have to go. Later, Mateo." Then she hung up and turned to Holden with an eager expression. "Well?"

"Call came from the Westin," he announced. "You were right, Cate. He's with the wife."

Chapter 27

"We've got a visual on Camila Rivera," Ash reported two hours later.

Liam nearly sagged over in relief when the rookie's voice filled his ear. He and Sully had barely exchanged ten words in the hour they'd been holed up in this hotel room and he was getting tired of the silence. It gave him way too much time to think about the way his friend had looked in the shower yesterday. On his knees, heated eyes peering up at Liam, hot lips wrapped around Liam's dick.

They hadn't fooled around since, and although Liam's head insisted that it was probably for the best, his body was primed for another round. He'd been walking around with a semi ever since. Sooner or later that need would spill over and he and Sully would wind up naked again.

"Is she alone?" Liam asked Ash.

"Negative. Got a female friend with her. No sign of Mr. Rivera."

Sully spoke from the other double bed. "Noelle—permission to roll?"

"Not yet," she answered over the feed. "Give Cate and the rookie five. We need to make sure she's not just making a quick pit stop."

"Roger that," Liam said.

The moment the comm went silent, his agitation

returned. Sully's gaze was glued to the door, not once straying in Liam's direction.

He knew exactly why he was being frozen out—because of last night's heart-to-heart in the barracks. That was Sullivan Port's MO. When shit got too real, the man shut down.

For as long as Liam had known the guy, Sully had always held a part of himself back. He'd share that his mother abandoned him on the front steps of a church, but never reveal the crushing sense of abandonment it had caused. He admitted to never knowing his father, but left out how much that hurt him. He described the shitty conditions of the foster homes he'd grown up in, but neglected to mention the loneliness he'd felt.

Yesterday, when Sully spoke about the girl he'd loved, it had given Liam insight into his friend that he'd never had before. Sully passed himself off as a cocky ladies' man. He had a reputation for fucking anything that moved and for never, ever taking life too seriously. He'd once described himself as superficial, confessed the belief that he'd make a terrible father or partner, but Liam saw through that bullshit now.

Sullivan Port was a coward, plain and simple.

"You're staring at me."

The flat voice broke through his thoughts. "Yes."

Sully glanced over warily. "Why?"

He shrugged. "Just figuring a few things out."

His teammate's gaze shifted back to the door.

"What, you're not going to ask what I'm figuring out?" he said lightly.

"Why would I bother? You're going to tell me anyway, aren't you?"

Oh yeah, Sully was definitely in shutting down mode. He only turned into an ass when he felt like he was in danger of exposing any vulnerability. And he'd exposed a shit ton of it yesterday. The pain in his voice had been so visceral when he'd spoken about Evangeline. And his boat, the fucking boat that Liam and the team mercilessly teased Sully about being his entire life . . . turned out it was a tribute to the girl he'd lost.

"You wouldn't have hurt her," Liam said, his voice low, cautious.

Sully's gaze flew to his. "I wouldn't have hurt who?"

"Evangeline. You loved her. You wouldn't have hurt her. And you would've kept your pants zipped if she'd lived."

There was no response.

"It's true," Liam insisted.

"Whatever you say, Boston."

"For fuck's sake, Sully." He drew a calming breath. "You go on and on about what a whore you are. You constantly remind me that you're an orphan and don't have a family. But truth is, it's you that doesn't want a family and it's you that can't keep a relationship. Not because you can't be faithful, but because you're too fuckin' scared."

Those gray eyes narrowed. "You're psychoanalyzing me again."

"Maybe you need to be psychoanalyzed."

"Yeah? Then I'll go see a shrink. I don't need you doing it for me."

"You do that, man. But any therapist worth their salt will figure you out in a heartbeat." Liam cast a challenging look. "They'll tell you that you're terrified of getting hurt."

"Sure," the other man muttered. "If you say so."

"You're really going to deny it? I see you, Sullivan. I see who you are deep inside. You're a scared little boy whose parents abandoned him. You're the guy who found someone to love, someone who mattered the world to you, and she left you too. That's what it boils down to. It's not about monogamy and it's not about you getting bored. It's about you being scared shitless."

Sully's lips curled in a sneer. "You really want to talk to me about scared? You're too chickenshit to tell your family that you're bisexual. Too chickenshit to tell them that you don't want marriage and kids and all that normal bullshit. You just let them believe that it's going to happen eventually, that you'll settle down once you get all the action out of your system. But we both know better. It'll never be out of your system."

Liam stiffened. That wasn't true. He *would* tell them . . . eventually. And he *would* have that normal life.

Except . . . when he thought back to all the things he'd dreamed of doing in life, having a kid wasn't one of them. He'd seen a house, sure. A home base to come back to in between his travels.

But he'd never pictured kids or a wife in that house.

He took a ragged breath and met Sullivan's accusatory eyes. The tension was back. Not of the sexual variety, but the strange animosity that kept cropping up each time they tried to have a meaningful conversation.

They'd been best friends for years. They'd talked for hours about anything and everything. But, he realized, they'd never truly dug beneath the surface.

Fuck. He was no better than Sullivan, now that he thought about it. He'd told Sully about his past, his family, his goals, but he'd never taken that extra step either. Never admitted how any of that shit actually made him *feel*.

Jesus Christ. Maybe *he* should see a therapist.

"Looks like she's gonna be here a while."

Ash's voice jerked them out of the tense stare-down, and once again Liam experienced a burst of relief.

"Good," Sully answered gruffly. "I'll get our girl Paige

on the line. Let us know if Rivera's wife ventures back this way."

"Copy."

Sully swiped a finger over his phone, then put it on speaker. A few seconds later, a polished British accent greeted them.

"You boys all set?" Paige chirped. She was the only one of Noelle's chameleons that Liam had yet to meet, and truthfully, he didn't know much about her other than that she was a tech guru hermit who lived in northern England.

"Yep," he told her. "How're things on your end, darling?"

"Almost ready."

"Are you sure we've got the right room?" Sully asked.

"The room's registered to Victoria Kern, one of Camila's known aliases. If she's staying at the hotel, this is our best bet."

The question was, was her dear old husband with her? That's what they were about to find out.

Liam stood up and drew his sidearm. "Just give us the word and we'll go in."

"One sec."

He and Sully headed for the door as they waited. The sound of fingertips moving over a computer keyboard clicked out of the phone speaker. Like Holden, Paige could make magic with a wireless connection and a laptop. It was all so over Liam's head that he never even bothered asking for explanations.

The typing lasted for several more seconds before Paige spoke again.

"Done."

"Thanks, love." Sully ended the call and tucked the phone in his pocket.

Liam touched his earpiece. "Noelle. We're all set."

"All right. Go do your thing."

As they stepped into the carpeted hallway, both men kept their weapons out of sight by palming them against the sides of their cargo pants. They'd already made sure that housekeeping was done with this floor, and the corridor was empty as they soundlessly approached the door across from theirs.

They nodded at each other. Sully raised his gun slightly. Liam reached for the knob. Paige had deactivated the magnetic key panels, disabling the hotel's entire lock system. The concierge would be dealing with a lot of confused and unhappy patrons soon, but Liam didn't worry himself with that.

He pushed open the door. His teammate slid inside first and they worked in perfect unison, Sully moving forward into the suite while Liam ducked into the small powder room to his right.

"Clear," he murmured.

"Clear," Sully murmured from deeper in the suite.

Liam entered the living area in time to see his friend's broad frame ducking into the bedroom through a pair of open French doors.

"Clear," Sully said again. There was no mistaking the disappointment in his voice.

Shit. It wasn't like Liam had expected Rivera to be sitting in the room patiently waiting for them to show up and kill him. But from the looks of it, he hadn't been here at all.

A search of the suitcase on the floor turned up nothing but women's clothing. A pair of black high heels sat on the carpeted floor near an overstuffed armchair. On the end table by the sofa was an empty wineglass with a pink lipstick stain on the rim. In the bathroom, Liam found women's toiletries. Sweet-smelling soaps, lotions, a makeup case.

All around them were signs of a woman's presence, but nothing that belonged to a man.

Still, they continued to flip the room, checking every drawer and cabinet and coming up empty-handed. The room safe wasn't even locked—Liam peered inside to find an empty space. Pressing redial on the phone directed him to the front desk. The last call out of this room had gone to room service.

"Son of a *bitch*."

The angry oath had him hurrying to the bedroom, where he found Sully standing in front of the closet. The door was open to reveal the full-length mirror hanging inside it, but Sully's muscular body blocked Liam's view.

"What's wrong?" he barked as he marched over.

Sully took a slight step to the side so Liam could see the mirror.

He instantly let out a curse of his own. There were four words written on the clean, shiny surface, scrawled in the same shade of pink as the lipstick on the wineglass by the bed.

Nice try, little girl.

Ash didn't know how Morgan did it. How he was able to work with Noelle in the field or stand idly by while the woman placed herself in one dangerous situation after another. The problems for Ash were twofold: he wanted to hide Cate in one moment, and in the next, he wanted to flip up that long gauzy skirt of hers and remind himself what she tasted like.

He smothered a groan as Cate bent over a market stall under the pretense of inspecting a handmade necklace.

"*¿Cuánto cuesta?*" she asked the merchant, holding up the amber-colored beads to the sun.

"For you, pretty lady? It is twenty-five American dollars."

"The drone is up and running," Holden said in Ash's earpiece. "Your target is coming out of the jewelry store and will pass you in"—he paused to do a quick mental calculation of speed, distance, and time—"three minutes, twenty-two seconds. Give or take."

He smiled and winked at the vendor who was still haggling with Cate. "I love you, man. Glad you're back."

"It's good to be back." Holden sounded surprised by his own words.

Ash fully understood it. Holden had suffered the worst blow a man could ever face. He'd lost his woman, and from the stories Ash had gleaned around the compound, Holden had been in bed with her at the time. That shit didn't just scar. It scooped out your insides and left you a shell of a person. That Holden had kept going was a testament to his personal strength, and Ash silently saluted that.

His gaze once again drifted over Cate's gorgeous body. He didn't know how he'd be able to handle it if Cate was taken from him. Then again, maybe he wouldn't have to worry about it. Morgan would probably shoot him on sight after he learned about the plans Ash had for Cate.

Ash had wanted to talk to her about those plans this morning, but she wasn't ready. He could tell by the panicked look that filled her eyes whenever he opened his mouth. Hell, last night she couldn't wait for him to leave. If he'd dallied any longer in the bedroom, he had a feeling she would've gotten up and dragged him out. One would think four orgasms would have driven out her self-consciousness, but apparently not.

Out of the corner of his eye, he tracked the jaunty gait of Camila Rivera. She had a friend with her and they were talking animatedly. You wouldn't know Guatana was on the brink of collapse by looking at Camila, who wore sky-high heels, tight white jeans, and a flowy top. On her wrist were half a dozen gold bangles, and the rings on her fingers sported rocks that Ash figured could probably feed an entire village for a year.

"Got her," he murmured loud enough for the mic to pick up. He laid a hand on Cate's back. "Go ahead and buy it, sugar. You know you'll regret it later if you don't."

Cate nodded and handed the money to the seller, who clapped his hands and promised her that she would be the envy of all her friends.

Straightening, Cate eyed their mark under the guise of readjusting her sunglasses. "How about we head over to the shop we saw earlier? It had a beautiful scarf in the window."

Ash bent down and pressed a kiss against her temple. "Anything for you." He hid a self-satisfied smile when he felt her tremble.

"Great. I think it's over there, right?" She deliberately pointed in the opposite direction of Camila Rivera.

"Try that way, sugar," he teased, steering her in the right direction.

She responded with a fake giggle and allowed him to push her toward their target. "Where do you think she's going?" Cate murmured when they were out of earshot.

"Who knows. It doesn't look like she bought anything in the store."

"This entire place looks so sad."

Ash couldn't disagree. Overhead, the remnants of colorful pennants hung on the crisscrossing telephone lines. Lining the stone streets were dozens of brick and metal stores painted in reds and teal greens, but most of the shops were closed. Tape, cardboard, and wood planks covered smashed windows, and the once busy city center was filled with more birds than tourists.

Up ahead, Camila Rivera and her friend walked briskly up one of the never-ending hills in Guatana City.

"It's no wonder all the women here look like supermodels," Cate groaned as they climbed a slope steep enough to require mountain-goat-like balance. "And she does it in heels."

"She's probably on drugs and can't feel a thing," Ash told her.

"Give me whatever she's on, then. And check out her ass—it's disgustingly perfect. I'm so jealous right now. How is she in her mid-forties?"

"Your ass looks fine, sugar. Feels good too." He allowed his hand to drop a little lower than was publicly appropriate.

"Ash, seriously," she grumbled. "We're on a mission."

"Yeah, you two are on a mission," Holden repeated in their ears.

He pulled his hand up reluctantly, because they were both right. "Where's she going, Holden?" he asked to distract himself, though it was damn hard with Cate's sweet body swaying next to his.

"She took a left turn on the next block. It's down an alley."

"This is no shopping trip. Not up here in the hills." He glanced around again. The neighborhood was far from affluent; the buildings were too shabby for that.

"Maybe she's going to meet Rivera," Cate said, her excitement evident.

Ash wasn't so sure. It couldn't be this easy, could it? When they turned down the alley that Camila had disappeared down, a buzz kicked up in his stomach and it wasn't one of anticipation. It was a warning. This particular alley had four-story-tall buildings on either side and was just wide enough to accommodate the tiny cars that were so common on the streets of Guatana. In fact, Ash could probably stand in the middle and touch both buildings with one arm span.

"I don't like this," he said bluntly.

He spared a sideways glance in Cate's direction, careful to make sure it didn't seem like he was checking up on her. He was sick of fighting with her, and any indication that he thought she wasn't performing up to task was bound to rile her. But he couldn't stop caring. That'd be like cutting off his arm or something. Even then he'd still have those phantom pains.

She looked all right, though, if not a bit tired. He felt a pang of guilt for keeping her up so late, but he hadn't been able to control himself last night. And she'd been so damn willing each time he'd reached for her, flooring him with her passion. Cate was wild in bed, willing to do anything, wanting to do everything. Ash had never experienced that kind of enthusiasm before.

He was dying to experience it again.

"As far as I can see, there isn't anything ahead of you except a couple old ladies hanging up laundry on the third floor. Nine o'clock," Holden reported.

Ash looked to his right and spotted the *abuelas*. "Nothing about this feels good, Holden."

His unease only heightened when Liam checked in with an update.

"We searched her room. No signs of Mateo Rivera. Except . . ." Liam hesitated.

"Except what?" Noelle barked. She was positioned across town outside the hotel, making sure Liam and Sully didn't encounter any unwelcome surprises.

"There was a message on the closet mirror," Sullivan finally reported.

"What'd it say?" Noelle sounded impatient.

"'Nice try, little girl.'"

Both Cate and Ash froze.

"Shit," Noelle swore.

"The message is meant for me," Cate mumbled. "He knows we're tailing his wife."

"Do we abort?" Ash asked.

"I think we have to," Holden said grimly. "You're coming up on a T intersection. Mrs. Rivera is heading left, which means she's going in a huge fucking circle."

"She's playing games," Noelle murmured. "It's a trap. I'm calling this off."

"I can send out my other drone," Holden suggested. "Maybe we can—ah, fuck. Hold on. There's someone coming up to talk to me. I—"

The feed went quiet.

"Holden?" Ash prompted.

There was nothing but silence on the other end.

"Holden. You there?" Sullivan demanded.

No answer.

The tiny hairs on Ash's neck prickled. "We're going back," he announced.

"What about Camila?" Cate asked.

"You heard Noelle. We're aborting." And Holden still wasn't fucking answering, damn it.

A good Marine never ignored his gut, and right now, Ash's gut was waving every flag in the book to get his attention. Something was wrong.

Something was very, very wrong.

Chapter 28

As urgency pounded in his veins, Ash grabbed Cate's arm and practically dragged her to the mouth of the alley. Rather than voice an objection, she fell into step with him and the two of them raced down the cracked sidewalk in the direction they'd come from. Fortunately, they were going downhill this time, making for a much easier trek back.

Ash couldn't remember the exact alley where Holden had been parked. Somewhere near the bank, maybe a few blocks north of that. He ran faster, ignoring the startled faces of a trio of cigar-smoking men sitting on a nearby stoop. He and Cate sprinted past them, nearing the bank building at the corner of the intersection and—there it was. He remembered seeing that rusted metal newspaper dispenser by the entrance of the alley.

Relief flooded his gut when he spotted the black Range Rover. He lunged into the narrow lane, only to lurch into a standstill.

It was the amount of flies around the open car door that alerted him.

Oh fuck.

"What's wrong—"

He flung out his arm and pushed Cate back before she could enter the alley. "Stay here," he ordered, and hoped for once in his life she listened to him.

He jogged forward, pulling the gun out from under

his shirt and keeping it tucked against his thigh. When he reached the car, his boots splashed in liquid. Sick to his stomach, he grimaced at the rust-colored puddle staining the pavement.

"What is it?" Cate called out.

"Stay there and don't take any pictures." He held up a hand. "Seriously, Cate. Just listen to me this one time. You don't want to see this."

Ash himself didn't even want to look, but he forced himself to. His pulse buzzed in his ears as he stepped closer to the Rover, his stomach a tight knot of nerves. He'd seen dead men before. He'd watched fellow Marines die, held their bleeding, broken, often in-pieces bodies in his arms and listened to them utter their last words.

He knew all about death . . . and yet nothing had prepared him for the corpse that used to be Holden McCall.

Someone had slit Holden's face, Joker style, from ear to ear. There were multiple stab wounds in the chest and arms. From the looks of it, at least a few of them were defensive. Holden's gun lay in the backseat as if it'd been knocked out of his hand. Ash hoped some of the blood on the ground was from the tangos.

Choking down his horror, he edged closer and saw that Holden's button-down shirt was gaping open, stained almost black from his blood. Then Ash's eye caught something else—a coil of . . . something, at Holden's boots. Was that a fucking *snake*? No, it . . . He leaned in even closer. It smelled like smoke . . . and meat.

Jesus Christ.

What he saw made his gorge rise. He backed up and took several deep breaths in an attempt not to throw up his breakfast.

"Ash?"

As his stomach continued to churn, he slowly turned around to face Cate, who'd crept up behind him.

She stared at him, wide-eyed, beautiful, and alive.

And suddenly he realized that the problem he had with Cate in the field didn't have anything to do with her competence. It had to do with *him*. She could be the best trained, most skilled, and lethal operative on the planet and it would change nothing for Ash. She'd somehow become his reason for living, and if she wasn't around, he didn't want to be either.

He wasn't going to be Morgan, who didn't give a shit if Noelle went on a hundred missions. He wasn't going to be Holden, who could somehow keep living after the loss of Beth.

Ash would never be able to survive it if something happened to Cate.

"Oh God," she whispered, her gaze traveling to the SUV.

"Don't look," he bit out.

It was too late. Whatever she'd glimpsed had drained the color from her face. "He's with Beth now," she whispered.

"I sure hope so," Ash said hoarsely.

"Rookie, we need a fucking report here," Noelle snapped in his ear.

He drew another breath before replying. "Holden's gone."

"He abandoned his post?" Sully said irritably. "Where'd he go?"

"Nowhere." Ash's throat ached so badly it was hard to talk. "He's gone. Dead. KIA."

A shocked puff of air blew over the line. "Jesus," Liam murmured.

Noelle broke the short silence with a harsh noise. "Get back to base. All of you. Now."

Ash wasn't about to argue. He wanted Cate out of this alley. Out of this city. Out of this goddamn country.

He approached her slowly, struggling for oxygen as he reached out for her with shaking hands. Then he pulled her against him and pressed one palm over her heart, nearly weeping when he felt the organ beating reassuringly beneath his palm.

But although she was breathing, Ash knew that the wave of fear that swept over him when he'd seen Holden's guts lying in a scorched pool at his feet wasn't going to subside until he had Cate under him, flesh to flesh.

It was hours later, nearing midnight, when Sullivan found himself alone in the dusty courtyard of the Guatana military base. He took a drag of his cigarette and sucked deep. Held the smoke in his lungs until they ached, then blew out a sputtering cloud that was instantly carried away by the humid air.

"I'm sorry about your friend."

A heavily accented voice broke the silence as Timo Varela came up beside him. The courtyard served as a recreation area for the Guatanan soldiers, boasting a handful of picnic tables on which several chessboards and decks of cards lay abandoned. The men came here to gamble, smoke, and drink, but tonight the yard was deserted. Earlier, the base had received word of a shoot-out in the city, so most of the units stationed on base had been dispatched to deal with the rival gangs.

"Thanks," Sully mumbled in response. "Holden was a good man."

He might not have had contact with Holden for more than four years, but they'd worked together a long time before the guy went off the grid. Holden had been a quiet, loyal man who'd gotten them out of many a jam during his time on the team. GPS, SOS calls, cell phone tracking . . . Holden McCall and his trusty laptops had always been there to save your ass.

It was just a damn shame that nobody had been there today to save his.

"Morgan made it back to Costa Rica safe and sound, eh?" Varela hopped up on the picnic table next to Sully. "I assume the rest of you will be moving out soon?"

He smiled wryly. "Eager to get rid of us, huh? Don't worry, I get it. Our presence here makes all of you a target."

Varela gave a wry smile of his own. "We were a target of the cartels long before you got here."

Sully took another drag.

"They don't like that Guatana has a military to protect it," the commander went on. "They don't want there to be opposition while they rip our country to shreds." He swiped the cigarette from Sullivan's fingers and took a quick puff. "You're better off getting the hell out of this country."

Varela tried handing the cigarette back. When Sully shook his head, the other man smoked it down to a nub before flicking the butt on the dirt.

"I'm tempted to leave myself," the commander admitted, wearily hopping to his feet.

"Why don't you?"

"This is my home. I plan on protecting it until my dying breath." Anger tightened his angular features. "But men like Rivera and Barrios and all the other cartel slime, all they care about is money, power. And they have enough of both to sway the government into doing their bidding. They've even turned high-ranking military officials to their way of thinking. How do I stand a chance against that?"

Sully didn't have an answer, but it was obvious Varela was speaking rhetorically.

Sighing, the man said, "Have a good night, friend." Then he ambled off toward the building behind them.

Sully forced himself to get up too. He couldn't sit out here all night. But he also had no desire to go inside and see everyone's stricken faces as they grieved for their old friend.

To his relief, every door was closed when he walked into the barracks. He entered his room and found Liam in bed, lying there in the darkness.

"Hey," came a gruff voice.

"Hey," Sully answered. He stripped naked and stretched out on the other mattress, propping one arm behind his head and resting his other forearm over his eyes.

"Ethan and Juliet flew out an hour ago with Holden's body."

"Montana?"

"Yeah. His parents still live there. And that's where Beth is buried. They'll probably bury him beside her."

He fell silent for a beat. "He should have had backup."

"We're spread thin," was Liam's bleak response. "There was no one available."

As frustrating as it was to hear, Sully couldn't argue. They *were* spread thin. Bailey and the Reillys had gone to New York with Isabel and Trevor. Everyone else had rushed off to protect their families. With him, Liam, and Noelle at the hotel, Cate and Ash in the market, and Ethan and Juliet watching Benicio Rivera, the team had been too shorthanded to provide Holden with the necessary backup.

Still, it ripped Sullivan apart to think that Holden had been ambushed by those cartel killers. That he'd died alone.

"Get some sleep," Liam advised. "We can regroup tomorrow."

He closed his eyes, but sleep didn't come. He just stared up at the speckled ceiling, grief weighing on his heart. His mind continued to race with thoughts of Holden, of Rivera, of the argument with Liam at the hotel. The angry accusations they'd hurled at each other.

Liam was wrong, though. Sully wasn't afraid of getting close to people. He did it all the time, for fuck's sake. Maybe he didn't have any biological relatives but he absolutely considered the team his family.

His aversion to relationships had nothing to do with fear either. After Evangeline's death, nobody had been able to hold his interest for more than a few weeks. So, what, he should purposely lead his lovers on? Screw that. Better to keep things casual right off the bat. That way nobody got hurt.

It had nothing to do with fear. He was just being *considerate*.

Tamping down his agitation, he rolled onto his side and tried to get comfortable. He heard Liam's steady breathing but wasn't sure if the other man was asleep.

We'll regroup tomorrow.

Would they? What the fuck did *tomorrow* mean anyway? Holden had probably woken up this morning thinking he'd have a tomorrow, and now he was fucking dead.

With a strangled noise, Sully sat up in bed.

"Everything okay?"

He ignored the drowsy-voiced question and weakly climbed off the mattress. His bare feet carried him the five steps required to eliminate the distance between the two beds.

"What are you doing?" Liam sounded startled when Sully slid in beside him.

"Kissing you," he mumbled, then cupped the back of Liam's head and brought their mouths together.

A feeling of rightness washed over him. Yeah. Kissing Liam was so much better than thinking about Holden and his lack of tomorrows. So much better than thinking, period.

His pulse sped up when the tip of Liam's tongue flicked over his. The kiss started off tentative, slow, the light brush of lips and lazy swirl of tongues, but it wasn't long before it transformed into something hot and desperate. Liam's hand curled around Sully's neck while they tried to eat each other's faces off. As need slammed into Sully's body, fast and hard, he rolled Liam over and climbed on top of him.

He wasn't worried about crushing the guy. At six-two and one hundred and eighty pounds of pure muscle, Liam could handle whatever Sully gave him. And he gave it back with equal force, his fingers biting hard into Sullivan's hips as the two men ground their lower bodies together. Their mouths were still fused, tongues slicking feverishly as heavy panted breaths heated the air.

"This is probably a bad idea," Liam grunted, yet his hands were already sliding down to cup Sully's ass.

Sully jerked when he felt the rough squeeze. "I'm the master of bad ideas," he muttered before burying his face in Liam's neck. He inhaled the scent of citrus and soap and man, kissed that strong column of flesh, and then licked a path back to Liam's mouth.

His friend groaned when their lips met again. Sully rotated his hips and the torturous friction of his bared cock rubbing against Liam's covered one sent both arousal and impatience streaking through him. He wanted them skin to skin, damn it.

Growling, he hooked his fingers under the elastic of Liam's boxers and peeled the fabric away. His mouth flooded with moisture when a long, thick cock was exposed to his gaze. Another bolt of desire shot through him, pushing him to action. He eagerly closed his fist around the velvety smooth shaft, eliciting a low moan from the man beneath him.

"We really shouldn't do this," Liam mumbled.

"Yes, we should." He peered down, a lump of regret forming in his throat. "Life is short, mate. We have no idea what's going to happen tomorrow. Might as well take advantage of tonight."

He didn't know if it was the philosophical words that caused Liam to surrender, or if it was the way Sully tightened his grip around the man's dick. Didn't matter, because Liam was suddenly thrusting into his hand, features creased in desperation.

Chuckling, Sully lowered his head and took the thick shaft into his mouth, getting it nice and slick with his tongue. His own dick was an iron spike, throbbing, twitching, pleading for attention. He pushed his hips into the mattress in an attempt to bring himself some hint of relief, rocking slowly as he continued to suck. Hard and fast, summoning tortured noises from Liam's throat.

"Jesus fuck, Sully. You trying to kill me?"

"No." He lifted his head and smiled. "I'm trying to get you off."

Liam groaned again. "I didn't realize it was a race to the finish, literally."

"I've been wanting to make you come again for two bloody days, mate." He gave a sharp stroke of the hand. "So now shut the fuck up and give me what I want."

His friend must have been just as on edge as he was because it didn't take long for Liam to come apart. A few more sucks, the swirl of tongue around the head, and Liam was shuddering in climax.

Salty flavor coated Sullivan's tongue and he lapped it up readily, quickly, not wanting to waste a single drop. Normally he took his time with sex. He was all about the foreplay, drawing out sensations until both parties were sweaty, gasping messes begging for release. Tonight, he was impatient. He was so hard it hurt, and each frantic *thump-thump* of his heart brought with it a hot bolt of excitement.

As the other man recovered from the orgasm, Sully hopped off the bed and walked over to the duffel bag he'd left near the door. He unzipped it, stuck his hand inside, and rummaged around until he found what he was looking for.

Liam raised a brow when he noticed what Sully was holding. "Seriously? You travel with lube?"

"Have you ever known me to *not* travel with lube?"

That got him a choked laugh. "Good point."

He wasted no time crawling back onto the bed and reaching for Liam again. He flipped him over onto his stomach and sat astride him.

It took a few seconds to realize that Liam was frozen in place. "What's wrong?" Sully murmured.

There was a beat. "Nothing."

"You sure?"

"Ah . . . yeah. It's fine."

"Good," he ground out. "Because I really need to fuck you now." Again, he didn't miss the way Liam's back tensed. As a pang of doubt hit him, he smoothed a hand over the man's muscular ass. "Unless you don't want me to . . . ?"

"No . . ." Liam sucked in an audible breath. "No, I do."

Thank God. Thank *God*. Sully could've been satisfied with a BJ or a handie—either would have succeeded in releasing the tension coiled tight in his balls—but he knew he'd come harder in the tight sheath of Liam's ass. A shiver ran through him at the mere thought. Christ, it had been so long since he'd fucked someone. The fact that he was about to fuck Liam only heightened the anticipation.

Taking a breath, he dripped some lube in his hand and then trailed a finger down the crease of Liam's tight buttocks. His friend's spine went rigid again when that finger breached him, but his ass pushed against the probing touch. The lube made it easy to slide in deep, and when Sully slowly rubbed the spot he knew would drive Liam wild, he was rewarded with a hoarse groan of pleasure. He wished he could see Liam's face but the man's cheek was pressed against the pillow, his eyes squeezed shut.

Sully added a second finger and watched a shudder run up Liam's sculpted back. "You okay?" he said huskily.

"Yeah," was the equally husky response. "Don't stop."

Yeah right. Like stopping was an option. He wanted this too much.

Liam grumbled when Sully suddenly withdrew his finger. "I told you not to stop."

"Not stopping. Just suiting up, mate."

He leaned forward to kiss the nape of Liam's neck, then tore open a condom packet and rolled the latex over his shaft. After he'd applied a generous amount of lubrication, he shifted forward on his knees, gripped Liam by the waist, and tugged slightly to adjust the angle.

Sully knew he was a big man and Liam sure as hell wasn't making this easy for him. The resistance was so strong he could barely work himself inside. But the tight suction around the tip of his cock felt incredible. He almost came right then, had to breathe through his nose to will away the tingling sensation in his sac.

Squeezing Liam's ass with both hands, he leaned in to whisper, "You've got to relax for me, Boston."

Liam drew another breath. This time when Sully

pushed forward, there was less resistance. He slid nearly half his length in.

"Fuck," Liam whispered, his fists clawing the sheets as Sully continued his slow entry.

"Feel good?" he rasped.

"Mmm-hmmm."

He'd never heard Liam sound this blissed out before. Soon the man began squirming in impatience, sliding backward against Sully's dick.

When he was fully seated, he cried out in pleasure that bordered on pain. So fucking tight. He'd never experienced anything like this before. Hell, he couldn't even stay upright—his chest sagged onto Liam's back, his whole body trembling as he valiantly fought for control.

"I thought you were going to fuck me," Liam taunted.

Sully croaked in laughter, but he still wasn't ready to move. Not if he wanted to last more than two strokes.

"Fuckin' hell," Liam bit out. "Fuck me. *Now.*"

Another laugh popped out. "How is it that you're the one giving orders when I'm the one with my dick in your ass?"

"How is it that your dick is in my ass and you're not goddamn moving?"

When Liam bucked back again, a wild curse flew out of Sully's mouth. Holy shit. He was so close to the brink that he couldn't see straight.

He pulled out carefully, then drove back in with equal care. As much as Liam clearly wanted to get drilled hard, the man was tight as hell and Sully didn't want to hurt him, so he maintained the slow pace, stroking Liam's hips with each gentle glide.

Lord, he couldn't believe they were doing this. Two years ago he'd flat out refused to, and now he was balls deep in this man and it felt so bloody amazing. He knew he wouldn't last long but if he was going to go up in flames, he was taking Liam with him. Luckily, when he reached around and gripped the man's dick, he found it rock hard again.

Liam groaned. "Yeah. Like that. A bit faster, man."

He barred an arm across Liam's chest to raise him up, so that he was on his knees and Liam was sitting astride him with his back glued to Sully's chest. Then he gave an upward thrust, as deep as he could go.

"Holy shit," Liam mumbled. "I . . . didn't expect this . . . so good . . . fuck . . ." He was mumbling incoherently now, lost in the same mindless bliss that was fogging up Sully's brain.

As he jacked his friend's cock, Liam twisted his head so that their mouths could meet. His tongue slipped inside Sully's mouth, and then both of them were coming, mouths locked together, bodies trembling.

The flood of pleasure stole Sullivan's breath. His heart was beating dangerously fast. So was Liam's—he felt it hammering against the palm he still had pressed to the man's chest.

Sully brushed his lips over Liam's temple before gently easing out of his body. Liam made a sound of protest, then collapsed on the mattress and rolled onto his back, wearing a sated expression that Sullivan knew matched his own.

Still fighting for breath, he rolled the condom off and dropped it on the floor. He'd get rid of it in the morning. Right now, he was too fucked-out to move. He settled in beside Liam and they lay silently on their backs, naked, still hard.

After a beat, Sully rolled onto his side and pressed his head against Liam's shoulder.

After another beat, Liam wrapped his arm around him.

The beat after that, Liam was fast asleep.

Sully, on the other hand, remained wide-awake, unable

to fight the undeniable truth that rose to the surface of his mind.

Liam was right. He *was* a coward. Because what happened between them just now? It scared the shit out of him.

He'd screwed other men before. Screwed a helluva lot of women too. And not a single one of them, male or female, had set his body on fire like this. Not a single one of them had evoked this feeling of pure belonging.

It was too confusing. Too scary. Too bloody much for his brain to process. And when a knock sounded on the door, he was so grateful for the distraction that he lunged out of bed in a heartbeat.

"Yeah?" he said.

"Pack up your shit," was Noelle's sharp reply. "We're moving out."

Sully furrowed his brow. When he glanced at the bed, he saw Liam sitting up, equally puzzled.

"Where we going?" Liam called at the door.

"The compound." Her voice held a rare note of joy. "Jim just regained consciousness."

Chapter 29

Turtle Creek, Costa Rica

"You look tired."

Cate had to smile as she met her father's dark blue eyes. She'd figured his first words after regaining consciousness were going to be sharp ones of rebuke. Instead, he was studying her intently, concern etched into his every feature.

"It's four in the morning," she answered, leaning forward to take his hand. "We flew out of Guatana the moment Sofia called to tell us you were awake."

Morgan stared at their intertwined fingers before lifting his gaze to her face. "Sofia said I was out for days."

Cate nodded. "We were all starting to get worried," she confessed. "Do you remember anything?"

He grumbled under his breath. "I remember getting shot."

Guilt pricked her belly. "What about when you were in the coma? Any dreams? Could you hear us talking to you?"

"No. All I remember is the pain in my neck. Blacking out. And then waking up to Sofia poking me with needles." He moistened his chapped lips with his tongue, then fixed her with a frazzled look. "Don't tell me everyone sat at my bedside weeping about how much they fucking love me."

"They did."

Her confirmation made him frown. Now *that* was what she was used to—her father frowning in disapproval. It was a relief to see it again. Yes, his skin was still pasty white and his features were drawn, but the fact that he could grumble and scowl meant she had her dad back.

"Don't get mad at them. It's not their fault they love you."

He snickered, but the effort it took quickly brought a pained flicker to his eyes. "My back fucking kills," he admitted.

"No kidding. The surgeons removed two bullets from it. And one from your neck."

He gave a slight wave of his hand, which was still hooked up to an IV. "I already know all that. Tell me the rest."

"The rest?"

"Yeah. The shit Noelle is all tight-lipped about. What happened after I went down?"

She bit the inside of her cheek. Crap. If Noelle hadn't filled Jim in on the details, then Cate sure as hell didn't want to. Jim was going to freak and she was tired of being the one with her neck on the line.

"Noelle will fill you in later." Ha. There. She'd slid the buck right back to her stepmother. Noelle was going to *love* that.

Her answer only agitated Morgan even further. "What the fuck is everyone keeping from me?" he demanded. Then, without waiting for another reply, he yanked the IV right out of his wrist, making Cate flinch.

"You can't do that!" she protested. "Lie still."

"Screw that." Her father was already throwing the thin white sheet off his body. He wore nothing but boxers beneath it, and Cate averted her gaze in embarrassment.

"Would you quit being such a stubborn jerk? You're not allowed to leave this bed until Sofia gives you the all-clear." She gave his chest a gentle shove when he once again tried to move. "Lie down, Dad. I'll tell you everything, okay? Just lie the fuck down."

"Don't fucking swear," he said automatically.

"Hypocrite."

"Brat."

Both their mouths began to twitch. Yeah, everything was back to normal, all right.

And yet . . . *nothing* was normal. Cate's humor faded as she remembered all the horrible events that had transpired since the team had arrived in Guatana to save her ass.

"Cate? What's wrong?"

She clasped her hands tightly in her lap and glued her gaze to them.

"Sweetheart?"

"People are dead," she whispered.

Wrong thing to say. Morgan was instantly attempting to get out of bed again. "Who?" he bit out. "Who did we lose?"

"Lie down," she begged. "Please."

After a beat, he went still. But he did slide up into a sitting position, rubbing days' worth of beard growth with both hands. "Tell me," he ordered.

"Rivera sent hit squads after us," Cate said in a shaky voice. "Isabel's father was killed in prison. Ash's grandmother was raped and murdered. Holden—"

Morgan's eyes narrowed. "What about him?"

"He came to Guatana to see you and help us out, and he . . ."

The words got stuck in her throat. Jim and Holden had been close. They'd met nearly two decades ago when they were both Army Rangers. This was going to kill her father.

"He what?" Morgan's tone was sharper than a knife.

Cate released an unsteady breath. "He was killed. Rivera's people killed him."

Silence crashed over the room.

Morgan scrubbed his hands over his face again. "Fuck," he muttered. *"Fuck."* Then he cleared his throat and met her sorrow-filled eyes. "Who else?"

"That's it. We got everyone else out of town in time." Her heart clenched. "And you already know about Riya."

"Your journalist friend. The first casualty."

"Yes." Agony burned her throat. "The first casualty of the war I started."

Her father reached out and pulled one of her hands off her lap. His cold palm covered her knuckles. "Sweetheart . . . Look at me."

It took a few seconds before she found the courage to look up.

"You didn't start this," he said firmly.

"I took that picture. If I hadn't, Riya would still be alive. Holden would still be alive."

"Maybe not." He shrugged, then winced as if the movement had caused him pain. "Someone would've eventually discovered that Rivera had faked his death. Maybe your friend Riya would've been the one to piece it together. Or maybe another journalist, another photographer. Men like Rivera bring war wherever they go. There would've been casualties regardless."

"But not *our* casualties."

His gaze became knowing. "That makes it better?

If civilians you *didn't* know had been the collateral damage?"

"No," she said grudgingly.

"At least this way, we can put him down. Another journalist might not have been equipped to do that. *We* can." His eyes glittered in fortitude. "And we will. For Holden. And for Riya."

Cate gave a weak nod. She wished she could be as certain as her father. But she wasn't. Every attempt they'd made to find Rivera had failed miserably. Morgan's coma had rendered him out of the loop. Once he realized just how ineffectual they'd been, his conviction might falter.

"Get Noelle in here," he told her. "I want to know what we're doing to find that bastard."

"Later." She firmed her tone. "Seriously, Dad. Can you please just rest for a few hours?"

He opened his mouth to object but Cate held up her hand.

"Everyone is asleep. You can start ordering them around in the morning." A note of panic crept into her voice. "Please. Let's wait until morning. I can't think about any of this right now. I just need a few hours of . . . peace."

Something on her face had Jim's eyes going soft. "All right," he finally murmured. "I guess it'll keep until morning."

"Enjoy your long nap, old man?" Ash mocked as he stepped onto the terrace.

Morgan was sitting in a chair around the large glass-topped table, looking a shade paler than a vampire. "Would've woke up sooner if I'd known you guys weren't getting the job done."

Ash rolled his eyes on his way to Noelle, who sat at the other side of the table smoking a cigarette. "Morning, beautiful." He leaned down and kissed her on the cheek before lowering himself next to her.

It was early. The sunrise was just peeking out over the top of the jungle. Below them, the pool and grounds were still illuminated by the outdoor lights where the sensors hadn't been hit by the sun yet. Only the jungle birds and monkeys were awake.

Ash winced when Noelle blew a stream of smoke right toward her husband's face. "Rivera was waiting for you to wake up, asshole." She shrugged. "At least your daughter's still breathing. You can thank Ash for that."

Ash didn't try to hide his surprised expression. "Cate took care of herself. I didn't do squat other than argue that she didn't belong in the field."

Noelle tapped her cigarette against the ashtray impatiently. "Have it your way, honey. I was trying to say something nice about your work down in Guatana in front of your boss, but if you don't want to take that praise, I can shove my foot up your ass instead."

"I'll take the praise," Ash said wisely.

Morgan was looking at the two of them with an inscrutable expression, so Ash made a small gesture that he hoped conveyed his *I have no idea what your wife is trying to do* message.

"What's the plan now?" Ash asked, changing the subject. "To draw Rivera out," he clarified when neither Noelle nor Morgan jumped in right away.

"He's not leaving his hidey-hole," Noelle drawled.

"So why come back?" Morgan asked bluntly. "Because I woke up? I don't need you here tending to me at my bedside."

"Do I look like a nursemaid, baby? We came back

because in Guatana we were sitting ducks. Rivera had all the advantages and we had none."

Ash nodded. "If we'd stayed in Guatana, he would've picked us off, one by one."

"So we give him an easier target by stuffing everyone here?" Morgan spread his hand toward the sprawling mansion they all called home.

Well, not all of them, at least not for now. Once Noelle had radioed the compound to report that everyone was moving out of Guatana, D and Kane had promptly moved the kids to an unknown location. Ash could tell that Cate had been hurt to hear that, because she'd gone from Morgan's bedside to her room without saying a word to anyone.

He'd followed her upstairs but she hadn't answered his knock and after ten minutes of fruitless silence, he'd left. But he hadn't slept well at all. When he'd spotted Morgan on the terrace just now, he'd figured he might as well get his ass in gear and start planning. The sooner Rivera was dead, the sooner Cate would be safe. And maybe then the two of them could figure out what the hell was going on between them.

Until then, he would concentrate on the barrier he could get rid of—Rivera—before contemplating the barrier he couldn't move—Cate's father.

"Let's pick a place, then," Ash suggested. "Anywhere that Rivera's sources are weak. We know he has contacts in the south and east."

"Do we have any idea where the hit on Isabel's dad came from?" Morgan asked.

"Boston mafia family," Noelle supplied. "The Pistasellis."

"He doesn't have strong contacts in New York, then, if he had to outsource it to Boston," Ash mused.

"Doesn't matter where we go, he's not going to come

himself," Morgan said with a shrug. "He'll send some-one."

"And that someone will eventually lead us back to Rivera," Ash argued.

"Using what bait?"

They all knew which bait would be the most effective but none of them wanted to say her name out loud. Hell, Ash hated even thinking about it, but he wasn't stupid. He knew the score.

Rivera had a hard-on for Cate. He enjoyed the cat and mouse game he was playing with her and seemed to want to drag it out for as long as possible. That was why he was picking them off slowly instead of sending a rocket launcher to destroy this quasi-military compound.

"Cate," Ash said finally. "We use Cate as bait."

The words were thick in his throat. Forcing that admission out was more painful than he'd anticipated.

"No. Not acceptable," the boss snapped. "Next idea."

Ash cast a plea for help in Noelle's direction but she busily avoided his gaze. Awesome. Looked like he was on his own here. "Then we get Isabel or Juliet to pretend to be Cate."

Morgan rolled that suggestion around in his head before nodding in approval. "Better. Let's talk to Juliet about it. I don't think Isabel's head is in the game right now." He turned toward his wife. "You're too quiet. You don't like this plan?"

She didn't answer right away. She and Jim stared at each other for a long, uncomfortable beat of silence until she spoke. "I don't have anything to say that you want to hear."

Morgan frowned.

With a shrug, she ground her cigarette butt into the tray and pushed to her feet. Gliding over to her husband, she captured his lips in a long, thorough kiss before backing away. "I'll talk to Juliet. I'm sure she'll be okay with this plan. One of you"—she waved a finger between the two men—"get to have the fun task of telling Cate she's being left behind. Again."

Ash stood up too, hoping to sneak back to the barracks before Cate came downstairs. As much as he didn't want her in danger, he also felt like she'd earned the right to be part of this op, and he wasn't going to be the one to tell her she was out.

"Wait a second, David."

He halted. David, huh?

The last time Morgan had used his given name was after a hairy mission when plans A through D had to be abandoned and they'd ended up shooting their way out of a safe house in Istanbul. After they'd made it to safety, their skin barely intact, Morgan had grabbed Ash by the shoulder and said, "You're a goddamned good soldier, David. Proud to have you as part of the team." And Ash had damn near hugged the man because he'd never heard the word *proud* used in conjunction with his name.

"Yes, sir?"

Morgan made a face at Ash's use of *sir*. The other man had never liked that. Said it made him feel old. "Cate listens to you. If I go to her, she'll accuse me of treating her like a child and then she'll do something we'll all regret."

"All due respect, sir, but I think her response to me will be the same."

Morgan shot him a cool gaze. "It's different with you, though, isn't it?"

Ash felt an uncomfortable prickle at the back of his neck. Shit. Did Morgan know about them? Had Noelle said something?

"In what way?"

"You really want me to spell it out?"

"Yeah. I do."

That earned him a cold look. "All right, then. Cate's always had a crush on you." Morgan shrugged. "So use that to get her to sit her ass at home."

"That's a little low, isn't it?" he said stiffly.

"Better to be underhanded than have a dead daughter."

With that, Morgan turned his gaze toward the jungle beyond the railing. The conversation was over. Ash was dismissed.

And for the first time in a long time, he felt like that piece of dirt under someone's shoe. Only this time, it wasn't a bunch of folks from Peterville, Tennessee, whose opinion he couldn't give two shits about. It was the man he looked up to as a mentor, a father figure.

As his insides twisted in resentment, Ash curled his fingers into fists and then spun on his heel and walked into the house.

He didn't know why, but it felt like he was walking away from the only life he'd ever really cared about.

Cate heard his boots again and wondered for the second time in twenty-four hours if the heavy treads were a warning. When Ash was training or out in the field, he moved soundlessly, all quiet sinewy muscle and lethal grace.

That she could hear him outside her door told her that his guard was down, that his warrior facade was slipping.

Last night she'd been on the verge of opening the door to him but her emotions had been too raw. She'd sat with Jim for an hour before Noelle came in to take her place, and from the hushed conversation between Jim and his wife, Cate knew that Noelle had been filling him in on everything that had gone down. She had no doubt that Jim and Noelle were planning a retaliation strike against Rivera—and she had no illusions that those plans would involve her in any way.

She'd be kept here at the compound under armed guard, a prisoner in her own home, until Rivera was caught and killed. The children had already been spirited away and once the rest of the team was dispatched to do their jobs, it would be her, a few guards, a mountain of C-4, and, if the walls were ever breached, an extended stay in the panic room.

She'd been down in that steel-lined two-room bunker once and didn't care to repeat the experience. No matter how safe it was intended to be, she still felt suffocated down there. There were no windows. Only a toilet with the tiniest drain, a hand shower, and enough army rations to feed a person for a year.

A survivalist heaven.

But Cate didn't want to survive; she wanted to *live*.

She dropped her face in her hands and wondered what she had to do to make her father understand that whatever life he'd dreamed up for her wasn't the one she wanted. Not now, and not ever.

Thump thump.

When Ash's boots passed her room again, Cate lifted her head and grumbled at the door. "If you're here to convince me that you guys don't need me, take your sad song elsewhere. I'm not in the mood and I already know all of the lyrics by heart."

"I'm not here for that."

Cate imagined him leaning one arm against the door, shaking his head wearily. "What are you here for, then?"

"Open up."

"Tell me first," she insisted, but her feet had hit the floor and she was standing.

"Open up, Cate."

The firm command had her gliding across the tile. "Don't make me regret this."

She pulled the door open and raised a brow at his disheveled appearance. He looked like he hadn't slept a wink. His dark hair was tousled, his jaw was coated with dark stubble, and his green eyes lacked that usual glint of energy.

Ash placed one big hand on her waist and marched her backward, closing the door with one booted heel.

"Do you still have the pen I gave you?"

She made a face. "What?"

"The night I visited you at Brown . . . I gave you a pen. Do you still have it?"

Cate wished she could say no, but that would be a lie. The damn thing was in the bottom of her backpack. She brought it everywhere she went.

"It was the worst gift I've ever received," she said bluntly.

The corner of his mouth curved up. "I don't doubt it, but I didn't ask whether you liked it. I asked if you still had it."

He touched her face and the palm of his hand burned hot against the side of her cheek. Or maybe she was the one burning him. His eyes had darkened to forest green, revealing so much naked need that it took her breath away.

They weren't talking about a pen. She knew that. He was asking her to jump and telling her he'd catch her. And as terrifying as that prospect was, there'd always been such a huge hole in her heart.

She wanted to fill it up with Ash.

"I still have it," she whispered.

In an instant, his mouth crashed down on hers. She tasted the morning on his tongue, fresh and new. She felt midnight between his legs, dark and heavy. With one move, he picked her up and spread her thighs until she was forced to cling to him as he walked her back to the bed.

His mouth never left hers. Not while he kicked off his boots. Not while his fingers found the elastic of her shorts and pushed them clear of her legs. Not while his hands tore at her T-shirt until it lay in two ragged lengths on either side of her chest. Not while he positioned his cock at her entrance and thrust forward with so much power she had to throw up her hands against the wall to prevent from going through it.

He just kept kissing her like he'd stop breathing if her mouth wasn't glued to his, and Cate wrapped her arms around his shoulders, her legs around his hips, and hung on. He plunged into her with furious, hard strokes. He was reckless and rough and she loved it.

She felt him everywhere. Beneath her heels, his ass cheeks clenched with every thrust. The muscles in his shoulders rippled as his whole body worked against hers. She kissed him back with an equal amount of ferociousness until the pleasure became so intense, she couldn't hold that contact for a second longer.

Her entire body bowed off the bed with the force of her release, and even then he didn't stop. He pounded into her and Cate could feel him struggling for control. His hips drove into hers while his hands pushed her down, as if he simultaneously wanted to come right this minute and hold off for as long as possible.

The former won out and Ash buried his face in her neck with a shudder. "*Coming*," he groaned.

She lay there under him, feeling his heart thundering against hers. He hadn't used a condom—again—and a warm trickle slid along the insides of her thighs. The rest of her hadn't come out unscathed either. Her lips were kissed raw and her nipples were abraded from rubbing against the wall of his hard chest.

She felt bruised and used and it was glorious.

Sighing happily, Ash rolled over, taking her with him, refusing to let her go. They remained like that for a long time, silent and joined.

"We need to talk," he said finally.

She closed her eyes in frustration. Couldn't she be allowed to enjoy this bliss for a few moments? She wasn't ready to face reality. Not after that earth-shattering experience.

"I thought men were supposed to be worn out after sex. Like aren't you supposed to be asleep by now?"

He captured her hand and brought it up to his mouth. "Is that your experience? Low energy guys who pass out after the first orgasm? No wonder you're willing to have a repeat with me."

"You're right. I'm definitely only with you because of my shitty past experiences."

"Let's not talk about your past experiences," he said, and his voice was a little tight.

Cate smiled in girlish pleasure at the sign of jealousy. "Let's not talk at all," she countered.

"No, we need to. I . . ." He hesitated.

"You what?"

"I . . ." Ash's fist clenched against her thigh. "Fuck, I don't know. I thought I could say it, but . . ."

"Say what?"

He was silent for so long she wondered if he'd fallen asleep. But then he made a frustrated sound and said, "Forget it. I've got nothing to talk about."

"Good." She grinned. "Then let's take a shower together."

Shower sex was high on her fantasy list of things to do with Ash, a list she'd spent years crafting. Maybe they could knock a few of them off today. She wanted to give him a blow job. She wanted him to bend her over the kitchen counter. She wanted—

"Actually, I have a better idea," she blurted out. "Let's go to the grotto."

But she knew that the suggestion was dumb even before it left her mouth. Even before he sighed and said, "No." Then, to her irritation, he shifted and sat up. "I didn't come up here for this. I spoke to Jim and . . ." He stopped again.

The warm glow of the sex was rapidly wearing off. She reached for the corner of her comforter and tried to cover herself up.

And that was when she realized that Ash still had his pants on. He'd ditched his shirt, but his pants he'd just pushed down to his thighs.

Wonderful. While she'd been crafting odes to the best sex of her life, Ash was still wearing his damn pants. The absurdity of it triggered a hysterical laugh.

Ignoring his mystified expression, she hopped off the bed and pointed to the door. "Time for you to go."

"What?" His confusion turned into shock.

"I can smell your guilt, Ash."

He raked a hand through his hair. "For fuck's sake, of course I'm going to feel guilty. Morgan just woke up from a coma and I'm up here with his daughter doing stuff he definitely does not want me to do."

She flinched. "Is that all I am to you? Jim's daughter?"

"No," he said hastily. "Of course not."

Cate didn't believe him. She marched over to the door and threw it open, uncaring that she was buck-naked. "Get out."

"Sugar—"

"Don't sugar me! I mean it, Ash, get out."

"Why?" He was visibly frustrated as he yanked his pants up to his hips.

"Because when I'm with a guy, I don't want my dad in bed with us!"

It was his turn to flinch. "Cate . . ."

"I swear to God, if you don't leave right now, I'm going downstairs and telling Jim how you just fucked his daughter." Bitterness scraped her throat as she swallowed. "And you certainly don't want that, do you? You'd rather sacrifice your life, your happiness, than upset my father. You'd rather see *me* upset than put so much as a frown on that man's face."

Ash's features creased. "That's not true."

"Like hell it isn't. Jim Morgan always comes first with you." She pressed her lips together to stop a sob. Her chest was throbbing so painfully it became hard to breathe, but she managed a quick, ragged exhale. "And Cate Morgan . . . God, that poor, stupid girl never stood a chance."

Chapter 30

Ash had no idea how he managed to attend the afternoon briefing without breaking down in front of everyone. But somehow, some way, he found the strength to keep his cool. To adopt a vacant expression. To ignore the state of agony that Cate's dismissal had put him in.

He'd gone upstairs earlier to try to talk to her about Morgan, to tell her that she was going to be left behind again. Instead, he'd gotten distracted by lust. And then, when he had the opportunity to tell her, he'd chickened out.

He couldn't do that to her, damn it. He couldn't shut her out, not when he truly believed that she'd earned the right to be part of this mission.

Morgan, however, was determined to deny her that right. As the briefing unfolded, Cate was turning to stone before their collective eyes. Each word that came out of Morgan's mouth turned her as hard as the marble that made up the terrace floor.

But Morgan was oblivious to the rage that was building up inside his daughter. As various suggestions for finding Rivera were tossed out and shot down, not once did he mention Cate, even though every single one of his people had glanced her way at some point in the conversation.

"So everyone's going but you and me," Cate muttered when her father was done talking.

"That's right. We'll have some alone time." He gave her a halfhearted smile, which earned him nothing but a disdainful glare.

Ash couldn't remember the last time his boss had misread a situation so poorly. Or maybe Morgan wasn't misreading it but intentionally ignoring Cate's unspoken demands for recognition.

It was a mistake, though. Why couldn't Jim see that he was losing her?

Panic hit Ash square in the chest when he saw the frustration in Cate's eyes give way to resignation. Oh fuck. They were *all* going to lose her. She wasn't going to fight Morgan any longer.

Instead, she was going to leave.

In the four years they'd known each other, she'd told Ash more than once that she was tired of everyone leaving her behind. She'd admitted to constantly feeling abandoned—by her mother, who'd died before she was born; by her grandfather, who was supposed to love her but had kept her from her father; by Jim, who'd taken her in and then refused to value her in the same way he valued the members of his team. Maybe even by Ash himself, who'd chosen Morgan's loyalty over Cate's schoolgirl love.

Back then he'd believed what Morgan had preached— that Cate deserved to find a normal rich boy and live a normal, privileged life.

Now, he wasn't so sure anymore. He wasn't sure of anything other than he couldn't live without her. But he didn't know how to tell her that. Or if she'd even believe him or want to hear it.

Sure, she'd slept with him, but that didn't mean shit. Ash had slept with lots of women and not one of them had triggered a second thought. Cate, on the other hand, had lived in his head, and his heart, for nearly half a decade.

But he wasn't sure she felt the same about him.

"Actually . . ."

Cate's calm, even voice jolted him back to the present.

"Your alone time is going to have to be just that—*alone* time." She walked over to her father and leaned down to brush a kiss against his cheek. She did the same with Noelle, kissing her lightly, before moving toward the patio doors. "I'll text you when I get there."

"When you get where?" Morgan asked sharply. "Where're you going?"

"I'm packing. And then," she paused with a hand on the doorjamb, "I don't know. I'll text you when I get there," she repeated.

Morgan rose unsteadily to his feet. He'd already been pale from his injuries, but now his face was as white as the bandage on the back of his neck.

"Cate. I've gone easy on you. I let you traipse around the country taking photos and putting yourself in situations that result in stuff like this."

Stuff like this?

From across the table, Ethan threw Ash an incredulous look. At the railing, Liam and Sully shifted awkwardly from one foot to the other. Juliet, who was leaning against the pillar near the door, looked ready to throttle Morgan.

And Cate . . . well, she went ballistic.

"Stuff like *this*?" she yelled. "Like this? This happened a grand total of once!"

She thrust her index finger upright, though Ash didn't think it was the one she really wanted to wave at Morgan.

"I'm not the one putting myself in constant danger," she ranted. "I'm not the one who runs toward guns. I'm not the one whose entire life is spent with one finger on the trigger."

"And I came to Guatana and saved your ass!" Morgan roared in return. "So you best be damn glad I know how to use my trigger finger!"

Cate reeled back as if he'd punched her. Ashen-faced, she inched closer to the doors. "You know what? I'm sorry I called you for help. So fucking sorry."

And then she whirled around and ran inside.

"Damn it, Jim." Noelle's chair scraped across the stone floor. "When are you going to start watching your mouth with her?"

"She drives me crazy." He slammed his fist on the table. "I'm trying to keep her safe."

"You're a dumbass." Noelle sighed. "I love you, but you're a dumbass."

The others seemed to be fighting laughter as Noelle strolled into the house without a backward look at her husband. Ash was too worried about Cate to even crack a smile. She'd looked and sounded . . . devastated.

"Ash, get in there and tell Cate to settle her ass down." Morgan jerked his thumb toward the second floor in the general vicinity of Cate's room.

Ash's shoulders went as rigid as the stone columns on the patio. How many times had he done everything Jim asked? A thousand, at least.

He'd jumped when Morgan said jump.

He'd killed when Morgan said kill.

He'd talked Cate into going to college when he'd wanted nothing more than for her to stay.

He breathed deeply, trying to loosen the tension in his body. It didn't work. Cate's wounded blue eyes continued to flash through his head. Her weak voice when she'd whispered to her dad—*"I'm sorry I called you for help"*—continued to buzz in his ears.

He exhaled in a rush. "No. I can't do that."

Morgan's eyes narrowed. "Why not?"

"Because Cate is as vital to this op as any other person here. We're not dragging Rivera out of hiding unless we have Cate with us." He hesitated. "She's willing to put herself on the line and make a sacrifice to keep the rest of us safe. And I . . ." He gulped. "I'm going to respect that."

"You're willing to put someone you love in danger? Jesus! Do you even have balls between those legs?"

Ash crossed his arms tight to his chest before he gave in to the urge to clock Morgan. "I'm going with your daughter, sir." Then he stopped and corrected himself, because as Cate had said so pointedly this morning, she was more than Jim Morgan's daughter. "I'm going with Cate. If that takes her to Guatana, I hope the team is there to back us up. If not"—he shrugged—"then I guess it'll just be Cate and me."

He moved toward the door, turning his back to the man who'd saved his life and his dignity five years ago. To the only father figure he'd ever known.

Morgan's cold words rang out clear in the midmorning air. "If you leave, don't come back. You won't be welcome here."

Ash swung around and raised his right hand to his brow. As bitterness rose in his throat, he gave Morgan a sharp salute. "Yessir."

It was the last order he'd ever take from Jim Morgan, and they both knew it.

After the shit show on the terrace, Liam couldn't escape fast enough. He excused himself under the pretense that he needed to call his family, leaving the others to deal with the mess. Though honestly, he wasn't sure if any amount of cleanup could make this mess go away.

Ash had quit.

Cate was upstairs packing.

Noelle was pissed at Jim.

Jim was pissed at everyone.

With the threat of Rivera still hanging over their heads, Liam couldn't handle any more drama. Morgan would get his shit together, he always did. Until that happened, Liam was perfectly content to hide out in his room.

He made a beeline for the private bath, ducking inside to take a quick shower because he hadn't gotten around to doing it last night. After he'd washed himself clean, he wrapped a towel around his waist and entered the bedroom that he hadn't slept in for two years. Before that, this room had been his home, and he was gratified to find that nothing had changed in his absence. The navy-blue-and-beige color scheme, the king-size bed, the cozy sitting area, and huge flat screen mounted to the wall. Morgan's housekeeper Inna had either cleaned the room regularly or tidied it up right before his arrival because there wasn't a trace of dust and the hardwood floor gleamed beneath his bare feet.

He sat on the bed and ran a hand over the impossibly soft bedspread. He'd been living in Boston for the last two years, yet the apartment he was renting didn't come close to feeling like home. Not the way this room did. He'd loved living on Morgan's compound. Being surrounded by his teammates. Having the mountains, jungle, and ocean at his disposal, the gun range and training course where he could expend his energy.

Fuck, he'd really missed this place.

A knock sounded on the door. From the macho *tap-tap-tap*, it wasn't hard to guess who it was.

"Come in," he called.

Sure enough, Sully stepped through the threshold. He

wore olive-green cargos, flip-flops, and a white wife-beater that revealed the roped muscles of his big arms.

"So that was interesting, huh?"

Liam snickered. "Understatement, dude. Morgan looked ready to slit Ash's throat."

"Yeah. But I'm with the rookie on this one. Cate's a tough cookie—she can handle this work, if that's what she wants to do with her life."

He nodded in agreement. "She might be tougher than all of us combined."

Shifting awkwardly, the blond man shut the door and then glanced around the bedroom. "Uh. So. You happy to be back?"

"Yeah. I am, actually. I was just thinking about how this place feels like home."

"I thought the same thing when I walked into my old room," Sully admitted. "It's weird, but when I was growing up, I never really felt like I belonged anywhere. And somehow I wound up with not one, but two places that I consider home—here, and on my boat."

Liam swallowed. "That's . . ." He stopped, averting his eyes as the heat of embarrassment rose in his cheeks.

"That's what?"

"Forget it."

"What were you going to say?" Sully approached the bed, his fingers hooked loosely in his belt loops.

"That's my list too," Liam finally mumbled. "Where I feel most at home—here, and on your boat."

Their gazes locked. Something traveled in the air between them. Not tension or hostility, but . . . fuck, it felt like regret.

And in that moment, Liam understood why Sullivan was standing in front of him right now.

"You're leaving," he said flatly.

Sully gave a quick nod.

"We haven't found Rivera yet."

"You don't need me for that, mate. The boss is awake now—he can coordinate the op from his bed if he needs to. He's got Noelle, Ethan, you. Trevor and the rest of them will be back from New York soon. Plenty of manpower to go around."

"You don't want to see this through to the end?" The question held a double meaning and they both knew it.

But Sully only addressed the obvious one. "What, you're going to accuse me of being a coward again because I'm bailing on this op?" There was a bite to his tone.

Liam shrugged.

"You guys don't need me here," the other man insisted, as if he were trying to convince himself rather than Liam. "I came to Guatana to say good-bye to Jim in case he croaked, but he's alive and kicking and I'm feeling restless, craving the water. I need to go."

Liam offered a nod. He could have called bullshit, but he didn't. No point. He knew damn well why Sullivan was leaving. And yes, it *was* because he was scared. Last night, when their bodies had been pressed together, the connection between them had been impossible to deny. They'd experienced a sense of closeness that Liam had desperately missed.

The depressing thing was, Sully had no idea how monumental last night had been. It was the first time Liam had let another man fuck him. It had been a major exercise in trust, a moment of sheer vulnerability for him, but he wasn't about to tell Sullivan that. Hearing it would just send the man running even faster.

Still, he couldn't stop himself from voicing at least some of what he was feeling. "We are," he said thickly.

A dark-blond eyebrow arched his way. "We're what?"

"Friends." He laughed under his breath. "We keep saying we're not, but that's a load of bull, dude. We're always going to be friends. Even if you walk out this door right now and then show up again in fifteen years, it still wouldn't change that. We're friends for life."

A sad smile lifted Sully's lips. "I know."

Liam took a breath. His brain screamed for him not to keep talking. To simply shake this man's hand, say good-bye, and let him walk away. But the words popped out before he could curb them.

"I could come with you."

Sully looked startled. "What?"

"I could come with you," he repeated. "I meant what I said before—I feel at home on your boat. I feel at peace there, just like you do." His throat tightened. "We could be at peace together."

The silence that followed was like a dull blade to the gut. Yeah. He should've kept his mouth shut. Of course Sullivan didn't want him to come along. How could Sully hide away and pretend he wasn't scared shitless if Liam was there to witness it?

"Not a good idea, mate." Sullivan ran an agitated hand over his scalp. "We're not . . . you're . . . if you come with me, it won't end well . . ." He snagged his bottom lip between his teeth. "I can see in your eyes what you're really asking."

"And what am I really asking?"

"Whether or not we can continue . . . this . . ." Sully gestured between them. "But we can't. I told you, I'm not interested in relationships."

"Yeah, you said that."

"I'm not interested in loving someone again."

"Yeah, you said that too." He got to his feet.

Sully's nostrils flared when Liam stepped closer. "Boston . . ."

It was a warning.

Liam ignored it. He slipped his hands under the hem

of Sully's shirt and slowly dragged the material up his friend's chest. Heat rippled through him as his palms glided over defined muscles and heavy pecs.

"I'm . . . I'm leaving," Sully muttered.

"Yeah, I got that, man. But you're not leaving until I do this."

He undid Sully's pants, then slid his hands inside and groaned when Sully's bare ass filled them. The man never wore any boxers, which was not only hot as fuck, but it definitely made life easier.

"Until you do what?" Sully croaked.

"Make sure you never forget me."

The man's breath hitched. "What are you talking about? I could never forget—"

Liam silenced him with a kiss, and as usual, his heart took off in a gallop the moment their lips touched. It was so jarring kissing a man after he'd spent a year kissing Penny. So different. The scrape of stubble against his chin, the dominating thrust of tongue.

Groaning, he tugged on Sully's waistband. In response, Sully kicked off his flip-flops, ditched the pants, and pressed his long, muscular, naked body flush against Liam's. Liam had expected a little more resistance but his friend was kissing him back in desperation, frantic hands already fumbling with the knot of Liam's towel.

And then they were both naked and stumbling toward the bed. Sully fell onto his back with a soft thud. Liam lowered himself over him and their erections slicked over each other.

Jesus.

So good.

He groaned again and wrenched his mouth away. "You're going to remember this," he said hoarsely. "When you're in the middle of the ocean, sitting alone on that deck and staring out at the water . . . you're going to remember this."

Then he kissed his way down that hard, male body and took Sully's cock into his mouth, lapping up the salty, masculine flavor. He sucked him all the way to the base, then teased the shaft with decadent licks before kissing his way down to that tight sac.

"Boston," Sully said helplessly.

"I'm here," he murmured. "Don't you fuckin' forget that."

He left the bed briefly to grab a condom and lube, then resumed the task of driving the other man crazy. He sucked, licked, pumped, tormented. He twisted his fingers inside the impossibly tight passage. Nuzzled the man's thigh and jacked his cock until Sullivan was panting in desire. When he felt the motion of Sully's hips speed up, he tore his mouth and fingers away and rose up to his knees, quickly sheathing his aching cock.

"You're going to remember this," Liam promised.

Gray eyes, burning with need, peered up at him.

Liam was swamped with sensation the moment he slid inside. Sweet mother of God. It was incredible. Tight and hot and . . . home.

It was fuckin' home, and as he drove in to the hilt, he finally grasped the true meaning of that word. Or at least, what it meant to *him*. Those two places he'd named . . . the compound . . . *Evangeline* . . . the only reason he considered them home was because of Sully.

Home was Sullivan Port.

His eyes felt hot all of a sudden. Christ. His pansy-ass was close to weeping. He didn't want to say good-bye to Sullivan again. He couldn't.

Blinking rapidly, he pushed aside the sorrow and focused on the pleasure, the relentless tingling at the base of his spine, the snug warmth squeezing the hell out of his cock. He'd planned on dragging this out, but urgency overtook him now, his hips pistoning as if they had a mind of their own.

Sully let out a husky, pleasure-laced sound. *"Yes."*

Liam leaned forward on one elbow, fucking him harder. Watching as Sullivan's eyes glazed over with arousal, darkening to metallic silver.

He wasn't going to last much longer. He was damn certain of that, so he reached down and took hold of Sully's dick, jerking it in time to the fast, deep thrusts of his own cock.

"Come for me," he growled in Sully's ear.

"Fuck," was the choked response.

It ended way faster than Liam had intended, but when release hit . . . holy hell, it was spectacular. A full-body orgasm that pulsated through every square inch of flesh, turning his limbs to jelly. Sully shuddered and came in Liam's hand, and Liam instantly dipped his head and captured his friend's mouth in a kiss, swallowing up his moan of pleasure.

His heart was still hammering uncontrollably as he gingerly pulled out. He sat up and studied Sullivan's expression. The man looked dazed. Stunned. And . . . afraid.

Yeah, Sully was definitely freaked out again. Liam suspected that his friend would've already been tearing out the door if it weren't for the ringing phone that captured both their attention.

Naked, Liam stood and grabbed his cell from the night table. His brother's name brought a grim smile of satisfaction. Good. Maybe Kevin had finally come to his senses and was ready to leave Boston.

"Kev. You changed your mind?"

"No, that's not why I'm calling. Is this a bad time?"

Liam's gaze traveled to the naked man on the bed.

He closed his eyes briefly, wondering what his brother would say if he told him he'd just fucked another dude. Kev would either spew a litany of homophobic words or go into cardiac arrest. Neither scenario sounded appealing at the moment, so Liam kept his mouth shut.

"It's fine. What's up?"

"I've got one of your cartel buddies locked up in my interrogation room."

Liam froze. "What? Who? *How*?"

"The motherfucker just waltzed into the building," Kevin answered, sounding amazed. "Told the guards downstairs that he was there to deliver a message."

"And you let him up?" Liam said incredulously.

"He was unarmed. Didn't have anything on him except a very detailed file on you."

A flicker of unease tugged at Liam's insides. A file? What kind of file? And what did Kev mean, *detailed*? What the hell did it say?

"He speaks English but has a Spanish accent. Dark skin, dark hair, tattoo on his wrist—a bleeding rose. That's the Rivera brand, no?"

Fuck. "Yes. It is." He paused. "So I'm assuming since you're calling me, that you managed to take him down?"

"No takedown necessary. He came up to my office, sat down, and assured me he wasn't going to hurt me or the family. Said he needed to talk to you."

"To talk?" Liam echoed. He glanced at Sully, who was watching him warily. "Who the fuck is this guy? Send me a pic so we can ID him."

"No need. He was more than happy to introduce himself," Kevin answered in a flat tone. "It's Benicio Rivera. Mateo Rivera's son."

Chapter 31

Boston, Massachusetts

Seven hours after the most incredible sex of his life, Sullivan was in the passenger side of a black Escalade. In the driver's seat, Liam pulled up to the curb in front of Kevin Macgregor's security firm in South Boston. He killed the engine and jumped out of the car, while Sully hopped out of the passenger side and sidled up to him.

A moment later, an identical SUV pulled up behind them. Two doors slammed. Cate and Ash joined them on the sidewalk.

They all looked toward the four-story brick building, which was located near Summer and A Streets, in an area that was mostly commercial and not at all busy.

"So this is where you're working these days?" Ash teased Liam. "Is it as boring inside as it looks from the outside?"

"Pretty much." Liam's tone was distant. In fact, he'd been aloof ever since they'd boarded the jet back in Costa Rica.

Sully knew the guy wasn't thrilled to be back. He, meanwhile, had no idea what the hell *he* was doing here. He could've piloted the twin-engine Cessna at the airfield and flown himself to Aruba, where *Evangeline* was waiting for him. That was the plan, after all. But . . .

Sully couldn't let Liam do this alone, damn it. Not after Liam's confession about how much he hated his life in Boston.

He'd come along for moral support. Or at least that's what he was telling himself. It wasn't that he wasn't ready to say good-bye to Liam yet. Nope. Not that at all.

"How do we know this isn't a trap?" Biting her lip, Cate voiced the question she'd already asked ten times before. Her blond hair was arranged in a long braid that hung over one slender shoulder, and she wore a tight tank that showed off a pair of spectacular tits that Sullivan shouldn't have been admiring.

But hey, at least he wasn't the one touching them. The rookie had probably had his hands all over those beauties. And he must be really attached to them, otherwise he wouldn't have been so quick to go against Morgan.

"We don't," Ash replied for the tenth time. He glanced at Liam. "Though I've got to ask—are you sure your brothers can be trusted?"

Liam offered a stony look. "I trust them with my life."

"All right, then. If we're walking into an ambush, I lay all the blame at the Macgregor door."

They headed for the front entrance, but it wasn't until they reached the doors that Sully realized Liam had remained at the curb.

He gestured for Cate and Ash to wait, then strode back to where Liam stood. With his black pants, black Timberlands, and black long-sleeve shirt that hugged every contour of his perfect chest, Liam looked like he should be creeping through a dark jungle. Or walking the runway of a Calvin Klein show. Either way—sexy as fuck.

"You okay?" Sully asked tentatively.

Liam nodded. "I'm fine." And yet he still didn't move. "We need to go in."

Liam's chest rose as he took a breath. Then he followed Sullivan to the entrance and swiped a key card on the panel mounted to the wall. After the doors buzzed open, the four of them walked in to find a secondary security area.

"Harry. Tyrone." Liam greeted the two guards with a brisk nod.

"Hey, man! How was the vacation?" the taller one— Harry—asked.

Liam's shoulders tensed. "Great. My brothers already up there?"

The guard's friendly expression faded. "Yes. And they requested we pat everybody down. No exceptions."

"Go nuts, man." Liam grinned, but it didn't quite reach his eyes.

The guards stepped forward to search them, then waved the small group off to the elevator banks. Cate continued gnawing on her bottom lip as they stepped into the elevator car.

Sully knew she was still worried about the possibility that this was a trap and he didn't blame her. Everyone was worried about it. Morgan had all but tried to lock his daughter in the compound's basement tunnel after he'd found out she was going to Boston.

Surprisingly, Noelle had been the voice of reason. There was absolutely something fishy about Benicio Rivera brazenly showing his face at MG Security but Noelle insisted that they couldn't afford to not follow up on the lead.

Still, with the rest of the team scrambling to protect their families from Rivera's hit squads, she and Jim could afford to send only a small crew to Boston—and they all knew that Morgan was not happy that Cate was part of that crew. Wasn't happy that the rookie was coming along either.

Hell, nobody on the elevator looked too happy right now. Cate was worried. Ash was eyeing her in concern. Liam's expression was bleaker than Sully had ever seen it.

When the doors dinged open, they found two men waiting for them in front of the elevator.

Sully's breath instantly got trapped in his lungs, because . . . holy shit. He was looking at Liam's clones.

Kevin was in his mid-forties, Denny was forty, forty-one, but their resemblance to their younger brother was unreal. They were as tall and muscular as Liam and just as attractive, and being in the vicinity of three drop-dead gorgeous Macgregors had Sully feeling like he was mingling with celebrities at an Oscar after-party.

Cate's jaw dropped at the sight of the two men. "Are there any more of you?" she blurted out. When Ash narrowed his eyes at her, she glanced over defensively. "What? *Look* at them."

One of the men cracked a smile but the other had a frown firmly set in place. He was staring at Liam. "You got here fast," he remarked. "I take it you didn't fly commercial."

"No. We have a jet." Liam peered past the man's shoulders. "Where is he?"

"You're not going to introduce us to your friends first?"

Liam seemed to be gritting his teeth as he muttered a quick introduction. "Sullivan, Cate, Ash, these are my brothers, Kevin and Denny."

"It's nice to meet you." Cate warmly extended a hand.

Kevin and Denny shook it, skepticism flickering in both their expressions as they assessed Cate. "How old are you?" Denny asked warily.

"What does that matter?"

The defiance sizzling in her eyes had Denny taking

a step back. Sully stifled a laugh. Cate was a formidable woman. Definitely a chip off her old man's block.

"I guess it doesn't," Denny backpedaled.

"There," Liam said grimly. "You got your introductions. Now where's Rivera?"

"I'm not taking you to him yet," Kevin retorted. "Not until you answer a few questions."

Liam gave him an incredulous look. "Questions? What the hell are you talking about, Kev? You want to *interrogate* me? Fuck that."

"You can argue with me all night, little brother, but you're not seeing Rivera until I get my answers."

A vein throbbed in Liam's forehead. He rubbed the bridge of his nose. Drew a deep breath, as if he were trying to calm himself down. "Fine. Whatever. Let's get this over with."

"My office," Kevin said.

He and Liam took off walking, their body language as stiff as their tones.

The others hesitated for a beat. Sully shrugged and followed them. He walked alongside Denny, who offered a rueful smile.

"Don't be alarmed if they start yelling at each other. It's the Macgregor way."

"Really? I don't think I've ever heard Liam yell. Like, ever."

"No shit? That's surprising. That kid can be a real dick when he's pissed."

"Maybe the Macgregors bring out that side of him," Sully countered.

Rather than take offense, Denny grinned again. "Yeah, we do tend to bring out the crazy in each other."

They walked past the empty receptionist's desk toward the offices in the back. Kevin pushed open a door and led them into a spacious office with hardwood flooring and a huge window that overlooked the street. Nobody sat down despite the presence of a sofa, two armchairs, and a big leather desk chair.

"We're wasting time here," Liam grumbled, crossing his arms over his chest. "What do you want to know?"

Kevin scowled. "Which side of the law you're on."

"What the fuck is that supposed to mean?"

"It means—which side of the law are you fuckin' on, Liam? You call me three days ago telling me you're caught up in the middle of some cartel war, that they're killing people's families. You order Ma and Dad to get out of town, scaring the shit out of Ma, by the way. Then the son of a cartel leader shows up at my place of business saying he needs to talk to my little brother. Why would he need to talk to you?" Accusation dripped from Kevin's tone. "What are you involved in?"

"I told you what I was involved in. Suddenly you don't believe me?"

"Criminals don't just request meetings with the good guys! They request meetings with other criminals!"

"You calling me a criminal?"

"Are you?"

"Boys," Denny started.

"Fuck off, Denny."

"Shut the fuck up, Denny."

Sully couldn't stop a laugh. All three Macgregors turned to glare at him, throwing off so much testosterone that the room temperature spiked.

Cate stepped between the two warring brothers and planted a hand on each of their chests. "How about we all calm down?" she said quietly. She focused on Kevin. "Your brother's not a criminal. He works for my father."

Suspicion clouded Kevin's eyes. "Who's your father?"

"James Morgan."

"Yeah? Never heard of 'im." The man's Boston accent

made Sully smile. Kevin sounded so much like Liam. They even scowled the same way.

"What does your father do?" Denny asked Cate.

"He's a . . ." She paused, as if trying to find a nicer way to say *mercenary*. "He's a private contractor. These men"—she gestured to Ash, Sully, and Liam—"are just a few of the soldiers on his team. They're all former Marines, Rangers, SEALs." She grinned. "It's pretty much an all-star lineup over there."

Kevin didn't smile back, nor did he seem appeased. If anything, he looked angrier as he swiveled his head toward Liam. "You're a gun for hire? Seriously?"

Liam frowned.

"First you're a narc and now you're a *merc*? Jesus Christ. Dad's gonna shit a brick when he finds out about this."

"Well, you can tell him all about it later." Liam slammed an angry hand on the desk. "We're in the middle of an op here. That bastard's father sent hit squads after all of us." He pointed to Cate. "He tried to kill her—twice. If she wasn't such a wily little thing, she'd be dead already. So please, save your judgment for later. We need to talk to Rivera." He directed his gaze to his other brother. "Where is he? Conference room one or two?"

"Two," Denny murmured, which earned him a scathing look from Kevin.

Liam took a step to the door, only to halt in surprise when it opened without warning.

A tall, bulky man in faded jeans and a blue button-down froze in the doorway when he spotted all the bodies crammed in the room. Brown eyes rested briefly on Liam before shifting to Kevin.

And whoever the stranger was, his presence had rattled Liam. Sully watched as his friend's shoulders instantly tightened, blue eyes narrowing in displeasure.

"What the fuck?" he barked at his brother. "You involved the cops?"

"No. He just involved me," the stranger answered for Kevin, his sharp gaze continuing to sweep the office.

Yeah, this man was definitely a cop. That heightened awareness just screamed law enforcement.

"Detective Joe Conley," he told the newcomers. "Boston PD. I'm a friend of the family."

"Sullivan Port." Sully shook the man's hand, all the while fighting his unease.

Conley was undeniably attractive, with rugged features and a hard, toned body, but the way his gaze kept straying toward Liam was really bloody annoying. And his expression . . . there was something in it that made Sullivan's instincts hum, and not in a good way. Liam didn't seem to like it either, because his gaze dropped to his boots.

Who the fuck was Joe Conley and why was Liam so uncomfortable in his presence?

"I called Joey for advice," Kevin said defensively. "It's not every day that the heir to a drug empire shows up on my doorstep."

"And what advice did Joe give you?" Liam mocked.

"I told him not to do anything until you showed up." The cop had a deep voice. It was kind of . . . sexy.

Oh, for fuck's sake. Sully swallowed another rush of annoyance. He wasn't allowed to evaluate the sexiness of this man's voice, especially when there was obviously history between Liam and this fucker.

Childhood friends, maybe? Nah. Conley looked to be at least ten years older than Liam, so that didn't make sense.

Another idea occurred to him, but Sully banished it before it could take root.

"We need to talk to Rivera," Liam was saying. "So how about you all just get out of our way and let us figure out why he's here."

"What, are you gonna torture him?" Kevin asked, sarcasm dripping from his every word. "Who taught you how to do that? The DEA or your mercenary boss?" He glanced at the newcomer. "Little bro's a soldier of fortune, how about that?"

Nobody missed the condemnation in his voice.

Conley's lips twitched. "Ah, so he finally told you."

Betrayal shone in Kevin's eyes. "You *knew*?" He angrily turned to his brother. "You told him before you told us?"

The cop answered for Liam. "Hey, go easy on him. It's not his fault I'm so fuckin' easy to talk to."

Liam snickered softly.

Sully's hackles rose again. Oh yeah, there was definitely something between these two. Liam hadn't told his own brothers what he did for a living but he'd told this man? This cop? Who the fuck *was* this guy?

It took every ounce of willpower to extinguish the flames of jealousy heating his blood. He couldn't afford to be distracted by . . . this. Whatever this was. Besides, he had no reason to be jealous. He was leaving town the second they got Benicio Rivera to talk.

"Okay, enough of this shit." Clearly tired of the discussion, Liam stalked to the door.

Sully hurried after him, with the others on their tail.

Liam knew exactly where he was going, marching across the office space toward another set of doors. The one he stopped in front of was labeled CONFERENCE TWO and required a key card to unlock it. He impatiently swiped his card, waited for the door to buzz, then pushed his way inside.

Coming up beside him, Sully conducted a cursory sweep of the room. It contained a table with two chairs on either side, a blinking camera in the corner of the ceiling, and nothing else. It was more of an interrogation space than a conference area, which made him wonder what kind of meetings the Macgregors held in here, and with who.

There was a man sitting at the table. He wasn't bound or gagged and he shot to his feet at their entrance, his gaze flying from Sully to Liam. His clothes looked bedraggled and dusty, as if he'd been wearing them for days. His hair was dark and his eyes were even darker. Nearly black.

"Macgregor. Liam Macgregor." Benicio Rivera stared at Liam, then nodded to himself. "I recognize you from the pictures."

"What pictures?" Liam replied in a frosty tone.

"The file. My father compiled a file on you. All of you. But yours was the only one he gave me. I was tasked with eliminating you and your family."

"I see." Liam sounded bored, but Sully knew better. Pure, volatile energy radiated from his big frame. "You claim you're Benicio Rivera?"

"Yes." Benicio's expression went sullen, giving him an air of insolent youth. He was in his early twenties, more of a boy than a man. "If you don't believe me, I'm sure your contacts in the American government can verify my identity. Send them a picture."

But there was no debate. Sully recognized him from the pictures they'd already received from the DEA. And he had those eyes, those snakelike Rivera eyes. Though while Rivera Senior's eyes held a deadly, calculated gleam, this pair conveyed obvious fear.

"I'm told you want to talk to me," Liam said coolly. "What's this about?"

The young man shook his head. "No, I'm not here to talk to you."

Liam raised a brow.

When Benicio's gaze shifted to the side, it took Sullivan a second to realize that Cate had come up beside them.

A chord of desperation rang in Benicio's voice as he addressed Morgan's daughter. "I'm here to talk to *her*."

Chapter 32

Cate blinked in surprise, shifting uncomfortably under Benicio Rivera's unwavering gaze. "Me?" she squeaked.

Out of the corner of her eye, she saw Ash stiffen and waited for him to lodge a protest. To tell everyone in the room that she didn't belong there. Frankly, as she looked at the armed men all around her, she had to acknowledge that she was more comfortable pointing a camera than a gun. She wasn't cut out for mercenary work. Had never wanted it.

But Jim had pushed her into a corner and so here she was.

Ash remained silent and grim. He'd barely said a word to her since they'd boarded the plane for Boston, and his lack of words was almost as bad as Jim's yelling.

"Yes," Rivera's son said firmly. "You."

She straightened her shoulders. "Good thing I'm here, then."

Benicio lowered himself onto a small metal chair and clasped his unbound hands on the table in front of him. She supposed restraints were unnecessary given the number of armed men in the building.

"Sit," he urged.

After a moment of hesitation, she strode forward and took the seat across from him. She extended a hand and said, "I'm Cate, which you already know. I'm beginning to think your whole family has a crush on me."

He gave a halfhearted limp shake in return. "Benicio, as you already know," he mimicked. His lips curved slightly. "And yes, I think my father likes you. He's always been attracted to fiery women. My mother is"—he paused, searching for the right word—"incomparable."

There was reluctant admiration in his voice, along with a tinge of regret. Cate didn't hold the same warm feelings that he had, not after Camila had led them on a goose chase that resulted in Holden's brutal murder.

"So terrorists love their mamas. How sweet." She placed her hand on her chin, trying her hardest to look like she was at ease. "I'm struggling to figure out why I shouldn't have everyone in this room take turns plugging you with holes."

Sullivan snorted from the doorway.

Benicio's smile turned chilly. "I come in good faith, Ms. Morgan. I'm here to stop these endless killings."

"I see. And how are you going to do that?"

"How are *we* going to do that," he corrected.

She raised one eyebrow.

"We can work together."

Cate sensed Ash coming up to stand behind her. "Or we can just kill you," he drawled, his Southern accent rearing up.

Benicio's mouth twisted. "My death is just one. If we don't stop my father, you'll be grieving for dozens." He stretched a hand around the room. "Can you really tell me that my life, just one life, is the equivalent of all your loved ones?"

"It'd be a good down payment," Cate answered. The remark generated a few snorts and bolstered her confidence. "So let's talk. You want a deal, huh?"

"Yes."

"Fine. Tell us what the terms are. What you want and what we get in return."

Benicio leaned forward. "When I was a child my mother would call for us to come to the table. Adrián and I were to race each other and the first to the table would get a prize. Sometimes it would be money, sometimes a small privilege, such as skipping a lesson or extra time with our friends. It was very small, but we were to fight for it nonetheless. My brother would trip me, push me down. A few times he would tie me up." He frowned deeply before continuing. "I learned to stay close to the kitchen and I made friends with the cooks. And before long I was the first at the table. I did not have to use force like my brother. I used my head." He tapped the side of his skull. "It's why I am here and he is not."

"Your brother got shot up by our team. That's why you're here and he's not," Ash said coldly.

"Americans see things in such finite terms," Benicio scoffed. "You on one side, we on the other. Adrián is dead, and while I mourn him, I also acknowledge the necessity of it. He was a violent man. Maybe with his death, there'll be less violence in this world."

"Your brother must've beat you to the table a lot."

"Many times," Benicio admitted. "He excelled at using brute force to win all arguments."

He reached down. In a blur of movement, Ash was between them with a knife at Benicio's throat.

"Keep your hands where we can see them," Ash growled.

Benicio raised one arm into the air. "I am just showing her a scar. Nothing more."

Ash still didn't move, not even when Benicio's shirt came up to reveal a jagged line of white puckered skin below the young man's rib cage.

"My brother gave me this when I was nine. I picked a few flowers for Mama and she showered affection on me, telling me I was her most beautiful boy. He didn't like the compliments and skewered me with a dull knife. His mistake, though. Mama could not be torn from my side until I had healed."

He lowered the shirt and placed his hands on the table. Ash backed away until he was once again at Cate's side. The knife remained in his hand.

She wanted to reach out and reassure him, but didn't want to give Benicio any more ammunition. He was already flicking curious gazes between the two of them.

"I'm sorry your brother sucked, but as you said, his death was necessary."

"And so is my father's."

This time Cate couldn't keep in her gasp.

"This shocks you?" Benicio said with amusement. "You've spent a week in Guatana trying to kill him. Surely it cannot come as a surprise that others may want him dead, even his own son. Do you not want him dead for nearly killing your father?"

"You know I do. I'm just trying to understand why a son would want to kill his own father."

"Because while he still breathes, my own life is in danger. And as much as I love my mother, I love myself more. So this is my deal—I lead you to my father and you kill him. That is what you Americans call a win-win, correct?"

He slouched back, looking satisfied.

"That's it?"

"That's it. Of course, you'll have to come back to Guatana with me."

"And why is that?"

"It's the only way I'll be able to get back into my father's good graces, if I tell him I've captured you for him. He would not agree to meet otherwise. As I said, he likes fiery women and he's anxious to get his hands on you."

Cate didn't miss Ash's reaction to that. If the man turned any stiffer, he'd crack like a sheet of ice.

She had no idea how he managed to hold his tongue. If the situation were reversed and Ash were the one being threatened, Cate would've been on Benicio in a heartbeat. But Ash didn't move a muscle. He remained the silent guard at her back, never once trying to make her look weak or unqualified in front of Benicio, even though Cate felt completely out of her depth.

"Well?" Benicio prompted. "Do we have a deal?"

She glanced over her shoulder at Ash, Liam, and Sully. All three men offered barely perceptible nods, and then Ash leaned over and placed a burner phone on the table.

"Call your father," Cate told him. "Set up the exchange."

Benicio didn't hesitate. "How long will you need to sufficiently prepare?"

Ash answered in a cold voice. "Today, tomorrow. It doesn't matter so long as it's soon."

"All right." Taking a breath, Benicio picked up the phone and dialed a number. He put the call on speakerphone so they could all hear what was being said.

It took six rings before a sharp male voice came out of the speaker. "Yes?"

Rivera's son leaned forward. "It's Benicio. I'd like to speak with my father."

"Where are you?" was the suspicious reply.

"In the States. I have something my father wants. He will want to talk to me."

"One minute."

It took longer than that. At least five minutes passed before a familiar voice filled the room.

"Benicio, where are you?" Mateo Rivera barked.

"I am in the States. Boston, to be precise. It's a sad city, Father. Very drab. You wouldn't like it."

"You should return home. I told you I didn't want you going anywhere."

"I know." Benicio paused. "But I had to do this."

"Do what?" Rivera's tone hardened with disapproval. "What have you done, Benicio?"

Cate didn't miss the way Benicio's face darkened at the implication that he'd done something wrong. She knew from her conversations with Rivera Senior that the man thought his son was a fuckup, and though she didn't want to feel sympathy for anyone whose last name started with R and ended with IVERA, she couldn't help but feel sorry for the young man across the table.

"For once, I've done something you're going to like," Benicio told his father, a trace of bitterness in his voice.

Rivera snorted. "Somehow I doubt that. But I'm willing to entertain this. Go on, tell me."

Benicio paused, long and measured. Cate had a feeling he was going for dramatic effect.

"I have Catarina Morgan," he announced.

Silence.

"Father, did you hear me?"

"I heard you," Rivera said coldly. "I don't, however, believe you."

"I have proof," his son protested.

A chuckle echoed in the air. "Oh, you do, do you? By all means, let's see this proof."

"One moment." Benicio covered the mouthpiece and sent an imploring look to Ash. "We need to make it sound real," he murmured, his voice barely over a whisper. "You must hurt her."

Cate hardly had time to blink, let alone process the absurdity of that statement. One minute she was sitting down. The next, strong fingers were thrust in her hair, yanking the long strands hard enough to make her cry out in pain.

"That fucking *hurt!*" she roared, glaring up at Ash.

He pressed one finger to his lips while his other hand released her, and she suddenly realized that Benicio had uncovered the mouthpiece.

There was a loud hitch of breath over the line. "Is that you, little one?"

Cate never thought of herself as much of an actress but she happened to be damn good under pressure. As Benicio eyed her expectantly, she leaned toward the phone and hissed, "Fuck you! And fuck your stupid son! If he lays a hand on me again, I'm going to rip his balls off and—"

"That's enough," Benicio snapped. "One moment, Father. I'm gagging the bitch again."

Cate's peripheral vision caught Ash glaring at Benicio for calling her a bitch. She turned to see him stroking a thumb across the blade of the knife that he still hadn't sheathed.

"She's not a very nice girl," Benicio remarked.

There was another silence. "Why have you done this?" Rivera asked his son. "What do you want?"

"A chance, Father. A chance to prove that I am worthy. Isn't that what your goal was?"

More silence.

"Father?"

Rivera's steady breathing filled Cate's ears.

"Father?" Benicio said again.

"Bring her."

Cate's gaze flew to Ash, who offered a grim look in return.

"Where?" Benicio said eagerly.

"Salana. Tomorrow at noon."

The call disconnected, leaving Cate slightly stunned.

Benicio slid the phone back across the table. "Tomorrow. I assume that's not a problem for you?"

"Tomorrow," she echoed before unsteadily rising to her feet.

When Ash took her arm, she gratefully leaned against him, needing his strength. A part of her hadn't believed Rivera would actually agree to this. She shook her head, dazed, as Ash guided her to the door.

"I want your agreement!" Benicio cried out from behind them. "I'm upholding my end of our bargain. I need to know you're going to uphold yours!"

Ash propelled Cate through the door without a response. In the hall, they were joined by Sully, Liam, Liam's devastatingly handsome brothers, and the strange cop who for some reason was still lurking about.

"Are we really going to do this?" she asked.

"It's probably a trap," Ash answered, his uneasiness written all over his face.

"Probably," Sully agreed.

"More than probably," Liam said lightly.

Cate glanced from one man to the next. "But are we going to do it?"

"It's your call, sugar." Ash's response sounded like it was being dragged out of him by a thousand horses.

She bit the inside of her cheek, her gaze dropping to her feet. God. She did *not* want to make this decision. But at the same time, she'd always known that it would come down to her. This whole mess had begun with her, and it was fitting, in a strange and horrible way, that she would see it through to the end.

"Cate?" Ash prompted. "Are we doing this?"

With a tired breath, she lifted her head and met his eyes. "I think we don't have a choice."

As expected, Morgan was livid when he was informed of the plan. With each shouted obscenity that blared out of the phone, Sullivan found himself cringing, and he thanked the lord above that he hadn't been given the task of telling the boss.

He, Liam, and Ash had been about to draw straws to see who would be losing his balls, but Cate proved she had bigger balls than the three of them combined because she'd picked up the phone and called Morgan herself.

Although Sullivan had never felt comfortable using one of his people as bait, Cate was adamant and there was no talking her out of it. When Liam suggested using Isabel or Juliet to pretend to be her, Cate insisted that Rivera wouldn't fall for a decoy. Ash had reluctantly backed her up on that, and even Sully had to admit that a decoy ploy worked only about half the time.

Cate would need to be at that village. In person. Anything less than that and Rivera wouldn't dare to show his face.

Now all that was left to do was hop on a plane to Guatana and carry out this crazy plan. Sully didn't particularly trust Benicio Rivera but at this point they didn't have many other options.

Since they were heading out soon, he went looking for a bathroom, ducking his head into various doorways before he found one. He took a leak and washed his hands, just shutting off the tap when he heard voices in the hall.

"Got a sec?"

He froze. That low baritone belonged to none other than Detective Conley.

A frown marred his mouth when he heard Liam respond.

"Not really."

There was a quiet chuckle. "I know you're in a hurry

to jet, but what, you can't spare five minutes? Not even for me?"

The intimate note in Conley's voice had Sully's hands clenching into fists. He resisted the urge to slam both into the door. Instead, he crept closer. He didn't typically make a habit out of eavesdropping but he was dying to know more about Conley. Or rather, more about Conley's history with Liam.

"No, I've got time for you."

Sully bristled. Like hell he did. They needed to get to the airport. What was Liam doing, making small talk with this man? This Boston fuck with his stupid Boston badge and his dumb Boston accent.

"I miss you," Conley said gruffly.

Oh hell. This wasn't small talk. It was *big* talk. It was gi-fucking-gantic talk.

"I know you don't like to do the whole heart-to-heart bullshit," Conley hurried on. "Normally I don't either, but"—a pause—"Kev said you and Penny broke up."

"We did."

"Did you end it or was it her?"

"Her, but it was mutual."

"Ah. Okay." Conley stopped again. "Liam . . . I've been miserable this year. No—don't say anything. Please just let me finish. I know I scared you off by trying to get too serious, too fast. You weren't ready. And I blame myself for you calling it off. I drove you away when I asked you to move in with me."

Sully's eyebrows shot to his hairline. The motherfucker had asked Liam to move in with him?

Oh. Hell. No.

He inhaled through his nose. The air burned his nostrils, seared his throat. He wasn't sure where all this rage was coming from. Jealousy, sure, he understood that.

But this red-hot fury boiling in his gut caught him off guard. He was two seconds from Hulking out and smashing right through the bathroom door.

"This last year, I kept thinking back to our relationship and I realized that I was offering you something I couldn't even give you at the time." Conley gave a self-deprecating laugh. "I wanted you to move in, and yet my plan was to tell Kev and our families and my co-workers that we were roommates, that you were just crashing in the guest bedroom. That was fuckin' stupid of me. No, it was unfair."

Liam sighed audibly. "I get it, man. Of course you couldn't go public. You have your career to think about, right? I mean, even with all these new PC initiatives and non-discrimination policies, it isn't easy being a gay cop in Boston. Especially in Southie."

"No, it isn't. And last year I wouldn't have even considered coming out to the department. Or telling my family—Christ, you know what homophobic fucks my folks are. I've been living in the closet my whole life. I would've been content to stay there forever." He stopped. "But not anymore."

Sully's jaw tightened.

"Joe . . ."

"Let me finish." Conley cleared his throat. "I spent this entire year missing you. I went out with a few guys, and none of them were you. And that made me realize . . ."

Don't say it, Sully warned silently.

"I'm . . ."

Don't say it.

"I'm in love with you."

Bloody hell.

The wave of outrage almost knocked him on his ass.

His pulse thudded in his ears, making him miss whatever Liam said. But he heard Conley's next sentence loud and clear.

"If you want to give it another go, I won't be pulling any punches this time. I'm all in, babe."

Babe?

"I'll tell the captain, the department. We can tell our families together. Just . . ." A heavy breath sounded behind the door. "It's rare for me to connect with someone, you know? And I never expected it to be Kev's little brother. But then you moved back to town . . ." His voice grew so soft that Sullivan began to miss words. ". . . beers . . . St. Patty's Day . . . and we went . . . and then that first night . . ."

An eddy of emotion slashed violently in Sullivan's body. Jealousy. Anger. And now there was a strange sting in his eyes, like he was going to bloody cry or some shit.

What the hell was wrong with him? Why did he care if this cop professed his love to Liam? He couldn't be with Liam. He couldn't be with anyone.

When Evangeline died, she'd taken his heart and soul with her. In the years that followed, he'd fucked every woman and man who crossed his path. He hadn't given a shit about anyone. Still didn't.

So why did the thought of Liam giving Conley another chance send a jolt of panic through him?

"Joe . . ."

The other man cut Liam off. "Tell me you'll give it another shot. Penny's not in the picture anymore, so what's stopping us? We can start over. Be a real couple."

Liam sounded slightly stunned. "You know how much shit you'll get at work, Joey? If you come out, you're bound to get harassed by some of the other boys in blue."

"I don't give a shit. They can harass me all they want

during the day as long as I'm coming home to you every night. A man like you doesn't come along every day. I'll risk anything for you."

"Joe." Soft and gentle now.

Sullivan's throat ached, because he knew what Liam was about to say. And despite his overwhelming jealousy, despite the fact that he wanted to punch Detective Joe Conley in his chiseled Marlboro Man face, Conley seemed like a decent guy. Like someone who might actually be worthy of Liam. Someone who was willing to risk his career, his relationship with his family and his friends, just so he could come home to Liam Macgregor.

"Don't say no yet," Conley blurted out. "Just take some time to think about it."

But Liam had never been one to lead anyone on. "I don't need to think about it, Joey. Truth is, I didn't break it off because it was moving too fast. I mean, it was, but that wasn't the main reason I ended it. I don't feel the same way about you as you do about me. I don't see a future for us."

Conley cleared his throat again. "I see."

"You're a great guy. An amazing friend. Kev is lucky to have you. *I'm* lucky to have you. But . . . you and me . . . it's not in the cards."

There was a short silence, followed by an awkward laugh. "Hey, it was worth a shot, right? I know I would've regretted it for the rest of my life if I didn't at least ask. Risks, right? Sometimes they pay off, sometimes they don't."

Their footsteps slowly moved away from the door. Their voices grew fainter.

". . . heading back this way after your op?"

"Yeah. Still got some family shit to deal with and I can't leave Kev in the lurch . . . help him find a replacement . . . don't think I'll be working here anymore."

Conley laughed. ". . . always knew this wouldn't be long-term for you."

". . . suppose it isn't."

Their footsteps retreated. The corridor went silent.

Sully took a breath and leaned his forehead against the door.

Fuck.

Liam and Conley would probably be mortified if they found out he'd overheard their exchange. Hell, a part of him wished he'd never heard a damn word of it.

Every single thing they'd uttered was branded into his mind now. He had a goddamn ocean of emotions swirling inside him and he couldn't even begin to dive deep enough to make sense of all of them.

Chapter 33

She was nervous. Her hands were sweaty, just like Eminem had rapped about. The ham sandwich she'd eaten on the plane felt like a lead weight in her stomach. Why had she eaten anyway? That was stupid.

Oh right, because Ash said she should. Ever since they'd left for Boston, she'd done everything he'd told her to do because she was so damn grateful that he'd taken her with him. That he'd included her.

"How're you feeling?" he asked now.

They were still on the jet that Benicio had chartered, but it was sitting in the hangar of a private airstrip. Any second now, the transport Rivera was sending for them would arrive. Cate felt like throwing up when she thought about having to leave the safety of this plane.

"I'm nervous as hell," she admitted.

"Me too." He rubbed his hands down her arms. "You'll be with Benicio and the tangos but we're always behind you. Okay?"

She nodded, her head bobbing up and down a little too manically. "Are you sure I should take the weapons?"

At Ash's insistence, she had a small pistol tucked inside her boot and a knife at her waist. The waist one was intended to be found; Ash maintained that if Rivera's goons found the blade, it might stop them from searching the rest of her.

"It's worth the risk," he said briskly. "If they confiscate them, so be it, but if they're careless at all, at least you aren't completely defenseless."

"How far behind will you be?"

"Two clicks. No more."

Clicks. Short for kilometers. She made herself do the math. "A little over a mile, then."

"That's right. Let's go over what you're going to do when you get there."

"Stall for as long as I can so you can get into position," she recited obediently.

Liam, Sully, and Ash had drilled this plan into her during the six-hour flight from Boston to Guatana City. According to Benicio, there would be one driver, along with a high-ranking member of the Rivera cartel. The two goons would take her and Benicio to meet Rivera.

Cate was supposed to plant a small GPS signaling device inside the vehicle. Using that, the men would follow behind, radioing the directions to the rest of the team, who'd flown to Guatana to assist them. The goal was to surround the building where Rivera was located, kill him, and extract Cate without harm. Extractions were something Morgan's team excelled at. They hadn't lost a "package" yet, Ash had assured her.

She just prayed to God that the streak continued, at least for today.

"That's right," Ash said again. He smiled gently. "You're brave, sugar. Kinda stupid, but brave."

She had to laugh. "Thanks."

His hands fell to shackle her wrists. "Be smart today. Take as few risks as possible. I know that Rivera likes to spar with you, but be careful you don't take it too far. I'd rather have you be alive and cowardly than dead and brave."

"Why are those my only two options?" she joked.

The grip around her wrists grew tight to the point of pain, but she didn't care. She was just happy to have the contact. Ash had come to her room last night to say good night, but he hadn't stayed long and he'd looked so troubled that she hadn't asked him to. And now she was afraid of saying the words that had hovered on her tongue and swam in her blood since the moment she'd met him. But she was also afraid *not* to say them.

She peeked at the back of the plane where Liam and Sully were standing, pretending not to notice the drama unspooling in front of them.

Ash's lips curved. "Smart and brave, then."

The smile gave her courage. "I've been afraid before, but not about this. I know you won't let anything happen to me. And I want you to know—"

"Don't." He cut her off before she could finish her sentence. "Save that thought for when it's all over. But you're right, sugar. As long as I'm alive, no one will touch you."

"It's time," Benicio interrupted, crossing the luxurious cabin toward them. "Shall we go?"

He held out a hand toward the open door of the private jet. The stairs had been attached and at the base of the metal staircase Cate saw a Land Rover with two black-clad men standing at attention in front of the vehicle. One was bald and the other had a head full of thick, curly hair. They both had submachine guns slung across their chests with a sash full of replacement magazines.

She wasn't ready. God, she wasn't ready at all, but she had to go. She leaned forward against Ash's broad chest and borrowed as much strength as she could. Then she nodded to Benicio.

"I'm ready." But at the door, she turned back to Ash. "Do you know why I kept that pen?"

He shook his head.

"Because you gave it to me."

"Cate, I—"

This time it was her turn to cut him off. She pressed her fingertips to her lips and blew him a kiss before disappearing through the doorway.

She imagined that the walk down the stairs was like walking the plank on a pirate ship. There was only doom at the end. She tried to regulate her breathing, counting each inhale and exhale, each step forward.

In front of her, Benicio's shirttails flapped as he strode toward the Rivera men. Overhead, the clouds hung low and the smell of rain was thick in the air.

A few feet away from the car, Benicio stopped and held up his wrist to display the bloodied rose. The two men did the same.

Semi-hysterical laughter burbled in Cate's throat. She supposed that was their secret handshake and was tempted to make fun of it, but she held her tongue. *See, Ash? I'm being smart instead of a smart-ass.*

"This her?" the bald one asked in a vaguely insulting manner.

"It is. Pretty, isn't she?" Benicio continued walking toward the Rover. "But you can't touch her. She belongs to my father."

"After he's done, then."

Benicio merely shrugged. "You'll have to take it up with my father." He opened the door to the backseat and gestured Cate forward.

The bald man made a sound that could have been either an agreement or a fuck-you as he climbed into the passenger seat. The curly-haired thug slid behind the wheel and two seconds later they were driving away.

Cate resisted the urge to bolt out the opposite door and run back to Ash. The Rover was stripped down inside with a glass partition between the front and the rear seats. It wasn't anything like the luxury vehicles they were billed to be in the US. Here they were prized for their off-road capabilities, which worried her. They wouldn't need an all-terrain vehicle if they were meeting somewhere close to civilization.

"Where are we going?"

Benicio peered out the window. "Salana," he replied, as if that told her anything. She'd never heard of the place.

"Where'd your father get those guys?" she asked mockingly. "Soldiers-R-Us?"

"They're ex-Guatana special forces. Rodrigo, the bald one, has over two hundred kills. He's one of my father's favorites. I hear that his favorite thing to do during sex is choke a woman. Sometimes they live, sometimes they die." He shot her a smarmy grin. "He prefers when they die."

For some reason, Benicio's taunts actually chased some of her anxiety away. Benicio was a man so weak in power that he was betraying his own family, running to a bunch of American mercenaries to hire out a hit on his old man because he couldn't do it himself. His only weapons were his words.

Cate leaned against the door. "You guys are going to run out of prostitutes if you keep killing them during sex."

"Possibly, but where there are drugs, there is a never-ending supply of women. Or boys, as some like . . ." He paused. "I understand your Mr. Ashton was pushed out of the military over a young boy."

Horror shot through her. What? He had to be lying. Cate didn't know why Ash had been discharged other than honorably from the Marines, but if that was the rumor, she knew with absolute certainty that it wasn't true. Ash lived his life with rigid honor. He would never, ever touch a boy.

"You need to work on your intelligence network. They're giving you bad information," she informed Benicio.

She crossed her arms at her waist to hide the fact that she was pulling a button from her pants pocket. It popped off easily and she let it fall down into the well between the seat and the door. No one seemed to notice it. The tangos in the front didn't stop, and Benicio was too busy staring at the passing countryside.

Together, they watched as the city faded in the distance. And the farther they got away from the city, the worse the roads were. The Rover bumped around for another hour and a half before Cate spoke again.

"Where are we?"

"Home, *querida*," Benicio mumbled, his face still glued to the window.

The paved road gave way to a dirt lane big enough for only one vehicle. She wondered how Ash and everyone would be able to get through here without being spotted. The sparse jungle foliage on either side of the vehicle didn't provide much cover.

Finally, the Rover came to a stop at a clearing. A large tree-covered hill loomed in the background. Dark clouds hung low over the hills, casting ominous shadows that made Cate shiver.

In front of her, she counted about a dozen buildings, some of which were just lean-to structures composed of bundles of thin logs bound together to form walls and sheets of corrugated metal resting against each other like two playing cards.

Her hand itched for her camera because the whole scene would've made a breathtaking picture, with the lush green peaks and foreboding sky serving as a backdrop for the dilapidated village.

"Your father is here?" she asked in surprise.

Before his "death," Rivera had been known for his posh lifestyle. Had he really been hiding out here in this abandoned village for the past three months? It would definitely explain why no one had seen him.

The door opened. Baldy, the sex choker, dragged Cate out of the backseat. Benicio exited on the other side and walked slowly to the center of the clearing, where a small depression in the ground was filled with rocks, discarded wood, and ashes. Baldy pushed Cate forward, his gun brushing against her arm.

Damn it. She was supposed to delay them so that the team could get into position but Baldy's pace was quick, his strides lined with purpose.

Taking a breath, Cate pretended to stumble. But the man simply hauled her upright and then half dragged, half carried her next to Benicio, who balked loudly.

"She's my captive," he snapped. "I'll be the one to bring her to my father." He tugged her out of Baldy's grip with enough force to bring a sting of pain.

"I thought you were supposed to be more gentle with the merchandise," she muttered as she pulled her arm free. She peered up at the ominous sky. "Think we can get on with this? It's going to rain soon."

Benicio looked around uncertainly before turning to her. "Stay here. I'll go see where he is."

He stepped forward, while the two goons remained behind her, hands on their submachine guns, feet braced shoulder width apart. It felt creepy with them at her back. Hopefully Ash had a red dot trained in the middle of each of their skulls.

Discreetly, Cate examined her surroundings for somewhere to hide if the shooting started. The best place would be behind the engine block of the Rover, but that meant she'd have to run directly past big men with guns. The shacks would provide almost as little coverage as any of the trees, so her best bet seemed to be to just sprint to the jungle.

Her gaze traveled to Benicio, who was approaching one of the shacks. When a gust of wind whipped his shirt up, Cate caught sight of the dull black metal of his Glock. She quickly revised her plan. She would grab the unholstered gun first, and *then* run like hell for the jungle.

She inched closer to Benicio's back and nearly slammed into him when he suddenly stiffened. "What's wrong—"

The question died on Cate's lips when Camila Rivera stepped out from one of the larger structures.

"Mama!" Benicio cried in surprise.

He held his arms out for an embrace but Camila stopped out of reach. She wore red from head to toe, a scarlet slash against the darkening backdrop. Her face was utterly expressionless.

Meanwhile, her son stood awkwardly, holding his arms wide for a beat too long before lowering them to his side. "I've brought her," he announced, hastily pulling Cate forward.

"Do you remember this place?" Camila asked quietly.

Benicio nodded. "Grandmother was born here."

"Your father too," Camila reminded him. "He was born of the dirt of this village and it was only through his relentless hard work that he was able to move beyond this life. He did it all for you and your brother."

Good God. Was she going to have to listen to some twisted rags-to-riches story before Camila led them to Rivera? As surreptitiously as possible, Cate glanced around, trying to pinpoint the locations of Ash and the team. She saw nothing but trees, scraggly bushes, and dirt.

"Yes. Yes." Benicio was nodding. "I know the story."

"He was tired. The business was exhausting him and we thought one of you could take the reins and give your father the rest he deserved."

Cate was getting a headache from the effort it was taking to keep from rolling her eyes. Because killing people to run a more efficient and profitable drug business was so terribly taxing? She could think of a thousand things that were more stressful than being a murderous, amoral drug lord.

"We did our best," Benicio said weakly. "I know Father believes I failed him." He cleared his throat and jerked a finger in Cate's direction. "That's why I went to Boston and captured this whore for him."

Be smart and safe. As Ash's advice echoed in Cate's head, she clamped her teeth around her tongue so she wouldn't say anything that would piss the two of them off, at least not until she had a gun in her hands.

"But how," Camila said, and it wasn't a question. "How did you, my weak son, manage to capture this girl? A girl whose father operates one of the most dangerous mercenary teams in the world." The older woman looked around. "Where are they hiding?"

Benicio shifted uncomfortably. His hand dropped to his side, pushing the back of his jacket up. Cate rose on the balls of her feet, ready to spring forward.

"I don't know what you're talking about," Benicio lied.

Camila's pretty face took on a sad expression. "If you would be honest with me, I could save you."

"Mama—"

"But I see that honesty is just another one of the traits you lack." She waved a hand toward the tangos. "Now I feel like my only option is to ask Rodrigo to execute you."

Benicio's eyes widened.

Cate saw the danger before Camila did, probably because Camila believed her son was weak. But the boy surprised his mother, whipping out his gun and spinning around with shocking speed to release a flurry of shots at the guards behind him.

It happened so fast that the two goons didn't even have time to shoot back. Their bodies jerked from the force of the bullets, dropping to the ground.

Oh boy. Shit had just gotten real.

As adrenaline spiked in Cate's blood, all the training Jim and Noelle had provided her kicked in. In one swift motion, she crouched to her knee and pulled the gun from her boot. The pistol was small, which meant its accuracy would suck, but Camila was only about twenty feet away, offering a short-range target that even Cate, who was more used to shooting photos than guns, could manage to hit.

Benicio rose slowly, his shirt spattered with blood.

Crap. One of the guards must've gotten a shot off.

"Mama," he said softly, staring at Camila.

His mother stared back. One arm rose, a perfectly manicured hand gripping a black semiautomatic that was pointed right at Benicio.

"You brought danger to our family. I loved you. I pleaded for your life. And this is how you repay me? By betraying us?"

Cate's eyes darted toward the tree line. Should she bolt now or—

Camila pulled the trigger.

Holy *shit*. The woman had just shot her son in the head.

And as Benicio's lifeless body crumpled to the dirt, Cate realized she wasn't going to be able to get out of this alive by merely running.

Without another conscious thought, she raised her own gun and fired, but the first shot went wide to the right. *Fuck*. She fired twice more in rapid succession and her second and third shots struck Camila in the shoulder and chest.

The older woman stumbled backward, her hand clutched to her chest, her gun falling to the ground.

Before Cate could pull the trigger again, an animalistic roar blasted through the air, like a lion in the Serengeti. Then a stocky figure shot out of the shack Camila had first emerged from, careening toward Cate in a blur of limbs and dark hair and wild eyes.

Mateo Rivera.

Chapter 34

Ash watched through the scope of his rifle as Rivera ran toward his wife.

Finger hovering over the trigger, he nearly took a shot, but the drug lord didn't lunge at Cate like Ash had expected; he raced past her, ignoring the body of his son and the two dead tangos, and threw himself on the ground next to Camila.

Even from a hundred yards away, Ash could hear the man's cry of agony.

"Leaving my post," he muttered into the comm. "Cate needs backup."

Nobody objected to that.

He felt weak in the knees as he left the safety of the tin structure he'd been holed up in. A pretzel of fear had been lodged in his gut ever since he and the others had left the hangar and tailed the Land Rover to this no-name village west of Guatana City.

They'd hung several car lengths behind, tracking Cate electronically, to see how many other cartel members would follow. It was a good thing they had, because two Humvees had swiftly fallen in behind Cate and Benicio. Ash and the team hadn't taken them out until the Humvee crew had stopped to rendezvous with a few other Rivera foot soldiers on the outskirts of the small village.

Despite his shaky legs, he felt comfortable emerging

out into the open. Morgan's team had already neutral-ized the heavily armed guards they'd found on the pe-rimeter of the village and Benicio had made their job easier by killing the two goons in the clearing. Ash had been seconds from taking out Camila when Cate had done it for him.

Cate's blue eyes widened when she spotted him. She still had her pistol trained on Rivera, who was now cra-dling his dead wife in his arms, but that didn't stop her from releasing a choked sob at the sight of Ash.

"Oh my God, I'm so happy to see you," she blurted out.

"I got you, babe. You're safe now." He came up be-side her, his sniper rifle replaced by an AK that he trained on Rivera.

"Camila," the man was whispering, his voice thick with tears. "*Mi amor*. Please." He hugged the lifeless woman tighter, the word *please* leaving his mouth over and over again.

Ash wasn't sure what the man was begging for her to do. Open her eyes? Come back to life? Either way, Rivera was completely oblivious to the two weapons pointed at him. He was inconsolable, his face wet with sorrow, his stocky body trembling wildly.

When Rivera finally registered the threat hanging in the air, he raised his head. Weakly, as if it was a strain to do so. His black eyes locked on Cate but there was no malice in them.

"You killed her," he said quietly.

"I killed her," Cate confirmed, her voice equally soft.

Ash slid his finger over the trigger. The world would be a better place without this asshole. One shot was all he'd need. One shot to make Cate safe.

But the man on the dirt posed no threat to Cate. Rather than spew violent promises, taunt her the way he'd done over the phone, condemn her for shooting his wife, Rivera simply dipped his head again and held his wife tighter.

"*Mi amor*," he whispered.

Swallowing, Ash lowered the gun to his side.

Fuck. The man was grieving over his wife, and Ash couldn't bring himself to kill him. They could dispose of him later. It didn't feel right—

A shot rang out right next to him, making his head jerk back.

Ash watched in shock as blood bloomed in the center of Rivera's chest, the viscous liquid spreading until it mingled with the stains on his wife. He hugged Camila tight and then slumped over her body.

What the . . . ?

Ash turned to find Cate lowering her pistol.

She looked up at him with tears in her eyes. "He would have come after us."

His throat tightened. Jesus. She'd just killed a man in cold blood, and yet Ash couldn't say he disagreed with what she'd done. He'd allowed Rivera's grief to touch him, but the Marine in him knew that delaying the inevitable would've been a mistake.

"You're right." He cleared his throat. "That was the smart and brave thing to do." Then he tugged the gun out of her hand and lifted her shaking body into his arms. "Come on, sugar. It's time to get the hell out of Guatana."

She wrapped her arms around his neck. "Agreed." Her voice didn't sound at all steady as she began babbling. "If I ever see this place again it'll have to be by force. I'm avoiding all places starting with G. No Greece, Georgia, or Grenada. No London because they have the Greenwich meridian. No Galveston, but I hate Texas anyway. It's too hot. No . . ."

He let her mumble about more G places until she

eventually passed out from shock and exhaustion in the car ride back to the airport.

There were two jets waiting on the runway. One was going back to Costa Rica. The other would fly the team members who didn't live on the compound down to Florida, where they'd all board different charters headed for their various homes.

Ash . . . well, he'd be on the plane to Florida, where he'd decide what he was going to do with the rest of his life. Hire his gun and skills out to another mercenary group, he supposed.

With Gran dead, there wasn't anything in Tennessee that he wanted to see. The only place he wanted to be was next to Cate.

He wasn't sure what her plans were, but she hadn't said a word about going back to the compound. Morgan definitely wouldn't be thrilled about that, but Ash hoped the man learned a lesson from all this. Cate had lived through a harrowing experience and she'd survived. She'd proven that she was all grown up. That she deserved to make her own choices. That they couldn't try to force their own expectations on her.

And while every atom in his body wanted to clutch her tighter to him, spirit her off to some cabin in the woods where they'd live by themselves forever, he forced himself to loosen his grip around her sleeping body.

"How's she doing?" Liam asked, twisting around in the front seat of the SUV.

"I think she's had better days." Ash smoothed a bit of hair away from her forehead and eased her into a sitting position.

"You should tell her how you feel, brother."

Ash's eyes flicked up to meet Liam's. After a beat, he said, "Your family is important to you, isn't it?"

It wasn't a fair question. Everyone knew Liam had a huge family in Boston that he loved dearly. The other man nodded. "Yeah, they are."

"Well, Morgan is all Cate has. I'm not going to come between that."

"Rookie—"

He cut Liam off by giving Cate a tiny shake. "Time to wake up, sugar. The plane's ready."

But Liam spoke anyway. "Morgan isn't all she has. She has you, doesn't she?"

"I'm not enough. For anyone." He laughed ruefully. "I appreciate the pep talk but the best thing for me to do is to let her go."

Liam gave a frustrated look as he got out of the car. Ash figured from the tension between him and Sully, Liam had his own issues to work out.

He turned back to Cate and smoothed his thumb along her cheek. "Wake up, sugar."

"Ash?" She blinked slowly. "What happened?"

"You saved the day and now it's time for your hero's reward," he teased.

"Did I pass out in the car from shock?" She sat up and looked around in dismay.

"Maybe?"

"Oh my God! That's so embarrassing!"

Chuckling, he opened the door and gestured for her to hop out. "Come on, time to go."

"Well, that was a baller way to finish the day, wasn't it?" she grumbled as she exited the Rover.

"Shock is a normal response to what you just went through," he said roughly. "Don't beat yourself up over it."

Cate glanced around the tarmac. "Why two planes?" she asked warily.

He hesitated. "One is taking the Costa Rica folks home and the other is headed for the States."

"Oh." She nodded as if that made sense to her. Then she held out her hand. "Come on, then. Let's go home."

He stared at those slender fingers that were steady and waiting for him to take them. Clearing his throat, he said, "I'll call you."

Her eyebrows knitted together. "What the hell does that mean?"

Beside him, Liam made a disgusted sound. Ash had totally forgotten he was even there. It was hard to notice anything or anyone else when Cate was around.

"Ash?" she demanded when he didn't reply.

He shifted reluctantly.

"Ash."

To his annoyance, Liam answered for him. "Ash isn't allowed to come home. Your old man said if he allowed you to be part of this op, he wasn't welcome back."

She gasped.

"Fuckin' A, Boston. I told you that wasn't any of her business."

Cate whirled on him, her eyes blazing. "You're not allowed to go home?"

"It's more like I got fired," he mumbled, trying to downplay the whole thing.

"But it's your home! You've lived there for how many years?"

"Four," Liam piped up.

"You're not helping, man," Ash warned with narrowed eyes.

Liam grinned. "The hell I'm not." He gave Ash a lazy salute and walked over to the Florida plane, where Sully was smoking a cigarette and chatting up the Reilly brothers.

Ash swallowed his discomfort as Cate continued to glare at him.

"Where do you plan to go?" she said tightly.

"I hadn't thought that far ahead. The plane is dropping everyone off in Miami. I figured I'd get a hotel and start a job search."

She raised her arms in exasperation. "You're ridiculous, you know that? Ridiculous!"

"No. I was unaware." The more she yelled at him, the lighter his heart got. He felt a grin starting to spread.

"Well, you are. Talk about stupid. Do you have anything but rocks in that head?"

The smile broke the surface. "Doubt it. I think I need someone around to tell me what to do."

The indignation in her eyes dissolved into something warm, gentle. She took a step closer. "Is that right?"

"Yup. And since I'm out of a job, I was thinking I could hire on to a magazine as a camera helper. What are they called?"

"Assistants. That's what they're called." Cate looked like she was trying not to laugh.

"No special job title?"

"Nope." Her lips twitched. "Do you have one in mind?"

"How about"—he pretended to think it over—"'Cate Morgan's man'?"

Her breath caught. "What?"

"You heard me." And suddenly he couldn't last any longer. He closed the distance between them and scooped her up in his arms, burying his face against her smooth, delicate neck as the wave of emotion inside of him spilled over. "I love you and I don't care what your father has to say about that. I'm sorry I hurt you. I'm sorry I was going to let you get on that plane without me."

She tugged on his hair to jerk his head up, then gave him a teasing look. "There. Was that so hard?"

He blinked.

"For you to say," she clarified at his confused expression. "I've been waiting years for you to get your head out of your ass and say those words to me, David Ashton."

"Aw shit. You're double-naming me again?"

"I wouldn't have to do that if you weren't so dumb. I think you *do* need me around. And of course you love me. Duh."

Duh? He professed his love and got a *duh* in return? Fuck, he loved this woman.

Her small hands cupped his cheeks. "I love you too, Ash. I've loved you since I was seventeen and I can't imagine ever stopping. I kept that stupid pen, didn't I?"

His smile was so wide, he wondered if his face was going to split from happiness. "You sure did."

Then he kissed her hard, crushing her body against his because he was afraid this might be some sort of sad illusion his lovesick mind had conjured up. But no, she was really here, and her mouth opened beneath his, her tongue attacking him with the same fervor that he felt in every pulse of his body. It wasn't a dream. It was all very real. Too real maybe, he had to acknowledge as his hard-on throbbed in his cargo pants.

He broke away from her mouth reluctantly. "As much as I love kissing you, sugar, you know what happens to me when my tongue is in your mouth, and I don't think the folks on the plane want to watch while I take you on the tarmac. So we better stop now."

Her lips curved into a naughty smile. "Who knows? Maybe they'd enjoy the show."

"I thought we hated Guatana."

"Oh we do." She wiggled out of his grasp and took his hand. "But I can wait a few hours. Can you?"

Not really, but he'd try his damned hardest.

*   *   *

Ash couldn't stop holding her hand on the flight to Florida but somehow he found the strength not to kiss her, touch her, fuck her. At the airport, they exchanged hasty good-byes with the team and checked into the nearest hotel, and only then did he allow himself to lose control.

He had her shirt off before the door had even closed behind them. "I can't wait another minute," he growled as his mouth ravaged her neck.

"Then don't," she growled back, her fingers already tearing at his clothes.

They fell to the bed in a tangle of naked limbs. When he reached between her legs and thrust two fingers inside of her, he found her wet and hot and willing. A motherfucking dream. Her inner muscles tightened around him and Ash immediately imagined his cock in the place of his fingers and nearly came.

"Next time, I'm going to fuck you for hours," he rasped. "But right now, I gotta be inside you before I come in my pants from just fingering you."

She moaned against his lips. "I love knowing how much I turn you on. Fucking. Love. It."

"You have no idea. Just watching you walk around makes me hard." He took himself in hand and positioned himself at her entrance. "And when you look at me like that . . ." He trailed off, the emotions thick in his throat.

Cate drew a hand over his face, down his cheek, to stop at his mouth. Her fingers hung on his lower lip. "When I look at you like you're my world?" she supplied. Her voice was just as hoarse as his. "It's because it's true. You've always been in my head, no matter how hard I tried to drive you out of it."

"I love you," he whispered, then ducked out of her grasp to kiss her as he slid home.

It didn't matter where they stuck their bags, parked their shoes, hung up their coats. Nothing mattered as long as he could have her, like this, his cock inside her tight channel, her arms around his shoulders, her essence seeping into all his cracks and crevices, healing up those painful empty spaces.

She threw back her head and arched into his embrace. Her hips rose to meet his thrusts, and Ash threw himself into fucking her, wedging himself so deep that a crowbar wouldn't have been able to separate them. Nothing would separate them. Not Morgan, not terrorists, and most of all, not himself.

He whispered his promises of love and she gave them right back, until the sweet agony of release swept over both of them. And when it was over, he picked her up and carried her to the shower, where he paid homage on his knees and lapped at her pussy until she was too weak to stand and he had to hold her up with his shoulders and arms. Even when she begged for him to stop, he couldn't. There were years of want built up inside of him and he couldn't get enough of her.

"You're going to kill me with all these orgasms," she mumbled hours later.

Their last bout found them back on the bed. The sheets were on the ground, the blanket crumpled beneath their sweat-soaked, sated bodies. It wasn't the least bit comfortable, but Ash didn't give a shit because Cate was beside him.

"Nah, I'm filling you with life." He grinned at the ceiling and waited for her smart-ass response.

"Is that what we're calling it? Because I'm pretty sure your soldiers are dying on my thighs."

"It's an honorable way to go."

She snorted and then laughed, the mattress vibrating with her mirth. "Speaking of honor . . ." The humor in her voice faded into a far more serious note. "You never told me why you were dishonorably discharged from the Marines."

He gave her a wry smile. "Technically it was a discharge other than honorable, but it means the same. You did something wrong, something very bad."

He flopped onto his back and stared up at the ceiling. Fuck. Nothing killed the mood more than talking about ancient history. Especially when that history sucked balls. "It's a shit story, sugar. Wouldn't you rather fool around?"

"Ash . . ."

"All right." He drew a breath and gave in. "I was on my second tour and I'd taken a bullet here." He squeezed his right side. "It wasn't a big deal but I couldn't go outside the wire."

He arched an eye to see if she knew what that meant. She did.

"So you were stuck inside the camp?"

"Right. There was a delegation of Afghani troops there. A couple higher-ups. We were taking them into the village to do some PR, community-building shit. I was riding point, doing some personal body protection for the higher-ups when we spotted a couple of boys selling cigs on the side of the road. We stopped to hand out some candy. The general got out, gestured for the boys to come over. They talked and then the boys climbed inside the back of the truck." Ash exhaled slowly. "Peterson, he was the driver, looked over at me, but I didn't know what the fuck was going on either."

Shit story, indeed. Hell, not many of his stories of deployment were full of sunshine and rainbows.

Cate's hand crept down to grab his, and he squeezed her fingers tight before continuing. "We went back to the base with those boys in the back. One of the translators took them away. I didn't see them again, but later, Peterson came to get me. He took me to the med tent and one of the boys was there. He was . . . lying on his stomach and there was blood on the sheet, down below his waist." Ash swallowed hard.

"You don't have to finish," Cate whispered.

He gave her a grim smile. "Might as well. Anyway, Peterson asked what we were going to do, but we both knew we couldn't do shit. And I suppose if I hadn't run into the general the minute after seeing that boy, nothing would've happened. But the sick fuck came to the tent to collect his property and I laid him out. One punch and maybe I would've gotten off with a warning, but I decided one punch wasn't enough." Ash closed his eyes. "When I was done, his jaw was broken and his eye socket was smashed in. He couldn't see. I was shipped back to the States the next day and given my walking papers."

"Oh, Ash." She crawled on top of him. "You did the right thing."

"Did I? I never stopped it from happening in the first place. I should've known. Hell, I think I did. I'd heard rumors about it. Tea boys, they called them." Guilt crept up his throat. "I should've told those boys to run off the minute the Humvee stopped. Or maybe told Peterson not to stop the truck."

"No," she argued. "You're one man who did what he could. And you keep doing it—I love that about you. You're the most honorable guy I know. Isn't that why you stayed away from me for so long? Because you wanted to honor what my dad did for you?"

He nodded. "I'll always be grateful for what Morgan did," he said gruffly. "He took me in, gave me a shot when the military had written me off."

Cate sighed and sat up. "Where's my phone?"

"Why?"

"I'm going to call Jim. I need to let him know where I am and that I love him."

Ash felt a flutter of fear in his heart. Shit. Did that mean Cate was going to leave him?

She seemed to read his mind because she laughed softly. "I'm not going back to Costa Rica without you," she said in a firm voice. "I want Jim to know that. I can love both of you, but if I have to choose, it'll be you."

A smile tugged at his lips. "Just like I'm choosing you."

Smiling back, she swiped the phone from the nightstand and dialed. Morgan must've been waiting by the phone because he answered right away.

"Hey, Dad," she said softly. "I'm with Ash and I wanted you to know we're okay."

Ash couldn't hear what Morgan said in return, and he wasn't sure he cared. Nope, the only thing he cared about at the moment was that Cate was snuggled up beside him again.

As she spoke quietly into the phone, he put his arm around her shoulder and held her close to his side. Then, without letting go of her, he found the room service menu on the end table and started reading while Cate mended fences with his future father-in-law.

The grin on his face widened. Yeah, he hadn't asked Cate to marry him but that was just a technicality. They were a unit now.

Forever and always.

Chapter 35

"So you're not gay."

"No."

"But you like men."

"Yes."

"And women."

"Yes."

"So you like both men and women."

Liam raked both hands through his hair and fixed his younger sister with a glare that made her wince. "Yes, Becca, that's what bisexual means. I like to fuck both men and women."

Becca's cheeks turned redder than the apples in the bowl that sat between them on the kitchen counter. "God, Liam! Don't be crude!"

"Then don't be stupid," he growled. "I'm bi. I'm attracted to both sexes. Why does that require a game of Twenty Questions?"

She had the decency to look sheepish. "I'm sorry. I'm just trying to wrap my head around it."

The slight crack in her voice chipped away at the armor he'd shrouded himself in before he'd pulled Becca into the kitchen. The rest of the clan was enjoying the Macgregor Sunday brunch in the dining room but Liam had wanted a private moment with Becca. He felt like a shit for ignoring her texts for a week and a half, and he'd known from the moment he'd walked into the house that she was anxious for an explanation.

Well, now she had one, and she was taking it a lot better than he'd expected, if he was being honest.

"Have you ever dated a man?" she asked curiously, twirling a strand of hair between her fingers.

Liam nodded.

"Who?"

"Nobody you know," he lied, because even though he and Joe were no longer together, he still respected the hell out of the man. He'd never out Conley like that.

"Are you dating one now?" Becca pressed.

A jolt of pain shot up his chest and pierced him right in the heart. "No." Although his tone stayed light, his body had never felt heavier.

He hadn't seen or heard from Sully in five days. They'd both been on the plane to Florida but the moment they'd landed, the Australian tracked down a charter and took off back to Aruba. Hadn't even said good-bye. Nope, not even a handshake or a backslap. Sully had simply disappeared.

Like he always did.

"When are you going to tell them?" Becca jerked a finger at the kitchen doorway. Beyond it, the loud voices of the rest of their family could be heard from the dining room.

Liam smiled when he heard one of his nieces shriek in horror. Sounded like Katie, and either he was mishearing shit or she was accusing her cousin Bobby of spitting in her food. Kevin promptly reprimanded his son in his usual no-nonsense style—"You spit in her food and I'll spit on you, you little jerk"—which got Kev a sharp chastising from their sister, Kelsey—"You can't call your child a jerk!"—which in turn led to a heated parenting discussion between Kev, Kelsey, and their sister Monica, who'd dubbed herself a parenting expert because she had the most kids.

Yeah. He loved those fuckers. He really did.

"Eventually," he said in response to Becca. "I mean, I'm single right now, so there's no sense in rocking the boat, right? But depending on who I end up with"—if he didn't spend the rest of his life alone, that was—"I'll have no choice but to tell them."

Becca pursed her lips thoughtfully. "I think they'll be okay with it."

He arched a brow. "Even Dad?"

"Hey, Daddy's cooler than you think," she protested. "Did I ever tell you he came with me to pick out my tattoo?"

Liam couldn't hide his surprise. "Bullshit."

"Yes shit."

"*Yes shit* is not the opposite of *bullshit*," he said with a sputter of laughter.

"Whatever. He still came with me. Why do you think I ended up with the cross instead of the sailboat I wanted?"

His heart clenched at the word *sailboat*. Damn it. Couldn't he go ten seconds without thinking about Sully?

"Sully's here!"

Liam froze when his eight-year-old nephew came careening into the kitchen. Okay. He was losing his ever-loving mind here because no way had Denny Jr. just said the words *Sully's here*. That wouldn't make any sense. No, of course it wouldn't. *Pizza's here.* That was probably what D.J. had shouted. So what if they never ordered pizza for Sunday brunch? That was clearly the *only* thing D.J. could've said.

"Uncle Liam, did you hear me?" The little boy waited expectantly in the doorway.

Liam blinked a couple of times. "Do you need me to pay for the pizza?"

"What is happening right now?" Becca asked, shaking her head in confusion.

He ran a hand through his hair again, unable to understand why his sister and his nephew were staring at him as if he'd sprouted horns.

"Your friend Sully is here," D.J. said emphatically, slowing down each word. "That's what he said his name was—Sully. He's at the door."

What?

Liam shot out of his chair like his ass was on fire. Sullivan was *here*? In Boston?

"Grandma let me answer the door." D.J. gave them a proud smile. "And I was like, *Who are you?* And the man said, *I'm here to see Liam.* And I said, *Uncle Liam?* And he said, *Yes.*"

Hysterical laughter bubbled in Liam's throat at his nephew's unnecessary, step-by-step account of his door answering. "You did good, kid." He ruffled D.J.'s black hair on his way out of the kitchen but his hand was shaking and his legs felt weaker than pool noodles.

What the hell was Sully doing in Boston?

The question ate away at his brain as he marched unsteadily to the door. A part of him still thought D.J. was full of shit. Sullivan was in Aruba, on his boat. Why would he—

Liam skidded to a stop when he reached the front hall.

His nephew was right.

Sully *was* here.

The big blond man wore a cautious expression as they locked gazes. "Hey, Boston."

Gravel filled Liam's mouth. He coughed. "Hey, Aussie."

A long, long silence descended over the small entryway. Long enough for Liam's mind to run through a million scenarios. Long enough for his heart to pound faster and faster until it was in danger of stopping altogether.

Long enough for Liam's mother to pop her head out and release a happy exclamation. "Why, hello there! Are you a friend of Liam's?"

Sullivan blinked and broke eye contact, shifting his head toward Mary Macgregor. "I am," he answered cheerfully. "Sullivan Port. And you must be Liam's gorgeous older sister."

She blushed prettily. "Well, aren't you a charmer! I'm Mary, Liam's mother."

"Liar," Sully shot back with a wink. "You would've had to have him when you were five."

She giggled.

Liam had never in his life heard his mother *giggle*.

Clearing his throat, he brought his gaze back to Sully. "What brings you to Boston?"

Hesitation flickered in those gray eyes. Sully opened his mouth but before he could answer, Mary latched her hand onto his big, muscular arm and dragged him forward. "You can tell us all about it over brunch! There's plenty of food to go around—we always make extra in case we have guests."

Liam gaped as he watched the two of them disappear into the corridor. Jesus. What the hell was going on? He would've appreciated some warning. And he definitely would've liked a moment alone with Sully. Instead, he was going to have to sit there for God knew how long while his nosy family cross-examined Sully over brunch.

Awesome.

When he entered the dining room, he found that Sully had already been ushered to a seat at the table. Liam's mother was piling up a plate for him, while the nieces and nephews crowded Sully's chair demanding to know who he was and why he was there and if he—a total stranger—had brought them any presents.

Liam caught the man's eye and offered a wry smile, which Sully returned ruefully.

"So you're a friend of Liam's?" At the head of the table, Callum Macgregor folded his hands on the crisp tablecloth and studied Sullivan from head to toe.

"Yup," the other man said easily.

Liam's father narrowed his eyes. "How do you know each other?"

"He's one of his mercenary buddies," Kevin spoke up, his tone lined with bitterness.

Liam stifled a groan. He'd been back in Boston for five days and Kevin still refused to forgive him for not telling the family about his work. Liam's older brother, of course, had already blabbed about the mercenary thing to everyone. Thanks to that, Liam had been bickering with his parents all week. His dad hadn't been happy to hear he'd been a merc and his mom had guilted the hell out of him for keeping it a secret. At least his sisters didn't seem to care—they were too busy with their gazillion children to care about what their brother did for a living.

"Indeed I am," Sullivan confirmed, his accent growing more pronounced.

Callum's gaze went even sharper. "You're one of those Brits, huh?"

"Actually, I'm one of those Australians." Sully looked like he was holding back laughter.

"Huh," Callum grunted. "So what brings you to Southie?"

Tension gathered in Liam's shoulders as he waited

for the answer. He hadn't sat down and Becca kept glancing over to where he stood in the doorway, shooting him curious looks.

"I'm visiting my boyfriend."

All the air in his lungs whooshed out in a fast gust. Okay. He was hearing things again.

"Your boyfriend?" Kevin sputtered in shock.

Or maybe he wasn't.

Liam stared openmouthed in Sully's direction, unable to understand what the hell was going on. Sully steadily held his gaze and there was no missing the crease of vulnerability on the man's face.

"You're gay?"

The tension returned at Callum's slow, measured words. Liam searched his dad's face for any hint of disgust. To his surprise, he found none.

"Bi, actually," Sully replied. His gray eyes traveled to Kelsey, who was undeniably the prettiest of Liam's sisters. "Blokes, birds, I love 'em all."

When Sully winked at her, Liam could swear Kelsey sighed in pleasure.

"Oh. Okay. So you've got a man in the city?" Kelsey asked.

Liam couldn't tell if his sister was disappointed or intrigued or both.

"I hope so," Sully answered with a shrug. "I'm not exactly sure how he feels about me these days."

"You're gay?" Kevin said dumbly.

Liam's mother shushed him loudly.

"Jeez, Kev, we've already established that he's bi," Liam's older sister Monica grumbled from the other side of the table.

"What's bi?" six-year-old Janey piped up, tugging on her grandmother's shirt.

"It's nothing, honey," Mary answered. Her face

looked strained at the edges as she glanced over at Liam. "Sit down already, would you?"

He stepped forward and gripped the back of his empty chair, wondering if he wanted to kiss Sully or kill him. The man disappeared and then showed up out of the blue claiming he was in love with a man? Or was it just in lust?

Callum interrupted Liam's confused thoughts, repeating Mary's command. "You heard your mother. Sit down." More cordially, he nodded toward Sully and said, "So you and my son work together."

"Used to. I've been on an extended sabbatical and am just now getting my sh—stuff together," he quickly corrected himself. "But Liam and I worked a lot of jobs before that. He was the best partner I ever had. I could trust him with my life or, if I had family, their lives too. He's a good man. You should be proud."

Liam remained standing, still confused by the whole situation—Sully showing up, Sully announcing he had a boyfriend, Sully snapping Mary's linen napkin before settling it across his lap.

"Of course we're proud of him," Callum said gruffly. "He's got a good head on his shoulders."

"Liam, honey, sit down," Mary insisted. "You're making me antsy standing there like—"

"I'm gay," he blurted out.

A shocked silence fell over the table.

"Ah, I mean, bi," he said hastily. "I'm bi."

Everyone continued to stare at him. No, to *gape* at him. As the silence dragged on, the back of his neck started to itch. His gaze collided with Sullivan, who was watching him in astonishment. Liam had always believed that nothing could shock the man but apparently announcing to a table full of Macgregors that he was bisexual was too much for even Sully to handle.

Why the hell wasn't anyone saying anything, damn it?

His family had the biggest, loudest mouths on the planet. *This* was the day they decided to shut their traps?

To Liam's amusement, his nieces and nephews were the first ones to break the silence.

"You're bi too?" Janey asked as she climbed into the chair next to Monica.

"It means he loves boys *and* girls," eleven-year-old Simon announced.

"Girls are gross!" D.J. yelled.

"No, boys are gross!" Delilah, Monica's oldest, yelled back.

"I wanna be bi like Uncle Liam!" Robbie the toddler declared.

The last exclamation set off an eruption among the adults.

"God!" Kevin gasped. "Do you see what's happening? This is what's wrong with the world. A three-year-old asking these questions!"

"Since when are you such a bigot, Kev?" Becca shot from across the table.

"Since Angie Kearney told him that she wasn't interested because she swung the other way," Mary said primly.

Liam's jaw dropped at his mother's matter-of-fact remark.

"Don't worry," Mary told Kevin's wife, Hailey. "That was before he met you."

Hailey's lips twitched in barely suppressed laughter. "It's all right. I know all about Angie Kearney and suspect you're right about why Kev is so uptight about LGBT rights."

"That's not true at all!" Kevin said hotly.

"So you're saying your mother and I raised you a bigot?" Callum asked with a frown.

Liam's head swung toward his dad in surprise, while

Kevin flushed bright red. "Course not," he mumbled, his eyes fixed on his plate.

"I didn't think so." Callum scowled at his son. "All your mother and I want is for our kids to be happy." He shrugged. "And if being bi or gay or whatever the hell you want to call it makes one of you happy, then that's the way it is."

The rest of the table fell silent under the glare of Callum Macgregor's forceful eye.

"Mommy, I want more juice."

Janey's plaintive voice, followed by her mother's hissed "Not now, sweetie," shook Liam out of his shocked stupor.

"Um." He cleared his throat. "Ma, Dad, you mind if Sully and I excuse ourselves? We've got a couple of things to talk about."

Callum raised his fork. "Go on, then, but you best hurry back before lunch gets cold."

"Yes, sir." Liam jerked his head toward the kitchen. "Come on, Aussie."

Sully carefully rose from his chair, his somber gaze shifting toward Liam's mother. "I'm sorry about causing a scene here, ma'am. We'll be right back."

"You better. No fooling around in my kitchen," Mary warned, but then smiled, because apparently no woman was capable of not smiling at Sully.

Including Kelsey, whose hungry eyes followed the Australian's ass all the way out the door.

"I think my sister wants you for herself," Liam remarked with a sigh.

"Which sister?"

"Kelsey." He paused. "Hell, probably all of them. Becca was practically drooling."

"Should I tell her I'm taken?" Sully asked lightly.

He swallowed, not sure how to respond to that.

They stepped into the spacious kitchen, which Sully spent a long time examining. He studied the cherry-wood cabinets that Liam's dad had built himself. The gleaming appliances. The shiny tiled floor beneath their boots.

Banishing the filthy thought of bending Sully over the counter and fucking him from behind, Liam rested his forearms on the counter. "Why did you come here?" he asked gruffly.

Sully heaved out a deep breath, dragged a hand through his hair, and then closed the distance between the two of them. "The night Rivera's son showed up at your brother's office . . . I, ah, overheard your cop guy tell you he loved you."

Liam rocked back in surprise. "You did?"

Fuck. That talk with Joe had been insanely personal. And uncomfortable. Christ, so fuckin' uncomfortable.

"Yeah. I did. And while I was standing there, listening to him say all that shit to you, I thought to myself, damn, now here's a guy who doesn't even know if his feelings are returned but he's willing to lay himself out emotionally and possibly lose his job just so he could be with you." Sully's voice grew hoarse. "And here I am, hiding on my boat with my dick in my hands."

A reluctant grin spread across Liam's face. "Literally or figuratively?"

"What do you think?" Sully smirked in return. Then his face grew serious. "I should've never walked away from you, man."

He gulped. "Then why did you?"

"Because you were right—I *am* a coward. My life has been one shit show after the other. Everyone I've ever given a damn about has left me. Some of them did it intentionally, like my folks. Some of them didn't have a choice, like Evie. But that doesn't change the fact that they're gone. They'll all fucking gone." Sully breathed deeply and rested a hand on the counter, as if he was trying to steady himself. "I'm scared, okay? I'm scared if I let myself love you, you'll go away."

An arrow of pain sliced into Liam's heart. Jesus. "That would never happen," he said thickly.

"It could." Another heavy breath heated the air. "It really could, and I wasn't willing to take that risk before. But I'm taking it now." Sully's eyes shone with emotion. "You don't belong in Boston. You belong in a jungle or a war zone or the middle of the ocean. You belong with me."

Liam arched a brow. "That so?"

"Of course it's bloody so. You and me, Liam. That's how it should be. Nah, that's how it *is*." Sully offered a look of challenge. "You telling me I'm wrong?"

Liam's response was to haul the Australian flush against his body and kiss the hell out of him.

Without missing a beat, Sully kissed him right back, his hands clutching Liam's shoulders to pull him in closer.

They were both breathless by the time they came up for air. They stood there for a moment, foreheads resting against each other and lips inches apart, a fog of arousal hanging over the kitchen.

"I think I might be in love with you," Sully muttered.

Liam choked out a laugh. "I think I might be in love with you too."

In a heartbeat, Sully's tongue was back in his mouth and a massive erection was poking his thigh. Liam pushed his own hard-on against the other man's groin, summoning low groans from each of their throats.

"Fuck," Sully croaked before wrenching his mouth away. "We gotta stop."

"Yeah," Liam agreed huskily. He reached up to

smooth his rumpled hair. "We should probably save it for your boat."

"My boat, huh?" Sully cocked one eyebrow. "Try again."

Liam had to clear the emotion from his throat before speaking. "*Our* boat."

His best friend nodded in approval. "Our boat."

Liam watched with undisguised interest as Sully stuck his hand down his pants to adjust his erection. When their eyes locked again, Sully flashed his trademark killer grin.

"C'mon, we better go back out there. I don't want to get off on the wrong foot with my soon to be father-in-law."

Liam's jaw gaped open as he followed the other man to the door. "For real? This is how you're going to ask me to marry you?"

Sully snickered. "Don't tell me you're *that* type of bloke, all old-fashioned and shit."

"Hey, I'm not saying I need hearts and flowers, but make an effort, man."

"Sure thing, Boston. I'm going to effort you so hard tonight that you'll be crying for mercy."

Liam smacked the man's ass as they left the kitchen. "Bring it on, Aussie. Bring it on."

Epilogue

Three years later

"There are a lot of unhappy-looking women in the crowd," Ash remarked.

Cate swept her gaze over the hundred or so people that littered the spacious restaurant overlooking the marina. Ash was right—an unusual amount of glum faces could be spotted in the crowd tonight. And while there was an inordinate number of gorgeous but obviously taken men, Cate hazarded a guess that the real source of consternation was the two males currently laughing their heads off at something Denny Macgregor was saying.

The two men weren't holding hands or snuggling, but sometimes, when they were in a group, Sullivan clamped his hand around the back of Liam's neck. Cate couldn't deny that the possessive grip was so freaking sexy.

Sully's free hand held a bottle of water, which made her smile. A few years ago the Australian had given up drinking, smoking, and anything else that could be considered addictive. He'd told Cate with a wink that Liam was his drug of choice, and if the women here tonight could've seen the lascivious look Sully had cast toward Liam when he'd drawled that, there would've been two dozen spontaneous orgasms.

"Two gorgeous men just took themselves off the market," Cate said with a sigh. "It's a day of mourning."

"For you too?" A smile played around Ash's sensual mouth.

She couldn't help herself—she leaned over and planted a wet kiss against it.

"Yeah, I've always had a thing for Hollywood." Her kiss had left a smear of red on Ash's lips and she was tempted to leave it there as a mark of her territory. That seemed more civilized than peeing on someone's leg.

"You should probably wait until you pop out your pumpkin before you try to steal Liam away from his new husband." Ash smoothed one hand over her stomach, lingering on the rise of the small swell.

"Maybe not. Some guys are into the pregnant thing."

His grip tightened possessively. "I know I am. I'd do you right here if you let me."

Cate's heart thumped loudly in response to the heat in his eyes. "I never knew you were into showing off."

"I'm into you." He dragged her out of her chair and into his lap, where he proceeded to bury his nose in her neck. "And I'm fucking impatient as hell, so I don't care who sees me."

The evidence of his arousal was digging into her ass. "I'd be willing to do it with you in public but preferably not while my father is glaring at us."

Ash heaved a massive breath and leaned back. Then he caught Jim's eye and waved impishly.

Cate watched as her father tensed, fisted his hands, and then forced himself to relax.

"You're going to give him a coronary," she murmured as she blew Jim a kiss.

"Only because he thinks I knocked you up out of wedlock." Ash stroked a broad hand down her back.

These past three years, he'd never missed an opportunity to touch her. He'd sheepishly admitted that he was making up for the four years he'd missed with her, but Cate suspected there was more to it than that. He was filling up that thirsty heart of his from the twenty-nine years he'd spent believing he was alone.

As for her, she lapped up all his obvious affection because she too had grown up without a lot of love in her life. She and Ash were perfectly matched, which she'd always known. She had instantly recognized her own sorrow and need in him, but because he was a stubborn jackass who was blinded by honor, it had taken him a while to come around.

But now?

There wasn't a more devoted lover, husband, or soon-to-be father.

"Seriously, when are you going to tell Jim you made an honest man out of me after Christmas?" Ash asked her.

"I don't know. Thanksgiving?"

He snickered. "You're evil."

"I know, but Jim deserves it for the way he gave you the silent treatment for so many months after the thing with Rivera."

She nestled backward against Ash's broad chest and his arms automatically came up to circle her. Beneath her, she felt his leg kick out and watched as he caught a nearby chair leg and dragged the seat over. Gratefully, Cate slipped off her shoes and propped her stocking-clad feet on the white linen cushion.

"Aw, go easy on him. He eventually came around."

She rolled her eyes. Ash kept insisting that he didn't want her holding a grudge, but her dad happened to be an even bigger stubborn jackass than her husband. Jim had been on her case again ever since he'd learned that Cate was knocked up and without a ring on her finger.

"It still surprises me how traditional Jim is," she admitted.

"It shouldn't. He wifed Noelle right away, didn't he? Just because he's a fighter doesn't mean he doesn't harbor deep-seated traditional beliefs."

Cate hid a smile because she knew Ash wasn't just talking about Jim. He'd wanted to marry her the minute they'd gotten back from Guatana but Cate had put him off—and kept putting him off, telling him that she didn't need a ring to know he loved her.

After nearly three years of bickering about it, he'd finally shouted in frustration that it was *him* who needed the ring. And, well, how the hell could she deny him after that? The next day, they'd flown to Vegas and she'd said "I do" under the beaming smile of an Asian Elvis.

She'd planned on telling everyone the next day but Ash had been called away on a mission. When he got back, Cate landed a plum assignment in Indonesia covering the election and Ash had gone with her. These days, he was hardly ever far from her side. When she went on assignment, he tagged along, leaving her only to do his work for Jim. Then he'd pick back up wherever she was.

She couldn't deny that she adored their life. It was full of adventure. New discoveries. Freedom. A few months ago she'd asked Ash if he missed home, worrying that he didn't like the nomadic life as much as she did, but he'd told her, between deep, passionate kisses, that his home was with her.

She was pretty sure that was the night they'd created this little person growing inside her.

"Remember your nineteenth birthday party at that golf course in Providence?" he whispered in her ear.

The slight puffs of air across the top of her earlobe sent shivers down her spine. "Yeah?"

"I wanted to fuck you then. You were wearing this top that was so filmy I swear I could see your tits through the fabric. I wanted to flip your skirt over your head, bend you over the railing, and nail you from behind."

Lust crept into her veins, heating her blood and making her nerves stand at attention. She shifted in his lap, hissing slightly when his erection stabbed insistently against her ass cheek.

"I would've let you. You know I wanted you then too."

"Your dad was there. He was staring at me, just like he is right now."

The ache between her legs throbbed so hard that she could barely see two inches in front of her, let alone all the way across the marina restaurant. "I don't think I would've cared," she confessed hoarsely.

When she moved again, Ash's fingers bit into her hips. "I swear to God, sugar, you squirm one more time and I'm going to do you right here in the middle of Liam and Sully's wedding reception—"

"Cate!" a happy voice shouted, and she cringed when J. J. Woodland materialized at their side. The six-year-old was sneakier than a ninja.

She hoped to hell he hadn't heard what his uncle Ash had just said.

"They're gonna play a slow song next and you promised me a dance," the little boy pleaded.

"So I did."

She swung her feet off the chair and slipped her shoes on, ignoring the whispered "cockblocked by a six-year-old" from her husband.

Tossing a coy look over her shoulder, she took the boy's hand and said, "Ash has something to share with my dad anyway, so this is perfect."

Ash rolled his eyes. As he got to his feet, he adjusted his tux jacket. "J.J., dude, we gotta work on your timing."

"My daddy sent me over," the boy said solemnly.

"Okay, we work on your old man's timing, then."

Cate glanced over to see Abby and Kane grinning broadly at them. Jerks. They'd probably guessed what Cate and Ash had been on the verge of doing.

"You having a good time, J.J.?" she asked.

"Not really." He shrugged. "But I got to eat three pieces of cake so that was okay."

"Well, I'm having a wonderful time," she told him, ruffling his sandy-blond hair.

It looked like everyone else was enjoying themselves too, if you didn't count all the unhappy single ladies who'd come in hopes of hooking up with one of Jim's men. There were still a few Macgregor men available, though. None as handsome as Liam but they were still hot as fuck.

Not as hot as Ash, though.

She slid her husband a mischievous look. "How about you, baby? You having a good time?"

She figured he'd grunt a *no* now that his fantasy of public sex had been interrupted, but he surprised her with a smile so beautiful that she nearly tripped on her long, green dress.

"Yeah. I am. I'm with you, aren't I? You're all I need to be happy."

"That's gross," J.J. declared and then tugged on Cate's hand. "Don't let him kiss you. You're gonna marry me."

She bit the inside of her cheek hard so she didn't laugh and hurt the little boy's feelings. "If I could marry you, J.J., I would. You're my favorite man next to Ash."

"There's nothing special about him," J.J. argued. "He isn't even as cool as my daddy."

They'd gotten close enough for Kane to hear that and he swiftly swung the boy up in his arms. "Who's not as cool as me?"

"Ash isn't as great as you," J.J. said with all the earnestness his little body could hold.

"Ash is great!" Gabriela Pratt cried from the other side of the table. D and Sofia's five-year-old daughter had had a thing for Ash since the moment she was born.

"You're dumb," J.J. told her.

"No, you are!"

Cate turned her face into Ash's jacket to muffle her laughter. Those kids were too damn adorable and now she was having one of her own with the man she loved. How could she not be happy? How could any of them not be happy?

Around her, she was surrounded by couples in love and precious babies. D's lap was full of his twin baby girls; Sofia kept popping them out like she was a baby Pez dispenser. She was already on her third pregnancy. Isabel and Trevor had adopted a two-year-old a few years ago and then gotten pregnant a year later. Bailey and Sean had Irish twins: a girl born just eleven months after her brother.

Only Juliet and Ethan were the holdouts. Cate didn't think it was something they wanted, but there were plenty of young ones around to play Aunt and Uncle with if they ever needed a kid fix.

"Think you'll have kids?" she asked Liam and Sully, who'd separated themselves from a pair of well-wishers to join their group. No, their *family*.

"Doubt it," Liam admitted. "But my sister offered to serve as a surrogate if we ever decide to do it."

"How bloody badass would that be?" Sullivan piped up. "The rugrat would have Macgregor *and* Port blood." He draped a casual but possessive arm around Liam's back. "But it might be hard to raise kids on a boat. And I ain't giving up the boat."

He gestured with his hand toward *Evangeline*, which was docked in the harbor and all ready to whisk the two men away on their honeymoon.

Liam rolled his eyes. "Nobody's asking you to give up the fuckin' boat, dude."

"Don't swear in front of the kids," D grunted.

Half a dozen astonished gazes swung toward him.

"Holy sh—sugar," Ash said. "I think hell has frozen over."

"What?" the tattooed mercenary said defensively.

"Who are you and what have you done with Derek Pratt?" Liam asked gravely.

"D's a family man now," Kane said with a smirk.

"Aren't we all?" came Morgan's dry voice.

Cate's father joined the group and placed a large hand on Cate's shoulder.

She greeted him with a smile. "Hey."

"Hey." His tone was gruff. "Thought I'd come over and see if my daughter would dance with me."

Her jaw fell open. "You hate to dance."

Jim shrugged. "Hate it," he confirmed. "But I know you like it, so . . ."

A broad smile filled her face. "I would love to. Oh, but . . ." She looked down at J.J. "Kiddo, you mind doing me a solid and letting me dance with my dad first?"

The little boy heaved an exaggerated sigh. "Fiiiiiiine."

"You rock," she told him, bending over to smack a kiss on his chubby cheek.

As she followed Jim to the dance floor, she caught Ash frowning at her. *Tell him,* he mouthed.

Later, she mouthed back, because she had no desire to spoil the festivities. Jim would no doubt gripe and grumble about Ash and her eloping. He'd bitch about feeling left out and then she'd bitch back and then

Noelle would step in and bitch at both of them, and . . . well, the bitching could wait until tomorrow.

Tonight, everything was good and right in Cate's world.

And she wanted to hold on to this feeling for as long as she could.

Don't miss the latest book in
New York Times bestselling author
Elle Kennedy's Outlaws series,

RULED,

available now.
Continue reading for a special preview.

"Everyone's in position. Just waiting on your word."

At the sound of the deep male voice, Reese shifted her gaze from the high-voltage electric fence in the distance to find her most trusted friend emerging from the shadows. Sloan wore black from head to toe, and he was armed to the teeth. So was she. They all were.

She bit the inside of her cheek. *Just waiting on your word.* Because it all came down to her. Her word. Her plan. Her decision to rob this munitions depot.

The weight of leadership was heavier than normal tonight. The crushing losses she'd suffered, the unceasing guilt she harbored . . . they were light and airy compared to this burden. Before, her raids had involved teams of three at the most, but this one consisted of more than triple that. She was holding too many people's lives in her hands, and she didn't fucking like it.

"You want to abort?" Sloan studied her face, his hazel eyes piercing through the armor that always turned from steely to flimsy when he was around.

He knew her well. Too well. Four years ago, when this strong, silent man joined up with her small band of outlaws, it had taken mere seconds for Reese to trust him. Something about Sloan had compelled her to confide in him, to lean on him, to seek him out whenever a decision needed to be made.

It was no surprise that his simple prompting lifted

the lid on the self-doubt she'd been trying to contain. "This could backfire on us. People could die."

"We all die eventually." His tone didn't hold a trace of emotion. "If it happens tonight, at least it'll be for a good cause."

"Will it?" Her teeth dug deeper into her cheek. What cause was she *really* fighting for? Freedom?

Or was it vengeance?

She wanted the Global Council to burn. She wanted to kill every single council member in the Colonies, every single Enforcer that carried out their dirty work. If she succeeded, the citizens living behind the city walls would be free. The outlaws living in secret outside those walls would no longer be hunted. But Reese would be lying if she said her motives were selfless.

The council had stolen everything from her. Every goddamn thing that she'd ever held dear. She despised them for it, and when that red-hot hatred burned as hot as it did now, it stripped away all notions that she might be doing this for anything other than pure revenge.

As usual, Sloan read her mind. He chuckled. "Doesn't matter that the cause—for you, anyway— might be tangled up with a bunch of other shit. It's still a cause, sweetheart. It's still something we all want." He jerked his head toward the small warehouse several hundred yards away. "We want those guns. We want to kill the bastards who are guarding those guns. And we're going to succeed."

A smile ghosted across her face. "We will, huh?"

"We've been planning this for weeks. Those motherfuckers don't stand a chance against us."

The rare flicker of humor in his eyes wore away at her hesitation. If Sloan was confident this could work, then she had to be too. He was right—meticulous planning had gone into it. They knew where every perimeter guard was posted. They knew exactly how many Enforcers were manning the interior. They knew the codes to deactivate the fence. They knew how to disable the cameras and the backup alert that the Enforcers would try to dispatch.

If they followed the plan to the last letter, they *would* get out of this alive.

Probably.

Maybe.

Fuck. She was doubting herself again.

Reese stared at the warehouse and wished there were more places around it to use for cover. The wooded area spanning the rear and east side was advantageous for only half her people; approaching the front of the building would be impossible to do covertly. The warehouse's location was completely isolated, which made sense because the structure, for all intents and purposes, was a gigantic time bomb. With all the potential ammo, weapons, and explosives inside, one tiny accident could kill everyone in the vicinity. The blast barriers might absorb most of the damage, but either way, an explosion wasn't the outcome Reese hoped to get out of this.

She wanted those weapons.

But she also wanted her people to stay alive.

"Maybe we should do this alone," she told Sloan, wincing at the note of panic in her voice. "You and me. Send the others home."

His handsome features creased. She couldn't tell if he was worried or annoyed. Probably the latter. God knew she was pretty fucking annoyed with herself right now. Why was she acting like a scared little girl?

"They know what they're doing," Sloan assured her. "We made sure of it."

They had. Reese had assembled her best-trained

people for this raid. And Connor Mackenzie, the leader of a small camp not far from hers, had sent three of his best men as well. Rylan, Pike, and Xander were used to these types of dangerous missions. In fact, Xan's technological prowess was what made the entire plan possible.

"Give the order, Reese," Sloan said softly. "We've wasted enough time."

She swallowed. Then she reached for the radio strapped to her belt. One shaky jab of her finger and she was addressing her soldiers. "Go time," she murmured. "The front guards will be switching rotation in three minutes. Xan, disable the fence now."

"Copy," came Xander's faint reply.

There was no outward sign that the fence would no longer zap anything that came in contact with it, but Reese trusted Xander when he reported a moment later that they were all set. The fence and cameras had been taken care of.

"Rylan, get ready," she said into the radio.

"Born ready," the bane of her existence drawled back.

She pictured him lying flat on his belly like a snake, hidden behind the small rise in the landscape that was hardly considered decent cover but was their only option. If the night breeze rustled even one strand of his hair, the Enforcers at the front gates would spot him. Though Rylan probably got off on that. From what Reese had seen, the man was addicted to danger.

She really wished Connor hadn't sent Rylan to join the party. The gorgeous blond outlaw got on her nerves, big-time. But he was also one of the most lethal fighters she'd ever met, thanks to the years he'd spent training recruits for the now defunct People's Army, an outlaw military group that had risen decades ago to fight the GC right after the war.

She might not like Rylan, but she needed him.

She glanced at Sloan, who was getting his rifle in position. "Let's do this shit," she said with a sigh.

His mouth quirked up in an almost smile.

The radio crackled to life again. "Shift change about to happen," Pike reported.

Reese took a breath before voicing the command. "Go."

There was only a split second of silence between her orders and the gunfire that blasted through the night.

Reese and Sloan burst out of the tree line, rifles up, fingers on the triggers. All her people had been given the same order: shoot to kill. They weren't taking prisoners.

Four Enforcers stood at the back gate, identifiable by their black tactical gear with red stripes down the sides of their pants. Two were behind the fence; two were posted at the gate beyond it. Reese didn't hesitate as she took aim on her enemies and opened fire.

Between her and Sloan—and the element of surprise—the guards at the gate dropped like flies, dead before they even hit the pavement.

The two behind the fence were a different story.

"Take cover," Sloan shouted as they charged toward the fence.

Reese dove for cover behind a military Jeep parked nearby. Sloan threw himself beside her as bullets whizzed above their heads. The Enforcers were shouting sharp, muffled orders to each other that Reese couldn't make out over the gunshots. The odor of gunpowder filled the air and she breathed it in as she repositioned her rifle and turned to Sloan.

"Head for the gate. I'll cover you."

He nodded, waited for her silent count, then flew forward with a surprising amount of grace and dexterity for such a large man. Reese popped up and provided cover fire, crowing in triumph when one of her bullets connected with her target. The assault rifle clattered out of the Enforcer's hands as a pained shout left his mouth. She'd hit his shooting arm. Good. That meant one less weapon being aimed at Sloan as he stormed the gate.

Shots continued to explode from all directions, but she refused to think about what was going on outside her assigned quadrant, refused to consider that her people might be caught in the cross fire she was hearing all around her. She focused on backing up Sloan, protecting Sloan.

"Clear!" he called less than a minute later.

Adrenaline surged through her blood as she hurried toward him. The cameras affixed to the tops of the fence weren't blinking green, but she still angled her face away from them, ducking her head as she ran.

Sloan trained his rifle on the rear doors. Reese did the same. She expected those doors to fly open at any second. The Enforcers guarding the interior would panic once they realized their lockdown procedures had been thwarted, a notion that brought a cruel smile to her lips. This station and its security protocols were wholly dependent on the technology that kept it operational. Thanks to Xander, all systems were down.

Her smile widened when muffled gunshots sounded from inside the warehouse. "They're in," she murmured to Sloan.

He didn't look as thrilled by that. "We should be in there too." But he didn't make a move toward the doors.

"We stay in position," she told him. "Stick to the plan, remember?"

And the plan required them to secure the rear and take out any Enforcers who tried to flee. Rylan and the others were doing their part inside.

It felt like an interminably long time before the gunfire died down and her people began reporting in.

"All clear." Beckett, who was with Nash on the west side of the warehouse.

"Clear." Davis and Cole from the east.

"All good here." Xander, who was monitoring the tech from one of their trucks.

"You guys can head inside now." The final report came from Rylan, sounding mighty pleased with himself.

Reese clicked on the radio. "Any casualties?"

A chorus of *no*s rang out, though she didn't miss the note of hesitation in Pike's voice. Shit. She hoped all her people were in one piece.

"Let's go," she said brusquely.

Weapons drawn, she and Sloan raced toward the two metal doors that swung open at their approach. A beaming Rylan appeared, his blue eyes dancing with mischief. "Hey, guys. Fancy meeting you here."

Sloan rolled his eyes.

"Is everything a joke to you?" Reese asked irritably.

"Gorgeous, we just raided a weapons depot and didn't die. I think I'm allowed to be in a good mood right now."

He had a point.

As they followed Rylan into the fluorescent-lit corridor, the ringing in Reese's ears eased, replaced by the wild hammering of her pulse. Holy fuck. They'd done it. They'd actually done it.

"Everyone okay?" she asked Rylan.

He shrugged. "More or less."

"What the hell does that mean?"

"Your girl Sam took a bullet, but she'll live."

A rush of concern overtook her, spurring her to walk faster. Damn it. She'd been torn about bringing Sam along, but the woman was one of the best sharpshooters

in Foxworth, the small town Reese had commandeered
years ago.

"Where is she?" Reese demanded.

Rylan gestured to the set of doors at the end of the hall.
"Pike's stitching her up. Don't worry, everything's fine."

Reese only moved faster. She'd be a fool to take Rylan's word for anything—the man could be bleeding out
from his femoral artery and still insist everything was
"fine." She rarely saw him without some injury that was
"no big deal, gorgeous," although he was always quick
to ask her to kiss it and make it better.

She pushed at the doors and found herself in a cav-
ernous room filled with endless rows of shelving soaring
almost to the ceiling. The scent of metal, gunpowder,
and blood assaulted her nostrils as she stepped through
the threshold. She paid no attention to the bodies strewn
all over the cement floor. Dead Enforcers meant nothing
to her.

Apparently they meant nothing to Rylan too; he
didn't even glance down as he carelessly stepped over
the bloodied body of an Enforcer who'd taken several
bullets to the chest.

"See? She's fine." Rylan sounded exasperated as he
pointed across the warehouse.

Reese relaxed when she glimpsed Sam. The slender
brunette was sitting on a plastic chair, wearing a stony
expression as Pike tied what looked like a piece of his
shirt around her upper arm.

"You okay, Sammy?" Reese called out.

"Peachy," the woman called back, then offered a
thumbs-up.

Appeased, Reese walked over to the nearest aisle
and poked her head around the corner. Stacks upon
stacks of wooden crates met her eyes, and then she spotted Beckett already hard at work, prying a crate open

with his crowbar. He grinned when he saw her, then shoved aside a sea of packing peanuts to extract a gleaming assault rifle from the crate.

"Nice, huh?" he remarked.

Her heart started pounding again, this time from excitement rather than adrenaline. When she'd been gathering intel about this warehouse, all her sources were unclear about whether it would contain weapons or ammunition. Most depots weren't equipped to handle both, and it would have been pointless to get their hands on a shit ton of ammo when they had no weapons to use it with.

But Reese's gut had told her that West Colony's council members didn't have enough manpower to guard multiple munitions warehouses, particularly with the new colony that they were supposedly terraforming along the west coast. She'd banked on the council's consolidating both weapons and ammo in one place, and her gamble had paid off.

These weapons were hers now. The endless boxes of ammunition were hers. It was all hers.

Her pulse sped up at the thought, but there was no time to bask in her victory. Once the Enforcers they'd killed missed their hourly check-ins with headquarters, the city would send backup.

Reese clapped her hands together, and the sharp sound echoed through the massive space. "Load the trucks," she ordered. "We have fifteen minutes to take as much as we can. Let's not waste time, people."

The Killer Instincts Novels
by Elle Kennedy

Enter the high-stakes world of deadly
mercenaries and kick-ass assassins, dangerous
men and the daring women who love them....

Find more books by Elle Kennedy
by visiting prh.com/nextread

"[Kennedy] leaves you breathless."
—*New York Times* Bestselling Author Vivian Arend

"Hard-core romantic suspense loaded
with sensuality."—*USA Today*

ellekennedy.com
AuthorElleKennedy
ElleKennedy